Family and Fate

LEGACY OF LEGENDS
BOOK TWO

ANGIE COLLINS

Cover Design: Kelly at Lacuna Author Services

Editing: Cassie at Weaver Way Author Services

Formatting: Cassie at Weaver Way Author Services

I hope you love this book as much as I do. In case you're wondering after reading the dedication from the first book, my daughters did not read it, but they have stopped saying I'm too "vanilla" for the books I read.

For those that like some plot with your smut, luckily I am a huge fan of both.

For the women who don't believe they can achieve all the things, take it from a girl who had always been told she would achieve nothing, you can do whatever you set your mind to. Just don't half-ass it, put your whole ass into that shit.

Content Warning

This book contains mature subject matter including, but not limited to graphic sex, violence, and other potentially triggering themes.

Chapter One

LAYLA

I'm running, but the faster I run, the closer he seems to get. Panic threatens to overtake me. Every corner I turn, every alleyway I duck into, only serves to heighten my sense of desperation as I realize that there's nowhere left to go. The walls close in around me, trapping me in a labyrinth of fear and uncertainty, with no way out.

My breath comes in ragged gasps, each inhale feeling like a struggle against the suffocating grip of panic that threatens to overwhelm me. My pulse pounding in my ears, a relentless drumbeat that echoes the rhythm of my racing heart.

As suddenly as it appeared, the nightmare begins to fade and is replaced by the sound of Caspian's voice winding its way through my thoughts, chasing away the lingering feelings of dread.

"Layla, wake up." His warm breath tickles the shell of my ear, sending shivers down my spine. My eyes flutter open and I am suddenly thrown back into reality.

Rio is dead.

Nova is dead.

1

I look into those gorgeous blue eyes and see sadness radiating from their depths. He leans in and presses a firm kiss to my mouth before sliding the covers back and getting out of bed. I can't help but admire his broad shoulders, strong back, and tapered waist. My mouth waters at the way his muscles bunch and ripple as he moves. The intricate tattoo that winds up one side of his body that looks like the dips and waves of the ocean, a symbol of his wielding ability, makes me want to trace every curve. This beautiful man of mine is all power and strength.

"You were having the dream again. I had hoped that being here would somehow make it stop," he says with a note of worry in his voice. Caspian is well versed in my dream, the one that I now believe to be my father dream walking into my subconscious, trying to find me as I sleep.

"Damian taught me how to shield myself. It helps, but with everything going on, I just forgot," I say, scooting out of bed after him, wrapping my arms around him from behind, placing a kiss on his back. He laces a hand with mine, looking out of the window at the beautiful valley below us.

"This place really is beautiful," I whisper. The house is small but clean and well-stocked. It's set near the portal to Earth we came through, specifically stationed for his family to use as they leave or enter the realm. Beyond it is a lush green valley covered in flowers of various shades of lavender and yellow. It looks like something out of a fairy tale.

"What kingdom is this?" I ask him, hungry to know everything there is to know about this part of my heritage.

"This is the kingdom of Verdantia, ruled by Freyr, the god of fertility, prosperity, and peace. He rules here with his twin sister, Freyja, the goddess of love, fertility, and beauty. Their father is one of the sea gods—he oversees the waters on the other side of Aetheria."

"So, there is more than one god of each thing?

"Yes, just like there are multiple rulers on Earth. But they are ruled by Nyx. Think of Nyx as the president and the rulers of each kingdom as state senators that live forever and don't get voted in, but appointed gods of areas depending on the powers they are born with."

"Gotcha."

He turns to face me, sliding his hands to my face and dipping down to capture my lips in a kiss. I eagerly open for him, moaning as his tongue slides across mine, heat flooding my system. When will my body stop instantly going molten just because he touches me? I lean in, pulling him closer as he moves his hands down my back and lower, cupping my ass.

"*Cas, please,*" I whisper through our link, not wanting to break the kiss to physically say his name, begging for more.

He picks me up and lays me on the bed, sliding a hand up my T-shirt. A loud banging at the door stops us in our tracks. Cas's hand stills an inch away from my breast, and I groan in frustration.

"Please, for the love of the gods, tell me you two are not in there fucking," Damian grouses. "There are other people in this house and unless you want to learn to shield your damn thoughts better, one of said people does not appreciate the deviant thoughts you happen to be thinking about my cousin, Caspian."

"Damian, just because you haven't gotten laid for a while doesn't mean the rest of us should suffer. Go away, damnit," I laugh as he bangs on the door again.

"Not happening, cousin. We have things to sort out and teach that damn pretty boy how to shield, or you will never be getting laid again when I'm around."

"Are you seriously calling me a pretty boy, Damian? Have you looked in a mirror lately?" Cas looks down at me, his lips curling up as he places one more kiss on my mouth and gets up, throwing on some pants and handing me my clothes. "I'm going to fuck you senseless later, and I'm not going to shield on purpose." The wicked gleam in his eyes makes my skin tingle in anticipation.

"I heard that!" Damian yells from somewhere deeper in the house.

I shake my head and open the door, a smile playing on my lips at these boys of mine. I find Damian in the kitchen making breakfast. His mother, Enthralia and my brother, Brennan, are already up and seated at the table.

"We need to talk. Cas, you know there is going to be backlash for bringing Brennan here. Mother, that you are aware of, has there ever been a full mortal brought to Aetheria?" Damian looks to his mother for answers. Of all of us, she is the most knowledgeable about these things.

"Not that I am aware of. It should be impossible for them to portal through, but I think he was able to because of the shield Layla put around him and the connection to her power."

"Now that father is dead, do you think it's safe for us to return to Shadowfell?"

"None of your father's men were particularly loyal to him. With him dead, unless Nyx decrees otherwise, it rightfully passes to you. As long as your uncle remains on Earth, I think it's safe to return, but do you really want to rule? I never thought you had a desire to run the kingdom."

"I don't know if I want to or not. I just don't want any of his bastards to try to lay claim to it. Can you imagine if some of them were in a position of power?" His eyebrow arches as he looks at her with worry in his eyes.

"No, I cannot."

"I think we should take Layla and Brennan to Shadowfell. Cas, I'm assuming you need to return to your kingdom soon? You have a few things you need to take care of, don't you?" A look passes between the two of them that makes the hairs on the back of my neck stand on end.

"What the fuck is going on, Cas?" I narrow my eyes at him, cross my arms, and wait for an answer, "What exactly do you need to take care of?"

"Shit. Thanks, Damian, you fucking asshole."

"You were going to have to tell her eventually."

"Tell me *what*?" I growl, a clear hint of warning in my voice.

"Fuck, don't panic, okay? I'm going to take care of it as soon as I get back. I don't care if I have to give up my position as heir. I. Will. Take. Care. Of. It." He enunciates each word, and a lump begins to clog my throat. "Princess Nerine is currently staying at my family's palace."

"Who the fuck is Princess Nerine?" I don't need to ask the question—I know the answer, but I need to hear him say it. My heart is racing and my vision clouds, power rising with my growing agitation, the sky outside darkening as thunder rumbles in the distance and shadows dance around the surfaces in the kitchen, racing to swirl around me.

Caspian is silent, so Damian opens his mouth. "Oh, for fuck's sake, she's the woman his father betrothed him to. Calm your ass down, Layla, before you destroy something."

"I kinda hoped this had already been taken care of," I say through gritted teeth.

"Look, I'm sorry, but you don't know my father. He doesn't listen to me or take into consideration what I want."

"It's true, he's a massive ass," Damian pipes in.

"I need some space." I throw on my shoes and storm out of the house. I know I'm being ridiculous, but I can't help the feelings churning inside of me. I don't know this girl, but I don't want her hurt in all of this either, and I've been sleeping with the man she

5

thinks she's going to marry. The guilt sits in my stomach like a ball of lead, and I don't enjoy the sensation.

"Hey, wait up!" Brennan runs to catch up with me.

I whirl around, lightning crackling in the sky above me as the wind picks up, mirroring the torrent of emotions swirling inside me.

"Fuck, Layla! Calm *down!*"

The fear in his eyes is like a dagger to my heart. I never want him to be afraid of me, and until a few days ago he had no idea I had powers or was only half-human. I can't imagine what he's feeling, and here I am about to kill us both because I can't get my shit together.

I close my eyes and call my power back to me, taking deep breaths trying to collect myself. "Sorry, the storm stuff is new, and I don't exactly have it under control yet. Plus, something about being here makes my powers feel stronger, easier to call to, and get out of control."

"I can't pretend to understand what any of that is like, I'm still freaking out a little about this whole thing, but you need to cut Cas a break. It's Cas. You know he's crazy about you. Let him get things sorted and don't freak out on him."

I let loose a weary sigh, "It's not that—I know he does. It's the guilt I'm struggling with. I'm essentially the other woman. That poor girl thinks she is going to marry him, and here I am sleeping with her fiancé."

He winces at that, "Well, that was TMI, but I get it."

Tears well in my eyes, "I already feel so much guilt about Rio, Nova, and you. Cas is supposed to be my safe space, you know? And now there's guilt attached to that."

"It's not your fault your psycho father kidnapped me. It's not your fault Rio and Nova are dead. You and Damian are the ones who saved me, and I know you would have saved them too, if you could have. Stop beating yourself up."

"Come here, kiddo." I open my arms, and he steps into them, resting his chin on my head. I release him and take a step back, looking out over the sky that is now back to a crystalline blue.

"Can you go get Cas for me?"

He nods and walks back toward the house. Plopping myself on the ground, I pull my knees to my chest. A moment later, Cas is settling in next to me, leaning back, supporting his weight on his hands, his long legs stretched out in front of him, ankles crossed. He's so damn beautiful it makes my heart ache to look at him.

He's quiet, waiting for me to speak. "I'm not mad at you, Cas. Well, I kinda am. You should have taken care of this before we got to this point. I can't ask you to give up your kingdom for me. I already carry enough guilt—don't put that on me, too."

"It wouldn't be for you, Layla. It would be for me. I want you more than I want to breathe. I can give up a kingdom—what I can't give up is you. Do you understand that? It's you I can't live without, what I *won't* live without." He grabs my hand, lacing our fingers together.

I nod, the knot still twisted tight inside my stomach. "I think I should go with Damian while you go back to your kingdom. Take care of what you need to take care of, and join us. Damian will train with me. I'm guessing my grandmother will want a word, and it will be easier to do with Damian. He says he's her favorite grandson, so maybe she will like me?"

He leans over and places a soft kiss on my temple. "Of course, she will like you—you are amazing."

Chapter Two

LAYLA

I'm not sure what I expected of a place named Shadowfell that was ruled by the god of doom, but this isn't it. It's actually quite lovely. The palace lies in the shadow of a mountain and the rest of the land spreads out until it touches the sea. According to Damian, this kingdom is smaller than most, the castle half the size of the ones in neighboring lands, but to me, it's perfect. The stone structure looks sturdy and regal, surrounded by a fence made of the same material as the castle itself. A large open archway is cut into the center, an opening for the road leading in and out of the palace grounds.

The homes and shops all look clean and well-maintained. As we pass through the city, the people happily greet Damian and his mother by name.

"This is not what I was expecting." The awe in my voice is impossible to hide. "It's really beautiful."

Enthralia beams. "It wasn't always like this. When Moros joined forces with his brother he was not here often, and the care of the people fell to me. I worked hard to earn their trust and help our kingdom thrive. Moros was content to let me because our coffers stayed full, and it pleased his mother that the people here were happy, so that helped him stay in her favor."

"I thought you were a prisoner?" I regretted the question as soon as it left my mouth. Sometimes, I don't think before my big mouth opens all on its own.

She nods. "I was. I had less freedom in the last several years as he discovered he could use me to control Damian, but that mostly meant I was watched by guards at all times, and the threat of violence was always there if Damian stepped out of line." She smiles sadly at her son as he grabs her hand, squeezing it tight, no doubt remembering how difficult things were.

Damian's entire demeanor changes as we enter the palace. Gone is the sensitive, funny man I have grown to love, and in his place is the ruthless killer I know he can be.

Two guards approach him almost immediately. "Castor, Hector, gather the other guards and members of my father's court. Meet in the throne room in thirty minutes." There is no room for argument in his tone. He doesn't wait for a response as he bounds up a set of stairs. "Mother, show Layla and Brennan to their rooms. I will see you in the throne room—dress appropriately and get her into some midnight leathers, a bodice, and a pair of runed boots."

His mother nods to him and turns to me. "Come, Layla." I follow behind her, a little overwhelmed, trying to take in every detail of the castle as we hurriedly move up the stairs to a wing only used by the ruling family. "Your room will be next to Damian's and Brennan's across the hall. I will send for the leathers. For now, quickly wash up." She gestures toward the door on her right before turning to my brother. "Brennan, I'm going to ask you to please stay in your room while Damian announces his father's death and lays his claim to the throne. Things could get a little...messy."

He nods and I squeeze his hand before he slips into his room, and I walk into mine. There's a large, canopied bed in the middle of the space covered with a midnight blue material, dotted with what looks like hundreds of tiny stars. A large window covers the opposite wall, and a door leads out to a balcony. There's a sitting area also decorated in shades of night. The furniture is all beautifully detailed in sun and moon patterns, with different constellations. I love it—it feels like it was made for me. Attached is an adjoining bathroom, and I make my way in there to quickly shower.

I'M CLEAN AND WEAVING MY HAIR INTO A SIMPLE PLAIT when Enthralia knocks. "Come in," I say. She enters, holding a set of black clothing in her hand.

"These articles are meant for warriors. I will assume he will either present you as a warrior or just let your presence near him make the statement for itself. All these pieces are enchanted with shadow magic, the fitted bodice is made from supple leather, featuring intricate lacing along the front. It provides support for the torso and enhances the wearer's agility in battle."

I run my fingers along it—it's impossibly soft and supple.

"The boots are crafted from sturdy leather, providing traction and stability on treacherous terrain while muffling the wearer's footsteps. I had to guess at your size, but I think they will fit nicely. The Midnight Leather pants are form-fitting leather armor dyed a deep black, offering both flexibility and protection in combat. They are enhanced with enchanted runes, or sigils, for added resilience. These are all symbols of a powerful warrior and will aid you in controlling your magic, as well as enhancing it. Now get dressed, quickly." She waves me in the direction of the bathroom and waits while I change.

Checking myself out in the mirror, I wish Cas was here to see me. I look like a badass. My hair is as dark as the leather—my fair complexion and red lips stand out even more, giving me an almost otherworldly appearance. Practicing my serious face in the mirror, I look slightly terrifying but sexy as the leather hugs and accentuates every curve of my body. I walk out and Enthralia's lips slowly turn upward.

"You look fierce and beautiful, a deadly combination. Come now, Damian will be forced to put on a show; do not be fooled by the mask he will wear as he declares his claim on the throne."

I laugh, "The first time I met him, he was in character. I am well versed in the many sides of Damian. He is quite the enigma. A soft teddy-bear one minute, a deadly killer the next."

She smiles, "I believe the two of you have that in common. It's no wonder you are so close—you are very similar creatures."

We enter the throne room and Damian stands in front of the center throne on the dais, a massive wolf standing next to him. The animal is so large his back is nearly to Damian's waist. That must be Chaos. His mother takes her place in front of the throne on the left, the one to the right sitting empty. I guess that used to be the one Damian occupied when his father was alive.

"You will stand beside the center throne, a clear symbol of importance. He may not want to reveal who you truly are, but you will need to be given a title of import so it will not be brought into question why you are with him often. Hopefully, the similarity in your looks will not give the two of you away."

I nod, and as I go to take my place, the wolf growls low in its throat. "Chaos, hush," Damian whispers, and the wolf quiets but looks back at me with narrowed eyes.

I know nothing about dire wolves, but I think I remember reading something once about not showing fear, so I bare my teeth and growl low in my chest right back at him. His ears quirk and his eyes widen in surprise as he quiets and looks forward once more. I hear a low chuckle rumble from Damian.

The room is circular, the walls covered in intricate tapestries that tell the story of the kingdom. There are large paintings hung around the room, several of Damian at various stages in life. He is clearly his mother's pride and joy. On the wall opposite us, above the main entrance to the room, is a portrait of his parents on their wedding day. His father looks bored, and his mother seems so full of hope for her future it makes my heart hurt a little thinking about how it turned out for her. I wonder if she would like to see the picture burned. I would if I were her.

My attention snaps back to Damian when he begins to speak. He changed out of his typical dress clothes for something that looks more appropriate for a king about to do battle. Clothed in a black leather form-fitting tunic that makes his body seem even larger, hugging every line and muscle, he seems fiercer, if that is even possible. It's adorned with intricate silver embroidery and buttons. His pants are similar to mine, but his boots come to his knees. Instead of a traditional crown, Damian wears a circlet crafted from twisted black metal decorated with dark gemstones, each etched with a different rune that glimmers in the dim light.

As he addresses the room, his commanding presence fills the space, drawing all eyes to him with an undeniable magnetism. His stature is tall and imposing, his posture regal and confident, radiating an authority that demands respect.

"My father is dead." He pauses as the room erupts in murmurs. He gives them a moment to settle before he continues, "As his son, it falls upon me to assume the responsibilities of leadership. I stand before you not as your prince, but as your rightful king. I'm ready to lead our kingdom with strength, wisdom, and compassion.

"My mother will continue to serve as queen regent until I marry and take a queen of my own. Together, we will ensure the prosperity and well-being of our people, upholding the values and traditions that have guided us for generations.

"But I cannot do this alone. In these uncertain times, we need strong and capable allies to safeguard our kingdom and protect our people. That is why I have chosen to appoint Lady Layla as my personal guard. She possesses unique abilities to wield the powers of night and storms, making her an invaluable asset to our kingdom's defense.

"Together, we will face the challenges that lie ahead with courage and determination. We will honor the legacy of those who came before us and pave the way for a brighter future for generations to come."

With each word he speaks, his voice carries a deep, resonant timbre that reverberates throughout the chamber, capturing the attention of all who listen. His words are measured and deliberate, spoken with a calm yet authoritative tone that brooks no argument.

His eyes, sharp and penetrating, scan the crowd with a keen intensity, taking in every detail with a shrewdness that betrays his strategic mind. There is a steely resolve in his gaze, a determination to lead his kingdom with strength and wisdom, to be everything his father was not.

"I ask for your trust, your loyalty, and your support as we embark on this journey together. With your strength and resilience, there is nothing we cannot achieve.

"Long live Shadowfell! Long live its people!"

The crowd erupts in cheers, and they begin to chant. "Long live, King Damian!"

Pride blooms in my chest. Love and admiration swell inside me until it feels like I may burst. I have zero doubt in my mind he will be an amazing ruler. It takes everything in me not to make a fool of us both by tackling him in a hug. I'm pretty sure it would be frowned upon for his guard to assault him, so I refrain. My shields are down, and I hear him snicker in front of me, Chaos looking up at him, then back at me.

"Does that damn dog read minds like you do because I swear it looks like he understands what is going on?" I throw that thought out to him, knowing he can hear it and wishing he could talk back to me like Cas does.

He takes a half step back and whispers to me. "With all the powers you wield, I bet you can read me, look into your mind and give it a shot. You seem to have every other damn power in the world." He mutters the latter half of that statement, amusing me with his obvious exasperation of my growing abilities.

I concentrate on Damian, searching my mind and trying to connect it to his. *"I'm going to have to keep an eye on Lyra. His thoughts are giving him away, he does not support my claim to the throne, the asshole."*

"I did it!" I mentally scream at him.

"Yes, you did. Now stop smiling and look fierce, and don't scream in my head before you give me a headache." His words contradict the laughter and pride in his tone.

After what seems like hours of him shaking hands and listening to the ideas of his court, everyone finally cleared out of the throne room. Damian sags in relief. His mother gave up and turned in an hour ago.

"Come on, I want to show you something before we head to bed for the night." He grabs my hand and leads me out a side door down a long corridor. He makes several turns, and we seem to be in the far back corner of the building before he stops in front of a large wooden door. Chaos stays on our heels, his footsteps so light they don't make a sound against the stone floor.

"Chaos, make sure she is on her best behavior." I swear the damn wolf huffs out a breath before Damian opens the door and lets Chaos walk in first. He follows behind, flipping on a light before opening the door enough for me to step in.

Holy shit.

In front of me are two other wolves, one almost twice as big as Chaos, the other about the same size as him. The smaller one sits quietly, but a rumble that sounds eerily like thunder vibrates through the chest of the larger one.

"Vengeance, this is Layla. Layla, Vengeance." I stare, slack-jawed at the beast before me. Her fur is steel gray and her eyes a deep, midnight blue, unlike anything I've ever seen on an animal before. It's hard to tell they are from the same litter; their looks are so different. Chaos has deep brown eyes and a reddish coat, and Havoc's are a softer hazel, almost the same color as his fur.

She continues to growl, baring teeth that are several inches long, saliva dripping onto the floor as the fur on her back stands on end. I narrow my eyes at her and bare my own teeth, growling back. It worked with Chaos, so I figure it's worth a shot.

I am oh so fucking wrong. It has the opposite effect; it pisses her right-the-fuck-off. With speed and agility I've never witnessed before, she leaps for me. I throw up a shadow that knocks her on her ass. The other two quietly observe the spectacle from the opposite end of the room, staying perfectly still, content to watch the drama unfold before them.

My temper snaps. "Look, you little bitch, I didn't do shit to you for you to lunge at me like that, so you can calm right-the-fuck-down, or I will pin you with shadows until you can act like you have some damn sense." I wag my finger in her direction, trying to infuse my tone with as much authority as I can muster.

Her ears twitch and she stops growling at me, sitting back and watching me curiously. *"You are a shadow wielder."* The feminine voice fills my head, and my eyes grow wide. I turn toward my cousin and the smile on Damian's face is so wide I'm surprised his face doesn't crack.

"She spoke to you, didn't she? I fucking knew it! Congrats, cousin, you now have a dire wolf." He runs over to Chaos and ruffles his hair as Chaos jumps around, growling and nipping in play, Havoc joining in.

"Explain," I demand.

He stops playing and looks at me, a shit-eating grin still plastered on his face. "When a dire wolf bonds with you, they connect to you the way Cas does and you can speak to each other. Dire wolves are known to be used in battle—they are deadly and intelligent. It's a formidable advantage and not one many people have. They are notoriously picky creatures and don't find many people worthy."

"So now I have a dog if I want one or not?" Vengeance growls again. "Sorry, you are much prettier than any dog, I meant wolf." That seems to appease her.

"Basically, yes. I knew you two were meant for each other. I love it when I'm right. Let's head to bed. Vengeance will sleep with you —Chaos sleeps in my chambers when I'm home."

"What about Havoc? We can't leave him here alone," I say, horrified at the thought of him being all by himself when he's used to having his siblings with him. "Havoc, you can sleep in my room with me and Vengeance."

Damian shrugs his shoulders, and we file out of the room. Havoc appears happy to be included, padding along behind us. "I'll have someone send up beds and bowls for them, and a servant will come let them out a few times during the day," Damian informs me.

"You don't have to sleep in a bed on the floor. My bed is big enough for the three of us," I tell them. "You won't eat a servant that comes to let you out, will you?" I level a look at Vengeance.

"I make no promises."

"Okay, let me rephrase that. You will *not* eat anyone nice enough to come let you out to relieve yourself, understand?" She makes no comment, and I sigh. "I think I'll be taking her out." I run my hand along her fur and marvel at the sheer size of her.

"Didn't you tell me they're still pups? They are fucking *massive.*" The awe in my voice is obvious.

"They are, they still have some growing to do, but not much more. They're about nine months old now."

"Where is their mother?" I ask Damian.

"She was killed by a hunter, an asshole who murdered her just for sport. They were too little to survive alone, so I brought them here and raised them." His voice is quiet.

"What happened to the hunter?"

"I killed him. It's illegal to hunt a dire wolf in this kingdom. I pushed for that law myself. They are intelligent creatures and revered in most places. They don't attack us unless provoked, so there is absolutely no reason for our kind to kill them, and yet they were hunted to near extinction."

I'm glad he killed the asshole. We reach my door and say our goodnights as I enter with the two massive wolves. "Don't eat me in my sleep, understand?" Her head swings around to look at me and I swear she looks annoyed at the suggestion.

Chapter Three

DAMIAN

The sound of screaming wakes me from sleep. Terror grips me as I bolt upright and fly out of my bedroom to see what the hell is going on. A million fears grip me at once.

Are we under attack?

Has my uncle come to kill us?

Did the court decide to rebel?

The screaming is coming from Layla's room, her door is open and growls rumble from inside.

Oh shit.

Vengeance.

Did I make a mistake, and that vicious beast of a wolf decided to attack Layla? Is someone attacking her and the wolves are trying to protect her? I can't get in there fast enough. I open my mind trying to read what's going on. No thoughts, just panic and fear, which now adds to my own growing sense of terror.

Fuck!

Each second feels like an eternity. My heart races, matching the tempo of my frantic footsteps. Dread coils in my chest, tightening its grip with every passing second. I push myself harder, driven by a primal instinct to reach her side, to protect her.

I fly over the threshold and see a terrified Anika and Brennan having a staring contest with the wolves while Layla stands between them, wagging her finger in Vengeance's face, lecturing her about scaring people half to death. Thank fuck everyone is okay. My heart is still hammering in my chest as I try to calm down, taking deep, steady breaths.

"You all took about a hundred years off of my life—I thought we were under attack," I snap. They all turn to look at me. Anika's gaze sweeps down my body and back up again, a blush spreading from her neck up to her cheeks before her eyes finally meet mine. Heat simmers there for a moment before she narrows them at me in disgust.

"Put some clothes on, Damian," she snarls and looks back at Layla. In my hurry to see what was going on, I forgot I was in nothing but boxer briefs that are tight enough to leave little to the imagination.

"Excuse the fuck out of me for not stopping to throw on pants when I thought someone was in here being murdered. Next time, I will be more considerate of your delicate sensibilities, Anika."

She snorts, and I leave the room long enough to throw on a pair of sweats, grinning at the memory of Layla wanting to take a picture of me in this exact getup and send it to Anika. My feet and chest still bare, I walk back into the room.

Vengeance has decided to behave after her scolding and is lying on the bed, curled up in sleep. Havoc is quietly watching the trio seated on the couch in the sitting area while Layla gives them a rundown of everything that's happened.

I see Anika visibly tense as I approach, her eyes lingering on my chest and stomach before looking back at Layla. I smirk and sit directly across from her, stretching an arm out over the back of the couch to be an asshole and putting as much of myself on display as possible. She can pretend she hates me all she wants, but I see the way she looks at me. She might hate that she wants me, but she wants me.

"So, is no one going to explain the giant wolves in the room?" Brennan nervously asks, with an eyebrow raised.

"Oh shit, sorry, Brennan, these are dire wolves. Apparently, the menace on the bed is mine now—her name is Vengeance," she points at the bed, then at Havoc, "and that's her brother, Havoc. Damian has one, too—his name is Chaos."

As if she summoned him, Chaos comes padding into the room on silent feet, laying directly in front of where I am seated.

"Vengeance is the only one that seems to have an attitude problem," Layla grumbles, and Anika laughs.

Chaos's ears prick at the sound. *"Is that your female?"*

"No, why do you ask?"

"Because it's obvious by your scent that you want her."

"Well, she hates me."

"Hmmm...that's not hate I smell coming from her."

"That's enough of that. Mind your business, you mangy mutt."

"I'm less mangy than you. Havoc likes her."

My eyes roam over to Havoc—his ears keep twitching, and he is openly watching her with interest. A part of me has been hoping he would bond with Brennan, but with him being human, I wasn't sure how that would work. Now I find myself hoping he bonds Anika.

"Think he will bond her?"

"Possibly, but he will take his time choosing a human, if he takes one at all. Of the three of us, he is the most cautious and thoughtful."

"Damian?" Layla looks at me with furrowed brows, the corners of her mouth turned down. "Anika asked you a question."

"Sorry, love, what was the question?" I swing my gaze to her, waiting expectantly.

Her tongue darts out over her bottom lip, and now I'm staring, hoping she does it again, my cock hardening at the thought of it sliding across its head.

"I asked if you would let me train here with Layla. I want to be able to protect myself. Protect those I care about." Her eyes drift to Layla and Brennan with clear affection before coolly regarding me.

"Absolutely not, Anika," I say with determination as I meet her gaze. "I cannot allow you to put yourself in harm's way. It's too dangerous."

Anger flares deep within those emerald green depths, and she kicks her chin up a notch. "I was already training with Cas and Layla before coming to Aetheria. You can either train me when you train her, or I will find someone else. I would much rather continue training with her, but I'm doing this with or without your help."

I run a hand over my face. Damn this fucking hard-headed woman. "Fine," I growl, "you might as well stay here at the castle so you aren't traveling back and forth each day for training. Be warned, I will not baby you."

"I wouldn't expect you to. I'm tougher than I look, *asshole,*" she all but spits the words at me, and damn if it doesn't make me want to yank her over my knee and spank that perfectly round ass of hers.

Fuck me, my damn dick is hard again. What is it about her that makes me react this way? I need to get this red-headed vixen out of my system. I have a damn kingdom to run and can't walk around with a hard-on every damn time she walks in a room.

"Anika, be nice," Layla says with a hint of warning in her voice. "Thank you, Damian. She really is good at hand-to-hand, and she isn't bad with weapons either. She's a damn good shot and has deadly fucking aim when throwing daggers, so watch your balls." She leans over and presses a kiss to my cheek. "And thank you for sending for her, it was a nice surprise, despite Vengeance trying to eat her," she laughs.

"Anything for you, dear cousin." I smile and meet her familiar brown eyes. There is no one in this world I have as much faith in as her. Being able to read people's thoughts has its advantages from time to time, one of them being that I know she is the most fiercely loyal person to those she loves, and I can trust her with my life, as well as my secrets.

Chapter Four

LAYLA

I miss Cas. The gnawing feeling in the pit of my stomach grows each day he doesn't arrive, making me feel particularly violent. Especially wondering if *she* is still at his castle. Does she flirt with him? Fantasize about tracing those gorgeous black lines of his tattoo up his arm, his neck, down his chest, across his hip? I land a particularly vicious punch to Damian's abdomen and he grunts in pain, darting away from me.

"Dammit, Layla!" he bellows, "Knock that shit off! This is training, not a fucking MMA match."

I blacked his eye earlier.

"She's sexually frustrated," quips Anika, one corner of her mouth turned up in a smile as I snap my head around and flip her off.

"Oh really, then what's your excuse?" Damian arches an eyebrow at her.

"She's sexually frustrated and sexually repressed," I glower as she sticks her tongue out.

"I am *not* sexually repressed." She doesn't bother denying the frustrated part.

"Gods, give me patience! If you don't chill, I'm going to go find that prince of yours and drag him back here myself so you will lose the attitude before you seriously hurt someone, shields be damned, I'll just leave for the fucking night." He runs a hand through his hair in frustration and I feel satisfied knowing we are getting on his last nerve.

We all seem to be a little on edge. The wolves lay a few feet from where we are, silently watching the exchange. Vengeance and I have come to an understanding, and she hasn't tried to eat anyone lately. I'm pretty sure she has grown some in the last few weeks, her head nearly touching my shoulder. She will be as big as a damn horse if she grows much more.

Learning how to share space with a set of massive wolves takes some adjustment. Last week, I gave her and Havoc a bath. Trying to bathe two massive beasts with that much fur took me hours and left me exhausted. Havoc was well-behaved; his temperament is much calmer than his sister's. She made several threats, growled through the entire thing, and was pissed at me for two days afterward. At least she doesn't smell like a wet dog anymore. She retaliated by peeing on a pair of my favorite shoes. Jackass.

"Damian!" Enthralia comes rushing across the grounds, excitement ringing in her voice as she approaches. "I just received a report that Umbragon has been spotted flying this way!"

Damian's earlier annoyance dissipates as his eyes light up, rushing to his mother. "Truly? It's been ages since she's been home."

"I know, she left shortly after you did for Earth, but the report says there is a wing of dragons headed this way, and she is among them."

"A wing of dragons?" I ask, not sure why they are excited—it sounds terrifying.

"Yes! Remember how I told you that the closest thing I found on Earth to a dragon was riding a motorcycle? Umbragon is my dragon. Well, I guess it would be more appropriate to say I am her person. I'm not sure dragons would consider themselves belonging to anyone."

He's talking a mile a minute; his excitement would rival that of a kid on Christmas morning. "You all have strange ideas for pets around here, they are all huge and terrifying," I say, eyeing the wolves while Vengeance growls at me. *"You just proved my point with that menacing growl you threw in my direction. A golden retriever wouldn't do that."*

"A golden retriever won't save you in a war, either."

"They might, Malinois go to war all the time."

"A war where the people can wield the elements? I think not."

"Point taken."

Suddenly, shadows pass over us and a deafening roar slices through the quiet day. My eyes turn to Damian, watching his reaction to the dragon's majestic flight overhead—his excitement is palpable, radiating from him.

There's a gleam in his eyes, a spark of anticipation that dances across his features as he watches her soar through the sky. It's as if every beat of her wings ignites a flame of exhilaration in him, filling him with energy and excitement.

The corners of his mouth curl into a wide grin, his expression one of pure delight. It's a sight to behold, witnessing Damian's unbridled enthusiasm as he revels in the sheer thrill of his dragon's return, one that lightens my heart and makes me smile. I love seeing this side of him. It gives me a glimpse of what he might have been like as a boy, before his father and the world hardened him.

With each graceful swoop and turn, Damian's excitement seems to grow, it's infectious as it spreads to everyone around him. It's as if, at this moment, all his worries and cares have melted away, the burdens of the last few weeks disappearing.

He turns to me, his eyes bright, "I can't wait to take you flying! You thought you liked the motorcycle? Just wait!" I look at him dubiously, a dragon and a motorcycle are two very different things. Sure, both can be deadly, but only one can eat you.

I glance over at Anika, and she too is watching Damian, a smile playing on her lips. Another thunderous roar reverberates through the sky, so loud the earth beneath our feet trembles. There are five dragons in all, all varying shades of night. They circle a few times before one of the largest, with a final, powerful beat of its wings, begins its descent. It folds its wings close to its body, angling its massive form toward the earth below with a controlled grace.

As it nears the ground, it extends its wings once more, using them to slow itself and guide its landing. With a thud, it touches down on the grass, its powerful legs absorbing the impact.

The ground trembles beneath the weight of the dragon's massive form as it settles into place. As it comes to rest, it lets out a deep, rumbling growl. The other four follow in quick succession, the field now full of the massive beasts.

Once they have all safely landed, Damian takes off running with Chaos tight on his heels. He's heading for a large, midnight-black dragon in the center of the wing. The beast lowers its massive head, and Damian all but throws himself at it while the creature nuzzles him with its nose like a damn puppy. Its head is three times the size of Vengeance's.

"Layla!" he yells, waving his hands at me to join him.

"I'm coming, just don't let it eat me," I shout back at him. I begin walking toward them, admiring the sheer beauty of the beasts. I can't fucking believe dragons are real, and I'm walking up to a wing of them like a sacrificial lamb. One is such a dark navy blue; from certain angles, it looks almost black.

The largest is a deep purple. At its darkest points, the purple-black hue verges on the edge of obsidian, its depths so profound that they seem to swallow the light around them. It's the most stunning creature I've ever seen.

The last two are both dark shades of silver-gray. They are considerably smaller than the others but no less terrifying.

I stop in front of Damian and the dragon. His smile is bright as he runs his hands over the dragon's snout, an affectionate rumble from deep in its chest causes him to chuckle. "She loves to have her nose rubbed. Umbra, this is my cousin, Layla." He rests his forehead against her cool scales before softening his voice to nearly a whisper, "She killed my father."

The dragon's golden eyes seem to widen in surprise, then narrow into slits as she studies me. She sniffs the air around me and I stay perfectly still. Damian is still grinning like a damn fool.

"*I like her,*" the smooth, feminine voice fills my head and my jaw drops to the ground.

"She spoke to me." I look at Damian, my eyes wide.

"I know, I heard. They speak to us much like the wolves, except they speak to whomever they choose, not just the person they bond with. Want to go for a ride?"

"I, um, is that okay?" I look her in the eye, I would hate to just assume she would be okay with me jumping on her back.

"*Of course, Damian will show you how.*"

She lays down and Damian climbs up her back, me following closely behind. There is an area at the base of her neck that is clearly a space for a rider.

"It'll be a tight fit, but it will work. You get in front of me so I'm not blocking your view." I sit where he directs me, the scales smooth and warm to the touch. Damian fits himself in behind me, his chest flush with my back. "Hold on to that raised area right there," he directs, and I do as I'm told. "If you are nervous, you can use your shadows to hold yourself in place."

All I can do is nod. The excitement and fear running through my veins are a heady combination, but I enjoy the adrenaline rush that makes my body tingle with anticipation.

"She's breathtaking, Damian. This feels like a dream." He throws his head back in a carefree laugh, the sound vibrating through me as he squeezes me in a light hug, placing the side of his face against mine.

"I forget how new all of this is to you, I'm glad I get to see you discover these things for the first time. Umbra, let's go!"

She takes a few steps away from the others and launches into the air, leaving my stomach back on the ground. Tears gather in my eyes as the force of the wind makes it hard to see. She climbs higher and higher until, finally, she spreads her wings, leveling out and gliding through the bright blue sky.

"This is amazing." My voice is breathless as I take in everything. The feeling of freedom is exquisite. "This is so much better than the motorcycle."

"Told you." Damian squeezes me, joy radiating off him like a tangible thing. "When my father would be in one of his moods, flying with Umbra was one of the only escapes I had. He was furious she chose me for her rider when no dragon would even speak to him, but he wasn't about to make her angry. He was an asshole but not an idiot. She's incredibly powerful and he enjoyed the idea of controlling her through me."

As we ride, Damian and Umbra both point things out to me and tell me stories. Umbra is a nightwing dragon, and she's one of the most powerful of her wing. She has night vision, can hide herself completely in shadows and darkness, can fly soundlessly through the night, and can manipulate the minds of enemies, filling them with terror. I repress a shudder, mentally calculating the amount of damage she could inflict before anyone even knew she had targeted them. I'm really glad she's on our side.

It's nearly dusk when we return. I'm tired and hungry, but I also feel happy and at peace. "Thank you, Umbra, that was wonderful." I scratch her nose and plant a kiss on her scales. She purrs in delight, making me giggle.

"You are very welcome, Godslayer." I flinch at the name she uses and look over at Damian.

"They are very intuitive creatures," is his only reply as he shrugs his shoulders, and we head inside to grab food.

"Thank you for that, Damian. I didn't realize how much I needed it."

"I needed it too, cousin." He smiles at me and bumps my shoulder affectionately.

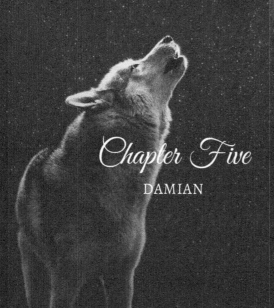

Chapter Five

DAMIAN

I find myself drawn back outside to check on Umbra and the other dragons one last time before retiring for the night. Truth be told, it's not just a matter of duty; I simply yearn to lay eyes on them once more. The presence of Umbra, returned safely home after an uncertain absence, offers me a semblance of peace. I had feared that my prolonged presence on Earth would have led her to seek out another rider, but seeing her nestled within the Dragonhold brings a sense of relief.

Built at my mother's behest after Umbra chose me as her rider, the Dragonhold stands as a haven for them. Resembling a large barn, it offers spacious stalls filled with soft hay where the dragons can rest if they wish.

However, it's not uncommon for them to retreat to the caverns of the mountain, nestled above the castle. While one might assume the Dragonhold to be the epitome of dragon comfort, Umbra and Dryvhn, as mates, often prefer to spend time away from the others. And so, they occasionally seek solace in the quiet seclusion of the mountainside caves.

When I exit the castle, I'm surprised to see Anika sitting in a chair, watching the dragons from afar. The look of longing on her face is obvious, whisps of red hair blowing around in the breeze. The urge to brush them back behind her ears is so strong my fingers twitch involuntarily. Her lips curve wistfully before she sees me and startles, rising from her seat to leave.

"Don't leave on my account. I was just about to check on the dragons," I hesitate for a moment before adding, "Would you like to come with me?" The want in her eyes is obvious, but she doesn't want to say yes to me. "I can take you for a quick ride if you'd like?" I raise my eyebrows, curious as to what she will do. She looks like she truly can't decide if she wants to accept my invitation or bolt.

She bites her bottom lip while a war wages within her. She's obviously curious about the dragons but doesn't want to be alone with me. "Come on, I won't bite." I smile at her and wish I could read her thoughts. I have no idea why, but I have never been able to see anything coming from her, and it's as infuriating as it is intriguing.

She takes a deep breath, her desire to see the dragons overriding all else. Crossing her arms, she finally begins to walk. I fall in step beside her, dying to get to know her better. "Have you ever seen a dragon before?" I ask quietly, afraid I might scare her away, desperate to keep her with me as long as possible.

"No, I was raised on Earth. I came here the first time shortly after my parents died." Sadness seeps into her as her shoulders sag slightly. It's a stark reminder that her parents are dead because of my father. Guilt sits heavy in my chest, making it difficult to breathe. I know I'm not responsible. I did everything in my power to thwart his efforts and save as many people as I could, but it doesn't ease the ache in my heart or the profound sense of regret for the ones I couldn't help, like her parents.

"I'm sorry, Anika."

She gives me a smile as we approach the dragons and it feels like a shot of dopamine through my entire body. She is so damn beautiful. I would do anything to see her smile more often, especially if it's directed at me.

"Umbra, are you up for another ride?" I pray she says yes. Her golden eyes look at me. *"Please,"* I beg silently.

"Did someone miss me, or is this more about that female you can't take your eyes off of?" Umbra teases and I am thankful she only sent that thought my way, slightly embarrassed that I'm so obvious in my ogling of Anika, not that she seems to notice.

"Can it be both?" I flash my teeth and give her a wink as she huffs at me with affection.

She slides herself into position for us to mount and I sigh in relief. I climb up first, showing Anika the way. When we reach the saddle, I say, "You will sit in front of me, just like Layla did. It will be a tight fit, but it will be easier for you to see and me to keep you on."

She nods nervously and sits down. I slide in behind her, and fuck, being this close to her is a bad idea. I'm already uncomfortably hard and feeling her pressed tight against me, smelling the lemony scent of her shampoo is the worst kind of torture. I reach my hands around her, and she stiffens.

"Grab on here, and make sure you hold on tight, okay? Lock your thighs as well." My voice is huskier than I intend, and my words come out strained. Every time she moves in the slightest, it sends a jolt of pleasure to my cock. She nods. I can feel her breath quicken as Umbra launches into the sky. Anika's entire body tenses until we level out and then she relaxes, leaning back into me enough that I have to grit my teeth to keep myself from grinding into her delectable ass. I steal a glance at her, and a few tendrils of hair have escaped the confines of her braid, the flaming red curls whipping around her face. Those pouty red lips are spread wide into a gorgeous smile, and her eyes are dancing with excitement.

I'm utterly enchanted by her reaction. I barely pay attention to the flight, so absorbed in watching her. I've quickly discovered that she wears her heart on her sleeve and can't hide her emotions for shit. She is so unguarded and unapologetic about it. It makes me wonder what it's like to be able to be that free with your feelings.

Flying at night is nothing like flying in the day. It fills you with a mix of excitement and apprehension. As we glide through the darkness, the world below is veiled in shadows, casting an aura of mystery over our journey. The cool night air rushes past, carrying with it the scent of earth, heightened by the absence of sunlight.

In the darkness, we are more attuned to the subtle sounds and movements of the nocturnal world around us. The whispering of the wind, the rustle of leaves, the distant calls of unseen creatures— all become amplified in the quiet. Maybe that's why these feeling cracking open my chest seem so large, so overwhelming. The beat of my heart seems faster, louder in my ears. I'm acutely aware of every place her body touches mine, her heat seeping into me, igniting a yearning in my soul for this fiery woman in front of me. Her gasps and giggles are like music to my ears. The breeze and proximity envelop me in her scent until all my senses are full of her. I never want this to end. I've never felt this alive, this light of soul and I crave more of it, more of her.

Despite the darkness, there is a sense of freedom, a feeling of liberation as we soar through the star-studded sky. The celestial canopy above stretches out before us, a vast expanse of twinkling lights. She tilts her head up to admire the brightness, the column of her throat exposed, and I can't help but lean in close enough to brush my lips lightly over her skin. She turns to meet my gaze, but instead of surprise or anger, I see heat in those brilliant emeralds. A slow smile spreads across her face, and I grin back at her like a fool, tightening my hold on her more than necessary just because I *need* to touch her.

Each beat of Umbra's wings propels us further into the darkness, her powerful form cutting through the night with effortless grace. As we fly, I marvel at the beauty of the woman in front of me and revel in the simple pleasure of watching the wonder on her face.

"Are you having fun?" I whisper, feeling her shiver as my breath tickles her ear.

"This is exhilarating!" she exclaims, her cheeks flush with the pleasure. She throws her hands up in the air as her ass rubs against me, and I grit my teeth at the explosion of desire that sweeps through me so fast and hot that I ache. There is no way she doesn't know exactly what she's doing, surely by now, she has felt my cock pressing into her. Then I remember the look in her eyes when my lips touched her neck. Maybe the little vixen knows exactly what she's doing, at least I can hope.

We fly for a bit longer, being pressed up against her is a torture I don't want to end, but Umbra needs her rest. We land and Anika is still delightfully giddy, which I find all kinds of sexy. I climb down first, and she follows. Grabbing her waist, I lift her the last few feet, bringing her flush with my body as she reaches the ground. Surprisingly, she doesn't move away. Her erratic heartbeat against my chest makes me hyper-aware of every single place our bodies are touching, her soft curves pressing into me in delectable ways that make me hungry to touch every inch of her.

Holding onto my shoulders, her fingers splay out as she looks up at me—I see desire once again swimming in those beautiful green pools. We both move at the same time, me inching closer as she rises on her toes, stopping a mere inch apart as our chests heave and breaths mingle. I hover above her parted lips for a heartbeat before I lose all common sense and lay claim to them. Her taste is like the sweetest wine, heady in the way it makes my head swim. She groans and opens for me and it's all the invitation I need. I eagerly slip my tongue into her mouth and devour her like a man starved, twisting her braid around my hand to hold her in place, angling to explore her deeper. I want more of her, all of her. Anything and everything she is willing to give. The need to claim her sets a fire in my blood like nothing I've ever felt before, tearing through me. Consuming me in its flames.

She wraps her arms around my neck, and my hands slide down her back to grab her ass, grinding into her hips. I want to rip her clothes off right here and now and take her on the ground like a feral beast. I break the kiss so I can get my mouth on the column of her neck. The way she gasps makes me insane with need. I'll do anything to hear that sound again, to hear her say my name as she shatters.

I snake one hand around and slide it up the material of her shirt to the peak of her breast. I can feel how hard her nipple is through the fabric, and she arches into my touch as I rub a thumb over that sensitive flesh.

Her hands are in my hair, fingers scraping over my scalp as she begs, "More, Damian, please." By the gods, there it is, my name on her lips, begging me to touch her. The breathy way she says it makes me nearly come undone. I unbutton her pants and slip my hand down below the fabric of her underwear to find her swollen clit. I brush my thumb over it and she bows her back—the sound that escapes her is music to my ears. Her lips part, her eyes close, lost in pleasure, pleasure I am bringing her.

"You are so fucking beautiful, Anika. I wonder how wet you are for me?" My voice is rough with desire as I slide a finger into her pussy and find it drenched. "Fuck, baby, you are soaked. I want to bury my cock inside that tight little cunt of yours and feel you shatter around me."

"Yes!" she screams as I slide in a second finger. Damn, she is so tight I'm about to lose it just thinking about her around my cock. I move my fingers in and out, rubbing her clit with my thumb faster and faster. I can't take my eyes off her face. Watching her come undone is now my favorite thing in the world. I can tell she's close; her breaths are coming faster and she is shamelessly riding my hand with abandon. I catch her mouth in another kiss, and I fuck her harder until I finally feel her clench around my fingers, her thighs trembling as she screams my name. I keep touching her until she comes down from that peak, loving the look of wonder that fills her eyes as she meets my gaze.

I pull my hand out of her pants and put my fingers in my mouth, eyes closing as I memorize the taste of her. I hear her breath catch and she reaches for my pants, hands trembling. She strokes me through the fabric, and I grit my teeth and press harder into her touch.

"I'm not sure what I'm doing," she says nervously, "you'll have to tell me what you like."

My whole body goes rigid. "Anika," I have to take a second to collect myself before continuing. "You're not a virgin, are you?"

She blushes, and it's the most adorable thing I've ever seen. "No, but I have only been with one person, and we only had sex a few times." She looks away, embarrassed. I grab her chin and bring her gaze back to mine. "And I never...you know."

Oh shit. It hit me; she never had an orgasm before tonight. "Are you telling me that tonight is the first time you have ever found pleasure?"

She gets even redder, "No, yes, well kinda. I have with myself, but not with someone else." The thought of her getting herself off is an image that won't be leaving my mind any time soon, but the thought that the man she was with, not making sure she was thoroughly sated when he was done rankles me.

I suddenly realize Umbra is gone. Fuck, I was so caught up in Anika I lost my head and almost fucked her in the grass where anyone could have seen.

Her hand is still slowly sliding up and down my shaft, and it takes every ounce of willpower I have to step away from her.

Confusion and hurt flash in her eyes. "Listen to me, when I fuck you, and I will, I want it to be in a place where I can take my time and show you how it's supposed to be done. I am going to fuck you so thoroughly well that you will forget your own name. I am going to take you in every way possible and make you come so many times you beg me to stop." My voice is low, filled with dark promises as I whisper the words in her ear.

"What?" she says, sounding pissed. "So, you aren't going to sleep with me? This is a one-time offer, Damian."

"No, not tonight, but mark my words, I will fuck you." I grab the back of her neck and roughly kiss her lips. She stands perfectly still for a moment before I pull back. I can feel the anger vibrating from her.

"No. You won't be." She turns and quickly walks into the house, the sounds of my laughter filling the night as she flips me off over her shoulder. I hate that I hurt her feelings, but when I take her, I'm going to make sure she is so satisfied she never wants to leave my bed.

Chapter Six

LAYLA

"He turned me down!" Anika moans, burying her head in my pillows, "It was *so* humiliating!"

"Wait, he literally turned you down?" I ask, thoroughly confused. I've seen the way he looks at her.

"Yes! I have never thrown myself at a man like that before, and to have him tell me no," tears spring to her eyes as heat stains her cheeks, "I will never be able to look at him again!"

"So let me get this straight. He kissed you in a way that made your knees weak, then within minutes, he gave you a mind-blowing orgasm—your words, not mine—with just his fingers after an incredibly romantic evening, then he pats you on the head and sends you on your way?"

"Yes! Well, I confessed that it was the first time I had ever...you know...and he asked if I was a virgin. I told him no, but that I had only been with one person, and it wasn't very good for me, and then he gave me some bullshit excuse, but I'm pretty sure he was turned off by my lack of experience."

I can see the hurt and uncertainty in Anika's eyes. Damian and I will be having words later. "I thought he wanted me. I mean, I had my hand on him, he was as hard as a rock, I literally *threw* myself at him, Layla."

"I'm sorry. I don't know what's up his ass, you are gorgeous, sexy, and any man would be lucky to even breathe the same air as you, much less get into your pants."

"He's essentially a king now. Maybe he just doesn't think I'm good enough." Her voice is so quiet and full of hurt—my heart aches for her.

"Knock that stupid shit off right now." I hate the way she is beating herself up over this. "I am so kicking his ass."

"No! Layla, you *cannot* say anything to him, I will *die*!"

"Fine, I won't say anything, but I'm not promising I won't hurt him." I stand to leave as she rolls her eyes at me and I flash her a grin before slipping out the door to find the object of my irritation.

"*Where is he*?" I ask Vengeance. I know she can track Chaos, and where Chaos is, Damian is.

"*He's in the throne room.*"

"*Thanks. Stay here; it's going to get bloody.*"

I walk out of the room, and true to form, she listens to nothing I say and quietly follows after me.

"*Stubborn mule.*"

"*Stubborn, yes, but I'm following along for the entertainment this should provide.*"

Shadows swirl around me, ebbing and flowing with each step I take. I enter the throne room and Damian's eyes lock on mine, surprise flickering there as he sees the anger radiating from me.

"Excuse me a moment, Lady Layla seems to need a word," he says to whatever pompous ass he had been engaged in conversation with.

I jerk my head toward a door and start walking that way, him a few steps behind. "Layla." There's a warning in his tone. I whirl around and punch him right in the fucking nose.

"Dammit, Layla! What was that for?"

"Quit being a baby, I didn't even hit you hard enough to break it," I snarl. His eyes are watering and I smile in satisfaction. "That's for the hour I had to spend consoling Anika this morning because you rejected her."

"You *cannot* be serious right now. I did *not* reject her. Bloody hell, you females are so damn frustrating!"

"Then what happened? Because she seems to think you did. Did you or did you not tell her no?"

"Well, I did, but..." He doesn't get another word out before I punch him in the stomach, and he doubles over. "You hit me one more time, and I'm going to hit your ass back. Now stop and listen to me, you jackass!"

I cross my arms and narrow my eyes, waiting for him to speak.

"I had every intention of bedding her, hell, I almost threw her down in the grass and mounted her like an animal. But dammit, Layla, she's only been with one man, and he didn't even have the decency to make it pleasurable for her. I told her when I took her, it would be when I could take my time and show her how it's meant to be done. I don't just want to bed her, Layla, you should know me better than that, I *want* her."

Realization dawns on me. He actually has feelings for her, and he wants it to be perfect. It's sweet. "You *like* her."

He glowers at me, "Just now catching on to that, are you? And I thought you were intelligent. Guess I was wrong." He rolls his eyes and I laugh.

"Well, the way you two bicker, it's kinda hard to tell. I knew you were attracted to her, I mean, who wouldn't be? But I had no idea you actually *liked* her, liked her." Why does this conversation make me feel like I'm seventeen again? "Well, you are going to have some groveling to do because, as of right now, she never wants to see you again."

"Fuck."

"Good luck, cousin." I clap him on the back and walk away, grinning from ear to ear. "We are going to skip training today, meet me by the dragons instead."

"You do realize I'm the king and I should be giving you orders, right?"

I ignore him as I walk away, a grin on my face as I flip him off.

"What the fuck is up with all the females in this house giving me the damn finger?" he snarls as I leave a trail of my laughter in his wake.

A few hours later, I find my way to the field where the dragons are. As the midafternoon sun casts its golden glow across the landscape, I sit in the grass, cautiously observing the majestic creatures before me. I'm hesitant to approach too closely without Damian.

My gaze settles upon the two smaller dragons, their sleek gray forms shimmering in the sunlight. They exude youthful energy, engaged in a lively game of roughhousing. With playful growls and nips, they chase one another across the field, making me smile at their antics.

Meanwhile, the three larger dragons recline in the sun-soaked grass, their massive forms a testament to their power and grace. With eyes half-closed, they appear content, their scaled hides absorbing the warmth of the June day.

I watch with a mixture of awe and trepidation, captivated by the sight of them. Though fear tugs at my heartstrings, there's also a sense of wonder, a deep appreciation for their beauty and the power they wield.

I hear Damian approach and he sinks down next to me, "They are magnificent, are they not?" The affection he feels for them is obvious and it eases some of the fear thrumming through my veins.

"I want to ride one on my own today. Do you think they will let me?" I ask, the uncertainty in my voice betraying the lack of confidence I feel.

"Only one way to find out." He leaps to his feet with unnatural grace for a man his size and holds out his hand to me. I take it, and he yanks me up with a little more force than necessary, causing me to stumble. "That's for punching me earlier," he laughs, and I shove him. We begin the short trek across the field as he affectionately throws an arm around my shoulders.

We reach Umbra and start scratching her scales as she rumbles with delight. "Hello darling," he says as he lays his cheek against her face and I smile at the adoring way he looks at her. "Layla would like to give riding alone a shot today, what do you think?"

"She will ride me." A deep, commanding voice fills my mind, and by the look on Damian's face, it was said to him as well.

"Layla, it appears you will be riding Drayvhn today, Umbra's mate." His lips curve upward as he looks over at the massive purplish-black dragon. "He is the only night dragon more powerful than Umbra. His powers are similar to hers, but he can also breathe flames imbued with the darkness of twilight, capable of consuming light. It's slightly terrifying." He nods his head at Umbra and begins to mount her, climbing up her foreleg and easily scaling her shoulder to her seat, settling himself in, looking every bit like a warrior king on the back of his mythical creature. I mimic his movements on the back of Drayvhn, who is slightly larger. It takes me a minute to make the ascent and I'm less than graceful, but I reach the seat and hold on for dear life.

Damian and Umbra launch before us, but Drayvhn only waits a heartbeat before he follows suit. I feel myself slipping, so I lock my thighs and strap myself in with shadows just to ease my nerves.

It's no less exhilarating today. The feeling of freedom that comes with flying is addictive. I can see why this was an escape for Damian, I feel untouchable in the air on the back of this impressive beast. The adrenaline flowing through my system makes me feel giddy. I lower my shields so Damian can feel my unbridled joy and open myself to his mind.

"This is amazing!" I throw his way.

"It is, cousin! The next part of your training will be to teach you to wield from the back of a dragon."

I'm all for anything that gives me an excuse to fly.

"Hold on, Godslayer, I think we should challenge the King to a race." Drayvhn's voice is full of mirth as the smooth baritone of his words wrap around my mind.

I laugh, and Damian looks over at me with a mischievous grin that I can't help but return. I'm guessing he got the message because Umbra takes off faster than I thought possible. I lock myself in tighter as we follow suit. The thrill of the race courses through my veins as Drayvhn surges forward, his powerful wings beating against the air with rhythmic precision. Beside us, Umbra matches his stride, the midnight black dragon's sleek form cutting through the sky like a shadow.

At first, it's a friendly competition, our dragons weaving through the clouds with graceful agility. But soon, the playful spirit of the race takes hold, and Drayvhn and Umbra begin to play dirty. They nip at each other's wings, taunting and teasing as they jockey for the lead.

I can't help but laugh as Drayvhn dives and twists, his movements fueled by the sheer joy of the moment. Beside me, Damian shouts encouragement to Umbra, his laughter mingling with mine in the vast expanse of the sky.

Below us, I hear howls and see our wolves running along,

involved in their own race, playfully nipping at each other as they keep us in their sights.

With each beat of our dragons' wings, the exhilaration builds, the thrill of the race propelling us forward at breakneck speed. As we hurtle through the air, I know that at this moment, there's nowhere else I'd rather be than soaring through the clouds, racing alongside my cousin.

In the end, the race is too close to call, so we declare a tie as we land, our dragons panting with exertion.

"That was amazing!" I squeal, running my hands over Drayvhn's scales once I dismount, the fear I felt earlier completely gone, a warm affection in its place. "Thank you, I had so much fun."

"You did well today, Godslayer. It would be an honor for you to be my rider."

My eyes go wide, and I look over at Damian, who is grinning like an idiot. "You want me to be your rider?"

"Yes, together we will lay waste to anyone who dares threaten this kingdom."

"A little bloodthirsty, but I get it. Thank you, you humble me. I will do my best to be worthy." I plant a kiss on his snout. "You two go find some water; I'll see you tomorrow."

Vengeance, Chaos, and Havoc make their way out of the woods to walk back to the castle with us. I didn't even realize they had followed us until I saw them running. I look around, surrounded by so many wondrous things, and for the first time in a long time, I feel like I truly fit somewhere.

Chapter Seven

DAMIAN

Looking around the table at everyone talking and laughing as we prepare for the day makes my heart physically hurt. The sweet ache that consumes me must be love. I love this family we are making; even Brennan is growing on me. My mother looks more relaxed than I've ever seen her, relishing in a house full of life after all the years she spent mostly alone.

Layla laughs and snatches the last biscuit out of Brennan's hands as he tries in vain to take it back and our wolves lay about the floor, carefully watching for whomever will sneak them food, which is everyone.

"You all are going to get fat and lazy if everyone keeps sneaking you table scraps and you lounge about," I mentally say to Chaos. He doesn't bother giving me a response, just raises his gaze to mine and chuffs.

Even Anika's presence warms me, though she barely looks at me, and when she does it with a scowl of disdain despite my best efforts to appease the hurt I caused. I picked a bouquet of wildflowers and left them in a vase outside of her room a few days ago, and the minx left them sitting there until I finally caved and had them removed when they were mostly dead. I offered to take her flying and though I saw the want in her eyes, she coldly turned me down with a snarky reply that had something to do with the fact that she would rather spend the night in a den of snakes than do anything alone with me ever again.

My attention snaps back to Layla as she giggles, sneaking a piece of bacon to Havoc while Vengeance growls.

"Don't worry, sweetie, I've got a piece with your name on it too," she coos, "Chaos, come get yours since Damian is greedy and won't share."

"You know they are bred for battle, not to be spoiled house pets, right?" I can't keep the smile off my face when she sticks her tongue out at me. Does she have any idea I would burn the world for her? The fierceness in which I would protect her surprises me at times. Other than my mother, I'm not sure I have ever loved another being as much as I do her. The affection and gratitude I feel knows no bounds. This moment, this happiness that fills my soul, is boundless. The peace my mother has found would not be possible without Layla. I would literally do anything to keep her safe, to see her happy, *anything*.

She seems content enough, but she can't hide the shadow of misery behind her eyes as she waits for Caspian. It's been weeks and he's not so much as sent word. If he doesn't soon, he and I are going to have a conversation he will not particularly enjoy. I owe him a debt for rescuing my mother, but I can't stand to think of Layla hurting over him. Every time I see the pain in those eyes, so like my own, I fantasize about breaking his fingers, one by one.

We need to get moving. We have a limited window of time each day to train, but I am loath to remove myself from this moment, even though I have come to look forward to our daily sessions. Since our spat, training is the only time I can get my hands on Anika. She likes to pretend she hates me, but I feel the tension as we spar together, the way her thighs clench around my hips when I pin her. I insisted Brennan join us so I could assign Layla to begin his training, giving me an excuse to have Anika all to myself.

My cock hardens, making me shift uncomfortably in my seat as I remember the way those lips felt on mine, all hot, hungry, and desperate. I can't believe the fucker has the audacity to get aroused, considering the workout I gave it in the shower, imagining what that plump red mouth would feel like wrapped around it. I let out an involuntary groan at the thought, and every pair of eyes swings toward me as I cover my mouth and begin coughing, face reddening at everyone's confused looks. Everyone except Layla, she smirks at me, a knowing look in her eyes. Dammit, why did I teach her to read me? Not that she really needed to—she's smart enough to figure out what I was thinking.

"Damian, love," my mother begins, "how would you like to celebrate your birthday? It's nearly here, and we have made no preparations. The kingdom will be expecting a celebration."

Layla's eyes widen in surprise, "When's his birthday? We should go back to Earth and take him to a strip club!"

My mother cringes at that thought and Brennan rolls his eyes. Anika looks slightly intrigued, which makes me wonder what's going on in that beautiful head of hers. Would she be turned on watching women dance half-naked? Or seeing one grind themselves on my lap? Would she be jealous? I find I have no desire for the opposite sex beyond a mouthy redhead who enjoys putting me through hell daily, but I would gladly go to watch her take in the experience.

"That wasn't exactly what I had in mind," my mother sighs in exasperation but then smiles. The affection she feels for Layla is obvious, and she has taken on a motherly role, which Layla seems to bask in. "I was thinking more along the lines of a formal occasion, an actual party with dancing, music, wine, and food. What do you think?" She looks at me expectantly, hope shining in her eyes.

"Of course, Mother, whatever you want, we shall do," I say as I grab her hand and squeeze it, pushing off from the table, motioning for my band of misfits to follow me so we can begin training for the day.

"Get changed and meet me outside in ten," I demand. My eyes wander to the curve of Anika's delectable behind as she stands and walks away from me. The way it sways, barely covered by the material of her sleep shorts, makes my mouth water. Fuck, it's going to be a long damn day.

"YOU'RE TAKING IT EASY ON ME, STOP IT," ANIKA SNAPS. She's not wrong, I hold back when I'm facing her, but with Layla, it's more like a damn brawl. That girl fights dirty.

I narrow my eyes, the tension that has been drawn so tight between us causing my control to slip as I lunge, twisting her arm behind her back, bringing her flush with my chest, my lips against her ear.

"You might not want to push me, Anika, you won't like what happens." I lower my voice so only she can hear, my breath on her ear sending a shiver she can't hide from me when she's pressed so close. I swear I feel her arch into me just a fraction, and it makes me bolder as I nip at the place where her shoulder curves into her neck. She gasps and tilts her head to give me better access.

"Dammit, Layla! I think you broke it!" Brennan screams, holding his nose, Layla staring at him with her hands on her hips, looking annoyed. My head jerks up, remembering where we are.

Shit.

I release Anika, backing away from her like the distance might cool this raging inferno inside of me that makes me desperate to lay claim to her. Her cheeks are flushed, and her breathing ragged. Knowing she's turned on makes my cock so hard. I'm pretty sure just the tiniest amount of friction would have me coming in my pants. It's been way too long since I've gotten laid.

"Quit being a pussy, did you hear a distinct crunching sound? No? Then it's not broken, man up, dude." Layla rolls her eyes at him.

Brennan grabs a towel and holds it to his bleeding nose, his eyes shooting daggers at his sister. Dammit, we are all wound tight. Someone is going to eventually snap, and it's not going to end well. Between Caspian's absence, there being absolutely no sign of Layla's father, and the losses we have suffered lately, it's no wonder we are all so cranky. Maybe my mother is right, and we need a party.

"Damian, I need to talk to you," Layla demands as she begins to walk away from the others. When I don't start moving fast enough, she snaps, "*Now!*"

"Okay, calm the fuck down," I grumble. I follow her over to the spot she deems far enough away from the others and cross my arms, waiting for her to speak, assuming I'm getting my ass ripped over something.

"My magic is fading." Panic flares in her eyes and I'm stunned into momentary silence.

"Show me," I demand.

She tries to conjure fire and it stutters, barely holding for a few seconds before it dies out. "I can't call to the lightning either," she says, her voice wobbling as tears threaten to spill down her cheeks. I yank her to me, crushing her against me. Panic threatens to take control, fear of what this might mean weighs on both of us.

"What about your night-wielding?"

"It's still there," she says, her voice muffled against my chest. She tries to wiggle out of my grasp and I reluctantly let her go.

"I know you're scared, but we will figure it out together, understand? You and me. You are not in this alone." I hold onto her shoulders, looking her in her eyes, making sure she sees the truth in my face.

In my heart, I know what she's afraid of. She's afraid it means her bond with Caspian is fading. Heaven help him if that's the case because I might just kill the bastard.

Ending training early, I seek out my mother. I find her in the room she uses for an office, pouring over requests from people in the kingdom. She tries so hard to read every single one and help our people as much as possible. She rarely turns anyone away. I lean against the door frame, quietly watching her work. It only takes a moment for her to feel my presence and meet my eyes.

"Damian! What a surprise! What can I do for you, son?" she queries.

"I need you to cancel my appointments for the day. I need to have a talk with a prince," I say with barely leashed violence strumming through my veins.

She nods solemnly, "I was wondering when you would finally break. You've been watching her for weeks, and every day, you look angrier than the day before. Just don't do anything to bring their wrath down on us or Layla's on you. I love you, son, but if you do something stupid, I will stand back and watch her skin you alive." She pins me with her eyes, letting me know she means every word.

I nod to her and leave the room, heading out to the dragons. Umbra will be the quickest way to make it to Caspian's kingdom. His father will likely be pissed at my unannounced visit, but I've never much cared for proper etiquette anyway.

As I ride atop my dragon, the wind rushes past, whipping my

hair into a frenzy and carrying the salty tang of the sea. Beneath me, the kingdom of Pelagia unfolds like a painting of paradise, its verdant islands and sparkling waters stretching as far as the eye can see.

Despite the beauty that surrounds me, my heart is heavy. It's been weeks since we last heard from Caspian, and his prolonged absence has left Layla heartbroken and adrift. The hurt in her eyes leaves a perpetual ache in my chest.

As we approach Caspian's palace, nestled amidst the lush greenery of the islands, my grip tightens on Umbra. The thought of confronting Cas fills me with a tumult of emotions—betrayal, disappointment, and a simmering rage that threatens to boil over.

With each beat of my dragon's wings, I steel myself for the confrontation ahead. I know that it could piss Layla off, but I refuse to let Caspian's neglect go unaddressed.

As we land on the sun-kissed shores of Pelagia, I dismount from my dragon, my steps purposeful and determined. It's time to confront Cas, demand answers, and hold him accountable for the hurt he must know he is causing her.

Guards rush out to meet us, smart enough to keep a safe distance from Umbra.

"King Damianos, we were not expecting a visit," the head guard stammers as he watches Umbra who narrows her golden eyes at him.

"I know, I apologize, I need to see Prince Caspian urgently."

"Yes, sir, follow me."

He leads me into the castle and deposits me into the room designated for my wait. A refreshing sea breeze wafts through the open windows, carrying with it the scent of salt and sunshine. The chamber is bathed in soft, natural light, with sheer curtains billowing gently in the ocean breeze.

The walls are painted a serene shade of azure, embellished with delicate seashell motifs that shimmer in the sunlight. Artfully arranged driftwood sculptures and glass orbs filled with shimmering sea glass adorn the room, adding a touch of coastal charm to the elegant surroundings.

Seating options include plush armchairs upholstered in soft, ocean-hued fabrics, their cushions decorated with embroidered seahorses and starfish. A low table crafted from polished driftwood sits in the center of the room, adorned with bowls of fresh fruit and pitchers of cool, refreshing water infused with slices of citrus.

The sound of waves crashing against the shore can be heard in the distance, a peaceful soundtrack to the tranquil ambiance of the room.

It's a room designed to soothe the soul, but it does nothing to ease the knot that has taken residence in the pit of my stomach, waiting for Caspian's arrival.

As the minutes stretch on, I find myself growing increasingly restless, the weight of uncertainty pressing down upon me like a heavy cloak. I start to question if I'm doing the right thing. Should I be meddling in their relationship? My need to protect Layla was part of the reason I acted, but the fear in her eyes at the waning strength of her power is what set me into motion. Layla is rarely afraid.

Finally, the sound of approaching footsteps breaks the silence, and I brace myself for the encounter to come. The door swings open, revealing Caspian standing there, his expression a mix of surprise and confusion at my presence.

"Damian?" he exclaims questioningly, his voice tinged with disbelief. "What are you doing here? Is Layla okay?" Worry lines his face, a hint of panic to his words that dissipates some of my anger.

I meet his gaze evenly, "I feel like you left me no choice but to seek you out," I reply, my tone grave. "It's been weeks with no word from you. Layla doesn't complain, but the pain she is suffering is obvious, and her powers are diminishing."

As Caspian processes my words, I can see the wheels turning in his mind, his expression shifting from confusion to concern.

He drops into a nearby chair, looking nothing like a regal prince as his body seems to deflate, shoulders falling as he props his elbows on his knees and buries his face in his hands.

"Things are complicated, Damian. You know my father. He refuses to budge on the betrothal and to make matters worse, Aegir is in love with the princess and wants to marry her, and she him. The entire thing is a clusterfuck of epic proportions. I'm trying to find a solution. My father is riding my ass so hard it's ridiculous. I told him I was in love with Layla and would rather walk away from the crown than marry anyone else, and he literally threatened me with war on your kingdom if I didn't do his bidding."

"Let him bring war. I'm not afraid—Layla and I alone could decimate most of his forces," I say flippantly, even though we both know anytime a kingdom changes power they are vulnerable to attack, especially with the rumor of my father's death, an *immortal's* death, which is unheard of. The kingdoms are probably all frantically plotting, and I am pissed I didn't think about that before. I need to make preparations.

"Would you really? You would kill innocent men just to piss off my father? Face me in battle?" His eyebrow raises.

"Caspian, you and I both know you would not stand on a battlefield where Layla was the enemy. You could no more bring harm to her than I could." His eyes cloud over, and he goes quiet. "But there *is* another matter at hand. We need to talk about Layla's powers. What do you know of fated mates?"

"I know it's fodder for fairy tales, why?"

"Well, apparently, according to my mother, it's not. It just hasn't happened in a long while."

"And?" he questions.

"Apparently, you and Layla are likely fated mates if such things do exist, and your powers strengthen as your bond grows, hence why Layla's powers grew exponentially after she confessed her love."

Obvious pain flickers through his eyes as he remembers that moment. "Have you noticed a change in your powers as your relationship grew?"

"Yes," he whispers, eyes staring into the distance.

"Have you noticed them changing lately? Diminishing in any way?"

"Yes." He buries his head again, taking a deep breath.

"Does your father know it was Layla who killed Moros?" I hiss, furious at the danger that would put her in.

"No! He doesn't even believe the rumors that he is dead. He's been sending out people to investigate, which is another reason I haven't been able to leave. I'm trying like hell to protect her as much as I can. We both know she will be hunted if anyone finds out she can kill immortals."

"Cas, you need to find a way to come see her, if only for a short visit. Or would it be safe for her to come here?"

"No! Absolutely not," he says vehemently. "Your mother has already sent out notices for your birthday celebration. I will be in attendance for that, so will my brothers."

"And the princess?" I inquire with a raised brow.

He sighs wearily, "Yes, she will be as well. Please do not tell Layla. Let me explain things to her when I see her. Swear it, Damian, swear you will let me speak to her first."

I nod, "I will for now, but you better find a way to fix this, soon. Eventually her hurt is going to turn into anger. You and I both know how vicious she can be, especially if she's hurt," I warn before standing to leave.

"I wish we were seeing each other under different circumstances, but it was still good to see you, Damian." He looks so defeated I almost feel sorry for him.

"You too, Cas. Just please don't hurt her. I would hate to have to kill you." I smile as I saunter out of the room, leaving him to his misery.

Chapter Eight

LAYLA

Damian has been suspiciously absent most of the day. When I asked his mother where he was, she avoided giving me a direct answer, and Vengeance flat-out ignored me. Something is going on, and if I have to beat answers out of him, you bet your ass I will.

I head out to visit Drayvhn and discover Umbra gone. Hmm, the plot thickens. With the way everyone else has been ignoring my demands for answers today, I don't bother asking the dragon—getting pissed at something that can kill you in seconds might not be a smart idea, so it's better just to assume that would get me nowhere.

"Hey big guy, feel like going flying?"

"Always, Godslayer. Anywhere in particular you want to go?"

"No, just feeling restless," I reply as I begin the ascent up his leg and back. As soon as I settle in, he launches and the heavy feeling gripping my heart immediately loosens. We level out, and I see Vengeance and Havoc running below, and I wonder how far I can be from her and still communicate and if I can speak to her in my mind like I can Cas.

I close my eyes and concentrate on her, "*Vengeance?*"

"*Yes?*"

"*I was just checking to see if I could speak into your mind the way you can mine.*"

"*Of course you can,*" she says with an irritated huff.

"*How far away can we be and still speak?*"

"*It differs for each pair, but we are both exceptional creatures, so we can assume it will be a significant distance.*"

"*What do you all do when you follow us on our flights?*"

"*We hunt,*" she says simply.

I never thought about them hunting, but they are wolves. Even though we feed them, they still have predatory instincts.

"*I like to hunt sometimes too, but it's usually not for fun,*" I tell her.

"*Something tells me that while it may not be for fun, you still consider it so.*"

I just laugh because she's right.

I close my eyes and enjoy the feel of the wind on my face and the feeling of freedom that comes with flying. I hear a roar in the distance, and when I open my eyes, I see Damian and Umbra approaching us from the right as Drayvhn changes course, heading toward them.

It's obvious, even from this distance, that something is wrong. Damian's entire body is tense, and he's usually relaxed when he flies.

"Head home, Drayvhn. I need to speak to my cousin," I yell over the roar of the wind.

"*I think that is wise,*" Drayvhn replies and changes course, Damian and Umbra following suit.

We land and dismount. A chill creeps down my spine as Damian approaches, his usually composed demeanor marred by an unsettling tension. My heart quickens its pace, a gnawing sense of dread clawing at the edges of my consciousness. Instinctively, I know that something is off. I search his expression for answers, but his features betray nothing, leaving me to grapple with the unsettling sense of wrongness.

"You want to tell me what's going on, or do you want me to beat it out of you?" I plant my feet, cross my arms, and stand directly in his path.

"Not now, Layla," he growls.

"Oh, yes, *now*, Damian," I fire back at him.

He moves to walk around me, his long legs eating up the distance with ease while I scramble to catch up. I grab him by his arm and force him to look at me.

"You don't get to pull this shit with me. You are the *one* person I can always count on to be honest with me. You don't get to hide shit —I've had enough of that to last me a lifetime, so what the fuck is wrong?" I scream at him, this mounting pressure threatening to boil over and consume me.

He meets my eyes and the coldness there begins to melt. He lets loose a heavy sigh and his shoulders sag before he finally speaks.

"I went to see Caspian," he says quietly, searching my eyes, an overwhelming sadness in the depths of his.

"You went to see Cas," I repeat, my voice devoid of emotion as I try to process what he is saying. "What happened? Is he okay?"

"He's fine. Like all of us, he's just dealing with a lot right now. He will be here for my birthday celebration, and he sends his love." Some of the tension in him eases. He's being honest, but I get the feeling there's more he isn't telling me.

"Why didn't you take me with you?" It's impossible to keep the hurt out of my voice.

"I wasn't sure what kind of reception we would receive. I asked Cas about you coming to visit and he said it's not safe for you. His father is trying to find out what happened to Moros. If they discover you killed him, that you can kill the immortals, they will hunt you."

"Let them come!" I scream before realization settles over me. If they come for me, they will come for us all. Damian. His mother. Brennan. I can't let that happen. "I'm sorry, Damian, I don't mean that. I don't want to put any of you in danger." He wraps an arm around my shoulder and pulls me close, kissing the top of my head.

"I don't want them to come, but if they do, I will defend you with my dying breath. We do need to think about protecting the kingdom. I'm embarrassed I haven't been more diligent; any time there is a change of power, a kingdom is vulnerable. The news of my father's death has some kingdoms in an uproar—we need to be prepared for a possible attack."

I pale, fear settling into my bones. This is not a good time for my powers to be weakening.

"Tell me what you need from me, I will do whatever I can," I tell him vehemently.

"I'm going to meet with our soldiers—you need to be present for that. We need a strategy. It would be a good idea to train more people as dragon riders and for us to train with the wolves. Let's get together later tonight and brainstorm."

"Fine. Come here, your hair is a friggin mess." I reach up and try to tame the black waves that fall to his shoulders. It's a tangled mess from flying and he looks unkempt, which is adorable, but not very kingly. "You're hopeless, go shower." I shove him away and he laughs but does as he's told. "Plus, you smell like dragon ass!" I yell at his retreating back, earning a chuff from the dragons behind me, causing me to giggle and apologize to them.

A heavy weight still sitting on me, I decide to visit Brennan. He has adjusted well to the crazy that is now his life, but I know it's been a lot. I knock on his door and hear a distinctly feminine giggle from his room. Well, well, well...seems my baby brother is up to some tomfoolery.

He takes too long to answer, so I pound harder, a smile plastered on my face. "Brennan! I know you're in there, open the damn door, or I'll unlock it myself!" A flurry of motion comes from inside and some cursing has me almost doubled over with laughter. I'm such an asshole.

"What, Layla?" he pants as he throws open the door, half-dressed, his brown curls falling into his eyes, obviously disheveled.

"Whatcha doin'?" My eyebrows are raised so high they probably damn near touch my hairline, my face the picture of innocence.

"Well, uh, I was," he stammers. I can't hold it anymore. I burst out laughing.

"Brennan! You little manwhore! Come find me later when you are less occupied." I laugh as I walk away, heat creeping into his cheeks as he smiles and shuts the door once more.

I try Anika next, but she's not in her room. Shit. I guess I will be entertaining myself. We've been so busy I haven't had much time to read, so now is as good of a time as any to check out the library. Scanning through the shelves I find a few interesting reads. A few romantic-looking tomes and a couple on the history of Aetheria pique my interest. I head back to my room and drop them off before meeting with Damian to strategize.

Listening to his conversation with his mother, I enter through the open door and slide into a seat at the table, where they are engrossed in the details of party planning. I can't believe I didn't know when his birthday was until a few days ago. June twenty-second. I find this funny since mine is October twenty-second. Have we really only known each other for eight or nine months? In some ways, it feels like we have known each other our entire lives.

"So, the party is this Saturday?" I perk up at this bit of news, excited at the prospect of seeing Cas.

"Yes, and we have many acceptances. It will be wonderful!" she exclaims, happiness radiating from her like a shiny beacon of love and hope as she bustles out of the room. I have no idea how, with all she has been through, she is still so full of life and love. It's easy to see how Damian turned out to be who he is despite his father being a prick.

"Layla, come in. Let's roll up our sleeves and get to work," he says, closing the door behind us to ensure privacy. We settle in for what turns out to be an hour-long session, meticulously planning security measures for the upcoming party. Additionally, we outline a detailed schedule for the weeks ahead, focusing on training our men and gathering intelligence on the local forces. It's clear that we have our work cut out for us.

Chapter Nine

LAYLA

C as is here. I feel his presence even before he enters the building. Giddy with excitement, I follow the pull and take off running, the thrill of knowing I would be in his arms within moments spurring me on, joy radiating from me like sunshine on a summer morning. I round a corner, coming to an abrupt halt, when I see him standing in the middle of the hall, eyes drinking me in like a thirsty soul savoring his first drop of water. All the fears and worries melt away as I throw myself into his arms. He lifts me up as I wrap my legs around his waist and arms around his neck, kissing him with abandon.

"Room, now," he growls, and I slide down his body, grabbing his hand as we sprint down the halls and up the steps to my room. We don't have much time before the guests arrive, and I'm not about to waste a single second of it.

As soon as we are behind closed doors, we both start stripping as fast as we can, a flurry of clothing pieces being tossed around the room. When we are finally both naked, he picks me up and tosses me on the bed, his hands moving down to the apex of my thighs and lower as he slides a finger into me.

"You are always so fucking wet for me," he whispers.

"Cas, stop playing around. I need you to fuck me, *now*." I reach for his cock, placing it at my entrance and rolling my hips up, impaling myself on him as we both moan. He takes me rough and fast, an animalistic desperation to it, us both nothing but pure need. He fucks me like nothing in the world matters other than him finding his release, and I'm right there with him.

"Fuck, Layla. I've missed this, missed you," he whispers in my ear, sending shivers down my spine. I feel that pressure building and I'm so close I can taste that sweet release.

"Rub my clit," I demand. He puts a hand between us and rubs me in tight circles while he drives in faster, harder. "I'm going to come, Cas, don't fucking stop." I'm arching up into his thrusts, each one feels better than the last. He bites my neck and I claw at his back, teetering on that edge so full of pleasure it's almost painful until I finally explode, screaming his name, sobbing into his shoulder as tears spring to my eyes from the sheer force of my orgasm.

His rhythm breaks and his thrusts become even wilder, pounding into me so hard all I can do is hold on.

His grunts mingle with my moans as filthy words tumble from his mouth, and I scour my nails along his back.

"I love you, Cas," I say as I run my fingers through his hair and bring his mouth back to mine. His hips stutter and he thrusts into me one last time, spilling his seed, marking me, claiming me as his.

We lay in my bed for a few moments, him still inside of me, not wanting to move. "Why is it always like this with us? I feel like a fire rages through me each time you touch me, and you are the only thing that can put it out. I've never felt desire like this, the relentless need to be with someone. It's a little overwhelming," I confess as I play with his beautiful golden locks.

"It's the same for me. It's physically painful when I'm away from you." He runs a hand down my side and goosebumps dance along my skin. "I love you so damn much." His voice is husky as he pulls me close and kisses the top of my head before rolling off me.

"As much as I hate to, we need to get dressed. I have to be in the throne room as guests start to arrive. Thank you for coming early." I sit up, leaning over to press a kiss on his chest, before heading to my bathroom to clean up and get ready.

When I come out, I lean in to kiss him. It's meant to be quick, but he pulls me in, slowly exploring my mouth as he runs a hand down my back, making it hard for me to pull away. We finally break apart and I look at him, so much love shining from his eyes that my heart skips a beat before it expands, basking in the glow of being loved. I kiss him one last time and head out while he uses my bathroom to clean himself up. I hate letting him out of my sight, but I feel better than I have in weeks.

In the throne room, Damian's mother is running around checking on everything, and it gives me a warm, fuzzy feeling in my soul to see her bustling about, so damn happy.

Walking through the grounds of Shadowfell, I can't help but double-check every security measure we've taken for Damian's birthday, making sure everyone is in place. My steps are deliberate, my eyes moving over the dire wolves prowling the perimeter. They move like shadows, their presence comforting yet a stark reminder of the threats lurking beyond our kingdom. Above, dragons perch silently on ledges of the mountain, their eyes vigilant, ready to swoop down on any who dare disrupt our peace. Our troops are strategically posted inside as well as out, ever watchful.

Despite the immortality of Cas, Damian, and his mother, Enthralia, I can't shake the coil of worry tightening in my chest.

Anika and Brennan, woven into the very fabric of our lives, don't share this gift of eternal life. And me? Half-human, my fate is a question mark hanging over my head, my potential longevity still a mystery.

With Damian's ascent to the throne still fresh, I'm painfully aware that eyes are on us, seeing not the strength we project but perhaps an opportunity.

The fear of vulnerability isn't just about an external attack; it's about the internal cracks it could exploit and the damage it could do to our tightly-knit family. These preparations, while extensive, feel like a thin shield against unknown dangers.

As I finish my rounds, a mix of pride and anxiety settles in. We've done everything possible to prepare, yet the fear of the unknown haunts me.

Allowing myself a moment to just breathe, to feel the cool air brush against my skin, I find a brief respite from the storm of my thoughts. With a heart still heavy, I head back in to stand at Damian's side, standing protectively by my family, my everything.

Guests begin to arrive and I try to settle. They are announced one by one. My head snaps up when I hear familiar names being introduced, my lips curving into a smile as I see three golden-haired, blue-eyed men that I know based on looks alone are Caspian's brothers, Aegir, Nereus, and Delphin. The genetic pool in that family is insanely unfair.

They approach Damian to wish him a happy birthday. Their smiles speak of mischief and their eyes are full of laughter.

"Boys, let me introduce you to my cousin, Lady Layla," Damian turns to me, "this is Aegir," he points to one who is about as tall as Cas but broader. He's more rugged than pretty but still insanely handsome. "This troublemaker is Nereus." Nereus looks eerily similar to Cas. He's about an inch taller, putting him at a good six foot four, with a similar build. His hair is a little darker and cropped short.

Delphin walks closer and introduces himself, "He saved the best for last—obviously, I am Delphin, and you are Cas's Layla." He sweeps me up into a bone-crushing hug, and I am momentarily lost for words. Delphin is heartbreakingly beautiful. I think Cas is gorgeous, but Delphin is utter perfection. Tall and undeniably striking, his physical beauty seems to effortlessly draw the gaze of those around him. The tallest and largest built of the four, he possesses a poised stature that commands attention, his presence both imposing and inviting. His hair, a radiant shade of blond, is styled in a way that artfully balances between meticulous and carefree. The longer strands at the front fall just so, framing his face in a deliberate messiness that highlights his sharp features and strong jawline.

His eyes, a vivid blue, are piercing and alive with humor. They light up his face with a warmth and charisma that's hard to ignore. His physique, toned and well-defined, speaks of disciplined physical activity, but it's his effortless grace that truly sets him apart. Every movement he makes is fluid and confident.

There's a natural charm about him as well, a magnetism that's subtle yet undeniable. It's not just his physical appearance that captivates; it's the way he carries himself, with a blend of confidence and humility, that truly defines his allure. Despite his near-perfect features, there's an approachability to him, a sense of down-to-earth genuineness that makes him easy to like from the moment you meet him.

His youthful exuberance only adds to his appeal, and the deep timber of his voice settles in your bones and makes you want to sigh and just sit and listen to him say anything.

"It's so nice to meet you all. I've heard so much about you!" I laugh as Delphin finally puts me down, a grin plastered to my face.

"Cas never shuts up about you, at least when Father isn't around." He rolls his eyes and wrinkles his nose and I have the irresistible urge to boop it. He's so damn cute it's ridiculous. I burst with happiness knowing Cas talks to them about me.

I look at Aegir, and he's staring at the entrance, a thunderous look clouding his eyes, his lips pursed in a tight line, jaw clenched. I turn to see what he is staring at, and my heart stops. Suddenly, all the air has been sucked out of the room, and I can't breathe. At the entrance, being announced is Cas. My Cas. And on his arm is Princess Nerine.

Damian puts a comforting hand on the small of my back and whispers, "Open your mind to me, Layla." It's hard to concentrate enough, but I do as he requests.

"Layla, I had hoped he would have spoken with you before this, but by the look on your face, that isn't the case. He didn't have a choice. Look at Aegir. He's in love with her, and she with him. Cas is playing a part. He is still yours. Please do not panic, and for the love of the gods, please do not set something on fire or cause a thunderstorm. I've got you, understand?"

I nod my head, unable to form words, even in my mind. I can see the truth in Aegir's face, but it still feels like someone punched me in the stomach watching her walk in on his arm.

She's lovely, a fitting princess. Probably nothing like me with my rough edges and foul mouth. I can't picture her covered in blood or killing. She's the type of woman that he should have on his arm, and the realization almost makes my knees buckle.

"Layla, stop. I can hear those thoughts—stop them right now. He doesn't want a soft princess, that's not Cas. He wants you—you are beautiful, a warrior, and no one compares to you, do you understand? You are not a soft princess; you are a fucking goddess." The vehemence in Damian's voice makes me love him all the more. While it makes

me feel marginally better, the ache is still there, clawing its way through my heart.

"Cas, you couldn't give me a warning?" I throw the thought his way, but he has me shut out, which hurts almost as much as seeing her on his arm.

He walks up to wish Damian a happy birthday, eyes meeting mine for the briefest second, and I see the guilt swimming in those blue depths. The princess by his side curtsies and offers birthday wishes of her own, her voice as soft and lovely as she is. I see her gaze brush over Aegir, and he stiffens.

"Damian, I'm going to go check on the wolves," I say stiffly, not waiting for an answer as I turn on my heel and flee from the room like the hounds of hell are chasing my ass. My power rises, simmering along my skin, needing to break free to ease this torrent of emotion rising in me.

I make it far enough from the castle, let power surge forward in a rush, and fall to my knees. I feel the shadows flow over the grounds, blasting through the night, and it gives me a small moment of relief.

I feel a wet nose nudge me and look into the midnight blue eyes of Vengeance. She lays next to me, and I bury my head in the fur of her neck, sobbing into the softness.

"You probably think I'm pathetic," I sniffle as I hold on to her. It's the first time she's ever shown me any softness.

"I think you are someone who loves with your whole being. That makes you strong, not pathetic. Only the strongest among us can be broken and still find room in their hearts to love."

I feel as well as hear the growl rise from within Vengeance. I leap to my feet, looking for the threat as she bares her teeth. My spine stiffens as Cas approaches. I didn't even feel him.

"Layla," pain laces his voice as he eyes Vengeance wearily.

73

I lay a hand on her, "It's okay, this is Cas." She stops growling but eyes him warily and stays by my side.

He tries to take my hand, but I pull it away. "I'm sorry, I meant to tell you earlier. It's one of the reasons I came before them, but then we got kinda distracted." He gives me a roguish grin, "I'm sorry. Damian said he told you about Aegir."

I nod and take a deep breath. "I'm not going to pretend it didn't hurt to see you with her because it did," I say quietly as a tear slips down my cheek. "But it wasn't just that, Cas. She's the type of woman you should be with. She is everything a future queen should be. I'm nothing like that, our lives couldn't be more different. She's sweet and beautiful and probably hasn't had a single difficult day in her life and my life has been nothing but difficult days. I'm a fighter, not a princess, and you are a prince."

"Stop it, Layla." The anger in his tone takes me by surprise. "When have I ever given you any reason to believe I cared about that? I fell in love with you, knowing exactly who you are. I love that you are a fighter. You are fierce, fearless, and not afraid to kick my fucking ass when I need it, and I would rather you beat the shit out of me right now than see you sitting here crying because you somehow think you aren't good enough or that I don't want you. That's insane. You have known me for how long?"

The confidence in his words eases the pressure in my chest, but the image of them looking so perfect together still sits in my mind. He reaches for my hand again and I let him. He pulls me to him until our bodies are flush, taking my chin in his fingers, tilting my head up, and looking into my eyes.

"You. Are. Perfect. There is *nothing* I would change about you, not even your temper." He lowers his mouth, and my eyes flutter closed as he slants his lips over mine. "*I love you,*" he whispers into my mind. The intimacy of that connection is like a balm to my soul.

"We should head back. I am supposed to be standing in there

looking scary." He laughs and takes my hand in his. I turn to Vengeance and kiss her head before Cas and I walk back, hand in hand. I let go before we walk in, noticing the room looks exceptionally more crowded than when I left just moments ago.

"So, I take it Damian talked you into the wolf?" His eyebrow quirks up.

"Well, she decided I was hers after she tried to attack me, I called her a bitch and threatened her," I say nonchalantly, shrugging my shoulders.

His eyes light up and he gives me a full, genuine laugh. "Why does that not surprise me? She sounds perfect for you." That makes me smile as I scan the room for Damian.

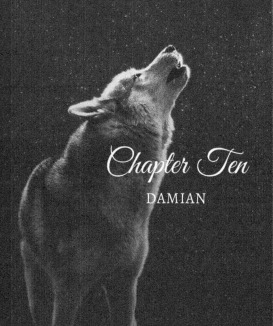

Chapter Ten

DAMIAN

My mother is bursting with excitement as guests pour in for the party. My nerves are frayed. The asshole, Caspian, didn't give Layla a heads up about coming with the princess, and I want to knock his teeth down his throat when I felt the hurt pouring off her.

Then there's Anika—the last few days of training with her have been torture. The tension between us stretched so taut there have been many times I've almost given into the temptation to haul her to my rooms and show her exactly how much I want her. I can't count how many times I have fucked my fist thinking about the way she sounded riding my hand and coming on my fingers.

Speaking of Anika, I have yet to see her tonight. Extracting myself from a particularly boring prince from a neighboring kingdom, I set off down the hall to look for her. Rounding a corner, I stop dead in my tracks as she steps out of her room. All thoughts leave my head and my mouth goes dry.

With the way she looks, there is no way I am going to make it through the night without putting my hands on her. Her hair is unbound, tumbling down her back in a cascade of fiery curls I desperately want to wind around my fingers. Her loose, flowy skirt has a massive slit up the side almost all the way up her thigh. The shirt is barely a scrap of fabric, her arms bare, several inches of the pale skin of her stomach showing, and *fuck me*, those shoes. The heels are tall, and they have straps that wind halfway up those long, fabulous legs that I have fantasized more than once about having wrapped around my waist.

My cock is instantly hard, straining painfully against my zipper. She turns toward me, and I see her eyes wander down my body, stopping at the bulge in my pants as she licks her lips before bringing her eyes back to mine. There is so much heat in those emerald flames she could easily set me on fire, and I would gladly die there if it meant having her. Before I know what I'm doing, I close the distance between us, trapping her against the wall, caging her in with my arms planted on each side of her head, leaning into her space. Her breath hitches as I take in her scent, feeling the heat radiating from her body as it reacts to mine.

"Hello, Anika. You look absolutely stunning tonight." My voice is low and husky, desire pulsing through me. The smell of jasmine wafts into my nose, and I've decided that is my new favorite scent, a smell that is distinctly Anika. Her pouty lips are painted red, and I wonder what my cock would look like sliding between them.

She kicks her chin up a notch, staring me in the eyes, challenging me.

"Damian," she says breathlessly, "shouldn't you be at the party?"

"I should, but I wanted to find you."

"Why?" She parts her lips and runs her tongue over that plump bottom one, and I groan.

"Because I can't seem to stay away from you." I graze the back of my knuckle across her cheek and her eyes flutter closed. My cock has its own heartbeat, all my blood rushing to it, robbing me of all common sense as I give in to the need eating me alive and capture her lips in a kiss.

It's soft for the briefest of seconds, but then she threads her hands in my hair and tilts my head, opening her mouth and stroking my tongue. My control goes up in flames, her taste, her smell, the touch of her tongue against mine consuming me. I groan into her mouth and place a hand at her waist, stroking the exposed flesh there. Her hips are grinding into me, and I'm about two seconds away from taking her up against this wall.

"Damian," she whispers as she reaches in between us and starts stroking my cock through my pants.

"Fuck, that feels so damn good, keep touching me just like that," I say through gritted teeth as I slide a hand through the slit in her skirt, slipping beneath her panties and rubbing her clit. She throws one of her deliciously long legs over my hip and is shamelessly riding my hand as I slip a finger into her heat while rubbing tighter circles, getting her closer to that peak.

We are both moaning and writhing against each other, not caring that anyone could happen upon us at any moment. Her breaths are coming faster and faster, the way she is moaning in my ear making me tremble with need.

Her fingers fumble as she unbuttons my pants and slides her hand in, gripping me so tight, sliding up and down me, squeezing as she goes.

"Don't stop, fuck, please don't stop!" she begs as she finally finds her pleasure. Clutching my shoulder with one hand, gripping my cock with her other, I feel her cunt clench around my fingers as she cries out my name. It causes me to lose all control and I tumble over that edge with her, coming in her hand like a horny sixteen-year-old boy. I lean my forehead against hers while trying to catch my breath.

"I love how responsive you are, the way you sound when you

come makes my knees weak. You are so damn sexy," I whisper before pressing another kiss to her lips, both of us trembling as we try to catch our breath. My eyes meet hers, and the wonder I feel is mirrored there as we search each other's gazes.

I remove my hand from between her thighs and bring it to my mouth. I lick one of my fingers, closing my eyes and moaning at her taste. "You taste fucking delicious. Open," I command, "I want you to taste yourself on my hand." She does as she's told, latching on to my finger, sucking it all, licking it with her tongue, making me instantly hard again. "Fuck, that's hot." I guide her hand back to my cock and press into it. "Look at what you do to me, I already want you again."

"Then take me," she quietly challenges, bringing her fingers that are coated with my climax to her lips, holding my gaze as she licks them clean one by one. The world could be crumbling around me, and I wouldn't have been able to tear my eyes away from those lips. When she finishes, I grab her hand and drag her to my room.

We cross the threshold and I kick the door shut.

"Sit," I say, pointing to the edge of my bed. She does, and it slightly surprises me that she is being so compliant. I kneel before her and put my hands on her thighs, spreading them wide. Pushing the material of the skirt back, I stare at her sex through the thin scrap of lace she's wearing for underwear. I grab them and rip the fabric, causing her to gasp, but she stays still, watching me. Savoring this moment, I slowly lean in and flick my tongue over her clit. She nearly comes off the bed as she gasps in pleasure, making me laugh as I do it again and again until she is arching up, her hands in my hair, moaning, wanting more.

"Tell me what you want, Anika," I say, my voice full of dark promises.

"Put your mouth on me again," she pants, and I eagerly comply. I slide a finger inside her and take up a rhythm that has her squirming and begging in moments, stroking that inferno that's growing inside her until she is grinding against my mouth shamelessly and I am lost in the taste of her, the feel of her slick heat.

So close, she's so damn close, all I can think about is making her come again, hearing her call out my name. I work in a second finger, and fuck, she is so damn tight I want to bury myself in her more than I want anything else in this world. I work my tongue faster, and a second later, her back is bowing, head thrown back, eyes closed as she threads her fingers into my hair and holds on for dear life as she crests over that pinnacle. I don't stop touching her until that last wave from her orgasm passes, and she is laying back on the bed, breathless and limp. I kiss the sensitive skin of her inner thigh and work my way up to her bare stomach, desperate to touch every part of her.

"Damian." The wonder in her voice makes me feel like I am on top of the world, knowing she's never found pleasure like that with another. Little does she know, I'm just getting started.

She sits up and I capture her mouth in a long, slow kiss that leaves her trembling. "I want to touch you," she says quietly as she reaches for my pants. I go perfectly still, letting her work them down my legs as I stand before her while she still sits at the edge of my bed.

She takes me in her hand and I'm lost. I've fantasized about this so many damn times, it's hard to believe it's real. I reach out and touch one of her curls, rubbing my thumb over the silky strands.

"Tell me what to do," she pants, looking up at me, a smile playing on her lips as she grips my cock.

"Hold the base, wrap your hand around it," I barely recognize my voice as it leaves me—it sounds like it's been raked across hot coals. She does it, and it takes every ounce of self-control I possess to be still. "Now use your tongue and swirl it around the head before taking it in your mouth." That first flick of her tongue has pleasure coiling tight at my spine, my balls drawing up, and she's barely touched me.

Fuck, fuck, fuck. Her perfect little mouth is wrapped around my head, and I want to come already. "Now, slowly slide down the shaft, taking as much as you can, then go back up. When you get back to the tip, rub your tongue over it," I don't even finish what I'm saying before she's doing it and I'm drowning in her. Watching her painted red lips around me, her hair spilling down, eyes looking up at me under those impossibly thick lashes. It's too much and it's been so damn long for me. It's so much better than any fantasy I've had.

A loud banging comes from the door. "Damian, are you in there? Your mother is looking for you." It's Layla, and as much as I adore my cousin, right now, I want to rip her fucking head off her shoulders.

"Don't stop, for the love of the gods, please don't stop," I whisper as I try so hard not to thrust myself into her mouth.

Layla knocks again. "Go the fuck away, Layla," I snarl. I can't hold back—it's only been a minute, maybe two, and my control has snapped. I'm thrusting into her mouth, my hands in her hair, seconds away from spilling my seed into those beautifully soft lips. "Just like that, baby, fuck, you feel so damn good. I'm going to come." She moans around me, and I'm done for. "Fuck!" I groan, my orgasm ripping through me with a force that leaves my legs trembling. It's barely been ten minutes since I found her in the hall, and I've already come twice. Damnit, I need to get myself under control.

I pull back and lie on the bed, pulling her into me as I try to control my breathing. "I'm so sorry, love. I don't normally lose control like that, but it's been a while for me."

"Really? How long?" she asks, running a hand up and down my arm.

"About fifty, maybe sixty years? I've lost count."

"No way!" She smacks my arm.

"I'm serious," I tell her, and a smile spreads across her face.

"I've never had anyone put their mouth on me like that. That was," she pauses like she's searching for the right word, "amazing. I don't even know how to put into words how that felt."

I pull her to me and kiss her mouth as Layla starts knocking on the door again.

"Give me five fucking minutes and I'll be down, you impatient brat," I yell, and she grumbles something I can't understand as she retreats.

"As much as I want to stay right here in this bed with you and do all sorts of depraved things, my mother will have my head if I do not get back to this party ASAP, and Layla will just take the door down. Once all the guests leave, I want you back in this bed, naked, understand?" I bite gently on her lower lip and she shivers.

Fuck, I'm hard again. I move away from her and pull her out of the bed, her gaze fixated on my cock as she runs her tongue over where I just bit.

"Yes, love, that is what you do to me, how much I want you, now be a good girl and go get ready and meet me in the hall." I swat her plump rear, and she giggles but gets moving as I find another pair of pants.

A few minutes later I am pacing the hall in front of her room, waiting for her to emerge. Her door finally opens and even though I just saw her a few minutes ago, the sight of her still has the same effect.

I take her arm and whisper into her ear, "Did you put on new panties?" My mouth waters remembering the taste of her.

Her lips curve seductively, her eyes flare with fresh desire. "No. Happy birthday, Damian."

"Bloody hell," I close my eyes and try to calm the storm within me, "I'm not going to last until the guests leave before I bury myself in you."

She gives me a satisfied smirk and I kiss her temple. Little vixen.

We reach the throne room where the party is currently underway. As soon as I enter, my mother catches my eye and waves me over. I reluctantly let go of Anika as she heads over to say hello to Layla and I make my way over to Mother.

"Son! Come meet Ceres's daughter, Flora, from the Verdant Valley Kingdom, our neighbors."

She holds out her hand and I dutifully take it. "It's nice to meet you, Princess."

"Likewise. The party is lovely." She smiles at me, and while she's beautiful with her blue eyes and long dark blonde hair. I know why my mother has introduced us, but apparently, I have a thing for redheads.

"Would you like to dance?" I ask, performing my duties to keep my mother happy.

"Delighted," she exclaims as she blushes. I lead her out onto the floor, and while I'm trying to be an attentive dance partner, my eyes keep scanning the room for a headful of bright red curls.

I finally see her standing to the side, looking uncomfortable as Flora's brother, Silvanus, has her cornered. My eyes narrow—he's always been an insufferable prick with an inflated ego, but if he keeps leaning into her space like that, I may rip him apart. She catches my eye and seems to be begging me to save her. She tries to extract herself from his attention, heading out to one of the halls. My heart hammers in my chest as he follows her.

"Excuse me, Princess Flora, I'm afraid something needs my immediate attention. Save me a dance later?" I bring her hand to my lips and press a kiss there.

"Of course, Your Highness," she giggles as she walks away.

I make my way out to the hall, trying to get my eyes back on

Anika. She's not here, neither is Silvanus. Nerves on edge, I check each room. I'm at the third door when I hear her.

"Get off me before I break your arm, you asshole." I rush inside, and he has her backed into a corner, his hand on her waist.

Before he realizes what's happening, my hand is around his throat, and he's pressed against the wall. Pure white-hot fury courses through me as I squeeze hard enough to cut off his air supply.

"Don't you ever touch what is mine again, understand?" I snarl at him as I squeeze harder.

"Excuse me?" Anika says, her eyes narrowing on me as I turn to look at her, my hand still around his throat. "I am *not* yours."

"Really? Because correct me if I'm wrong, but not thirty minutes ago, you were coming on my face, screaming my name."

Her blush is instant, desire flushing her skin even as anger flares in her eyes. "Let him go before you kill the fool," she hisses.

I blink. I had all but forgotten I was still holding the asshole as he starts to turn blue. I relax my hand, bringing my face inches from his. "Don't touch her ever again, or I will kill you, understand?"

He nods and drops to his knees as I release him. "Get out," I snap as he scrambles to his feet and practically runs from the room.

"I can't believe you did that! I had it handled!" she rages at me while anger still courses through my own system.

"Really? It didn't look like you had it handled. I believe what you meant to say was thank you," I respond tersely.

"Thank you for what? Embarrassing me? Un-fucking-believable. You're an ass." She tries to shove past me, but I grab her wrist. "Let me go!" she screams.

"Really, because earlier you were begging me to touch you," I whisper, my voice cold and dangerous. Her little tantrum makes me want to throw her over my lap and spank that perfect little ass.

"That was a mistake. You are an arrogant ass with your 'I am caveman, this is my woman' routine."

She tries to jerk out of my grasp, but I yank her closer. "You might not want to push me," I say as I pin her to the wall, pressing my hips into hers. Her body betrays her as she arches into me, even as anger floods her veins.

"Get off me," she grinds out through gritted teeth.

"I bet if I slide my fingers into that sweet little pussy of yours, I'll find that you're drenched, so turned on that you're dripping down your thighs." I trail my fingers down her body, and she shivers.

"Don't you dare fucking touch me," she tries to sound angry, but it comes out a husky whisper that feels more like a challenge than a threat.

I slip my hand through the skirt and feel her heat. We both moan as she presses into my hand.

"See? You love it when I touch you, don't deny it." I slip a finger inside of her and start moving it in and out. Her breathy little moans short-circuit my entire system. I pull her skirt away from her, throwing it over the backs of her legs as I grip her thighs and pick her up. She wraps them around my waist, and I rock into her core while kissing her with a desperation only she seems to have the power to bring out in me.

Her nails scrape across my back, and I wish my shirt wasn't in the way so I could feel them on my bare skin. She is kissing me back like she's just as needy for me as I am for her, chasing every stroke of my tongue, sucking it into her mouth, making me dizzy, my heart pounding in my ears. I can't wait anymore, I'm going to take her up against this wall right now.

As if she could read my thoughts, she reaches between us and frees me from my pants, bringing my head to her entrance, rubbing it up and down, moaning as she drags it across her clit, and I feel like I'm already about to burst. She presses it to her entrance, and I feel my legs tremble with the force of my need. I slip in that first inch and she's so fucking tight, so damn perfect. I gasp as my entire focus narrows to the feel of her.

"Damian!" she gasps as she arches her hips, greedy for more.

"I need a second, sweetheart, you feel too fucking good. If you move, I'm afraid I'm going to come, I can't seem to control myself when it comes to you."

I slide into her a little more, gritting my teeth. I slowly pull out and push back in a little further.

"Fuck, Damian!" She writhes and yanks my hair, kissing my neck, moving her hips against me, taking me a little deeper until I'm finally seated to the hilt.

Then the lights go out, and all hell breaks loose.

Chapter Eleven

LAYLA

W ell, well, well. Looks like the sexual tension that has been so thick between Damian and Anika you could cut it with a knife has finally been broken. Good for them. I could barely keep the laughter out of my voice as I banged on his door after clearly hearing the moans coming from his room.

He reappears a few minutes after I return to the party, his face unreadable with that mask he so easily slips into place in front of others, seeming every bit the deadly warrior king, as cold and formidable as he is beautiful.

His mother introduces him to a princess, and he politely takes her hand and leads her to the dance floor. Anika heads my way, but before she can reach me, she is stopped by a man I was introduced to but can't remember his name. I don't like the way he is eyeing Anika, but I get distracted when Delphin finds me and asks me for a dance. As much as I would love to take him up on his offer, I decline. All the other females are dressed in beautiful gowns, and I'm in my midnight leathers, so instead, he regales me with tales of him and his brothers growing up. His easy charm is infectious, and I see several young ladies eyeing him.

A moment later, Anika leaves the room, the man who had stopped her following close behind. Two seconds later, Damian follows. Grinning, I consider going after him, but it's probably best if I just stay out of the way.

Within moments of their departure, the man comes back in, his face red and looking frazzled. I can't help but smirk, I'm assuming that Damian did go after them and it went about how I imagined. I feel an immense sense of satisfaction at that. Poor Damian, Anika is going to have him running in circles, and I friggin' love it.

I'm chatting with a guest when panic overwhelms my senses, seeming to come from nowhere. *"Godslayer! Enemies are in the castle; I am on my way!"* Vengeance's voice is full of rage, and I look around, confused, frantically scanning the crowd. A blood-curdling shriek fills the room right before the lights go out.

A heartbeat passes, then two, before my instincts kick in. Damian's mother, she's the closest, I'll get her to safety first. These bastards don't realize that by putting us in the dark, they gave me the home-court advantage. Trying to keep calm until I can identify the threat, I take deep, steadying breaths. Once my people are safe and I find the culprits, there will be no holding back. I send out my power, finding my way to Enthralia. It takes me mere seconds; terror is rolling off of her in waves.

"Aunt Enthralia, it's me, I need to get you to safety so I can find Damian and the others." Vengeance bursts through a side door. That's my girl, perfect timing. "Vengeance, take Damian's mother out to the Dragonhold. Tell Umbra to guard the people as you bring them out. Have Chaos find Damian, go!" I hike Enthralia onto the back of my wolf, and she's off, sprinting her to safety. One down.

"Layla!" Caspian screams in my mind.

"Cas, get the princess and your brothers out to the dragons, they

will protect them. Vengeance has Damian's mother and will be back as soon as she's safe. She can lead you, just get them out before you come back to help."

People are running everywhere; I hear Cas and his brothers trying to get people to safety. I can't find the damn threat, so I send out my power to look for Damian instead. I follow its pull until I hear Chaos's growl and teeth ripping into the flesh of what looks to be one of our guards. What the fuck? I don't have time to process that information, so I file it away for now.

Anika is using her powers to light up the room. "Anika!" I hug her as Havoc throws himself into the room, eyes wild.

"Holy shit, he just spoke to me!" her voice trembles.

"Congrats, you have a wolf," I say, "Havoc, protect Anika. She's going to use her powers to help get people out to the Dragonhold—tear apart anyone who tries to harm them, understand? And I mean, tear them to fucking shreds. Chaos, I will keep Damian safe. I need you to go with Havoc and Anika. I trust you two to know friend from foe better than we would. Damian and I are going hunting." I smile at Damian, and he grins back. We are both pissed, and these fuckers have no idea the beasts that are coming for them.

"Are we leaving any alive?" I query.

"Let's capture a few so we can play a bit and see what they will tell us." He smiles like a feral beast. Our wolves and the people we love are being ushered to safety while we go hunting in the dark, where I am the fucking queen.

I steady my nerves, following Damian's lead as he calls to his own power, following trails of thoughts. "Damian. If you dampen power, will it block mine?"

"Probably not, but it will Anika's and Caspian's brothers. That bunch is fairly terrifying, so it's better to leave it open so they can defend themselves and others if need be."

I nod my head. I feel the night skittering across my skin, whispering to me. "Damian, someone is coming."

"Switch to thoughts only—stay silent," he commands.

"*Any idea who they are?*" I ask him, hoping he can collect some intel.

"*No, it's strange. Their thoughts don't seem to be their own. I can't seem to influence them either. Something is...off.*"

I don't like the worry that seeps into his words.

Feeling movement to my right, my shadows whip around and subdue the threat, holding them in place.

"*Fuck, Layla,*" there is actual fear in his words, "*your father must have sent them, they are all dead.*"

Anger, hot and incessant flares, and I send a flame out to incinerate the abomination. In seconds, it turns to ash before our eyes, and I immediately douse the flame.

"*Vengeance, is everyone safe?*" I can no longer hear screams or the sounds of people trying to flee.

"*Yes, Godslayer, these enemies are strange. Even when torn to pieces, they do not die.*"

"*They are already dead—flame will kill them. Have the dragons incinerate any parts you have ripped off.*"

"Well, if they are all dead, there's no point expending my mental energy reading you to communicate. Cover me for a moment—I need to concentrate—I'm going to send shadows out along the entire palace grounds and see what I can find. It's difficult with so many strangers in the palace, but the dead give off a different feeling, so locating should, theoretically, be easy. I'm just worried about missing someone alive who might be trying to kill us," I say to Damian.

"I've got you, and Chaos is on his way to cover us as well now that the others are safely guarded by the dragons."

I nod and close my eyes, calling to my power, opening myself fully to it, and then sending it out in all directions as far as I can. I can feel everything. Every piece of furniture, every speck of dust. The dead are everywhere, waiting for us. I can feel a presence, but it's too far for me to get a good read on it, but I know in my bones that it's my father.

My eyes open and I meet Damian's eyes as he speaks, "He's here, isn't he?"

"Yes, but I think he's watching from somewhere farther away—I can barely feel him," I spit the words out. Forcing my feet to move, I begin walking, Damian scrambling to catch up. "We need to clear the army of the undead. They seem to be...waiting."

"I got that feeling too." His face is determined as he takes my hand, and we walk through the castle together. I can feel them in the shadows, they seem to be suspended in animation until we approach, and then they attack. I easily subdue them with shadows and drag them along behind us—their guttural, unnatural grunts and moans are definitely not human.

"What are you doing?" Damian hisses, watching me gather a horde of them trailing in our wake, his face a mask of cold, unyielding anger.

"I already scorched one of the palace rugs. I am not about to incur the wrath of your mother for making a mess in the castle when I don't have to. I'll take them outside and have a fucking bonfire and hope my father is close enough to see."

Laughing, he shoves my shoulder. "Only you would be thoughtful enough to not want to ruin rugs in the middle of a battle."

"Hey now, I can take on an army of the dead, no problem, but your mother?" I shiver, "She actually scares me when she's angry." I grin and snatch another creature lurking in a corner.

Sending out my shadows through the castle once more, it seems to be clear of these vile abominations. I have about twenty undead in my collection when we arrive outside, and I'm momentarily speechless at the sight before me. An overwhelming army of my father's zombies have breached the palace gates, their rotting forms pressing relentlessly forward. Cas and his brothers are holding them back with the help of Drayvhn.

Caspian's dress shirt is rolled up to his elbows, hair whipping around his face, a rip across his chest exposing a red gash that would probably make me furious if I wasn't so damned turned on. Every inch of him looks like a warrior. The set of his jaw, the concentrated fury on his face, the way his muscles bunch and ripple with every confident movement. He is glorious, and I'm shifting my weight to try to ease the ache between my thighs.

I shake my head to clear my thoughts. I am really fucked up to be getting turned on at a time like this, but damn, he is breathtakingly beautiful.

His brothers are no less impressive, sending out some kind of pulse that causes a distortion in the air, but I don't understand the mechanics of what they are doing. The ripple that emits from their power can be felt by all of us, but it has the front line of the horde immobilized. They all look stunning and fierce, the playfulness from earlier completely gone as they work as a unit.

My eyes return to Cas as he wields a fire whip with precision, snaring the creatures a few at a time before flinging them into the air. Drayvhn, perched on a cliff that juts from the mountainside, awaits their descent, ready to engulf them in flames. The burning embers of their flesh scatter harmlessly against the mountain's side, ensuring that no unintended fires are ignited in their wake.

My head turns toward Damian, mouth agape. "Cas can wield fire," I whisper.

Damian looks none too pleased but not surprised. "It seems he can, cousin. I'm guessing it's an effect from the bond, much like with the powers you wield."

"Cas!" I call out, and he turns to me. Relief and something more primal shine in his eyes. *"This is going to take too long. I'm going to set them all on fire. You and your brothers wield water to contain it!"* I say through our link. He nods. As always, we work well together.

I toss my captives into the group, watching them land on top of the others before I rain fire down on them. Because there are so many, I can't burn them all as easily as I could one, so as they burn, they try to run.

Aegir sends out his power to immobilize them again, but I can tell it's taking a toll to do it on his own while the other three brothers contain the blaze.

Gathering my reserves, I send out as much fire as possible, my body trembling with the effort. Cas sees me weakening and adds in his own flames.

I feel Damian's hand on my shoulder. There's too many, and I've used up so much energy already that I'm not going to be able to take them all out.

"Cousin, let me help. Open your mind to me and take from my strength," he begs.

"What?"

"Just do it!" he snaps.

I close my eyes and feel for him. As soon as I open that channel, I feel his strength pour into me. My eyes open, and I search his for a moment, hugging him around his neck. "You will need to explain later, but thank you."

Glancing back at the group, now diminished to about half its original size, I take a deep breath and prepare to start again.

"Godslayer! They are in the town, attacking the people!" Drayvhn's roar splits the night as he launches, landing away from the horde of undead.

"Go, Layla! I've got this!" Cas screams at me and I run for where

Drayvhn landed, our thoughts perfectly in tune, Damian right behind me.

"Damian, call to Chaos, have him and Vengeance run below us, our people will be safe in the Dragonhold with Havoc and Umbra standing guard." I don't bother checking to make sure he heard me. I know him well enough to trust it will be done as I mount my dragon, with Damian following behind.

As soon as we are settled, he launches, flying at a breakneck speed to get us into the heart of the town in minutes. I can feel the fear pouring off Damian. The people he has sworn to protect are being attacked because of my father, his uncle. I don't have to read him to know guilt is consuming him.

"I can't set them on fire without risking the town," Dryvhn says.

"I know, big guy; just stay close in case we need you."

Damian and I dismount and run through the village streets. I whip out my shadows and grab hold of every threat we come across. I can already smell the tang of blood in the air as the undead kill without mercy.

I catch sight of a frantic mother trailing behind her child at the same moment Damian does. With swift agility, he reaches them, sweeping up the little girl into his arms as the undead close in, killing her mother. Fury whips through me, and I snatch the creature with darkness and set him on fire with a touch of my hand. I wait a heartbeat for him to turn to ash before dousing the flame.

A chilling shiver courses through me, freezing my heart in its tracks as icy tendrils of terror coil around my senses. My breath catches in my throat, and my pulse quickens with a surge of dread. My eyes widen in disbelief as the scene before me unfolds with surreal horror.

In a cruel twist of fate, the frantic mother I had just seen moments ago is now transformed, her eyes vacant and glassy, her movements jerky and devoid of life. The realization hits me like a sledgehammer to the chest—she has become one of the undead.

"*Damian!*" I scream, sprinting back to the dragon. Vengeance comes flying around the corner. "The people they kill are becoming part of the undead, so be careful!"

"I know! There's so many, and I don't know where to put the ones we save to keep them safe!" He's still clutching the child.

"Give her to Vengeance! She can run her back to the Dragonhold—it's the only place I can think of, but we need a better plan. We can't get everyone there!"

He throws the girl on Vengeance's back and as soon as she's securely on, my girl takes off. She's our best bet for the moment because she's the fastest and the strongest.

I run back through the streets, trying to focus on saving as many people as I can. I have a rhythm, whip out shadow, contain, burn, douse. Over and over. Damian is working on getting people to safety. My energy is waning. I can't keep this up. I should have practiced more, should have gotten stronger, should have been more prepared.

I'm so fucking angry. We are surrounded by so much death. I pick up another, burn, douse. Again and again. I'm so tired, all the way to my bones. I can barely lift my arms, my knees hit the stone pavement. I just need a little break.

"*No!*" I hear the unmistakable roar in my head. It's Cas. Everything goes dark.

Chapter Twelve

DAMIAN

Drayvhn roars and Vengeance howls in the distance as I run for her. One of the undead is closing in, and I'm not going to make it. Faster, fuck, I need to go faster! I try to use my powers to hide in a pocket of time until I can reach her, but I don't have enough reserves left for that. I'm too exhausted.

"*Layla!*" I scream. I will never forgive myself if she dies. Never. I hear Caspian screaming as he is running for her too, but I'm closer and still not close enough. Cas tries to send out a pulse to throw the creature back, but he's used up his strength and can't accomplish it from that distance. The creature is now only a few feet away. "Dammit, Layla, *move!*" I can't hide the agony in my words.

A dark, cloaked figure steps in front of her prone form and raises its hands. With a sweeping motion, the creature disappears, and a wave of dark energy pulses forward, sweeping through the town, instantly turning all the creatures to dust. I am almost to Layla, but the figure is in my way, so I try to mentally grab on to them and shove them away from her. The figure easily swats me away like I'm a mere child, knocking me on my ass. It does the same with Caspian as he arrives seconds after me.

The figure lowers their cloak and steps into the light. "Is that any way to greet your grandmother, boy?"

Holy shit. It's our grandmother, Nyx.

"Grandmother! I didn't realize, had I known, I'm so sorry," I stammer.

"I understand, Damianos. It looks like you may have been a bit... distracted." She looks around at the carnage with an arched brow. "My son's handiwork, no doubt?"

"Yes."

She nods and looks at Layla, gently brushing a loose strand of hair from her brow. "Wake, child," she whispers, and Layla's eyes flutter open. "There you are," she whispers, "how are you feeling? I would imagine you feel like you've been hit by a truck. Damian here is probably too exhausted to help, so let me." She reaches down and gently presses a hand to Layla's cheek.

"You too, boy, come let your grandmother see you. Happy birthday, by the way. Looks like some party." I do as I'm told as she presses a kiss to my cheek. "Close your eyes and let me give you my strength." My eyes close and I feel warmth spread through me, and the exhaustion I felt moments before has been washed away.

Behind us, Layla stands, her eyes fixating on Cas lying on the ground. A sob escapes her, and she races toward him, checking him over to make sure he's alive, cradling his head in her lap. "Cas! Please wake up, please!" she sobs, running her hand down his cheek as she gently rocks him.

"The prince is fine. He's tired from using so much power like the rest of you, but otherwise, he's fine," Grandmother tells her gently as she reaches down to touch Cas. His eyes flutter open, then he stands as Layla throws her arms around him and he holds her tight before releasing her, murmuring words I can't hear in her ear.

Layla smiles at him, looking relieved before finally shifting her gaze to look at Nyx, eyes widening in shock. "You're her, my grandmother?"

"I am, little one. I'm sorry we have not met before now. We have much to discuss."

Vengeance comes flying around the corner, baring her teeth and snapping her jaws. As Nyx begins to raise her hand, Layla throws herself in between them. "Don't you dare, she's *mine!*" she snarls, and I flinch. Did she really just snarl at the most powerful goddess in our world?

Yes, yes she did.

Nyx stops her movement, holding unnaturally still while Layla faces off with her, eyes narrowed as Vengeance growls from behind her.

"I wasn't going to harm the beast, but you can't very well expect me to sit here and let her attack me, can you?"

Layla blinks and her face relaxes. "Vengeance, stand down, this is my grandmother." Vengeance immediately calms, walks to Layla's side, and sits.

"Damian, let's get out of the street and head back to the castle, shall we? I think the theatrics are over for the night. Send troops out to check on your people. I've already called for some of mine to help with the cleanup and repairs to the city."

I nod and call for Umbra and the other dragons to help with transporting Cas, his brothers, and any injured that need to be tended to. "Grandmother, would you like to ride one of the dragons back?"

"No, thank you, I've got us covered; just have them help the others. I won't be able to transport the sea prince or the wolf, but you and Layla shall come with me." There is no room for argument in her tone as she holds out her hands to us. We take hold, and darkness swirls around us. When it's gone, we are standing in the throne room.

"Holy shit," Layla exclaims. "How do you do that?"

"It's a skill you also possess—you just have to learn to use it, my dear. Damian, start seeing your guests safely home while Layla and I talk."

Guests have started to pour back into the building, shaken but safe. I scan the crowd for my mother and Anika.

"Damian!" I hear my mother's voice across the room as she dashes toward me and wraps me in a tight embrace. "You're safe!" Her arms are a fortress around me, and as she clings to me, I catch sight of Anika stepping into the room. She appears a bit rattled but otherwise unscathed. A wave of relief washes over me, catching me off guard with its intensity. It underscores emotions I have yet to fully acknowledge or explore.

I kiss the top of my mother's head, "Of course I'm safe. Do you think Layla's stubbornness would allow harm to come to me?"

She throws her head back and laughs, "No, I suppose not." I let her go and move toward Anika.

"Are you okay?" I ask softly, I know I shouldn't ask in this crowd of people, but I can't help it, I reach up and rub my thumb across her cheek.

Her lips softly turn up, and she nods. "I'm relieved to see you are not hurt. Is Layla okay? Cas? Brennan?"

Fuck, I forgot about Brennan. We kept him in his room tonight, still not sure about how people will react to having a human in our world. Anika sees the realization in my eyes.

"I've got it, I'll go check on him, you go deal with this mess."

"Thank you." I grab her hand and place a kiss on her palm before she walks away.

I move to my throne, ready to address the crowd.

As I stand before the gathered faces, their expressions a mix of relief and lingering fear, my voice finds strength in the quiet of the aftermath. "Ladies and gentlemen, friends and family, tonight we faced an unexpected challenge, an attack that sought to shake the very foundation of the peace and safety we've come to cherish within these walls. But look around you—we stand united, not just unbroken, but stronger in our resolve.

"My heart swells with pride and gratitude for every one of you. Your courage, your willingness to stand and defend, to protect one another, is the very essence of what makes us great. We are a family, bound not by blood but by our shared commitment to each other's welfare.

"To those who sought to bring darkness to our doorstep, let this be a message: we are not deterred by fear, nor are we weakened by surprise. Instead, we rise, together, with a strength that cannot be underestimated, a force that will not be silenced.

"Tonight, we also remember that this unity, this unbreakable bond, is our greatest weapon. As we move forward, let us carry the spirit of this night within us. Let the memory of our resilience in the face of adversity be a beacon that guides us through whatever challenges may come.

"I want to extend a special thanks to our brave defenders, to the guardians of our walls, to the warriors who fought not just for a kingdom but for the person standing next to them. Your valor has saved lives.

"And to my family, my friends, and my beloved people, I promise you this: as your king, I will do everything within my power to ensure that threats like tonight's will find no foothold in our future. We will fortify our defenses, we will strengthen our resolve, and together, we will build a realm where peace reigns supreme and where such darkness cannot dwell."

I take a deep breath, taking a moment to look around the room and meet the gazes of several of the people standing before me.

"Tonight, we faced a terror that no one should ever have to endure. It was unexpected and horrifying, but together, we stood strong."

Pausing, I take a moment to let my sincerity sink in. "The safety of our people, of each and every one of you, is my highest priority. While the night has taken a turn none of us could have anticipated, I promise you this; we will take every measure to ensure that you all get home safely."

My voice grows firmer, more determined. "The roads will be patrolled, and escorts will be provided to anyone who requires them. We shall leave no one behind to face the dark alone." I let those words hang in the air, a solemn vow from their king.

I offer a reassuring smile, albeit a tired one. "Please follow the guards' instructions as we organize your safe passage home. And remember, we are a community, bound not just by land but by the unwavering spirit to protect and care for each other."

With a final nod, I step down, ready to lead the effort to ensure that every guest, every friend and ally, finds their way safely under the cloak of night. Tonight was a stark reminder of the threats that loom outside our doors but also of the strength and unity that define us. We will recover, we will rebuild, and above all, we will remain vigilant, together.

Chapter Thirteen

LAYLA

We walk into the room Damian uses for meetings and my grandmother takes a seat on the sofa, motioning for me to sit. I do, and Vengeance lays at my feet, ever vigilant.

She quietly studies me, so I do the same. Growing up in the human world, I'm used to grandmothers being older, but Nyx barely looks older than I am and is stunningly beautiful. I can't help but notice the stark contrasts and subtle similarities between us. Her hair, dark and flowing, cascades down past her waist—a mirror of the dark locks that Damian and I share. Her skin is pale, luminous almost, against the darkness of her hair, whereas my skin matches the shade but not the luminescence. Damian, on the other hand, inherited the warm, tawny tone of his mother's complexion. But it's Nyx's eyes that truly captivate me; deep navy blue, they hold the mysteries of the night sky, unlike Damian's and my dark brown gaze. Even seated, her presence is towering, and I can't help but feel slightly overshadowed in comparison.

"You seem to inspire quite a bit of loyalty in those around you.

That is not a quality you inherited from your father," she says with a measure of disdain.

"I wouldn't know, the one time I met him, he was an asshole and I had planned on killing him, but the fucker got away." If my crude language bothers her, she doesn't show it.

"So, is it true then? Are you able to kill immortals?" I flinch. Shit, we were supposed to be keeping that bit of information under wraps. "Don't lie to me, child—answer the question."

"I think so? I mean, I killed Moros, but it was kinda a spur of the moment, I was really pissed off kind of thing, sooo... Sorry about that?" I say sheepishly. I don't regret what I did, but he was her son, after all, so I'm not certain how she feels about it.

She purses her lips and waves her hand like she's brushing off my apology. "Moros was a horrid waste of air. The only thing he did right in this life was ensure the creation of your cousin." Her eyes soften at the mention of Damian, not bothering to hide her affection for him. "That boy was born to rule, even though he's never had an interest in the crown. He's fierce, loyal, and kind. Three words I could never use to describe either of my sons. The fact that he is so incredibly loyal to you speaks volumes about your character. He loves you very much."

A smile lifts the corners of my mouth. "I love him too. Besides my brother, he's the only real family I've had, and the more I get to know him, the more I admire him."

"Ahhh, yes, the human boy," she says, arching an eyebrow at me. "Don't look so surprised. I know you have tried to keep him hidden, but not much goes on in these lands that I don't know about. I wield the night, remember?" She raises her arms and shadows race out, covering the room in darkness to remind me of her power, the same power I wield.

"The night doesn't scare you though now, does it, child?" Her voice echoes from all around the room. To anyone else, it would instill fear—for me, it's just another day. My power rises in answer to hers, chasing it, then pushing it back.

When the shadows recede, she's grinning. "I knew you were powerful," she says with obvious approval. "I want to declare you as my heir." She takes my hand as my jaw pops open and I stare at her.

"But you barely know me," I stammer.

"I know all I need to know. You are fiercely loyal, kind, and protective. Dragons and dire wolves are discerning creatures, and you and Damian are the only two people in this kingdom who have bonded with both species. I would declare Damian as heir, but your powers eclipse his tenfold. He is strong, but you are stronger. I suspect that one day, your powers may eclipse even my own. Now, I've had thousands of years to hone mine, and you are still barely more than a babe in immortal time, but you will master yours by the time I am ready to step down or move on to the next realm, and you will be ready."

"What if I don't want it?" I ask quietly.

"No one will force you. That's why we are having this conversation. I'm not asking you to take up the mantle tomorrow; it will be years from now when you are ready, but I am hoping declaring an heir will make your father cease in his petty war before more of our people die."

"Wait, so am I immortal?" I've wondered about that lately. It's an odd concept when you grew up as a human.

"If I declare you as my heir, you will be. Otherwise, I believe so, but can't be sure."

"So, you can make me immortal? What about my brother? Can you make him immortal as well?"

"You, yes, him, no," she says, and my face falls, "but I can grant him an extended life like the people that live in our lands. You will need to speak with him first and see if that is what he wants. You need to be prepared for the possibility that he may want to return to the human world when it's safe, but for now, he can move about our kingdoms unharmed."

I nod my head. "Thank you, I'll talk to him and see what he wants. You know my father wants you dead, right?"

She lets out a long, drawn-out breath and then says, "Unfortunately, I do. It's not a surprise. He's been power-hungry for as long as I can remember, and when I refused to name him heir, he was irate. He would not be a fit ruler, nor is he powerful enough to keep these lands safe."

"What do you mean? Are there others out there that you have to keep us safe from?"

"Oh child, so sweet you are. There are always threats, always. Anytime there are positions of power, there are people that want them. That's why you have to be fair and ruthless to rule. Loving and vengeful. You can't just be one thing. It takes a delicate balance that few can master."

I think about her words, understanding what she means. It still doesn't make me desire a future where I rule over these strange lands that I still know so little about, but it does make me wonder what she may know about me and why I seem to be so different from everyone else. Even here, in a world where I should fit in, I don't.

"Why do you think I have all of these powers?" I've wondered why for a very long time but didn't have anyone I could really ask.

"One can never be certain, but the universe always requires balance. The balance here has been shifting. You've seen what the hunger for power can do. You had no desire for power, you just wanted to survive and yet you wield more of it than anyone. Even now, after saving as many as you did here tonight, it sits heavily on you. You don't feel worthy, you worry you will let people down. You don't crave the power you can wield, and yet when it comes to being able to defend the defenseless, you are thankful for it. You, yourself, are a perfect example of that delicate balance."

Her words leave me more confused than ever, but I think I somewhat understand.

"Now tell me about you and the sea prince. I know he is betrothed, but the two of you are obviously entwined."

"I love him. I'm *in* love with him. Damian's mother thinks we are fated mates."

"Ahh, well, she would know. Enthralia's powers enable her to see snippets of the future and read people's fates." The shock on my face must be obvious because she laughs at me. "I'm sure she didn't tell you that. Then you would wonder why she allowed herself to be shackled to Moros if she could see her fate? She can't see everyone's and definitely not her own. The only thing she knew about her own fate when she agreed to marry my son was that she would birth Damian, and she loves that boy with her entire being. She will tell you she would endure everything twice over to have him."

"I'm thankful she did, I had no idea how incomplete my life felt until he came into it."

"I feel much the same about the boy, and I think it will apply to you as well. I would like to spend time getting to know you, would you be agreeable to that?"

The thought pleases me more than I ever thought possible. "Yes, I think I would like that."

"Now, back to your prince, I will have the betrothal ended," she says matter of factly.

"You can do that?" I ask in wonder.

"Child, yes, I can do that. Consider it done."

"Good because she's in love with Aegir, and he with her."

"Perfect, then it's a win-win for everyone. Triton is an ass; I shall enjoy it."

That makes me giggle and I really think I am going to like her.

She smiles and stands, "Well, I best go check on the cleanup efforts and head home. It was lovely to finally meet you, I will visit soon." She pulls me into a hug, and I'm surprised by how comforting it actually feels. I head out to help with the chaos, feeling calmer than I have in weeks.

Cleanup is well underway by the time we emerge and the guests have all been seen safely home. We lost some guards, but the death toll was relatively small, given the level of attack. The town suffered the heaviest losses and true to her word, Nyx sent in people to help as well as fortify our defenses.

Cas and his brothers decide to stay at the palace, and don't think I didn't notice the princess slip into Aegir's room. I'm perfectly okay with that because I know Cas is sleeping in mine, not that I plan on getting a lot of sleep. I have all kinds of delicious, devious things planned for him. Just thinking about it causes heat to bloom between my thighs.

Wanting to check on Brennan before I head to bed, I find him in his room—his expression a mixture of frustration and resentment at being confined while others were out in the thick of the action. We argue about his safety, his annoyance with me is palpable.

"I'm not a fucking child, Layla," he reminds me.

"I know that, dumbass, but we are talking about immortals, undead and magical shit that I still don't even fully understand. I'm not risking you." We sit down to talk, and I explain Nyx's offer in detail. He listens intently, his brow furrowed in deep thought.

As we delve into the complexities of Nyx's proposition, Brennan is quiet. The weight of the decision hangs heavy in the air, and I can sense the turmoil brewing within him. It's a lot to process, I acknowledge, especially under the duress of our current circumstances.

Despite his initial resistance, I can see the gears turning in Brennan's mind. He's weighing his options and agrees to take some time to think it over. We say our goodnights, and I head back into the hall.

When I finally retreat to my room, a sense of exhaustion washes over me, dragging at my limbs like heavy chains. Pushing open the door, I'm met with the comforting sight of Cas reclined in the tub, the warm water enveloping him like a cocoon. He looks up at me with a weary smile, the lines of tension easing from his features as he welcomes me.

I move to his side, perching on the edge of the tub with a sigh of relief. The events of the day weigh heavily on me, but in this moment, the only thing that matters is the soothing presence of Cas. I reach out to him, running my fingers through his damp hair, a silent gesture of reassurance and affection.

Together, we sit in companionable silence for a moment, the gentle lapping of water against porcelain the only sound in the room. I watch as Cas's wounds slowly begin to heal, the water's restorative properties working their magic.

"Hey there, handsome," I say as I lean down to kiss him. "Want some company?"

"Always. Get your ass in here," he growls as he yanks me down for a deeper kiss.

I pull away and strip off my clothes, climbing over the side of the tub, settling in, leaning my back against his chest. The water is warm and soothing, and being in his arms feels right.

"I have some news," I say to him, excitement building in me.

"Mmm?" he says, kissing a path down my neck, making me gasp.

"My grandmother is ending your betrothal."

He stills. "Are you serious?"

"Yes," I say breathlessly as I turn to face him.

He cups my face and kisses me with wild need. "Out, now," he demands.

"What? I'm confused."

"I said, out. As in, get out of the tub, Layla, because I am going

111

to fuck you. If I'm not inside of you in the next thirty seconds, I think I might lose my mind." I stand and quickly step out of the tub, sloshing water everywhere. He stands behind me and picks me up, carrying me to the bed and dropping me on it. I giggle as I bounce, and true to his word, he is inside me within seconds.

Despite his threats, what he does isn't even close to fucking. He makes love to me like I am something precious and breakable. It's different from the rough and desperate way we usually come together, but it's no less fantastic.

He's kissing me in light, feathery kisses all over my face, whispering over and over that he loves me.

I lazily run my hands down his back as he rolls his hips into me. "I love you so much, Cas. I don't even have the words to tell you how big my feelings are."

"I love you too, more than you will ever understand. You are everything to me. I was so awed by you tonight; you are so damn strong and fierce. Sometimes I worry that you don't need me."

I push him off me and onto his back. Straddling him, I slide his cock back home and ride him. "Cas, I will always need you. I will always *want* you. Always."

I spend the rest of the night showing him just how much.

Chapter Fourteen

DAMIAN

A nger simmers under my skin as I pace in my room. I can't believe he attacked us. The loss of life in the city has guilt clawing at my chest. I rub my hand over it, trying to ease the ache there, to no avail. I should have been more prepared. This is my fault.

A knock sounds at my door.

Assuming it's my mother or Layla, I snap, "Come in!"

I stop my pacing when I catch fiery red curls in my peripheral. I turn to her as she walks in and shuts the door, standing against it, chewing on her bottom lip like she's nervous.

"Anika," I breathe her name, a fervent whisper, and stalk toward her with purpose. I place one hand on her waist and the other on her cheek. "Anika, this isn't the place for you. Given my state, gentleness isn't in the cards tonight, and I lack the ability to keep my hands off you if you don't go."

"Maybe I don't want gentle. Maybe, I just want you." I can feel her heart pounding against my chest, her breaths coming faster as desire flushes her skin. I know I shouldn't, but I want her too much to send her away. I lean in and capture her mouth in a bruising kiss that leaves her panting with want by the time I pull away.

"You have no idea the filthy things I dream about doing to you." I twist a curl around my finger, studying it, relishing in the softness sliding over my skin.

"Then do them. Do every single one. Do anything and everything you want, just please, touch me." She looks at me, chest heaving, eyes darkening with heat.

She completely destroys me with those words.

"Strip, now," I demand as I step back and watch her slowly take off her clothes, her fingers trembling.

I take my time sliding off my belt. "This is your last chance to leave, Anika," I warn, my words a deep rumble from my chest, laced with dark desire.

"I'm staying," she says with conviction, tilting that chin up at me with defiance that makes me want to take her over my knee and spank it out of her. I wrap my belt around her neck and pull it tight. She gasps but looks me in the eyes, unafraid.

"On your knees," I growl. She's so eager, such a good girl doing what I tell her. I hold the belt tight, wrapping it around my fist. "Undo my pants and free me." She makes quick work of it, a moan escaping those soft lips as my cock springs free, its thick length jutting out, jerking in desperation to be buried in its rightful place between her thighs.

She slides her hand down it, and I hiss—it feels so fucking good, her tentative touch driving me to madness. I pull the belt a little tighter. "I didn't say you could do that yet."

She stills, removing her hand and sitting back, waiting for instructions. I look down, taking her in. The flush of her cheeks, the part of her lips as her breaths come in pants, the way she shifts herself, trying to ease that ache I know has bloomed between her thighs, making me smile. She is so godsdamned beautiful it hurts.

"Wrap your hand around the base and keep it there, holding tight. Then I want you to open your mouth and relax. You aren't going to suck my cock—I am going to fuck your mouth, do you understand?" She nods and opens for me, and fuck is it a glorious sight. As soon as she's in position, I slide myself in between those perfect lips and moan. "Seal your lips around me." My voice is nothing more than a horse whisper. I start sliding in and out of her mouth, and it feels so damn good. She moans and tries to move with me. I pull the belt tighter. Not enough to cut off her air, but enough to make it a little harder for her to breathe.

"I said I was going to fuck your mouth; you are just going to sit there and take it like a good girl, understand? Look up at me, look me in the eyes." I keep her still with the belt while I look into her eyes and start thrusting into her willing mouth like a fucking beast. I fist my other hand in her hair.

"Fuck, you are so damn beautiful on your knees with my dick in your mouth. You feel *so fucking good*," I rasp. Her eyes flutter closed at my praise, and she moans, sending vibrations down my cock that almost makes me come so fast I have to pull away from her to control myself. I strip out of the rest of my clothes as I watch her.

Looking at her on her knees, her nipples hard, aching to be touched, her pale skin flush, lips swollen, something in my chest constricts as I realize I more than just want to fuck her—I want her to be mine. I pull her up, remove the belt from her neck, and wrap it around her hands. "Get on the bed, I'm going to tie you to the headboard." Once she is secure, I spend my time exploring her body, figuring out what makes her beg for more. I take one of her nipples in my mouth while I plunge two fingers inside of that slick, wet heat, making her hips buck under me. I lightly bite her nipple, and I feel her clench around my fingers.

"You like that, love? Like it when I bite you?"

"Yes," she pants. I bite harder and she screams. "Too much?"

"No, Damian, please. More," she begs.

I untie her arms and roll her over, pulling her up on her hands and knees. I slam myself into her, burying myself to the hilt in one hard thrust as I bring the belt down on her ass. She moans and presses back into me. "Fuck, you feel better than I imagined. I was so pissed we got interrupted earlier. I barely had time to feel that sweet pussy around me." I drive into her again, hard and bring the belt down again, on the other side.

I feel her clench around me, and I nearly lose it. I rub my hands over the pink marks on her perfect little round ass and start fucking her like I've wanted to for months. "Your ass is beautiful with these pretty pink marks on it."

She's moaning and panting, pushing her hips back, meeting my every thrust. I reach around and start rubbing her clit. "Fuck, Damian, just like that! I'm going to come! Don't you dare fucking stop!" I feel her tighten around me as she screams my name, sobbing as she rides those waves until she's limp from the force of her orgasm.

"That's my good girl, coming on my cock. I love the way you scream my name." I pull out and she groans in protest. I pick her up and carry her across the room to the couch, sitting down with her straddling my lap.

"Listen to me, I want you to ride me hard, use me to take your pleasure. Be rough, I want to feel you tear at my hair, rake your nails so hard over my shoulders and back that you leave your marks on my skin. Bite me, I don't care, just be rough."

She nods and slides herself on my cock, and it feels so good I close my eyes and lay my head back.

She yanks my hair, "I don't think so, Damian, you keep those eyes on me." Using my own words against me, I chuckle as she leans down and bites my bottom lip hard enough that I taste blood. Oh, fuck yeah. How is she so fucking perfect? I grab her hips and thrust up into her, I can't get deep enough—I want to be fused to this woman and never let her go.

She's riding me hard, and I reach around and grab her ass as I take her nipple into my mouth. She arches her head back and grabs on to my shoulders to hold on as I thrust into her harder and harder, her nails digging into me, that tinge of pain making the pleasure all the sweeter. I let go of her nipple and kiss the column of her neck, nipping and biting as I go.

"Harder, Damian! Harder!" she cries as sweat beads on our skin while I thrust into her harder, picking her up, not breaking the pace as I lay her on the couch and press one of her knees into her chest so I can get deeper, hitting an angle that has her coming unglued under me. I grit my teeth as I feel that pleasure building. I'm trying to hold back, but it feels so fucking good. Every thrust better than the last. Her moans are the most erotic sound in the world as she digs her nails into the skin on my ass, begging me not to stop until her cries echo throughout the room and she is clenching around me so damn tight I can't hold back anymore. I plunge into her one final time and roar with the force of my release as I spill myself into her.

I lay my head on her chest, careful not to crush her as she plays with my hair. I can feel her legs trembling beneath me.

"You're shaking—are you okay, love?"

"I'm perfect," she purrs, "and you're shaking too."

"So I am," I laugh and wrap my arms around her, holding her tight.

"Damian," she says softly.

"Yes, love?"

"Was that normal?"

"What do you mean?" Fear lances through me, terrified I was too rough with her.

"It's just, I know I don't have a lot of experience, but even hearing other people talking about sex, well, other than Layla, and you know how she is about sex. No one talks about it being quite like *that*. That was phenomenal. Is that normal?"

"Sex should always be quite good, and I'm sorry that it wasn't for you, but no, love, that was not exactly normal. That was more of an out of this world, out of body experience kind of fantastic."

Her smile lights up the entire room, and I feel the need for her stir again. "There're all kinds of ways to make it pleasurable, and I would say I'm sorry for how rough I was, but I'm really not. I'm going to show you all the ways it can be good," I say as I smile wickedly and pick her up, taking her back to the bed where I spend the rest of the night teaching her exactly how pleasurable sex can be.

When she's exhausted, and we are both so sated we can barely move, I tuck her into my chest and hold her as she falls asleep in my arms. I feel like the luckiest bastard on the planet.

SOMETHING WARM AND SOFT IS PRESSED TO MY SIDE. I jerk awake, started by the unfamiliar feel of someone in my bed. I smile, and my cock stiffens as I remember it's Anika. I take the moment to watch her in her sleep. She's on her stomach, tilted slightly to the side, arms above her head, and completely naked. Her hair is a mess from having my hands in it, spread across her back, the red a stark contrast to the black sheets and her fair skin. The blanket has slipped down across the swell of her ass, and I can't help but trace my hand from her shoulder, down her back, and finally trace the curve of her hip.

She moans at my touch, so I lean down and kiss the cheek of her ass, pulling the blanket down further, stroking the inside of her thigh. She shivers, and her eyes flutter open, turning to look at me.

"Damian." Her voice is husky, rough from sleep. I'm certain nothing has ever sounded sweeter.

"Good morning, love. How do you feel?" I continue stroking the inside of her thigh, moving a little higher, and she gasps.

"Sore, but fantastic," she purrs, stretching her body like a cat, opening her thighs further, a silent plea to touch her.

I lightly brush my hand over her clit and she arches her hips, a disappointed sigh escaping her when I move my hand down the other thigh. I trail kisses up her side and delight in the goosebumps that blossom on her skin from the touch of my lips. I reach her ribcage with my mouth and her breathing quickens. I get to her breast, and the perfectly dusky, pink-colored nipple is already hard, begging for my touch. I flick a tongue over it and she arches her back, desperate for more.

"Damian," she pleads, trying to pull me up her body, "please."

"How could I ever deny you when you beg so sweetly?" I whisper against her skin. I move my hand back to her clit and rub slow circles with my thumb, bringing my mouth to hers as she sucks my bottom lip, sending fire flooding through me.

"More," she demands, and I eagerly comply, slipping a finger into her heat and groaning at how ready she is.

"Fuck, Anika," I say breathlessly, "you are so damn wet, I can't function when you are near me. All I can think about is how much I want to kiss that mouth; how much I want to bury myself in you and fuck you until you are screaming my name when you find your pleasure." I plunge my fingers in and out of her until she's gasping and writhing beneath me.

"Fuck me, Damian, I need you inside of me, *now*."

I am powerless to do anything but her bidding. I settle myself between her thighs and slide into her with one long thrust of my hips, the feel of her squeezing me the most exquisite kind of torture. I still, laying my forehead against hers, as I try to memorize this moment. Her scent, her feel, the sounds she makes. I want it to never end, to lay here in this bed just being a man worshiping a woman instead of a king of a kingdom that has been broken.

She arches into me, silently pleading for me to move, so I do. I keep the pace slow at first, wanting to stay in this moment with her for as long as possible. To keep the problems we will have to face today at bay a little longer, and just feel her. I slowly explore her lips, kissing and nipping, making her whimper as that pleasure slowly builds, showing her it doesn't always have to be fast and reckless.

She's getting close, her hips meeting my thrusts, her breathing uneven as she claws into my back.

"Damian!" I look into her eyes and smile; I can see that frantic need mirrored there, as well as wonder. I love how new all of this is to her, to be able to be the one that shows her how good it can be.

"Take your hand and rub your clit for me," I command as I angle myself to give her room. She hesitates but does it. As soon as she touches herself, her eyes close, and she's lost in the sensation. I start thrusting a little harder, watching her face. Watching her is making it hard to hold my own release back, but I'm determined to take the plunge with her.

"Rub faster, Anika, harder. I can't hold back much longer," I plead, feeling that pressure build. She does and starts making those breathy little moans that I know means she's almost there. "There you go, love. Let me see you come so I can come with you. You are so damn beautiful, so perfect. I love seeing you come apart for me."

Thank fuck she finally arches and tightens around me as that first wave hits her. I thrust wildly into her now, and as she's in the throes of her orgasm, I find my own and spill myself into her, shuddering with the force.

I roll to my side, too spent to hold myself up any longer and bring her with me, tucking her into my arms, holding onto her like she might disappear at any moment. I love how perfectly she molds to me as we drift back into sleep.

Someone knocking at my door way too damn early wakes us. My lips curve upward at the sleepy but annoyed look on her face.

"Don't worry, it's probably just Layla," I whisper against her ear as I trail a finger down her naked back, and she purrs.

"Go away, have I ever told you how much of a pest you are?" This is twice in the past twenty-four hours that she has interrupted my time with Anika.

"It's me, jackass. Open the damn door, I have Brennan with me, and I need to talk to you both," Cas barks from the hall.

"Shit, I don't want them to see me in here," Anika says frantically as she tries to find her dress. It slightly annoys me that she seems to be embarrassed to be caught with me.

"Anika, we already know you are in there, so just hurry up, dammit, before Layla gets suspicious and comes looking. I want to talk to you too." Cas sounds frustrated and I smile. Guess we are officially busted, and I find myself all too pleased with the idea of everyone knowing about us, she, however, looks furious.

"Put on one of my shirts, love," I tell her as I throw on some joggers. I love the idea of seeing her in my clothes. She rolls her eyes and puts on her clothes instead, and I despise how that small act of defiance gets under my skin. I'll punish her later for it. I don't have time to really analyze why it bothers me so much before Cas is knocking again, and I throw the door open.

"What can I do for you, gentlemen?" I ask as they come in and take a seat.

Brennan shrugs his shoulders. "I was summoned, so I have no idea what this is about."

Cas runs his fingers through his hair as his knee bounces up and down. He looks nervous. So help me, if he tells me something that is going to hurt Layla, I *will* kill him.

Slowly.

Painfully.

With a smile on my face.

"I wanted to talk to the three of you because, well, with Rio gone, you are the most important people in Layla's life, and I, uh, didn't want to just talk to one of you and piss the others off so I thought maybe I should just talk to all of you at once."

I stand, crossing my arms and leveling a hard glare at him, waiting for him to go on.

"Nyx told Layla she was going to put an end to my betrothal. Once that business is behind us, I would like to have your blessing to ask her to marry me."

A huge smile spreads across Brennan's face and Anika jumps up, squealing as she throws herself at Caspian so fast he barely has time to catch her. Seeing her in Cas's arms opens something dark and feral inside me that screams to rip her away from him. I shake it off as Brennan claps Cas on the back and pulls him into a hug after Anika steps away.

"It's about damn time, brother!" Brennan exclaims, still grinning. Anika is glowing with excitement, a twinkle in her eyes as she turns to me. I realize I haven't spoken and they are all now facing me as they quiet down and look expectantly, waiting for my answer.

"It's not my decision to make. I will support Layla in whatever she wants. I approve of the match, but know that if you hurt her, I have no compunction about killing you. None," I growl. Anika playfully smacks me on the arm, and I smile. "But welcome to the family, Cas," I say holding out a hand to shake his.

Chapter Fifteen

LAYLA

The castle is bustling with the current addition of Cas and his brothers, and I must admit, I kinda love the chaos. They may all be grown men, but they tease and grumble like a bunch of overgrown children, constantly picking at each other.

Damian's mother seems to bask in the glow of a full table, and despite the events of the night before, everyone is in a relatively good mood as they sit down to eat.

"Hey fucker, I wanted that!" Delphin complains as Cas grabs the last sticky bun and takes a huge bite right in his baby brother's face. "You act like the fact that you slobbered all over it will stop me." He snatches it out of his hand and quickly moves out of the way so Cas can't snatch it back, running to hide behind me.

"Get him, Layla!" Delphin says as he playfully puts me between him and his current foe.

"Hey now, boys, I'm a neutral party, leave me out of this!" I laugh.

"I will have some more brought out; children behave!" The

laughter in Enthralia's voice and the sparkle in her eyes make me wonder if she wished she had more children.

Aegir and Nerine keep looking at each other, thinking they are being sly, but we all know she stayed with him last night, and if we didn't know it, we quickly figured it out based on the moans and screams coming from that end of the hall. I'm guessing they celebrated the end of her betrothal to Cas in much the same way Cas and I did now that she was free to give herself to Aegir. I'm trying really hard to hide the smirk on my face and can't, so I take a sip of my tea.

From my seat at the breakfast table, amidst the clinking of silverware and the boisterous conversations, I can't help but smile at Aegir and Nerine, the guilt I felt about sleeping with Cas while he was betrothed to her evaporating. Their attempts at discretion are almost endearing, if not entirely unsuccessful. From the corner of my eye, I catch them stealing glances at each other, their eyes locking for just a moment too long before they hastily look away, a flush creeping up their necks.

Aegir's gaze drifts toward Nerine with an undeniable warmth, his fingers absently tapping on the table as if channeling his nervous energy. Nerine, for her part, is no better at hiding her feelings. Despite her efforts to engage in conversation with Damian and his mother, her eyes invariably find their way back to Aegir, lighting up with a spark that wasn't there the night before.

It warms me, observing their silent, electric communication. It's as if they're in their own little world, connected by an invisible thread only they can feel. The rest of us at the table, including Damian's mother, aren't fooled for a second. There's an unspoken acknowledgment in the air, a collective amusement at the pair's not-so-secret secret.

Damian catches my eye from across the table, and we share a

knowing look. Everyone senses the shift between Aegir and Nerine, their thinly veiled feelings hiding behind casual glances and fleeting smiles. It's a gentle reminder that despite my father's attempt to destroy us, he failed as stories of new love play out over the morning breakfast table, unfolding right before us, hidden in plain sight.

Speaking of new love, Damian and Anika look a million times less tense around each other than they ever have, and they too keep sneaking glances at one another. I hope Damian doesn't think I don't notice how many times he has touched her this morning. A hand on her shoulder, a brush of his fingers across her arm as she looks into his eyes and smiles.

My heart swells with how much love surrounds this table. Brennan has already bonded with Cas's brothers, and they act as if they have known each other for years, laughing and teasing. My heart is so full, and then my eyes meet Caspian's, and it begins to gallop in my chest. I never knew this kind of happiness was possible. We are in the middle of a damn war, but these people here in this room make this fight worth it. I will go to the ends of the earth for them, to keep them safe. To give them the opportunity to live their lives happy and in love.

Lost in my own thoughts, I don't hear what Damian says to me.

"Layla?" He frowns, looking concerned as I turn toward him.

"Hmm? What's up?"

"I asked you how you felt about Cas's brothers and the princess staying here for a few days until Nyx handles that nasty business of the betrothal. It would probably be best for all involved if Triton has a few days to cool off before the boys head home, don't you think?"

"Oh! Yeah, I think that's a great idea! I'd love to see what kind of powers they have too. That was some awesome shit last night—what kind of shield were you throwing up that kept them back like that?"

Nereus, who is more reserved than the others, speaks up. "I'm sure you've heard of how dolphins and bats use a type of sound waves, right? Well, with our abilities in the water, we have similar capabilities except on land we can use it like you saw. With one of us, it doesn't do much, but together, it's fairly powerful."

I nod and look at Cas with my eyebrows raised as he squirms a little in his seat. "So, big guy, wanna tell us what other things you're hiding from us?"

"Well, I wasn't hiding it exactly. We just haven't really had much time to talk, and it's fairly new. I don't have quite the range of powers you do, but I do have a few that have popped up. Fire seems to be the easiest for me to command besides water, which is such a mindfuck for an Aquaborn."

"What else can you do? The stronger your bond becomes with Layla, the more powers she displays. She literally can wield almost everything at this point, to some degree, though they did wane a bit for a while. They seem to be back in working order now, I see," Damian states. "I know some people saw you two throwing powers around last night in the chaos, but we really need to keep a lid on exactly how much the two of you can do. This attack was meant to show weakness, but I believe it was also meant to expose you. Thanatos already knows you can kill gods."

Caspian's brothers all pale at this revelation. I guess Cas had not shared that particular fact with them. "I'm sure he suspects you might have other abilities too and he's trying to test his theory, which is why he sent the undead but stayed close enough to watch." Damian's face is grave as he reminds us of what we are dealing with, and all the joking from this morning quickly disappears.

Cas raises his hand a few inches and shadows race from the corners of the room, swirling about and filling the room with darkness. It's not quite as strong as when I do it, and the room isn't completely encased in shadow, but it rankles me a bit because water-wielding is still one of my weakest powers.

126

"Shit," Delphin whispers. "Who are you and what have you done with my brother?" Everyone laughs a little nervously at the joke. Cas obviously hasn't shared this power with his brothers. I am awestruck and more than a little turned on. He's sitting across the table from me in a T-shirt that hugs every damn muscular inch of his chest and arms, one hand resting in his lap, the other arm propped with his elbow, clicking and unclicking the top of the pen he holds over and over, obviously feeling a little anxious. Those blue eyes meet mine, and it hurts my heart to see so much uncertainty there. I'm guessing he sees the heat in mine because he sits up a little straighter and raises an eyebrow at me.

"*You are so fucking hot; I want to jump you right here and now,*" I say through our link.

"*Might be a little weird with both of our families sitting right here.*" There's laughter in his voice, but his face looks calm as he keeps his gaze locked on me.

"*Might be worth it.*" I get up from the table and prowl over to where he is. He stands and looks a little terrified.

"*You might want to stop looking at me like that, Layla.*"

"*Or what?*" I stand directly in front of him and wrap my arms around his neck. "*Take me upstairs, now.*"

He grabs the back of my thighs, and I wrap my legs around his waist as he carries me out of the room while his brothers all whoop and holler, and Damian groans.

"We aren't done talking, so hurry the fuck up!" Damian yells after us. I flip him off over Cas's shoulder.

As we make our way to the bedroom, I kiss Caspian's neck, biting it gently in all the places that he loves before reaching the lobe of his ear and tugging on it with my teeth.

"Fuck the bedroom," he growls as he throws open the first door we come to. A poor girl is in there cleaning and Cas scares her to death. "Out. Now," he demands, and I giggle.

"Sorry!" I say after her as he plops me in a chair. I try to stand, but he pushes me back down.

"Stay," he demands, unbuttoning his pants and freeing his cock. "That wasn't nice, Layla. Making me hard as a fucking rock right there in front of everyone. You want me? Want this?" He strokes himself, and I'm rubbing my thighs together to try and ease the ache that is so powerful it almost hurts.

"Yes," I pant.

"Good girl, you're going to suck my cock, I want your lips wrapped around me."

I reach out and stroke my hand down it and lean in to run my tongue over that ridge, watching his hips flex and his hands thread through my hair. I'm so damn glad I hadn't braided the long, dark mass. I love it when he tugs at it when he's in my mouth. I take him as deep as I can and I do it oh so slow, knowing it's killing him when he tries to urge me to go faster. He thinks he's in control, but I'm going to have him begging before it's over. I keep up the maddeningly slow strokes until I finally sit back, moving away from him as he growls, trying to reach out and touch me.

"I don't think so, sir." I pull my leg up, put my foot directly on his chest, and shove just a little. He barely moves, but he gets the point. "Sit," I demand, and he falls back into the chair across from me. I rise and slowly take off my clothes piece by piece, making sure to put on a good show. I allow him to touch himself while I do, but that's about to end.

Once I'm finally naked, he says, "Come here and sit on me."

"No." His eyes darken in fury as he starts to rise. "Don't you fucking dare get out of that chair," I say darkly. He does, and I pin him with my shadows as he growls. "Now, I'll let go if you promise to be a good boy."

He stares at me, eyes thunderous, but stays still, so I release him.

Satisfied he is going to play nice, I sink back down into my chair, draping one leg over the arm, putting myself on display for his viewing pleasure.

The hunger in his stare causes an inferno to blaze inside of me. I love knowing how much he wants me; it gives me a heady sense of power. I slowly play with one of my nipples, his eyes glued to my hand. I arch my back and moan, then slowly brush my fingers lower as his breathing gets harsher the closer I get to my clit. I rub it once, gasping at the jolt of pleasure that streaks up my spine, then lower, inserting my fingers into my wet pussy, bringing them in and out as I buck and moan at the sensation.

"Fuck, Layla, I *need* to touch you." I almost feel sorry for him; the look of pain on his face makes me nearly give in, but I'm not done.

"You want to touch me?"

"Yes."

"You want to bury your cock inside of me? See how soaked I am for you? Look how wet it is, Cas." I slide my fingers out and show him how they glisten before putting one in my mouth and sucking.

"*Fuck*, Layla!"

"I want you to beg."

"Please, Layla, please, have mercy. I need my hands on you. My mouth. I need my cock buried in you," he growls, the sound vibrating through the room, making me wetter.

I slide out of the chair and crawl over to him, swinging my hips as I look up at him and lick my lips. I crawl up his lap until I reach his face and thread my fingers through his hair, yanking his head back and running my tongue up the side of his neck before capturing his mouth in a savage kiss.

"Do you know how fucking turned on I was last night when I saw you out there fighting like some kind of warrior god? You looked beautiful, Cas, so damn perfect my heart hurt." I settle myself over him, lining him with my entrance as he grabs my hips and buries himself inside of me with one hard thrust. I can't believe we are still this hungry for each other as many times as I had him last night. This kind of insatiable need can't be normal.

This feels different, though—this is pure desperate fucking. His thrusts are savage, I may be the one on top, but he's in complete control, and all I can do is hold on to his shoulders as he pounds into me without mercy, punishing me for making him wait.

He's feral and I fucking love it.

He bites my shoulder and I claw my nails down his back. "Cas!" I cry.

"I know, baby, just stay with me, I want to come with you." He slides a hand down between our bodies and starts rubbing my clit as he thrusts harder. I love the sounds he makes when he's close, the grunts and moans that tumble from him. It makes heat coil so tight in my belly, the need so incessant I feel like I may combust at any moment.

"I'm going to come, Cas! Don't stop!" I cry out and close my eyes, fireworks exploding inside of me as I ride that wave of bliss. He groans one last time beneath me, shouting my name as I feel him throb inside of me as he finds his own release. Wrapping his arms around my back and holding me close, we stay like that, holding each other close as our breathing returns to normal, and he lazily rolls his hips, not ready to break apart just yet.

"Dammit, Layla, every time, it just gets better." He takes my face in his hand and places a quick kiss on my mouth, his breath still ragged as I lay on his chest, trembling.

"You okay?" he asks, kissing me all over my face.

"I'm perfect, I just think my bones have all melted. That was, just... wow."

"So, what I'm hearing you say is that I have ruined you for all men, right?" He smiles and those ridiculous dimples make an appearance, making my insides feel all warm and fuzzy.

"You are incorrigible," I say, giving him a loud kiss on the mouth before I move from him. I look over my shoulder and say, "But yes, you have ruined me for all other men. There's only you, Cas."

He yanks me back down, and in no time, I'm screaming his name again as he shows me exactly how ruined I am.

WE FINALLY EXIT THE ROOM, HIS FINGERS THREADED through mine, both of us grinning like fools. Everyone is still in the dining room, talking about the plans to check on the people in the city today and offering aid where we can.

Grandmother was true to her word and sent in a small army to help with the effort, which is great, but we all feel like we should be out there providing aid as well. Enthralia determines it will be a great show of camaraderie between our kingdom and Cas's for his brothers to be seen helping our people, so the decision is easily made. Triton may get pissed about it later, but none of the boys seem to care. Brennan and Delphin are going to stick together, even though Nyx said it was safe, we would rather him not be out wandering alone, especially with my father still on the loose. Not after he kidnapped him once already.

As we gear up to help clean up the city after my father's brutal attack, I can't shake the fluttering sensation in my stomach. It's like a swarm of butterflies swirling around inside me, reminding me of the enormity of what lies ahead of us.

With every step I take toward the wreckage, the butterflies seem to dance with more fervor, mirroring the mix of emotions swirling within me. Fear, uncertainty, guilt, and determination all vie for dominance, creating a whirlwind of sensations that I struggle to contain. I feel my power sizzling along my skin, mirroring my rising tide of emotions. I know I need to get them under control. Will the people blame me if they find out my father was the one behind the attack?

They don't need to blame me—I blame myself.

We are all quiet as we enter the city, the playful morning long forgotten.

As I survey the aftermath, a fresh wave of guilt washes over me, threatening to drown me in its depths. Vengeance senses my mood, nudging my hand with her nose. The streets are strewn with rubble and debris, a stark testament to the devastation wrought by Thanatos's rampage. Each broken building, each shattered window, bears silent witness to the lives lost and the suffering endured.

I can feel the weight of every death pressing down on me, a heavy burden I'm not sure I can carry. The innocent victims haunt my thoughts. I can't shake the feeling that I am responsible, that my very existence has brought this tragedy upon them.

But it's the memory of a young girl that cuts deepest into my soul. I can still see her tear-stained face, twisted in anguish as she watched the undead tear into her mother, hearing her screams as Damian whisked her away so she didn't meet the same fate. Her cries still echo in my ears, a constant reminder of the pain and suffering that I have caused.

These people would not be dead if my father had not come for me.

As I stand amidst the ruins of the city, I can't help but feel that I have failed them all.

The guilt is suffocating, threatening to consume me from within. I know that I can never truly atone for what has happened, but I vow to do whatever I can to make things right, to ensure that no one else suffers because of my father's desperation for power.

I try to swallow down the lump in my throat. "Where do we start, Damian?"

"Just go door to door and check on the people, see what's needed. Supplies will be here soon; we will pass those out." His voice is thick with emotion. Anika places a hand on his arm and offers him a weak smile, his eyes softening as he looks down at her.

The reality crashes down on us like a tidal wave as we contemplate the aftermath of the battle. "What do we do about funerals?" I voice the question that hangs heavy in the air, my words echoing with a somber gravity. "Every soul that died was turned, and we had to burn them all. There's not even anything for their families to bury."

It's a realization that hadn't crossed my mind during the chaos of the fight. During the battle, amidst the chaos and the roar of flames, the thought of no remains hadn't registered. But now, as the dust settles and the echoes of the conflict fade, the cruel reality becomes starkly apparent. My father, in his ruthless quest for power, has even robbed these people of the chance to properly mourn their loved ones.

Damian's expression darkens as he grapples with the same realization. Running a hand through his hair in frustration, he nods. "We cannot let their memories fade into oblivion," he declares, his voice firm with resolve. "We will hold a service for all of the fallen. I'll confer with Grandmother on how we should proceed to ensure the souls are not lost and end up in their proper place in the afterlife."

"How many people died?" Tears threaten to spill down my cheeks, but I can't show weakness right now, so I steel my resolve and promise myself I can feel all the feelings later.

"One hundred and twelve," Damian says grimly. "Many were killed when their loved ones turned, according to the reports that came in this morning. Parents mauled their own children. I couldn't

133

help myself, I looked into some of their memories, it was horrific." His voice breaks, and I can see the turmoil in his eyes, the guilt that weighs on him nearly as much as it weighs on me.

I grab his hand and squeeze reassuringly. He looks at me and squeezes back before we go separate ways to begin seeing to the needs of the people.

Chapter Sixteen

DAMIAN

Somehow, between the events of last night and this morning, I had convinced myself that the losses and damage were not this bad. In the light of day, the reality settles in as I take in the amount of destruction. We suffered very little death at the palace, but the rest of the kingdom was not as lucky.

I see an older gentleman cleaning up debris in his yard and I head over to lend a hand. The front door had been ripped off the hinges, too badly damaged to be repaired. I grab one end as the older gentleman struggles with it. "Here, let me help."

"Thank you, I appreciate—King Damianos! Sir! You should not be out here picking through trash!" the man exclaims.

"I would be nowhere else. Why should I not be out here helping my people in their time of need?"

He looks at me for a moment, lost in thought, before nodding his head. "All right then, let's put it over there for me to chop up into smaller pieces." We each take an end, carrying it across the yard, where I pick up the axe and start chopping. The physical work feels good—it gives me something productive to focus on, easing the knot inside of me with every swing. Once I'm finished, I continue working with the man as he regales me with tales of his youth, an easy camaraderie forming through physical labor and sweat.

"Can I ask your name, sir?"

"I'm so sorry, I plum forgot and lost my manners! My name is Jorah, Your Highness."

"It's nice to meet you, Jorah, please call me Damian," I say as I hold out my hand that he grips tight.

"Did you lose anyone last night?" I ask the question weighing heavily on my heart. He shakes his head.

"We were lucky—my wife is out of town, visiting her sister who just had her first grandchild. They just breached the house when Lady Layla came through the darkness looking like a vengeful goddess, whipping them through the air and setting them on fire. It was truly a sight to behold, and we are forever grateful to her."

"She is something, isn't she?" I smile. "I'm glad she's on our side. She's slightly terrifying," I say, my voice filled with laughter.

"Aye, she is, but she sure is a beauty. People have been wondering if you would make her your queen, but I suspect the two of you are close for different reasons. She favors you—anyone with some sense can see the two of you are related. A bastard sister, perhaps?" Bastard children were common among the immortals. I have several half-siblings running around if rumors are true, none worth a damn.

"We wondered how long it would take people to piece it together. Not a bastard sister, but a cousin. We met in the mortal realm, though she feels more like a sister, I suppose. We have grown very close. I think she may be destined for bigger things than our quaint little kingdom, and besides, she is in love with Prince Caspian."

"Ah, that's a solid match. He's nothing like his father—he's a good man and will make a fine ruler one day."

"I agree, he's running around here somewhere with those brothers of his, helping our people now. The four of them were invaluable last night. The casualties would have been much higher had they not fought with us."

Chatting for a few moments more, I move on to help others. Their stories and kindness throughout the day awaken something in my soul, a desire to be something more than I am, to be something worthy. The weight of my father's sins often sits like a stone, dragging me down to the depths of an ocean where there is no air or light to be found, only a darkness that bleeds into the very marrow of who I am.

Here, with these people who look to me with hope in their eyes, light breaks through the murky water and shines on a path out of the depths of guilt that consumes me.

Supplies begin to arrive, some carrying the crest of Shadowfell and some the crest of Nyx. My lips curve upward that she kept her promise to send aid, not that there was ever any doubt that she would.

Caspian and his brothers begin to unload the heavier items. Delphin, Nereus, and Brennan seem to have caught the eyes of some young ladies who are vying for their attention, the boys all too happy to indulge them as they strip off their shirts in the hot sun.

Aegir follows Nerine as she hands out sweets to children. She is proving herself to me much more than a soft, pampered princess. She has toiled out here doing as much manual labor as the boys while also chatting with the people, her gentleness putting them at ease.

"Caspian, where is Layla?" I yell up at him as he hands another bag of supplies down to Delphin.

He pauses, turning in a circle, scanning the surrounding area. "I'm not sure, I haven't seen her in a while."

My heart drums in my chest as I fight down the panic that

threatens to send me flying through the streets, screaming her name. Caspian catches my eye, and I can tell that he too is concerned.

"I'll go look for her—you stay here," I tell him, and he nods his head in agreement. I whistle for Chaos, and he comes padding out from between two houses where he and Havoc had been dropping off bags onto porches full of food that Anika had been filling for the people.

"Chaos, find Vengeance and Layla."

"They are safe, but I can smell the Godslayer, and she reeks of sadness."

We move in and out of houses until Chaos walks up the steps over a splintered door into a small home. A keening wail filled with grief and desolation pierces my heart and sends shivers down my spine. Vengeance's mournful howl reverberates through the air, and Chaos whines in response.

My breath catches—this is the home of the little girl I saved last night. The one whose mother died mere steps from her. There is no evidence of any others living in the home. It must have been just the two of them, and now the young girl has no one.

Layla is mourning for the child, the life that has been ripped away from her, the love of her mother that has been stolen by my uncle.

Seeing Layla like this, with her body wracked by sobs, each one seeming to tear through her as if physically ripping her heart from her chest, is a torment like no other. Every cry she emits is a blade twisting in my gut, her pain becoming my own. The sight of her, so vulnerable and shattered, awakens a fierce protectiveness within me, alongside a helplessness that claws at my insides. I want to reach out, to hold her, to somehow take this insurmountable pain and make it my own if it means she would find even a moment's relief. Yet, I'm frozen, feeling woefully inadequate in the face of her grief, not knowing how to ease the pain. The air around us feels charged with her sorrow, and it's as if I can physically feel the echo of her heartbreak. It's a sight that I never wanted to witness, Layla in such despair, and it leaves me feeling utterly powerless.

Vengeance nudges Layla as she lays on the girl's bed, her arms wrapped around a stuffed bear. Layla turns, burying her head in the fur at the wolf's neck. Chaos joins in, whining and nudging Layla until she looks up and meets my eyes. Another sob escapes her, and my feet move of their own volition until I am next to the bed, sitting down and gathering her in my arms.

"Shhh, it's okay, Layla, the girl is safe."

"Yes, but she lost her m-m-mother. Look around this house, Damian, her mother loved her and now she's gone," she cries. "It's my fault." Her voice was barely more than a whisper. "All of this is my fault. He was here because of me. These people are dead because of me. Why do I deserve to live when so many of them died? These people trusted us to keep them safe and I *failed* them, Damian." Her voice breaks as she says my name, and the tears flow once more.

"Listen to me, cousin, and listen closely." Anger races through my blood at her confession. "This is not your fault. You saved countless lives last night, countless. It is not your fault your father did this, that is on him, not you. You nearly killed yourself trying to save people that you don't even know. You didn't grow up here— you have only been in this realm for a matter of months, and yet you defended them with everything you have, ready to sacrifice yourself if need be. You can be sad about this, we all are, but these people need you too much for you to let this break you. Feel hurt, feel sad, I feel those things too, but you also need to be *pissed*. Pissed at him for doing this. This. Is. Not. Your. Fault." My chest is heaving when I finish, the overwhelming need to hurt someone scorching my veins.

She quiets for a moment and worry flickers in my heart, fear I may have gone too far. Vengeance whines, ears pinned back as she nudges her again, no doubt having her own silent conversation. I hold my breath, waiting to see what she does next.

She untangles herself from my arms and when her eyes meet mine, there is a determination there. I grab her chin with one hand and wipe her cheeks with the other before placing a kiss on her forehead. "There's my girl. You are the strongest person I know, Layla. I understand being sad. I feel it too, and the guilt. I have always said you and I are similar creatures. What we aren't is anything like our fathers. We will never be like them."

She throws her arms around me, and we sit like that for several moments. The strongest woman I know seems so fragile at this moment, but I know her vulnerability only makes her a fiercer protector.

The heavy thud of footsteps on the wood floor makes my body tense, but as I reach for their thoughts, the concern and fear shining through can only be one person, Cas. He reaches the doorway of the room and looks at us, worry etched on every line of his face.

I scoop Layla up, the emotional toil having worn her out, so she doesn't protest, and I hand her to Cas. "Take her back to the castle, she needs to rest. Try to get some food in her as well." He nods, and the love shining in his eyes as he looks down at her soothes some of the anger still simmering in my soul.

The fight that usually burns so brightly in her has almost completely burned out. A lump forms in my throat and the sting of tears in my own eyes has me gritting my teeth to keep them in check. I set about cleaning the small home, determination filling me. I will make it as orderly as possible so someone can come collect things for the young girl.

By the time we are finished for the day we are all dirty, sweaty, and exhausted. It's way past dinner time when we arrive back, and everyone quietly retires to their rooms.

"Stay with me tonight?" I nuzzle Anika's hair, taking comfort in the feel of her tucked into my side in the hall outside of her room.

"Yes," she sighs heavily. "Let me get cleaned up, and I'll be there soon."

"Take your time, I need to speak to my mother and will meet you when I'm done." I press a soft kiss to her mouth and head off, hoping my mother will agree to what I have planned.

Chapter Seventeen

LAYLA

Carrying me into my room, Cas gently sets me down and tells me to remove my clothes while he starts a bath.

"Soak in the tub while I go get us some food." He kisses my head and leaves the door open to the bathroom so Vengeance can lie on the floor while I slip into the warm water, sighing as it settles over my skin, the heat seeping into my bones.

"Godslayer, I understand your grief, but you must not carry the guilt for the actions of others."

"I know, Vengeance. I just can't help but think if I had killed him when I had the chance, those people would still be alive."

"You are not to blame. You are intelligent enough to know this."

All I can do is nod. I know her words are true, but it's difficult to separate what I know in my head from how I feel in my heart.

My eyes are heavy—I feel my power simmering pleasantly under my skin, lulling me into sleep.

"Layla, wake up." Cas brushes a piece of hair out of my face as my eyes flutter open. "I have food. Hop out of the tub and come eat."

I stretch and realize the water has gone cold as I pull the drain and stand, droplets of water pouring off my skin, making me shiver. Wrapping myself in a fluffy towel, I let my stomach follow the smell of food. Cas is stretched out on the bed with a smorgasbord laid out in containers as I climb up, folding my legs under me and digging in.

"You want to talk about it?" he asks softly, his eyes watching me carefully.

I put my food down, thinking about my words before speaking them. "I know I shouldn't feel this insurmountable guilt, I can tell myself all day long that this isn't my fault. I know this and yet my heart doesn't seem to understand it. It's just fucking unfair." The swell of grief and guilt that fills me threatens to spill out, tears forming in my eyes as I try to take deep breaths and collect myself.

"Come here," Cas says as he reaches for me, pulling me into his lap and cradling me against him. His strong arms encircle me, and the hard lines of his broad chest make me feel safe. The beat of his heart against my cheek calms me, its steady rhythm chasing away the thoughts parading through my mind.

He places a finger under my chin and tilts my head up to look at him. Lips softly meet mine as I let out a sigh of contentment. I could stay here forever just being kissed by this man.

"I love you," he whispers against my mouth. "I love that you care so much." He kisses me again. "You are the most amazing woman I've ever known." This time, the kiss is longer but still slow and sweet, making my insides turn to jelly.

Vengeance growls from the floor and hops on the bed, a clear warning to Cas.

I can't help but giggle.

"I know you are attached, so I won't kill him, but I can easily remove a hand if he doesn't keep it to himself and let you sleep."

"I guess she's telling me you need to get some rest," he says as he smiles against my mouth. He cleans up the food, making sure to give

Vengeance a few pieces, trying to win her over before tucking himself around me as we drift to sleep.

THE SHEER PANDEMONIUM ENSUING IN THE HALLWAY outside of our rooms wakes me the next morning. I jump up but it only takes me a second for my heart to calm when I realize it's just the boys emerging to start the day.

"They don't know how to be quiet, do they?" I groan. Cas pulls me back into his arms, cuddling closer.

"Nope. Try living with them for as long as I have. You get used to it." He places a loud kiss on my shoulder before moving out of the bed to get dressed. Vengeance hops down and waits by the door.

"The king is waiting for you downstairs. You need to hurry." Vengeance seems impatient. Curious as to why Damian needs me badly enough to have Chaos relay a message to Vengeance, I hurriedly put myself together, fighting over the sink with Cas while brushing our teeth. It reminds me of sharing a bathroom with him at the gym, and my heart hurts knowing the gym is gone, and so is Rio.

I shove down the feelings threatening to take me under already this morning and instead head down to find Damian. I thought he would be in the room where we usually meet, but he's in the dining room, which is already alive with chaos as everyone is getting seated and starting to eat.

"Took you two long enough. Can't you keep your hands to yourselves?" he grumbles, as I walk in, Cas quickly on my heels.

I start to open my mouth, but Cas snaps at him first. "Not that it's your business, but we are running behind simply because Layla was exhausted, and I wasn't going to wake her. She needed her damn sleep." His eyes narrow in a clear warning for Damian to back the fuck down.

Damian's eyes grow wide, then soften as they drift to me. "You do look better today, cousin. I'm sorry for snapping. I'm just a little anxious this morning. I have a few things we need to talk about."

The room goes eerily silent, all eyes shift to Damian. "First, the betrothal has been broken. Your father is furious and demanding you all return home this morning." The boys all start talking at once, obviously pissed off.

"We're grown-ass adults," Delphin shouts.

"I'm not going back, certainly not right now, maybe not ever," Aegir growls, taking Nerine's hand in his.

Nereus is quiet, but you can see the storm brewing in his eyes, the tension radiating off his body.

Cas, on the other hand, is completely silent. Weirdly so. His eyes meet mine, and the anger simmering there worries me.

"I won't go back without you, I'm not leaving you again, but something tells me you have no intention of leaving here," he says through our link.

"Damian needs me, so do these people. I won't leave them until I know they are safe."

He nods—he knows me well enough to understand I feel obligated to protect them.

"That's enough," Damian says forcefully enough that the room immediately quiets back down. "You do not have to leave. You are all more than welcome to stay here as long as you wish. You must send word to your father and make sure he knows it is your choice and that you aren't being held here against your will because he somehow thinks that is the case, despite Nyx telling him otherwise. Now, moving on to the next point. Aegir came to me this morning with a request once I told Nerine the engagement was broken. I'll let him take it from here before we move on to the rest of this discussion."

Aegir stands, looking down at Nerine with so much tenderness the entire room fills with their warmth. "I asked Damian if he would marry us. Being ruler of this land, he has the power to do so, and he asked Nyx to bless the union, and she has agreed. Father will be pissed, but he will not be able to undo what has already been done. We would like the blessing of all of you as well." Cheers erupt around the room, and everyone jumps to their feet and hugs the couple as the guys pound Aegir on his back.

I hug Nerine and congratulate her. "We shall be sisters one day. Would you please stand with me as my maid of honor?" she asks, flooring me with her request.

"Oh, course I will!"

"Thank you!" She squeals and hugs me again.

Damian clears his throat. "Now, if everyone could have a seat, I have another matter to discuss, especially if all of you will be staying here for the foreseeable future. I've already discussed it with Mother, and she's agreeable, so now I just need to know how you all feel and approval from you, Layla. I'm going to need all the help we can muster."

I look at him curiously and everyone else at the table is nodding their heads in agreement. "Whatever you need, Damian, you have but to ask," Aegir states.

"Mother, please bring Selena in."

Enthralia walks in, holding the hand of the little girl I had been crying over the night before. My heart lodges firmly in my throat. She's so young, maybe three or four years old. Her eyes are as big as saucers, and she shyly hides her face in Enthralia's skirt. Damian lifts her into his arms, and she buries herself in his neck as he rubs her back. The juxtaposition of her tiny, fragile little body in his massive arms makes me want to weep at the emotions that bubble inside of me.

"Hello, little one," he whispers as he smooths her hair, and she pops her thumb into her mouth. "Did you have fun seeing the dragons with Uncle Damian this morning?"

"Dragons?" She lifts her head and looks around. Damian's rich, velvety laugh rumbles through the room.

"No, the dragons are not in here, but we will go see them again soon, okay?"

"No dragons?" She looks so sweet, Damian's face splits into a huge grin, and he hugs her tight.

"You can go see the dragons if you wish. Mother?" He hands her back to his mother, and they leave the room, the little girl squealing in excitement about the dragons. Vengeance pads quietly after them. "Selena is three. She is one of about five children who lost their parents and have no other family members to take them in. We will look for suitable families to raise them, but for now, Mother is opening the wing that contains the nursery. The children will be staying there. We will all pitch in with them from time to time, but they will have governesses, and Mother will oversee most of their care. Is this agreeable to you, Layla?"

His eyes haven't left mine since he handed Selena back to his mother, waiting for my reaction. I am floored. I have no words. He knew exactly what I needed. I launch myself out of the chair and throw myself at him. He doesn't have time to brace himself and the chair goes toppling over as the room bursts into laughter. He picks us both up from the floor as I hug him tight, trying to speak over this tightness in my chest that seems to be stealing my air.

"Thank you, Damian. Thank you."

He holds me against him, rubbing soothing circles on my back, burying his head in my hair as he kisses the top of my head. "I didn't do it just for you, cousin, though I hated seeing you so broken. I needed this too, I've told you before, we are very similar creatures. It won't fix what these children have lost, but hopefully, it will make it a little easier."

He releases me and smiles at everyone around the table. "One last thing, Nyx will be here tonight to conduct a ceremony for the city to honor the people that we lost and to help usher their souls safely into the underworld. It begins at twilight, so be prepared. Now, we have a wedding to prepare for! Men, come with me, ladies, Mother will be back in shortly to start planning."

I smile as Anika and Nerine start talking about wedding plans.

The day passes quickly, and as twilight nears, we begin to prepare for the ceremony to honor the dead. I don my midnight leathers, dressed as a warrior, ready to lead the lost souls into their next phase of life. Damian, Cas, and his brothers are all dressed similarly. Anika, Enthralia, Brennan, and Nerine are dressed in simple black ensembles. The joy from wedding planning has quieted, replaced by a heavy somberness as we come together with the people of the city.

I stand amidst the gathered crowd, my heart heavy with sorrow as I watch the flickering torchlight cast dancing shadows across the faces of those assembled. The air is thick with grief, each soul present bearing the weight of loss in its own way. But amidst the somber silence, there is a sense of reverence, an acknowledgment of the sacredness of the moment. Before us stands Nyx, her presence commanding and serene as she presides over the ceremony.

Grandmother radiates a divine aura, her ethereal beauty illuminated by the soft glow of the moon overhead. I can't help but feel a sense of awe in her presence, a recognition of her power and wisdom, and wonder how she thinks I could ever take her place. I feel inadequate in comparison. As she begins to speak, her voice echoes with a haunting melody that resonates deep within my soul. She speaks of love and loss, of the fleeting nature of existence, and the eternal bond that transcends the boundaries of life and death. Her words are a balm to my wounded heart, offering a glimmer of hope in this shitshow.

Throughout the ceremony, I find myself drawn to her words, each syllable carrying a weight of significance that resonates with my own experience. I think of those I have lost, of Rio, Nova, and even my mother. As Nyx speaks of the journey of the soul, of the eternal cycle of life and death, I feel a sense of peace wash over me. After the ceremony, Nyx offers a final blessing, her words a benediction that seems to linger in the air long after they have faded away. I close my eyes, feeling the warmth of Grandmother's divine presence envelop me like a comforting embrace. In that moment, I know that my loved ones are at peace, and though the pain of loss will always remain, I find solace in the knowledge that they will never be forgotten and know how much they were loved when they were here with us.

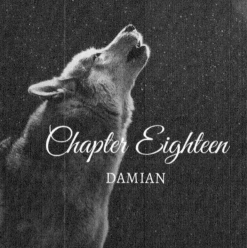

Chapter Eighteen

DAMIAN

"Are you absolutely sure, Cas?" I run my hands through my hair, mind reeling. I have no idea what to do with this information. "Can you trust this source?"

"Yes, Marcellus is a good friend, and while it irritates the shit out of me, he's rather fond of Layla too, so he wouldn't risk her."

Ahh, I remember Layla's little club boy. I can't help but smirk, knowing how much that probably gets under Caspian's skin. The thought quickly fades as I remember what we are discussing. "How many were killed?"

"He doesn't know for sure, but over a dozen. People are really starting to panic. He said the attacks are getting more frequent, and there's still a price for Layla's capture on Earth. He's trying to draw her out. With the attack here not working and Nyx getting involved, he's switching gears."

"Fuck. We have to tell her, and you know what that means." I level a stare at him, I need him on my side—it's going to take both of us to keep her out of this mess.

Anger is vibrating from his form, his rage palpable. I flinch when he draws a fist back and punches through the wall.

"Dammit, sorry. I'll patch that and paint it later," he grumbles, the tortured look in his eyes makes me feel a little sorry for him.

I wave my hand dismissively. I almost did the same to his face when he came in here and told me about the attacks. Guilt washes over me, knowing I'm not there preventing those people from dying.

"Invite him to the wedding this weekend, we will talk and get more information. Speaking of the wedding, Mother hasn't received confirmation that your parents will be in attendance. Have you heard anything?"

He snorts and rolls his eyes. "Nope. I still can't believe your mother managed to put all of this together in two weeks. Thank you for doing this for Aegir."

"It's nothing, I'm mainly doing it for Layla. I'm sure you are aware of how guilty she felt for fucking you." He scowls, which delights me. "She thought she was breaking that poor girl's heart. This makes her feel better, which, in turn, makes me happy." I really like Cas, but it's going to take a while for me to forgive him for the torment Layla went through over his engagement and then subsequent weeks of absence.

"Speaking of weddings, what the fuck are you waiting on? You asked us all for your blessing, and yet you haven't asked her," I query, more than a little curious as to why he hasn't popped the question.

He's quiet, looking out the window for a moment, gathering his thoughts before he speaks. "I want it to be perfect, and there's been so much going on. I also don't want to take anything away from Aegir and Nerine—this is their time, I don't want to overshadow that."

I nod, I respect his answer and understand the reasoning behind it. "I need to tell you something before I tell Layla because she is likely to try to cause me bodily harm before I can explain my reasoning to her." Cas quirks up an eyebrow at me but remains silent. "I have been dampening her powers. She could break through if she really wanted to, but with the two of you back in each other's good graces, I didn't want her to accidentally start a hurricane when she gets emotional. I let them lose the night of the attack, but other than that, I've been keeping a lid on them, which is starting to wear on me. They were naturally dampened when you were gone for so long and the bond between you had weakened, but before that, they were getting out of hand."

His eyes are wide, and he lets out a deep breath. "She's going to kick your fucking ass."

"I know, but I wanted to get someone here who could help her, and it took me a while to get in touch with him and get him to agree."

"Oh shit, you're not serious, you didn't, Damian."

I cringe. "You have a better idea? Plus, he only agreed if we would do one itty, bitty favor for him."

"Fuck me. What?" Cas runs his hands through his hair and over his jaw. I knew he wasn't going to like this.

"He has a daughter on Earth, Audra. She has no idea who he is, she is showing signs of having his powers, and he wants us to retrieve her. I can't do it alone—if she's as strong as he thinks she may be, I might not be able to manipulate her. I thought maybe Delphin could come with us. They are about the same age, and that boy can charm pretty much any female."

"I don't like the idea of him being anywhere near Layla."

"Come on, Cas, she won't fall prey to his charm. And besides, you are damn near as pretty. The only other person I could think of is Zeus and you know that asshole won't help. Thor is the only other option. Can you teach her to control those kinds of powers?"

"No, I'm still struggling to control some of the new ones I seem to have."

"Exactly."

"When do we leave?"

"As soon as possible, preferably before the wedding, which means I have to talk to Layla today and hope I come out alive."

"Well, let's go find her then." He stands and waits for me before striding out the door. Everyone should be out training at this time, so we head that way, each of us lost in our own thoughts.

Training looks more like pure chaos. Nerine and Layla are working on water wielding, with Nerine patiently teaching Layla how to pull water from things around her. Anika is on a mat with Delphin. My eyes narrow as I watch him put her on her back and pin her, a white-hot, unfamiliar feeling spreading through my chest as he touches her. My fingers curl at my sides, taking every ounce of control I have not to rip him off her and beat his face in. She forces him into a roll and is back on her feet within seconds. It takes him by surprise, and she lashes out, knocking him on his ass.

That's my girl. My lips curve upward, and pride replaces the ugly feeling from moments before.

"Layla!" Cas calls, waving her over. Her face lights up and she jogs to us, throwing her arms around him and pulling him down into a kiss.

"That's enough, children," I chide, and she laughs but doesn't release him. She whispers something in his ear and Cas lets out a deep rumble of approval at whatever she said.

"Damian and I need to talk to you about something. I need you to promise me you will listen until he's done talking. Then, if you want to bash his face in, I won't stop you." Her body goes rigid in his arms, and she slowly turns to look at me.

"It's not that bad, come on, let's talk." I motion to a set of tables and chairs closer to the castle for us to sit at. I explain to her about the attacks on Earth and tell her we will discuss a plan after the wedding. She seems content with that answer.

"Okay, so why would I want to bash your face in over that?" she asks warily.

I take a deep breath. Guilt churns inside my stomach, the bitter taste of it on my tongue. "That wasn't the thing I was worried about telling you." I take a deep breath. Fuck me, she's going to be pissed.

"You and I both know that when your storm powers started, you couldn't control them, and you were quite the menace."

She nods her head in agreement. "Yes, but I can't really wield that anymore." She tries and barely manages some gray clouds.

"Well, about that... I've been dampening your powers." I let go and thunderclouds form overhead as she pins me with a glare. "Listen to me, dammit. With Cas back, I was afraid they might get out of control, and until I could get someone here to help you harness them, I didn't want you worrying about hurting people."

"You could have talked to me about it first! You know how much it pissed me off when Cas and Rio would do that kind of shit to me, not trust me enough to include me in discussions that directly affected my life. I expected better from you!" She rages at me. Everyone has stopped what they were doing and is now staring at the spectacle unfolding.

"I know, I'm sorry. There were so many other things happening. I handled it poorly. I have someone willing to train—" She stands, rearing her hand back, and before I can react, punches me in the fucking face.

"Dammit, Layla!" I pinch the bridge of my nose to staunch the flow of blood as she stomps off. Why is her first instinct to punch me in the godsdamned face?

I go after her, still holding my fucking nose. "Layla, wait."

She whirls on me, putting her finger in my chest. "I get *why* you did it, I do. I'm not even mad about that. I'm *pissed* that you did it without talking to me. *That's not how you and I work!* You have always been the one person I could count on to treat me like an equal, not like something that needed to be protected. You don't get to make those decisions for me!"

"I know, I'm—"

"No! I don't want to hear your excuses or your apologies right now. Right now, I want to be pissed. When I'm done, I'll come talk to you—until then, leave me the fuck alone." Her face is flush, her breathing ragged, jaw clenched. Guilt coils in my stomach, and it's not a feeling I particularly enjoy. I nod and she turns and walks away from me.

I turn to Cas. "Go after her, make sure she's okay?"

"On it." He sighs and gets up to follow her at a distance. He's not dumb enough to get close to her right now.

Chapter Nineteen

LAYLA

The nerve of that fucking asshole! Of all people, I never expected this shit from him. That's what hurts the most. I stomp through the castle halls, heading to my room. I need to calm down; the rage boiling inside of me is going to spill over at any minute and I need to be away from everyone.

I throw open my door and slam it so hard the pictures on the walls rattle. Pacing back and forth, grinding my teeth, I hear my door opening and I freeze. So help me, if it's Damian, I'm going to do more than bloody his fucking nose.

Cas peeks around the door before stepping into the room and shutting it behind him. "I just wanted to check on you," he says quietly, concern etched on his beautiful face.

"Cas, I'm in the mood to fight or fuck, so pick one," I growl at him, throwing the words he said to me months ago back in his face.

"If I recall, when I said those words to you, you chose to fight." He folds his arms across his chest, and one side of his mouth lifts in a half-smile. He lowers his voice, "Is that what you want now, Layla? To fight? I'll be happy to oblige." I prowl toward him. Now he's grinning for real. His eyes darken, and I know we might be doing some wrestling, but I want to fuck.

I get close enough for him to touch me, and he roughly grabs me and pulls me flush with his body, fisting his hands in my hair to make me look up at him as our mouths collide. I don't bother with being gentle, I don't need that right now. Our tongues battle for dominance, my nails are already clawing into his back through the fabric of his shirt. I break the kiss just long enough to pull it over his head and toss it to the ground.

I throw mine off as well before fusing myself back to Cas. I need the skin-to-skin contact, for his heat to seep into all the places inside of me that had gone ice cold with Damian's betrayal. He grabs the back of my thighs, and I wrap my legs around his waist as he backs us up against the door. It wasn't gentle—he slammed me into it as he roughly moved his hands to my ass, squeezing hard, lifting me to grind himself into my core. The friction of his hard length causes me to gasp, the thrill of that electric spark flooding my system, making me arch myself into him, my nipples hardening as they rub against his smooth, muscular chest. I thread my hands through those thick blond waves, yanking his head back hard so I can kiss his throat, biting and licking my way up. His moans set my entire body on fire as he continues the delicious way he presses into me, making me nearly ready to combust.

"Naked. Now," I growl into his ear before nipping at the lobe. I feel his involuntary shudder before he lets me go. We both take our boots off, eyes watching each other appreciatively as we hurry. Shoes off, pants still on, he tucks his fingers into my waistband and yanks me over to him. He gets on his knees and unbuttons my top button, kissing the skin on my stomach as it's revealed, doing the same with each button as he opens them.

I grab a fistful of his hair and pull his head back so his eyes meet mine. "Faster. I don't want to play; I want to fuck. Get your pants off *now*."

He chuckles and stands back up, taking his off as I remove mine. I walk toward him, and he grabs me by my neck, squeezing just a little and kissing my lips, biting the bottom one hard.

"Your time for being the boss here is over—it's my turn, Layla. If you don't like it, you can fight me, but I'm going to fuck you the way I want, and you are going to shut up and like it. I don't want to hear another word out of your mouth unless it's you screaming my name or if I'm asking you a question. Understand?" This wasn't my playful Cas—this was the man who fought the undead like a warrior god, a man bred to command his father's army. His voice was dark and dangerous, and the tone left no room for argument. It's sexy as hell.

"I asked you a question." His eyes narrow at me, and for a moment, I'm tempted to knock him on his ass—we both know I can. He's asking me to submit to him.

"Understood," I grind out. He smiles at me; it's a smile of pure male satisfaction and my knees go weak.

"Good." He releases his hold and takes a step back. "Bend over the side of that chair and hold the fuck on."

I do, but he doesn't approach. Instead, he walks over to the armoire and gets something out. Walking back over me, he places a blindfold over my eyes.

"If you aren't comfortable with this, now is the time to say so." His voice is still commanding but a little gentler than before. I keep quiet, and he makes a sound of approval deep in his chest.

"I'm going to spank you, Layla, with my belt. If it gets to be too much, you can say stop." I nod my head, preparing myself for the sting, my clit throbbing in anticipation.

I hear him move and feel the bite of the leather against my skin. I inhale sharply, and Cas presses a kiss to the ass cheek he just smacked. He repeats the strike on the other side.

"Let's see how much my bad girl likes being spanked," he coos as he slides a finger inside of me. He groans, "Fuck, I knew you would be wet, but damn that pussy is soaked." He bends down and licks me, sliding his tongue in and out of me before sliding it up to flick my clit.

"Cas!" I gasp, trying to grind myself into him as he laughs and pulls away. The belt cracks across my ass again and I cry out, eyes watering.

"Such a greedy, greedy girl." I hear the belt drop to the floor and feel him rub his hands over my back and down to my ass. "I brought some toys back with me from Earth that I thought we might like to play with. I'm going to fuck you in the ass today, Layla."

Not being able to see has everything else heightened. Every sound and feeling sets me on edge. I moan, wiggling my hips, begging for his touch. I hear a cap open, and Cas unceremoniously plunges his cock into me with no warning.

"Fuck, you are so damn tight. I love fucking this tight little cunt." His thrusts are deep and hard, grunting and moaning as he pounds into me. "Is this what you want? Me to fuck your tight little pussy?"

"Fuck! Yes!" I pant. He reaches around and starts rubbing my clit. "I want you to come for me, Layla." He rubs harder and faster —I'm so damn close I feel like I'm going to explode.

I feel something probing my ass, and right as I am about to come, I hear something vibrating. He pushes it inside of me, the foreign feeling more pleasant than I would have thought. It sends me over that edge I had been balancing on, and I come apart, screaming Cas's name as he continues rubbing my clit and thrusting into me as I drift back down to earth, heart pounding in my chest.

He slides out of me, and I groan in protest at the loss. He

removes the toy from my ass. I hear the cap again. "I'm going to fuck your ass now, Layla, I'll be gentle. *This* time." I feel him press his finger into me and I hold my breath. "Relax, baby."

I breathe evenly, skin tingling in anticipation, a tinge of fear enhancing the excitement. He slowly slides his finger in and out of my ass several times before adding another. Pushing his cock back into my cunt, he adds a third finger, ever so slowly rolling his hips in tandem with his hand, making me feel deliciously full.

"Okay, baby, I think you're ready for me. It may hurt a bit at first." He removes his fingers before sliding his dick from me. I hear the cap once again and feel him rub lube all over my ass. He lines his cock up and slowly presses into that forbidden place where no one else has ever taken me before, a deep moan rumbling from him. I relax and he presses in farther, then pulls back out. He does this a few more times until he is finally seated to the hilt. He begins to move slowly. The stretch and the burn aren't overly comfortable, but I feel pleasure coiling in a different way, loving the fact that Cas is the only person to claim me like this. He rubs his hands over my skin, praising me over and over.

"That's it—look at how well you take me. You feel so fucking good, Layla. I am never going to get enough of this. All I want is to stay buried in your tight little pussy or this perfect ass." His uneven breathing and the way he is straining to keep himself controlled make that need build inside of me again.

"Cas," I plead.

"I've got you, baby." He reaches around and starts rubbing my clit with his thumb. His arms are trembling, and I reach into his mind, loving how hard it is for him to keep his control.

"*Let go, Cas*," I whisper through our link. It's not breaking the rules he set, I didn't say the words out loud.

"Fuck, I can't, Layla, I don't want to hurt you." He keeps his pace slow and gentle but rubs harder with his hand. He bends down and kisses my neck, whispering into my ear, "I'm getting so close, I need you to come for me, baby."

He bites my shoulder and rubs my clit harder. "Cas, fuck, I'm close! Rub harder!" I pant in desperation, my orgasm so close I'm lost to the need.

He ignores that I broke his rules and pumps a little faster, yanking my hair with his other hand, turning my face back to kiss me hard, biting my lip. Every thrust burns away the anger that's been simmering inside of me.

The bite of pain does it for me, my body convulsing as I scream his name, sobbing as I feel the throbbing pulses of pleasure as I come down from one of the most intense orgasms I have ever had in my life. He's almost there, his breaths coming faster in my ear, his pants my absolute favorite sound in the world. He thrusts one last time, "Aww fuck!" he grinds out, his body shuddering as he comes. His arms tremble as he presses his chest into my back, trying to catch his breath.

"Are you okay?" He trails kisses across my shoulder and pulls the blindfold off me.

A deep sigh escapes me as I gather my wits. How does this man always know exactly what I need? I feel a million times better—that coil of tension and anger completely gone.

"I am absolutely perfect. That was amazing," I say breathlessly.

I can feel him smile against me before he kisses my back again and pulls out of me. He picks me up and carries me into the bathroom, setting me down as he starts the water. He cradles me in his arms and sinks into the tub with me, sitting me between his legs.

"Are you sore? Did it hurt?" Concern laces his tone.

"Not at all, it felt a little weird at first, and it burned a bit, but it didn't hurt, no. When you started using your hand, I came harder than ever. It felt like my entire body broke apart and then came back together."

He makes that rumble of satisfaction deep in his chest that I love so much. It reverberates through me, making me smile.

"What does it feel like for you? Have you done that before?"

"It felt different and good, but I prefer fucking your pussy." He wraps his arms around me tighter, turning the water off with his foot. "And no, I've never done that before. It was a first for us both."

I have no idea why that pleases me so much, but it does.

"Are you ready to talk to Damian without killing him?" he asks gently, peppering kisses along my shoulder before grabbing a cup to pour water over my head. I sit silently while he puts shampoo into his hands and starts to wash my hair. I sigh, body relaxing. I love when he washes my hair.

I close my eyes and relish the feeling of his hands on my scalp, every ounce of tension leaving my body as I moan while his magical fingers massage my shoulders and neck.

"He was only doing what he thought was best, I know you feel betrayed, but he loves you." He begins rinsing me now, the warm water sliding across my skin, calming me almost as much as the night does when I call to it to help me sleep.

"I know. I'm still pissed, but I'll hear him out without punching him." My eyes feel heavy, and I lean back into him. "Maybe."

I feel his body tense under me, causing me to open my eyes. "What is it, Cas?"

"He's having someone to come help train you, he has a bit of a reputation," he grumbles, obviously not happy about this development.

"What kind of reputation?" I'm curious as to who could possibly have Cas rattled.

"As a womanizer. The fucker is stupidly handsome and charming. He may wield thunder and lightning, but he also has the power of seduction. He wants Damian and I to go fetch one of his half-breed children from Earth in exchange for working with you. I just need you to keep yourself shielded."

I can't help it, he looks so insecure and adorable right now, I laugh. "Cas, I can't imagine anyone being prettier than you, except maybe Delphin. Besides, I am hopelessly in love with you, so I think you can cross that off your things to worry about. Who is this mystery man?"

He rolls his eyes before answering me. "Thor."

"Holy shit, as in *the* Thor? The Norse god? Does he really have a hammer?"

"Yes, that Thor, yes he has a hammer, and he's not a Norse god, he's just one of ours, as all gods are, that just happens to be what people on Earth dubbed him as back in the day when he spent a lot of time there."

"If you are so worried about it, why not get someone else?" I still have a grin plastered on my face.

"The only other real option is Zeus, and he won't do it. Thor might be an ass, but he's also trustworthy. Well, he'd fuck you in a heartbeat, but he can keep a secret. We don't have to hide your powers from him—he hates your father and will do whatever he can to stop him. There're a few others that can wield weather and other elements, but none as powerful as you, so I'm not sure how much help they would be. Thor is one of the older gods, so he will be the best one to teach you. Considering how dangerous wielding lightning and storms can be, we can't afford to not have you get it under control, especially considering what kind of weapon that can be. Just *keep yourself shielded*."

I giggle, "Yes, sir!"

We finish cleaning up, and Cas offers to go fetch Damian while I wait in my room. This is a conversation that needs to be had in private.

The door opens and Cas makes his way inside. "He has

requested you meet him in his room if that's okay." He gives me a quick kiss as I make my way out of the room and down the hall.

His door is open, so I walk inside and shut it behind me. He's standing with his legs apart, arms crossed, body braced. I keep a serious face, but knowing he's worried that I'm about to kick his ass tickles me. I open my mind up to him and am flooded with so many images I cringe.

"Aww dammit, Damian, really?" He quirks an eyebrow at me. Throwing his words from the night he hunted me down at the club, I say, "Is there anywhere in this room that's safe to sit?"

He grins, "Did you read me, cousin? I wasn't even thinking about that, but now that you mention it...no, there is nowhere in this room that is safe to sit."

I sigh. "It's a good thing I'm not a whiny little bitch like you." I plop down on the couch. "Why the hell could I see all of that if you weren't thinking it?"

He shrugs, eyebrows knitting together, mouth pursed into a thin line. "My guess? I am struggling to contain your powers and your mind reading must be evolving beyond what even I can do."

Panic flares through me. All these powers are overwhelming, the pressure to be something more than what I feel like I am is daunting. The fear of failure is crushing.

"I'm sorry, Layla," he says softly. "I wasn't trying to hurt you or even keep it from you, not intentionally. There have just been so many things going on at once. I know I should not have made that choice for you, that wasn't fair."

The pleading in his eyes and the hurt I can physically feel wafting off him melt any lingering anger I was holding on to. I cross the room and wrap my arms around his waist. He hugs me back hard, and we just stand like that for several moments.

He puts a finger under my chin and tilts my head up to look at him. "Other than my mother, I've never had anyone in my family I care about the way I do you. I love you in a way I often don't know how to handle. It's what I would imagine it would be like to have a younger sister or a best friend.

"Wait, what? You've never had a best friend?" What kind of childhood did he have to not have a best friend?

"Sadly, no. My father wasn't fond of the idea of me having attachments that didn't serve him. Umbra and Chaos are the closest things to best friends, and that's because my father couldn't control them bonding with me, plus he thought he could use those to his advantage."

My heart breaks for him, it must have been so lonely growing up here. "Well, neither of us really know how to have healthy relationships, it seems, so we will just figure it out as we go."

"Yes, we are just two fucked up peas in a pod," he muses, and I laugh so hard I snort. "Did you just snort?" The dopey grin on his face looks ridiculous.

"What?" I say in mock innocence.

"That had to be the most adorable thing I have ever heard." He laughs and pulls my hair.

"I am *not* adorable! I am mean and badass... adorable is a direct contradiction of those things!" I yell at him, stomping my foot, cheeks flaming with outrage.

"Aww, Layla. You are so damn cute." Then he does the smartest thing he's done all day and darts out of the door before I kick his ass for real. Once he's out of sight, I allow myself to smile. Gods, I love him so damn much.

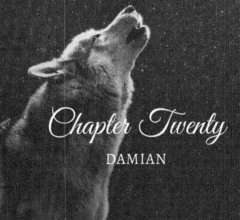

Chapter Twenty

DAMIAN

"So let me get this straight, we are going to Earth and leaving him here with the girls...without us?" Cas paces back and forth in front of my desk as we wait for the arrival of Thor.

"I don't like the idea either, but it is what it is. Is Delphin going with us?" I ask. Delphin has an easy charm, much like Thor, that I am hoping will work in our favor. Not to mention the kid is built like an ox and handy to have around when there's trouble.

"Yes, so Aegir and Nereus will be here to keep an eye on things," he grumbles.

"Look, I know you have a history with Thor, but he's our best bet, so get over it. Layla is not someone you have to worry about." It rankles me just a little that he doesn't have more faith in our girl than this.

"Where are the girls?" he asks.

"Outside training, they are going to be working in the nursery wing later today, and since things got interrupted earlier, they are finishing up." I stand to head outside, and Cas follows.

"How long do we have to retrieve her? The wedding is this weekend."

"We have exactly one day to get her back here because we will need tomorrow to finalize security plans before Saturday. Still no word from your parents?"

He shakes his head no. "So, what happens if we don't get her in time?"

"We will try again next week, but I don't foresee a problem."

We step outside, and both just admire the girls as they are training with Nereus. Layla and Anika are fighting hand-to-hand on a mat, and he has Nerine lifting weights with Brennan and Aegir.

We all sense him before we see him. Thor comes soaring from the sky, landing a few dozen feet from the training area. All three women stop what they are doing and look up, jaws agape.

He's even better looking than they portray him in the movies. He looks like he could be related to Cas and his brothers with the long blond hair and blue eyes, but they are more pretty. There's nothing soft or pretty about him—he is extremely masculine and brutally handsome. He's taller than any of us by a good inch or two, and his body is massive and very well-defined. The motherfucker oozes sex appeal.

"Well hello, ladies." He flashes them a smile, the deep cadence and lilt of his voice causing each of their faces to light up, which makes Cas roll his eyes.

Layla looks at Cas and I'm pretty sure they are having a silent conversation by the looks on their faces. I stride over and place a possessive hand on the small of Anika's back.

"Welcome, Thor! We appreciate you helping Layla. Cousin?" Layla walks up to stand beside me. Thankfully, she has her wits about her and is sizing him up with a grim look on her face.

"Hello, Lady Layla. It is an honor to meet you, I hope I can be of service." He takes her hand and kisses it. I'm fairly certain I hear Cas growl from behind us.

Thor looks up and sees him, letting go of Layla's hand. "Caspian! So good to see you! How have you been?" He throws an arm around his shoulder in a half hug before releasing him.

"We appreciate you being here. Layla's powers are unusually strong, and none of us know how to teach her how to control it. When she's upset, she really struggles."

"Come now, let's see it then. Show me what you can do." He rubs his hands together, obviously excited.

I let go of the little hold I have left and nod to her. She closes her eyes, and the sky darkens above us. Her brows furrow and sweat beads on her forehead. She raises a hand to the sky and lightning skips through the clouds.

Thor is now rubbing a hand across his chin, concentrating on Layla. "Can you make it rain?" he asks her softly. She raises her arms and thunder rumbles before big, fat raindrops fall from the sky.

"What else can she do?" he asks me, wonder lacing his words.

She opens her eyes, and the raindrops all stop in midair. "I can also wield water, but it was my weakest ability until recently." She lets go of her power, and the drops fall to the ground and the clouds depart.

"What power were you born with?"

"I control the night. Shadows and darkness." She raises a fist and shadows burst from the surrounding trees, swirling around us before moving back. It's harder for me during the day, but I can manage. I can also read minds somewhat, wield fire, and to a lesser extent, light."

His eyes are round. "Fuck me. I've never met anyone with powers like yours."

"Caspian has developed a few new tricks as well," I inform him. "He can also wield fire."

Thor looks at Layla like he wants to devour her, his eyes moving over her with pure, raw hunger. Shit, this could get ugly quick if Caspian can't keep his temper under control and trust that Layla can withstand him.

Layla crosses her arms and levels a stare at him. "Eyes up here, big guy," she says sardonically. I keep my face neutral, but I want to laugh. Obviously, we don't have to worry about her. I look at Cas with a raised brow, and he looks back with a slight quirk to one side of his mouth.

"Well, we should get going, Cas. Thor, is there anything else you can tell us about this girl before we kidnap her?"

"Just have a care; she's a bit wild and her powers seem to be strong. Her mother has passed and that I am aware, she has no other family to speak of."

I sigh. "Well then, the plan is for us to be back tonight. If we can't retrieve her in that time it will have to wait until after the wedding. Delphin, get yourself ready. Anika, may I see you for a moment?" Her eyes meet mine and she smiles, I feel like someone has a fist around my heart at the sight. She makes her way toward me, and we head inside together. Our bodies are so close I can feel her heat, but we don't touch.

As soon as we are inside and out of the sight of others, I grab her waist and haul her up against me. Her sharp intake of breath and soft moan as I press into her makes me wish I had time to say a proper goodbye to her. I lean in, so close to her mouth I can feel her breath on my skin.

"Be careful while I'm away." I nuzzle her cheek before kissing the dusting of freckles there. Her eyes flutter closed as I move to the other side and repeat the motion. "I'm going to miss you; I feel like I've barely seen you lately." I hover above her mouth, her tongue darts out to lick her beautiful lips.

"Have you missed me?" I can't help but ask. I hope I am under her skin half as much as she is under mine.

"Yes," her whisper is husky, her eyes pools of desire. I brush a soft, teasing kiss over her lips, and she makes a sound of protest before I finally settle my mouth over hers, running my tongue over the seam of her lips, begging her to open for me. She does, her tongue roaming over mine, a sigh of satisfaction tumbling from her as she molds herself to me.

I reluctantly pull away but smile down at her as she looks at me through hooded eyes, her body practically vibrating with need. Fuck. My smile quickly turns into a frown. Did I really just get her all hot and needy before leaving her here with Thor? Damnit to hell.

"What's wrong?" she asks, alarmed, hands splayed on my chest. I look around and see an empty room. Picking her up, she squeals in protest until my mouth fuses with hers once again in a demanding kiss full of need.

We enter the room, and I kick the door shut, pushing her back against it and quickly stripping her out of her pants.

"Damian! What—" she moans as I am on my knees before her, spreading her legs and lapping at her clit with my tongue. "Oh, gods, Damian, don't stop!" Inserting two fingers into her, I fuck her with my hand while devouring her with my mouth until she throws a leg over my shoulder and is shamelessly grinding herself on my face. In moments, she has her hands in my hair and is scraping my scalp with her nails as she comes in my mouth. I don't stop fucking her until I am sure I have wrung every last drop of pleasure from her and her legs are trembling.

I rise, and she gives me the most seductive smile I have ever seen, her breath hitching as she looks at me in awe. I had planned on just pleasuring her quickly before I left, but my cock is straining against my pants so hard it's painful.

All I can think about is her, the need to bury myself inside of her consuming my every thought. I don't care about who might hear us or walk in. The desperation for her is maddening. I can make this quick. I free myself and wrap her legs around my waist before I take my cock in my hand, line it up with her entrance, and thrust into her, seating myself to the hilt. I press my forehead to hers, reveling in the feel of her tight heat surrounding me. The pleasure flooding my system makes my knees weak. Her back arches as she cries out, and I seal my mouth over hers, wanting to be inside of her in every way I can. I take her up against the door, thrusting into her fast and hard. She is arching her hips to match my rhythm, taking me even deeper as she tightly wraps her arms around my neck.

The delicious sounds she makes against my ear have the pleasure quickly coiling tight inside of me, about to burst free. Fuck, I can tell by the sounds she is making that she's close. I change my angle so I'm hitting her clit with each thrust, and she starts grinding her hips to increase that friction.

"That's it, be a good girl and come for me, grind yourself all over me. You are so fucking beautiful," I say through gritted teeth. She buries her head in my neck, trying to muffle her cries as she thrashes wildly against me, her walls convulsing around my cock as she comes, and I can finally give in and take that tumble after her, plunging into her one final time, as deep as I can possibly go as I fill her with my release, the pleasure so intense I feel like I've died and gone to heaven. I slowly drift back down to the land of the living, heart slamming in my chest as I try to catch my breath. Knowing she's going to have me dripping down her thighs as she goes back out there gives me an immense sense of satisfaction. I sit her down and plunder her mouth one last time before I move away from her.

She's trembling slightly, her cheeks rosy, mouth swollen. Several pieces of hair have escaped the braid she wears today, and I feel a sense of distinctly male pride that she looks freshly and well fucked.

Maybe it's a dick move on my part, but I love it. I help her back into her pants as I adjust my own.

"That was one hell of a goodbye for someone who is just going to be gone for the rest of the day," she says, giving me a knowing look. "It wouldn't have anything to do with our guest, would it?"

I scoff. "Nooo, I have no idea what you are talking about." I sling an arm around her and walk into the hall, where I give her one last kiss before we say our final goodbyes and I go to meet Caspian and Delphin.

I make my way to the throne room and run into my mother, giving her some quick instructions about where we will be and what to do while we are gone. I hear voices in the distance, growing louder with each second as Cas and his brother walk in, in the middle of some kind of good-natured brotherly disagreement.

"You are an idiot, seriously," Delphin fires at Cas, as Cas rolls his eyes and shoves his shoulder playfully. Sometimes, they make me wish I had brothers growing up, but I have Layla now, and that is enough.

"You gentlemen ready to leave?" I quirk an eyebrow up at Cas, and he lets out an exasperated huff as Delphin continues his teasing.

"You sure we can't leave him behind?" He jerks his thumb in his brother's direction, and Delphin gives him the middle finger.

"Nope, he goes. The good news is we have a portal in the basement, so we can get in and out quicker." I shuffle through a stack of papers, waiting for this news to sink in.

"What the fuck, Damian?" Cas says, clearly shocked.

"That was my sentiment when I found out as well. Grandmother has enchanted it for us so no one may portal through without either me or Layla. That will keep it from being used for others to get into or out of the castle, and it now opens to my safe house, so at least it makes things easier for us." I inform them.

"Well, let's get this shit show on the road." Cas sighs as he and his brother follow me to the portal.

Chapter Twenty-One

LAYLA

I look at Anika as she walks back out, and a huge smile spreads across my face. "Well now, don't you look like someone who has been well and thoroughly fucked." Her face turns about twenty shades of pink, but she can't hide how pleased she looks.

"Girl, I never dreamed sex could be this good. Like seriously, that man can do some sinfully wicked things that make my knees buckle," she whispers. I cover my ears and pretend to be traumatized, considering she's talking about Damian, but I really am happy for her. She nudges me with her shoulder and laughs at my reaction.

"I've been telling you for years how great sex is," I tease.

"Well, yes, but my limited experience didn't leave me exactly begging for more. Now, all I can think about when he's around is how soon I can get his hands on me. Not to mention, I have discovered some kinks I've apparently unlocked." One side of her lip curves, and my eyebrows shoot up.

"Excuse me? Do I even want to know? Scratch that—if it were

anyone else you were fucking, I would absolutely want to know, but considering it's Damian? No, thank you."

Our conversation ceases when Thor comes back into view. Damn, he's hot. Like next level, insanely gorgeous, hot. "Is it just me, or is he...?" I question.

"Definitely not just you, he is." She lets out a breathy sigh.

Standing here, side by side, Anika and I can't help but fix our gazes on Thor. He's the most handsome god we've ever seen, a vision of pure allure. His presence commands the space, radiating a magnetism that's impossible to look away from. Despite his imposing stature, it's the striking beauty of his face and the intensity in his eyes that truly captivate us. Every movement he makes is filled with an effortless grace, a vivid contrast to the undeniable power and brute strength we know he possesses. His muscles seem to ripple with each movement, and damn if his smile and the lilt of his voice can't make every pair of panties in a twenty-mile radius drop.

Beside me, Anika's breath catches, mirroring my awestruck reaction. We share a quick glance, our silent communication speaking volumes. Thor's aura seems ancient, indefinable, and sexy as hell.

His laugh, rich and full, fills the air, coaxing smiles from us despite ourselves. The world around us seems to dim, his vivid presence outshining everything else. Anika squeezes my hand, a silent acknowledgment of our mutual appreciation of him.

Among gods and legends, Thor stands unparalleled, a paragon of masculinity that leaves us spellbound and utterly enchanted.

As the initial awe begins to fade, a flicker of irritation sparks within me. I catch myself, my brows knitting together in a frown. What are we doing? I mentally chide myself, feeling a sudden, sharp annoyance at how easily Anika and I have been reduced to hormone-driven puddles, ogling Thor as if we've lost all semblance of self-control. What the hell? This isn't like us, swooning over someone, no matter how sexy he is.

I shake my head slightly, trying to dispel the absurdity of the moment. Why should his looks have such an effect on us? I can almost hear my voice, tinged with a hint of disdain, mocking this uncharacteristic behavior. It's a jolt back to reality, a reminder that he's here to train me, not to be gawked at.

With a discreet roll of my eyes, I attempt to pull back, to regain some of the composure that seems to have slipped away for the moment. Anika seems to sense the shift in my mood, her gaze turning toward me, a question in her eyes. I offer her a tight smile as I mentally chastise myself for drooling over him, no matter how fucking hot he is.

The thought strikes me suddenly, a jolt of apprehension mingling with my irritation. How would Damian and Cas react, seeing us staring at him like this, drawn in by Thor's sex appeal? A twinge of guilt nibbles at the edge of my consciousness, an uncomfortable squirming in the pit of my stomach.

I can almost picture Damian's face, the tightening of his jaw, the slight narrowing of his eyes. He's insanely jealous—the idea of Anika checking out someone else, especially someone as potent as Thor, would probably make him bash Thor's head in. And Cas...a sigh escapes me at the thought. His reaction would be more visceral, a blend of hurt and a sense of betrayal, even if unwarranted. There's history there he needs to explain, but he clearly warned me and told me to keep myself shielded. I'm guessing this is why.

"Ladies," he says, the deep timbre of his voice sends a jolt of pleasure all the way to my toes. Dammit, this is going to be harder than I thought. "Layla, come, we need to get away from civilians. I know a place where we can go to train safely."

Before I can respond, he wraps an arm around my waist and

hauls me to him as we shoot into the sky. *Holy shit.* My eyes close as my stomach is left back on the ground with Anika. Wind whips around my face, and I bury myself into his chest to stop the assault. Oh damn, this wasn't a good idea either. Now his scent has worked its way into my nose, something musky and ridiculously masculine that causes tension to coil deep in my belly, my clit throbbing with need. This man is dangerous in so many ways. If I had met him before Cas and I became a thing, I would probably be rubbing myself against him like a cat in heat right now, begging him to put me out of my misery. If I am this turned on by his fucking smell, what would it be like for him to touch me? Have his mouth on me? I shudder and let out an involuntary moan as my nipples pebble from rubbing against his chest with the way he is holding me, the feeling having me ready to burst into flames.

He seems to sense my thoughts, or my misery, who knows, but the asshole laughs and being plastered to his chest, that deep rumble vibrates through my entire body, and fuck, if I am not so turned on. I press myself into his muscular thigh, seeking any kind of relief.

"We're almost there," he whispers in my ear, and I shudder. He hardens against me, his massively impressive length pressing into my stomach. *Please let us get there soon before I do something really stupid here.* I keep my eyes closed and think about Cas. The intense way he looks at me, the sound of him whispering into my ear, telling me how much he loves me. The way he holds me when I'm falling apart. I feel the raging hormones start to ebb, and I feel more in control of myself. Finally, we slow as he sets me down on a grassy ledge high on the mountain behind the castle.

He's still holding onto me with one hand, the other threads through my hair, tilting my head up to look at him. He has to tilt it way up because this fucker is seriously tall. He brings his face to mine, close enough I can feel his breath on my cheek.

"I won't pretend I don't want you, Layla. You are powerful. Beautiful. Sensual." Each word is said slowly as his face moves over mine, dangerously close and intimate, his breath skimming over my skin. It feels like a caress that has me all but begging for his touch. "I would keep you locked away for days on end, bringing you nothing but mindless pleasure until you begged me to stop. I would fill you with my seed until your belly grew round with our child, a being that would no doubt be one of the most powerful creatures in our world with our combined powers. You would rule by my side; nothing or no one could stop us. You intrigue me, Layla—you are something I've never seen before, and I want you more than I want my next breath, but know I will never do anything you don't ask me for. I will train you and no more if that is your desire. But with one word, I will have you naked on your back in seconds, filling you with my tongue and my cock until you scream my name."

His fingers on my skin send a jolt through my system, his mouth so close to mine all I would have to do is raise a fraction of an inch to taste him and the pleasures he can offer. One word, yes, is all it would take to be his.

His erection still presses into me, and all I can think about is the roaring desire that hums through my veins. The ache that he can ease, this need that he can satisfy if I just say yes... My eyes flutter open and I stare into his. Earlier, I had thought them to be as blue as the sky on a summer's day, but now a storm rages there, a darker hue mixed with gray. His hair whips in the wind as he looks at me so intently my entire body flushes with heat. The hand on my waist inches up, resting on my ribs, and I am desperate for him to take it higher. His thigh is still in between my legs, and he flexes it, pressing it slightly into my heat. I arch and moan, my nipples sliding across his chest, the fabric causing a delicious friction that makes me want more.

He nuzzles my ear, "Say yes to me, Layla. Let me show you pleasure like you have never known before," he whispers. Goosebumps erupt on my skin, the sounds wrapping around me, clouding my thoughts until all I want is to give him what he's asking and take what he's offering.

"Keep yourself shielded." Cas's warning from earlier slams into me, effectively dousing the flames that were burning me alive seconds before. I take a step back, out of his arms and shake my head, trying to clear it.

"Oh damn, you're good. I was two seconds away from letting you mount me like a damn beast and fuck me stupid right here in the grass." Now that I have some distance, I'm able to think clearly. I see why Cas was so worried, he is potent. Damn, I almost royally fucked up, I should have kept myself shielded, that's a mistake I won't make again.

He laughs, a full, genuine smile on his face, and fuck, it makes my heart stutter in my chest. "I won't say I'm not disappointed, but I am impressed you were able to resist me."

Cocky fucker.

"Yeah, well, in the not-so-distant past, I would have stripped you down and rode you like a pony, love does stupid things to a girl."

His eyebrows raise. "Love?"

"Yes, love," I say simply.

"Tell me, who is the man that has earned the love of a magnificent creature such as yourself?" he demands.

"I thought you knew. It's Caspian." His eyes grow wide at this, and he gives me an approving look.

"Caspian is a good man; it is a good match. Now, let's train." And just like that, the sexual tension is gone, and he's all business.

"You seem to be able to call a storm with thunder and lightning easily enough. Damianos said you have a problem controlling when you are upset. Is this true?" he asks.

"Yes, if I'm really stressed or worried, my powers tend to have a mind of their own. I can feel it simmering under my skin and it bursts free without me being able to control it. When I'm really angry, like the deadly calm kind of angry, I can control it with no problem."

"You need to work more on being able to control your emotions rather than your powers. You need to be able to stay calm no matter what obstacles you may face. Have you ever tried to meditate?"

"Uh no. Do I seem like the kind of girl that meditates? I'm more of a kick your ass now, ask questions later kind of person. I have a horrible temper and a mind that rarely shuts off."

"Then, yes, we will start with meditation." He sits close to the edge, the view of the kingdom and lands beyond is spectacular from here. He adjusts himself and tells me to sit next to him and mimic his pose. "I want you to clear your mind. The wind is an effective sound to concentrate on. Take deep breaths and stay put with your eyes closed until I tell you to open them. We will start small today, but eventually, you should be able to do this for days. It's an effective way to communicate with our ancestors when you fast and meditate for long periods."

"That sounds awful," I say as I get into position.

I sit cross-legged, attempting to emulate the calm poise Thor has shown me, his words on controlling emotions echoing in my head. He talks of meditation as a method to master the storm within. With a deep breath, I close my eyes, trying to reach for that promised tranquility, to touch the void that's meant to be devoid of all thought, all feeling.

But my darkness isn't empty. It's a screen, and my mind, uncooperative and relentless, starts projecting memories I've fought so hard to bury. My stepfather's voice, that cold, cutting tone, fills the silence, his words a barrage of abuse that I can't block out. I'm transported back to those moments of feeling worthless, seen only as a thing to be broken and used.

As I desperately attempt to push these memories aside and find that elusive center of calm, the effort feels futile. The memories don't just linger; they attack, each one a wave crashing over me, dragging me under into a sea of past horrors and fears.

Panic sets in, my breathing erratic, a stark contrast to the slow, measured breaths I began with. A bead of sweat trails down my temple, not from physical exertion but from the battle raging inside me. This isn't calming; it's a freefall back into the darkest corners of my mind.

Suddenly, the meditation isn't just failing; it's suffocating. My heart races, pounding against my chest as if trying to escape. The walls seem to close in, and I can't catch my breath. It's a panic attack, fierce and consuming, making my skin prickle with cold sweat.

I gasp for air, my eyes snapping open, the space coming back into focus. Thor's voice breaks through the turmoil, laced with concern. "Layla, what's wrong?" he asks, his brow furrowed, his posture shifting from tranquility to alertness.

I'm shaking, unable to form words, every breath a struggle. I want to explain, to apologize for this breakdown, but the words are just out of reach, trapped behind the flood of emotions and memories. Thor moves closer, his expression a mix of worry and confusion. "Talk to me," he urges, but how do I explain this storm inside me?

How do I tell him that the darkness I'm trying to escape is one I wasn't even aware was still there?

How do I explain to him that until now, I didn't even know that this was still lurking inside of me, just waiting to pull me under? There's a reason my mind never quiets. It's because when it does, the demons from my past invade and take over.

I stand, breathing hard, trying to shove all the memories back into that box I keep them in, deep in the recesses of my mind, but they have spilled over now and are running amuck.

Thor grabs my shoulders and pulls me up to look at him. "Breathe, Layla! I command it! Do as I do!" He takes a deep breath in and holds my gaze with his intense eyes. Then he breathes out. "Again," he demands. We do this over and over until my heartbeat stops thundering in my ears, and I'm calm.

His hands are still on my shoulders, his eyes never leaving mine. "Now tell me, what happened?" I shake my head; I can't tell him. "You *will* tell me." It's a command, not a request.

"Has anyone ever told you that you are a bossy asshole?" I ask.

"Not quite as eloquently as you, no. I cannot help you if you will not speak of what came over you." Something in his eyes makes me want to open up to him, to trust him. I want to know why this suddenly hit me like a train after all these years. Has it always been there lurking?

"It's an ugly story that only a very few people that I trust know about me, and I have only actually spoken of it to one, to Damian."

"I have lived over a thousand years, Layla, I know how to keep a confidence." He lets go of my shoulders and sits back down, crossing his legs at his ankles, leaning back, and bracing his weight on his hands.

"A thousand years, huh?" I sit next to him, thinking about what it would mean to live that long, and wonder how old my grandmother is.

"I was raised as a human," I begin. I tell him everything. Of the abuse, the rapes, the night I killed my stepfather, the months after when I was a shell of a person, terrified of my powers, of hurting someone.

I don't even realize tears are streaming down my cheeks until he wipes them away, a look of tenderness in his eyes that surprises me, given how cocky the asshole has been.

"You truly are a marvel. A will of iron and a pure heart. The reason you have a hard time controlling your powers when you are upset is because you fear them. You fear hurting someone that does not deserve it, and that fear makes it impossible for you to control it. You need to learn to embrace these powers, to respect them and then you will be able to control them."

Chapter Twenty-Two

DAMIAN

"She's a hellcat. I'm not going after her." We found the girl easily enough; the problem is we are all slightly terrified of her, and that's without her powers. We just witnessed her take on three men over twice her size in a bar and come out without a scratch on her, grinning like a damn maniac.

"Not it!" exclaims Cas, shaking his head as we watch her swing a bat at one of the men's crotches after he's already down, just for fun. We all wince, my balls shriveling up into my stomach, just bearing witness to it.

"Can you, like, do your mind-shit on her, Damian?" Delphin asks, a note of pleading in his voice.

"Maybe. I'd have to get closer, and I'm not sure I want to. I think she might be more vicious than Layla." I look at Cas, and he nods.

"Layla's only scary when she's mad—that girl just looks like she's having fun at this point. Guess you're up, baby bro. Work that charm." Cas smacks him on the shoulder, shoving him toward the bar and grill where the girl works.

"How is she already throwing people out like that? It's the middle of the afternoon. They should be serving lunch, according to their website, not needing to kick out a bunch of drunks." Delphin looks at Cas, a pleading look in his eyes.

"Dude, I don't think they are drunk," Cas says to his brother.

"Fuck." Delphin exclaims. "You all are going with me, let's go order lunch."

We walk through the parking lot, eyeing the three men trying to gather their wits enough to get up and get out of there. The place is run down, but the smells coming from the kitchen are actually tempting enough that my stomach growls, and Cas looks over at me with laughter in his eyes. There's a sign that says to seat yourself, so we pick a booth in a corner where we can easily watch the entire place. I see Audra behind the bar, wiping down the counter.

"I thought she was only twenty? How is she working at the bar?" Delphin asks.

"Maybe Thor was wrong. Maybe she's twenty-one or lying about her age." I reply. We watch the girl. You can tell she's Thor's daughter just by looking at her. She's stunning. Long, thick honey blonde hair that she has pulled back into a ponytail, the same striking sky-blue eyes, and a beauty that makes men look twice at her. She's small, an inch or two shorter than Layla, and petite but with dramatic feminine curves. She's wearing a pair of ripped-up blue jean shorts and a pink tank top that would make her look young and sweet, if not for the multitude of tattoos on one of her thighs and covering most of her arms. She turns her back and there's one peeking out of the top of her tank as well. A sheen of sweat coats her skin from the July heat and the workout she just had in the parking lot.

Her mouth seems to be permanently drawn into a scowl, but she looks to have full, sensual lips and a cute little button nose. She must get that from her mother. Her face is heart-shaped and if we hadn't seen her violent streak, one would think she was innocently adorable. She grabs a pad and pen then walks toward our table. Cas and Delphin both look a little wary, not that I blame them.

"Hi guys, I'm Audra, I'll be taking your order today. What can I get you boys?" Her voice is surprisingly pleasant compared to the attitude she displayed earlier.

Delphin turns on the charm, flashing the same dimples his brother has that make most women swoon. "What do you recommend?" he asks, his voice low and smooth, meeting her eyes while she assesses him, trying to decide if he's being genuine or just hitting on her.

"The burgers are my favorite," she says and raises an eyebrow at him.

"Great, three burgers, fully dressed, and fries," I say, handing her the menus.

"Hey, then, what are you going to eat?" Delphin laughs. I forgot how much that damn boy can pack away.

I roll my eyes. "I forgot the bottomless pit here can eat as much as a football team, so five burger plates." She laughs, an unexpected sound that shocks the three of us. The girl in front of us is a stark contrast to the one we witnessed in the parking lot mere moments ago.

"I like to eat too, so I feel you." She turns and goes to put in our order as we all look at each other while Delphin wears a dopey smile on his face.

"Damn boys, I think I love her," he declares, and I shake my head at him, amusement lighting up his brother's face, mirroring my own.

She comes back with our food a short while later and chats with us a little, Delphin happily digging into his burgers, giving a little appreciative moan as he takes his first bite.

"I told you they were good!" She rewards him with a full,

unguarded smile, leaning against the side of the booth near where he is sitting, seeming to enjoy watching him devour his burger. She seems relaxed, so I try to slip into her mind and frown. Her thoughts are open, but she is extraordinarily powerful and more than a little unhinged. The kid has been through some shit and is used to taking care of herself. She's not going to come willingly. I tentatively reach into her mind again, trying to influence her thoughts, feeling just enough give to make her pliant. I give Delphin a signal.

"Hey, what time do you get off? We are new in town, and these two goons have plans and are leaving me all by my lonesome, would you want to maybe hang out? Show me around a little?"

She hesitates—she's interested but wary. I give her a little shove. She fights against it, so I shove harder. I'm strong, but I've weakened myself holding Layla's power in check for so long, and Audra is not easy to push. I feel the strain it's causing me and realize how much I really need some rest.

"Um, sure. I get off at five. We could walk around for a bit; I can show you some of my favorite spots?" She frowns like she's not sure why she's agreeing to this.

"Great! I'll be back at five! My name is Delphin, by the way. It's nice to meet you, Audra."

"Nice to meet you too." She frowns and walks away.

"No way it's going to be this easy," Delphin says skeptically.

"Getting her to agree to meet you isn't exactly the same thing as getting her to Aetheria," I state, wondering how exactly we are going to do this without bloodshed.

"Maybe we should try telling her the truth? She knows she's not normal." Delphin shrugs his shoulders like it should be as simple as that.

"If you want to try that, I say go for it," Cas replies.

A few hours later, we are back. Cas and I stay in my SUV while

Delphin heads inside. In no time, they walk out, and *holy hell*, the girl is holding a motorcycle helmet. I scan the parking lot, and sure as shit, there's a pretty little purple and black crotch rocket parked in the corner that I would bet money belongs to her. She walks over to it, hooking the helmet to the side of the bike, chatting with Delphin, obviously telling him about the bike. Layla is going to love her.

She seems wary and has been frowning the entire time despite Delphin's easy charm and good looks. He towers over her, but I have to give her credit—she doesn't seem even a little intimidated by him. I'm curious if she can sense that he is like her or if she's more like Layla and has no clue.

The plan is for him to get to know her a bit, then we will come in and try to tell her the truth of what's going on. Worst case scenario, we tie her ass up and take her with us.

They start walking and we follow, keeping a safe distance. "You think the girls are okay?" Cas asks, a frown on his face, brows furrowed as he looks out the window.

"Why are you so damn worried about Thor?" I ask, genuinely perplexed.

He sighs heavily and looks miserable enough, I almost feel sorry for him. "He stole my first serious girlfriend. Well, not so much as stole, as fucked her at my twentieth birthday celebration. When I went looking for her, I walked in the room, and he was railing her on my father's desk and they didn't even have the decency to stop. It was humiliating. My father found it amusing. I did not. I was so pissed off about it, I threw a fit. It's one of the reasons my father sent me to Rio."

"Ouch. Well, Layla isn't like that," I assure him.

"No, but you know how she was before. Hell, even after we slept together, she went and had a threesome at the club with Marcellus. She likes sex, and she doesn't always see it as an act of love. I mean, damn, she knew how I felt about her and would have sex with other people in front of me and ask me to do the same. Not to mention, one of his powers is literally seduction, and he has a reputation for being a beast in bed."

"Cas, give her more credit. She knows you two are actually in a relationship now. She did the threesome because she was pissed about you being engaged and not telling her before she finally admitted there was something more between you two and slept with you after eight years. You took that choice away from her, and that is why she was pissed and hurt. She lashed out in the only way she knew how—trying to hurt you as much as you hurt her. If you are worried, have a bloody conversation with her about it."

Cas looks horrified. "Did she tell you all of that?"

"Yes! Because most of the time, recent events excluded, we *talk* like adults and share things with each other. She's probably my best friend, and for a while, I was the only person she had to talk to. You were gone, Anika was gone, and Rio was barely around. She was going insane."

"What the fuck?" Cas is staring out the window, mouth agape. I turn to see what he is looking at. Audra just grabbed Delphin by his belt and pulled him to her, wrapping her arms around his neck, standing on her tiptoes, obviously wanting him to kiss her. The height difference is too great for her to reach him on her own, he needs to bend down some, which he is all too happy to do. The boy wraps his arms around her and kisses her like he's about to strip her clothes off in the middle of the sidewalk and fuck her where everyone and their mother can watch.

"Damn, the kid is good," I joke and Cas laughs. "We are probably going to have to intervene before she takes him back to her place, and by the looks of the way she is rubbing up against him and he's palming her ass, it is going to need to be sooner rather than later."

He nods in agreement, "Can you dampen her powers if need be?" The sky above darkens and lightning flashes. "I think she's losing control."

"I'll give it a go, but I've been expending so much energy containing Layla's I'm not sure how long I will be able to hold it." Gathering my strength I mentally reach out and cast a mental net wide enough to encapsulate her and Delphin. Cas has proven impervious to my machinations, which will be beneficial if he needs to help contain her.

The clouds recede, and I let go to conserve my energy. "Yes, I can, but not for long. Let's go interrupt the young lovers."

Exiting the vehicle, we receive several appraising looks from people nearby. The women give us appreciative glances, while the men look at us warily—our size alone intimidates most.

"Hey baby bro," Cas says a little louder than needed, tapping Delphin on his shoulder. The couple breaks apart, a smirk on Delphin's face as he looks down at the she-devil in his arms. Her eyes are still closed, her lips swollen and parted, and she is breathing like she just ran a marathon. Her hands slide down to his chest and fist in his T-shirt as she steadies herself before opening her eyes.

Cas and I are both frowning at Delphin, who is smiling like the cat that ate the canary. He leans down and plants a kiss in her hair.

"Hey baby girl, I don't think I actually introduced you to these two morons with piss poor timing earlier. This is my brother, Caspian, and this scary-looking asshole is his girlfriend's cousin, Damian."

She seems to snap out of whatever trance she is in and takes a step away from Delphin. "Hi," she states, furrowing her brow as if confused.

"Can we go somewhere a little less public to talk?" I ask her, and she narrows her eyes at me suspiciously.

"Why the fuck would I want to talk to you?"

Cas groans, "Dammit, Delphin, you had one job. One. Talk to her." Delphin just raises his eyebrows and smirks. Little shit.

I reach into her mind. She's pissed, so she pushes back even harder, but I keep going. "Look, we know you're 'different' than most people. So are we, in a variety of ways. We just want to talk to you."

Cas holds out a hand and brings to life a small ball of fire, then creates a bubble of water that douses the flame. It's quick, and I'm blocking the view of others, so she is the only one who sees it, her eyes going wide. "We know you have the power to wield thunder and lightning. We just want to talk—we may even have some answers for you."

Her eyes are wild, a hint of fear there, but also, curiosity. Of course, I've pushed her mind to make her more agreeable as she climbs in my vehicle to go back to the safehouse for this conversation. We would like to come out of this with our manhoods intact.

As she gets comfortable in my backseat with Delphin, her gaze sharpens, eyes darting between the three of us with a mix of disbelief and caution. There's tension in her shoulders, a readiness that speaks of her preparedness for any deceit. Her brows knit together as she scrutinizes our faces for any sign of dishonesty. "How do you know about my powers?" she demands, her voice steady but laced with an undercurrent of suspicion. Her posture is defensive yet curious, betraying her interest despite her mistrust. The air is thick with unspoken questions and the weight of her wary gaze.

Carefully choosing my words, I say, "Well, for one, I can feel your power. Cas and Delphin can as well, but my cousin, Layla, is half-human like you and doesn't seem to have that ability, so I'm not sure if you feel anything like that from us or not."

She thinks for a moment, it's fascinating really to watch the wheels in her mind turn quickly as she tries to wrap her thoughts around what I've told her and decide what she wants to ask next.

"What do you mean by half-human?" Her eyes narrow when I meet her gaze in my rearview mirror as I drive. Cas fields this one.

"We are from a realm similar to Earth called Aetheria. From what we know, your mother was human, but your father is from our world, and he is who you inherited your power from. Not all half-breeds inherit power."

She snorts. "I don't have a father; he ran off before I was born." Cas looks at me with raised eyebrows, silently reminding me what he thinks of Thor.

"Well, about that, you do have one. He's currently at my castle," I say tenderly.

Her eyebrows shoot up so far they are hidden under her long, swooping bangs that frame her heart-shaped face. "Okay—first did you just say 'castle' as in you live in an actual castle? And second, my *father* is there?"

A long, weary sigh escapes me, but before I can respond, Delphin jumps in. "Damian here is the ruler of his kingdom in Aetheria, it's called Shadowfell. Cas and I are from the kingdom Pelagia. Cas is the heir to the throne there, and I'm the youngest of the four of our brothers."

"What the actual fuck? So, you're like a king, and you two are what? Princes?" She says it with so much disdain that we all cringe.

Delphin, being the dumbass he is, continues. "Well yeah, and technically, you are a descendant from a royal line too, *princess.*"

Hysterical laughter bubbles up from her throat as she wraps her arms around her middle and bends over, trying to catch her breath. "Do I look like a princess?"

"Well, Layla doesn't really look or act like one either, and yet she's a descendent of the most powerful goddess in our realm," Cas grumbles.

"So, please tell me, who exactly is this mystery man that is supposed to be my father?"

Fuck, I can already tell how this is going to go. It's not like he's not a well-known piece of mythology on Earth, and she obviously doesn't seem to be buying what we are selling. I pull into the garage, turn the vehicle off, and shut the doors behind us, engaging security protocols for when she inevitably tries to bolt.

"Thor. Your father is Thor." I rub my hand across my face, preparing for the tantrum.

"You all are fucking crazy," she whispers, eyes going wild. She looks all around like she is just realizing she is in a vehicle, in a strange house with three massively large males that she doesn't know. "Take me back to the restaurant. Now."

"Sorry, we can't do that. Your father has asked us to come bring you to Aetheria, he wants to meet you." I shake my head. I can feel her power rising with her panic. Please let her power be contained to outside like Layla's. If she can wield inside and I can't hold her, we are fucked. I try to slip into her mind, but her fear is overriding everything else, and it's not working to calm her. I do manage to dampen her powers, giving me a momentary sense of relief.

The relief is very brief indeed because right then, she loses her shit.

All hell breaks loose. And I mean All. Fucking. Hell.

Delphin reaches for her—her eyes are wild, looking for a way out of the car, but I've engaged the child safety locks so she can't from her current seat. Her fist slams into Delphin's nose, blood gushing as he curses. Grabbing me by my hair with one hand, she tries to gouge my eyes out with the other. Cas pries her off me, and she launches herself across the seat, driving her elbow into his face. While he's trying to protect himself, she manages to reach over and throw his door open, dropping herself onto the garage floor. Lightning quick, she is on her feet and running through the house.

Cas and I race out after her, Delphin screaming at us as he tries to scramble over the seat. I round the corner to the kitchen, Cas hot on my heels, almost slamming into me when I come to an abrupt halt, facing off with the she-devil, who is currently holding a knife.

"Little girl, I am immortal. A knife is just going to piss me the fuck off," I growl. Satisfaction fills me when her eyes give a momentary flare of fear. Instead of trying to go through me, she turns and runs, hurling herself at a window. Luckily, because it's a safe house, they are all bulletproof and damn near impenetrable. She bounces off it and lays on the floor as I approach her with caution. She rolls and is back on her feet, holding the side that took the impact before hurling herself at me, wrapping her tiny self around my body as she bites, claws, and punches.

"Son of a bitch! Some help would be nice, you assholes!" I bellow as I try to peel the spawn of Satan off me. Cas raises a hand, and the girl suddenly crumples to the floor.

Chest heaving, a heartbeat passes, then two before my mind clears enough to realize she's quiet. "Fuck, Cas, what did you do? Is she dead?" I reach down to check her pulse, thankfully she's alive. I let out a sigh of relief. Still crouched next to her I look up at Cas and Delphin, who both are staring at the figure on the floor, shocked.

"I'm not entirely sure. I thought I was throwing out a shield, but I kept thinking if we could just knock her out, this would be so much easier, and she crumpled to the floor."

"Interesting. New power?" Cas just shrugs. "Keep an eye on this feral creature while I get something to restrain her with." They both look at me like I've lost my mind. "What? Either of you want to try carrying the little banshee through the portal after the way she just behaved? She nearly took out three fucking immortals without any powers." They shake their heads. "That's what I thought."

I rummage through a bag and find what I'm looking for, zip ties. I make my way back to where Cas and Delphin are still staring at

her. She looks almost sweet and peaceful now that she's not trying
to kill us. I feel a pang of guilt as I pull her arms behind her and pull
the zip ties tight. Then I bind her feet—I'm not stupid enough to
think she can't do some serious damage with them alone. When I'm
satisfied, I haul her over my shoulder and make my way to the
bedroom where the portal has been created, the boys following
warily behind me.

Chapter Twenty-Three

LAYLA

Feeling a little raw after my session with Thor, working in the nursery is just what I need. Selena is lying on the floor with me, coloring pictures of her new favorite things, dragons. I'm coloring mine to look like Drayvhn, and she's scribbling hers gray, which I assume is supposed to be one of the juveniles, either Nox or Eclipse. Right now, they are both the color of stone, but when they mature, they will change and become some shade of the night.

Anika is bouncing a chubby little baby, softly singing a lullaby as she paces the room, snuggling into his sweet cheek. Nerine is reading to the older children and for the moment, we are all content.

"The boys are back," I announce, and Anika shakes her head at me.

"It's so weird how you can do that, how you know when Cas is near." Anika laughs.

"Hey now, it's not just Cas, I can feel Damian too, and I can tell you now, they don't seem happy."

A moment later the doorway darkens as a large figure fills it. I look at my cousin, and he is staring at Anika holding little Devlin with softness in his eyes and a small smile on his lips. I don't need to read him to tell what he's thinking.

Anika turns and sees him, her entire face lighting up. "Hi!" she says before she continues her song. He closes the distance between them, taking her chin in his hand to tilt her head up so he can press a feathery, soft kiss to her lips. My heart feels like it might explode watching the two of them, lost in their own little world where only they exist.

Selena looks up and notices Damian in the room, jumping up on her chubby little legs and racing over to him, wrapping herself around him. "Unca Damin!" she squeals. His face breaks into a smile, and he grabs her by her waist and flips her upside down as he raises her in the air.

Her giggles have everyone in the room grinning like fools. "What are you doing upside down?" he asks her incredulously. She points a chubby finger at him and giggles some more. "Ahh yes, I do believe it's my fault, very perceptive of you, little one." He flips her right side up and presses her close to his massive chest. "Have you been a good girl?"

"Yes! I good girl. Dragons?"

He laughs. "You certainly have a one-track mind, don't you? I will take you later to see the dragons. Uncle Damian has some work to do. He lifts her a little higher and blows raspberries on her tummy, throwing her into a fit of giggles as she tries to squirm away from him. He sets her down, and she runs back over to me.

"How did it go?" I ask. He turns, and surprise flickers across his features, like he is just realizing I am in the room.

His eyebrows raise and his lips turn down as he steps away from Anika before speaking. "It was a complete s-h-i-t show, but we have her. She's locked in a room downstairs, knocked out cold while we wait for Thor. How did it go with him today?" Anika snorts, and I shoot daggers at her with my eyes.

"Well, um, it was interesting. I'll fill you in later. Do I even want to know why she's knocked out?"

"Because, dear cousin, I think she may be an even bigger hellion than you."

I look at Damian and can't help but notice the shadows under his eyes, like bruises from sleepless nights. His shoulders, which usually carry him with such command and presence, now slump as if burdened with the world's weight. The confident aura that usually surrounds him—that makes him seem untouchable—has dimmed. Even his movements are slower, more deliberate, as if every step is a battle. Watching him, a wave of concern washes over me. It's as if he's moving through an endless night, bearing the weight of unseen battles, with the world's burdens resting squarely on his shoulders.

"Come on, take me to her. Someone should be there when she wakes, and it's probably better if it's not one of you." I hop up, kissing Selena before I leave, making sure the nanny knows we are heading out.

"Tell me about her," I ask quietly, curious about this girl who has more in common with me than anyone else in this castle. She grew up human like I did, had no idea who her father was, and is probably confused as hell right now. At least I had Rio and Cas.

"She's spirited. The first time we laid eyes on her, she was taking down three men twice her size with a baseball bat." He smiles at the memory, and I can't help but think I'm going to like her. "She's lovely. Evil, but lovely. She's a wisp of a thing, a little shorter than you, but powerful. Delphin is half in love with her already."

A laugh bursts from my lips. "That boy is a shameless flirt and is definitely a looker."

"Speaking of flirts. How did it go with Thor?"

I groan loudly. "Well, the training was insightful. He thinks I can't control my powers when I'm upset because I fear hurting people, so I have to work on a few personal issues." Taking a deep breath and letting out a very, very, slow exhale I continue, "He hit on me. Hard. Like no holding back, hard. Damian, I don't know how to tell Cas, but—"

He stops dead in his tracks and takes hold of my shoulders, leaning down to look me dead in the eyes with an intensity that frightens me just a little. "Please tell me you did not sleep with him, Layla. For the love of the gods, please tell me you resisted."

"Chill, I did not sleep with him." Damian visibly relaxes. "But I almost did. I was two seconds away from saying yes. If it wasn't for Cas, I would have climbed that man like a damn tree and—"

He releases me and holds a hand up to stop the words tumbling out of my mouth. "That's enough of that. Cas would have been crushed had you caved. He would have probably forgiven you, but he was really worried."

"What, he doesn't trust me?" I ask, slightly pissed.

"It's not that, exactly. Thor has the power of seduction, and apparently, there was an incident at one of Cas's birthday celebrations with Thor and his girlfriend. Then there's the whole history of the two of you and sex. I think he's afraid you miss having multiple partners, but you did not hear any of this from me, cousin."

As we descend the staircase and traverse the corridors of the castle, the distant sound of commotion reaches our ears. Turning down a hallway, the cacophony grows louder, a chaotic symphony of snarls, curses, and menacing threats echoing off the stone walls. Vengeance is sitting in front of the door, her head tilted to the side, ears twitching.

"What has you staring a hole in the door?" I ask her.

"I am curious about the female inside. She is like you."

"Want to go in with me, protect me in case she tries to kill me? Maybe look intimidating, growl a little, bare some teeth?" I'm fairly certain she gave me a look that is the equivalent of a dire wolf eye roll.

Damian pushes the door open for me and holds it for us to go inside. "Good luck, cousin. I have some things to see to, have Vengeance call for Chaos, or I will leave myself unshielded if you need to call for help."

Vengeance walks in first, then I duck under Damian's arm to follow, lightly poking his ribs as I go by. He retaliates by tugging my hair and then retreating with a chuckle.

As soon as my massive wolf is in Audra's line of sight, she starts screaming and thrashing.

"V, tell the boys she's fine so they don't come rushing in here." I walk around the couch she is lying on, and guilt gnaws at me when I see her restrained. "Calm down, I'm not here to hurt you, and neither is Vengeance. If you can settle yourself, I will take off those zip ties."

"The wolf's name is Vengeance? Oh, that's reassuring," she snaps. "Who the fuck are you? Where are the assholes that kidnapped me? I'm going to fucking *kill* them!"

I sigh. She is definitely feisty. "Good luck killing them. They are all three immortals. I'm Layla, Damian's cousin. I'm half-human like you and if I had to guess, you are probably fairly overwhelmed right about now. I had no idea this place even existed until about eight years ago, and had never been here until a couple of months back. This shit is straight from all the legends and fairytales we grew up with. I mean, there's dire wolves and *dragons,* for fuck's sake." I wave a hand at V to emphasize my point.

"Those crazy fuckers told me *Thor* is my father." She says the name like it's an expletive.

"He is. I was training with him earlier. He's quite the character."

"You are all fucking crazy," she whispers, eyes wild.

"Okay, let's think about this. You have powers. You have seen some of the boy's powers. You traveled through a magic portal to a different realm, are currently in a castle, and have a dire wolf sitting in front of you, but Thor being your father is what you are stuck on?" I raise an eyebrow at her and screw up my face in disbelief.

Her mouth snaps shut, and I can see the calculation in her eyes. "So, let's say I do believe you. Where is this mystery father?"

"He's on his way. If I let you go, will you behave? I will warn you, I'm not the boys. I'll put you over my knee and beat your fucking ass like a toddler. I'm powerful enough to do it, so don't try me." I narrow my eyes at her, and shadows encase the room, rushing along each surface, the embodiment of most people's living nightmares.

It has the desired effect on her, and her eyes go wide.

"Hold still so I can remove the ties." I have my shadows slide around her wrists and ankles, a loud snap sounds in the dark as she is released, and the shadows fall back to the recesses of the room. Audra looks like she might throw up as she rubs her wrists. "What questions do you have?"

"Am I stuck here? Can I go home?"

"I'm not sure. I don't know much about why you are here other than Thor wants to meet you. There are people on Earth hunting our kind, so he may want you here to keep you safe, at least for the time being. I'm sure he's not going to trap you here; we all can go to and from as we please. I know it's a lot to take in. You should have seen my face when Cas told me his father was Triton."

Her mouth drops open. "The sea king, like in *The Little Mermaid*?"

"Yep, except he has sons instead of daughters. The way Cas explained it to me was all the stories from Earth originated from somewhere, most from here. The gods used to spend quite a bit of time on Earth; some still do when they get bored, and that's how the stories started. They've been adapted through the years, obviously, but the basics are all still there."

The look in her eyes shifts to a wary understanding.

"I promise as long as you don't act like an idiot, no one will harm you, and you can hash out how long you are expected to stay with Thor. I'd love for you to at least spend enough time here to know this part of who you are. It helped a lot of things click into place for me. I struggled with my identity. I had no idea who my father was, my mother had passed away, and I knew no one else with powers until I met Cas. Being here just felt like I finally belonged somewhere."

She's quiet, her face looks serious, and I take the time to study her. She really is lovely, her tattoos a stark contrast to the sweetness of her face. Her thigh is almost completely covered with a skull that has roses threaded through it. Her arms have a variety of different things and I wonder what meaning each one holds for her.

"Well, I guess if I'm stuck here, you might as well show me around, I won't do anything stupid."

"Good because you can't get through the portal on your own, and we have a wing of traumatized children here. They don't need to witness anything else that might hurt them—they have already watched their parents die."

Her eyes go wide at that, and she nods her head in acknowledgment. I look at Vengeance. "*Can I trust her? You think it will be safe to give her a tour?*" I ask her through the link we share.

"*Yes, she will not do anything that would harm the children. If she proves me wrong, I shall eat her,*" V responds. We exchange a look, I trust her judgment more than any person I know, so I guess I am taking her on a tour.

"Let's go, you want to start inside, or start with the dragons?"

"What the fuck do you think? The dragons, of course!" A grin spreads across her face—the smile makes her go from beautiful to stunning. She looks a lot like Thor.

Chapter Twenty-Four

DAMIAN

My soul feels tired. Sleep has never been my friend—too many memories and worries dance behind my eyes when they close, and it's starting to catch up with me. If we can just get through the wedding this weekend, maybe I can take a day or two and hide away with Anika. Her image fills my mind, and my stomach knots and my heart squeezes. I'm hungry for the feeling of peace that finds me when she's curled next to me in bed, her wild hair falling over her skin, the warmth of her body pressed against mine.

For now, I have a Thor-sized problem on my hands. That and what I imagine to be a cage-match going on between Layla and Audra. Vengeance won't let her hurt Layla, at least.

I push open a door that leads outside and am surprised to see the ladies in question walking through the grass toward the Dragonhold, deep in conversation. I shake my head—when will I learn that Layla can wrap almost anyone around those fingers of hers? We should have taken her with us. Lesson learned.

To my left I see my mother and Thor walk out of another door, chatting about the children in the nursery. Worry flares, that's all I need is for my mother to be seduced by him, and while she's incredibly beautiful and deserves the utmost happiness, I don't think his wandering ways are what she needs. Thankfully, they look friendly, but she isn't showing any signs of interest so I can breathe a little easier.

"Ah! Damianos! I hear you were successful in fetching my daughter?" His smile is wide, and he looks genuinely pleased at the idea.

"We did, but I must say, you will have your hands full with that one. She's tenacious." It's not the word I would have liked to use, but it seemed the least insulting. "She's also lovely, and I believe the prince, Delphin, may be enamored with her."

"Of course, she is lovely. I am her father, am I not?" He smacks me on the shoulder and laughs.

"Mother, I saw the children today. They are looking well—how are the wedding plans coming along? Any word from Aegir's family?"

"They are all adjusting wonderfully! Everything is ready, but no, they have not replied." Her eyes soften, and she looks forlorn at that declaration.

I nod and turn to Thor. "Audra and Layla just walked out to the Dragonhold. Would you like to accompany me and meet your daughter?" I ask.

"Yes, I will update you on your cousin as we walk."

I don't bother telling him she has already spoken to me and let him fill the silence on the walk across the field. It takes mere moments to reach the Dragonhold, but Thor hesitates at the entrance when we hear distinct feminine laughter drift through the air. The confident, unflappable Thor looks nervous. I'll be damned, he really cares about her liking him.

"Come on, old man, it's time to meet your bouncing baby girl," I laugh as I grab his shoulder and steer him across the entrance.

Layla turns and sees us, her smile faltering a bit. Audra notices her change in demeanor and turns as well, narrowing her eyes on me then sliding them over to Thor. I watch her carefully and note the look of surprise that flares before she locks her feelings down.

"Um, hi!" Thor says, shifting his weight from one side to the other. "It's nice to meet you, Audra, I'm Thor, uh, your father."

Her jaw ticks before she raises her hand and throws a lightning bolt directly at his chest.

Layla gasps and runs over to Thor, "Are you okay? Thor, open your eyes, look at me." She can't keep the panic out of her voice. His eyes flutter open, and rage rolls off Layla as shadows race from the corners of the room to swirl around Audra, restraining her.

"Hey, Layla! Not cool! You said he was immortal, so I knew it wouldn't kill him, and come on, you know the fucker *deserves* it! He left me and my mom there to rot! Our lives were fucking *hard* while he was living it up over here—he deserves a lot more than that one hit!"

Something in Layla softens, and she lets her go but gives her a stern warning, "I get it, but that was the only shot you get. Next time, you will have to deal with me if you want to throw another tantrum." She levels a glare at her and holds her stare for several seconds before looking back down at Thor.

"You good to go? Can you stand?"

"Yes, of course, I'm fine." He blushes and gracefully leaps to his feet, brushing dirt off of his clothes. "Can you give us a few moments alone?" His eyes are glued to Audra as he quietly studies her.

"Think you can behave?" Layla asks Audra, who currently has her arms crossed, staring at Thor with narrowed eyes, suspicion and anger radiating from her.

"Yes," she snaps.

"Good, Thor, you okay if I leave V here?" Layla inquires, eyebrows raised at him.

"Yes, yes, that is fine."

She looks at me, jerking her head toward the door as she starts to walk out of it, and I follow after.

"V?" I ask, curious about the nickname she is now using for Vengeance.

She laughs and says, "She likes hanging with us in the nursery, and I felt like Vengeance sounded too scary to use around the kids. She doesn't seem to mind."

We walk in companionable silence for a few moments before she stops in her tracks and grabs my arm, turning me toward her. "Damian," she says softly, meeting my gaze, "are you okay? I'm worried about you." Concern swimming in those eyes that are mirrors of my own is almost my undoing. A lump forms in my throat. I don't know how to respond to having others care for me. For so many years I only had my mother, and that was only when my father allowed me to see her.

I pull her into a hug, resting my chin on her head. "I'm fine, cousin. Just tired. I've not been sleeping well, too much on my mind."

"Anything I can help with?" she says against my chest as she wraps her arms around my waist.

"Afraid not, but I will let you know if that changes. We should get back, Cas is probably looking for you right about now, and I want to see to a few things before we have to rescue Thor. Don't go too far in case I need you to wrangle in the she-devil." I kiss the top of her head as she chuckles.

"Sounds good." She moves away from me, and I find myself missing the warmth and comfort of her small frame snuggled against me. She may be her own little hurricane, but she brings a measure of peace and happiness to my soul that I didn't know was missing.

Back inside, I almost run into my mother as she rounds a corner. "Damian! I just received word from Aegir's father. He is requesting an audience with you and his sons tomorrow." Mother's face is lined with worry. I know she wants this wedding to be perfect, and after the disaster of my birthday celebration last month, she needs this.

I smile reassuringly at her. "Let him know that will be fine, set it up for whatever time he wishes. I will rearrange my schedule accordingly."

I make my way into the room I have turned into my office. Chaos is already lying on the rug in his favorite spot. I park myself at my desk and exhaustion rolls over me, settling into my bones. My hand runs over the back of my neck, trying to ease some of the tension there. The recent killings of our people in the mortal realm weigh on me. If I had been there, would I have been able to stop it? The killing of innocents, especially children, leaves a hollow feeling deep in the core of my being.

Raised voices pull me out of my intrusive thoughts. Thor and Audra step into the room, both looking tense, but I don't see blood, so that's positive.

"What can I do for the two of you? Did you have a good chat?"

"Yes," Thor says tersely.

"No," Audra scowls.

I laugh.

Thor pins her with a glare and she stares right back at him, the hard glint in her eyes challenging him.

"I know you have already done me a great service by safely bringing Audra here, but she has requested to stay here with Layla while she explores her heritage. Would this be agreeable? I will continue to work with Layla in the meantime, Audra can train with us as well." Audra's eyebrows raise, and she opens her mouth to speak before I raise a hand and stop her.

"Yes, that would be fine, Layla likes her, and they have a lot in common. I'm sure it will be good for them both. I would appreciate you continuing your work with my cousin, we need her to be able to wield her powers without putting others in harm's way. Audra, I will have Mother get you a room ready, I think the family wing is getting rather crowded, but I will put you as close to Layla as I can. Just be forewarned that part of the castle can get rather... rambunctious."

"Thank you," she mutters.

"Thor, will you be here for the wedding?" I ask.

"Yes, of course, I wouldn't miss it!"

"Perfect. Just make sure you don't end up balls deep in someone else's woman." I raise one eyebrow, and he looks a little mortified as he runs his fingers through his hair. Audra laughs so hard she snorts, which reminds me of Layla, causing me to soften just a fraction.

"Thor, go find Mother and have her show Audra her room." He nods and they walk out. With a deep sigh, I lay my head back in my chair.

"Chaos, find Havoc and get Anika in here, please." He raises his head without saying a word and silently pads out the door.

My eyes are closed, and sleep is close to claiming me when I hear the soft click of the door shutting. A moment later I feel her soft body fill the space in front of my chair as she leans against the desk. I open my eyes and meet her brilliant green ones. We both just stare at each other for a moment before I lean forward, laying my forehead on her. Her hands come up to thread through my hair and I let out a long, shaky breath.

"Damian?" she whispers, "Are you okay?"

I pull her onto my lap, and she lets out a little yelp at my roughness. "I just need you," I say, my voice raw with emotion. I reach around to grip her ass, and she rewards me with one of those breathy little moans that makes me instantly hard.

"Rough day?" She rakes her nails across my scalp gently, and I shiver at the pleasure of her touch.

"It was. It's much better now." I thread one hand through her unruly curls. "Fuck, I love your hair," I murmur.

"When I was a little girl, I hated it. I wanted anything other than my bright red mess. I dyed it blonde once in the ninth grade and straightened it. My mother nearly had a heart attack." She smiles at me, and my heart nearly explodes in my chest.

"Don't you ever fucking change it," I growl as I bring her mouth to mine. She moans when my tongue caresses hers and adjusts herself in my lap so she's rubbing against my cock, grinding on me with reckless abandon. The heat flares so bright and hot between us I get so fucking hard I'm about to bust the zipper of my jeans.

I stand her up, stripping her out of her pants as fast as I can before pulling her back into my lap. Sliding my hand in between us, I drive two fingers into her tight pussy and groan at how wet she is for me.

"Fuck, I love how wet you always are." Her nails dig into my shoulders as she rides my hand, getting closer and closer to that edge. I rub her clit as I fuck her, "I want to feel you come on my fingers, sweetheart."

"Gods, Damian, I love your dirty mouth."

"You do, do you? After you come on my hand, I'm going to bury my cock into your sweet cunt so hard and fast you are going to see stars. I can't wait to feel your tight heat coming around me."

"Fuck, Damian!" she screams as she convulses, her orgasm vibrating through her. I keep thrusting my hand and working her clit as she comes down from that high.

"The things you can do with just your fingers should be illegal," she says as she tries to catch her breath. I laugh darkly and bite the nape of her neck as she shivers.

I adjust just enough to get my pants undone and free my thick length, positioning her above me as I nudge the head of my cock into her entrance. Thrusting forward in one hard stroke, I bottom out and she gasps. *Fuck, I need more.* I can't get into her deep enough from this position. I lift her and place her in front of me, shoving my chair back as I stand. Grabbing her hips, I roughly turn her over, push her chest down onto the desk, and kick her legs wider apart. Sliding my pants off quickly, I press my cock back to her entrance, rubbing her perfect round ass with my hand before giving it a rough slap. A gasp escapes her as a bright pink handprint blooms on her skin. Moaning, she thrusts her rear back into me, begging for more.

I piston into her, slamming against her ass. She screams my name as I pound her over and over as she clamps around me like a vice. Fuck I needed this—to lose myself in her. I'm drowning in her —the way she feels, her scent, those moans that make me want to come unglued at the sound. The world could be burning around us, and I wouldn't be able to stop. I am as deep as I can go, but I still want more, still need to be deeper inside of her.

I drive into her relentlessly, items falling off the desk with the force of my thrusts. I vaguely hear something fall and shatter, but I don't fucking care. The only thing that matters is the need to be with her, to lay claim to her and mark her as mine.

"I can't get fucking enough of you," I say to her, groaning as I slam into her even harder. "Do you feel how hard I am for you?"

She clenches around me as she digs her nails into the desk, screaming with the force of the orgasm that rolls through her. She tries to arch herself, but my hand is pressed into the small of her back, keeping her still as I give her everything I have, fucking her harder than I have ever fucked anyone in my life. I'm so close, so close to the high of that sweet release from being inside of her. My other hand grips her hip so hard I know she will bear my marks there tomorrow, and the thought makes me feral.

"Fuck, Damian, yes!"

"You like the way I fuck you, love?" I barely recognize the growl that rumbles through my chest.

"I *love* the way you fuck me." she moans, her words sending me completely over the edge as my legs tremble and the force of my orgasm causes me to see stars, stealing my breath. "Fuuuuck, Anika!" I groan so loud I'm sure the entire castle can hear but I'm too lost to care. I lean over her, peppering kisses along her back as I wait for my legs to stop trembling.

"Are you okay? Was I too rough?" Guilt gnaws at me, worried I may have hurt her.

"Too rough? That was the hottest fucking sex I've ever had, feel free to fuck me like that any time. All the time, for that matter," she says with a contented sigh. I straighten and slide out of her. She gives a little moan of protest that makes me smile.

I strip my shirt off and use it to clean her up. She still hasn't moved, her ass bent over the desk, and damn, she looks sexy there, all freshly fucked and sated.

"Come on, sweetheart, we better get out of here and get to bed. Tomorrow will be a long day filled with last-minute wedding stuff to do."

She groans but stands. I help her dress, kissing her calves then thighs as I assist her into her pants. Once she's ready, I quickly get back into my clothes sans my soiled shirt.

I grab her hips, pulling her flush to my body, resting my forehead on hers. "Stay with me tonight?" I whisper.

"Of course, but only to sleep, you look exhausted. I'll rub your back."

We hold hands as we make our way upstairs to my room. I give her one of my T-shirts to sleep in and my heart expands at the sight of her in it, my exhaustion making me feel vulnerable, emotions tipping over. I don't deserve this wonderous creature sitting here in my room, giving herself so openly to me like I'm worthy of her. Her heart is so pure, and I have so much blood on my hands they will never wash clean, thanks to my father. Even with all the people I've saved, there's many more I didn't.

I'm starting to realize this goes so much beyond physical with her. She's quickly gotten under my skin in a way that my thoughts are never far from her, in a way that brings me peace when she's with me like nothing I've ever known. When the darkness of my thoughts starts to consume me, she brings me back to the light. For the first time in my life, I find myself falling into oblivion and relishing in it, not even caring if I ever land. If this is what falling feels like, I don't ever want to hit bottom. I just want to continue taking this leap with her, even though it terrifies me on every level.

Being with me could get her hurt. My mother was used against me, Layla's brother was used against her. The people we care for aren't safe, and that thought makes me feel like the biggest of assholes because I'm just selfish enough that I can't bear the thought of giving her up.

We go through our nightly routines together, and I love how easy it feels—how well we move and adjust to being in the same space. When we finally slip into bed, I try to slide behind her, but she stops me.

"No sir, roll over, I'm going to rub your back until you go to sleep, and then I'm going to snuggle you—you get to be the little spoon."

She looks so serious and adorable; I don't argue. Her hands and nails moving softly along my back feel heavenly. Every now and again, she moves up to my neck and my head, and I let out a content sigh. Beyond the ministrations of Layla after the last time my father had me whipped, I can't remember being taken care of like this, not since I was a very young boy before Father started telling Mother she was making me soft. I find that I like it.

"Anika?" I whisper as I slide into that warm place before sleep claims you.

"Hmmm?" she replies.

"I know I don't deserve you, but I have no intention of ever letting you go."

"Good," she says as I slip into nothingness.

Chapter Twenty-Five

LAYLA

C as is pacing nervously in Damian's office, waiting for his father to arrive. His brothers and Damian lounge about in different chairs, everyone tightly coiled, the tension in the air so thick it's almost suffocating.

"Layla, I'm not sure you being in here is a good idea," Damian reminds me for what seems like the four hundredth time, and it's starting to irritate the fuck out of me.

"I'm not leaving, end of story, so shut the fuck up!" I bark at him.

"He's not the only one who thinks that," Cas reminds me, and collective murmurs from around the room confirm their agreement.

"Guess what, boys? I. Don't. Give. A. Fuck. So, keep saying it and I'm going to set every one of your dicks on fire, understand?" I narrow my eyes and look at each brother, staring them down until I'm satisfied they will shut the fuck up about it.

"So damn violent," Cas grumbles but doesn't ask me to leave again.

Voices drift down the hall and everyone freezes, straining to listen, wondering if he's finally here. I feel my power simmer under my skin, skittering down my spine as I try to keep my emotions under control. This waiting feels like torture. Being late is a dick move, but Cas claims it's a pretty typical thing for his father to do. I take a seat, and my left leg starts bouncing furiously as I pick at my fingernails. I feel like I'm about to snap. I'm about to meet the father of the man I love for the first time, the man who tried to marry him off to someone else, and there are so many emotions inside me battling for dominance I can't sort them all out.

A door shuts down the hall, and the loud boom in the otherwise silent space causes me to jump as thunder booms outside.

"Layla," Damian says in clear warning, raising his eyebrows at me and pressing his lips into a thin line.

"Sorry," I mutter.

Finally, we hear Enthralia's soft voice echoing down the hall, followed by a rich baritone.

"Game face, kids," Damian reminds us.

"The boys are in Damian's office, right this way. They have been such a joy to have here, helping our people after the vicious attack we suffered. You must be so proud of them, all fine, caring young men." She opens the door and moves aside to allow him entry. I want to smile at her—she may be sweet, but she knows how to make people squirm just by being honest, and I love her for it.

Triton strolls in like he owns the place, and his presence overwhelms the room. His towering figure dominates the space like the ancient god he is. Every movement he makes seems to command attention, his presence radiating an aura of authority. His stern expression and steely gaze convey an unmistakable sense of power and importance, leaving no doubt that he is a force to be reckoned with. As he strides forward, his imposing frame seems to expand, filling every corner of the room with his formidable presence.

The boys favor him in looks, except his hair is darker and he has some gray at his temples. His strong jaw is covered in neatly trimmed facial hair, and his icy blue eyes scan the room, frowning when they land on me. The hairs on the nape of my neck bristle as he examines me like I'm something vile that should be scraped from his shoe.

"What is *she* doing here? I asked to speak to my sons." His thunderous voice drips with disdain and my eyes narrow at him, lightning crackling outside as my temper rises.

Damian and I go to speak at the same time, but Cas cuts us off. "I asked her to be here, whatever you have to say, you can say in front of her." His voice is just as commanding as his father's as he stares him down, daring him to argue about it. Pride surges in me. This is a different side of him, the future ruler of a kingdom that has grown into his own, no longer cowering to his father's demands. Even seeing that he has grown into his own man, I know this isn't easy for him—it's never easy to stand up to a parent, even when you know they are wrong.

"Fine, have it your way," he snaps, obviously not pleased that Caspian dared speak back to him. "Aegir, you are not marrying the princess. I forbid it."

"Father, they are in love. Do you not want them to be happy?" Caspian's voice carries a tinge of exasperation.

"Love," Triton sneers. "Marriages are arrangements, love has nothing to do with it. Her father wants her married to the heir so she will eventually be the queen of a kingdom. It was what she was bred for. It will unite our kingdom with Poseidon's. Marrying Aegir is tantamount to a declaration of war." He waves his hands around as he talks, his temper rising with each word that spills from him.

"Then I will renounce my claim to the throne," Caspian says with deadly calm. His eyes never leave his father's, his arms are crossed and feet apart, his stance making it clear he will not back down.

"The *fuck* you will! It's not just about ruling a kingdom! Her powers are the strongest of her lineage and yours are the strongest of mine! Breeding the two of you will ensure powerful future rulers!" he roars, face turning a bright shade of red as he gets in Caspian's face. We all stand, ready to jump in if he touches a hair on his head.

"If you want powerful rulers, then you should approve of his match with Layla. She's more powerful than all of us combined," Damian declares, his voice low and full of deadly promise.

Triton rounds on him, sneering, pure venom dripping from his words, "The half-breed bastard? I'll be damned if I see him sully our line with an illegitimate night-whore!"

"Who the fuck do you think you are?" I jump up, tired of being silent. Thunder rumbles outside once more, and shadows swirl around me, responding to my heightened emotions. Chaos and V come barreling into the room, both growling and baring teeth. Damian must tell them to be quiet because the growling stops, but they don't move, standing guard. Lights in the room flicker and another round of thunder reverberates shakes the walls of the room, electricity sizzling in my fingertips.

"I am the granddaughter of the most powerful goddess in this realm. I may be a half-breed, but my powers are far greater than even yours." Lightning flashes outside, and I feel Cas brushing the edge of my mind with our link and I shut him out. I raise my hands, ready to strike, but feel a hand grasp my wrist. I turn and Damian is pleading with me silently, letting the terror in his eyes speak to me in ways his words can't. I blink and take a deep breath as I command my shadows to fall away and the storm outside to settle.

"So, is it true then? Are you able to kill immortals?" He stalks over to me, invading my space until we are mere inches apart.

"Wanna find out?" I challenge.

Cas snaps, "Father, that's enough. Back away from her, *now*."

"*Let's see how well he fares when I rip his head from his shoulders,*" Vengeance threatens.

"*He's immortal, V.*"

"*Even asshole immortals are not immune to our bites.*"

"*What the fuck? Are you serious? That is information we will be discussing in detail, later. And did you just cuss?*"

"*Deadly serious,*" she states and then goes quiet again.

Triton turns and raises an eyebrow at Cas but doesn't move from me, and I'll be damned if I back down. "Or what, son?"

"Or you will be escorted from this castle. Remember, Triton, I am ruler here, and she is my cousin. You are just a guest," Damian intercedes.

He reluctantly takes a step back. "I want you boys to come home." He looks each in their eyes, waiting for an answer.

Nereus, the quietest of the bunch, speaks up first. "No, Father, we will be staying to participate in the wedding. Afterward, we can talk of coming home, but Damian has kindly offered for us to stay here, and I have grown rather fond of this kingdom."

Triton glares at him.

"I will be marrying Nerine, father, with or without your permission. Nyx has blessed the union," Aegir says with quiet resolve.

"I am never coming home, not unless you accept that Layla will be at my side. I plan on marrying her, so you might want to get used to the idea." My breath hitches and Cas holds my gaze, a small smile playing on his lips.

"I'm staying too, father," Delphin states.

"The four of you dare defy me? Dare to break your mother's heart? You were raised to be better men than this!" he bellows.

"I think Mother will be proud of us, and we are way better men than you raised us to be," Delphin says.

He whirls on Damien, "This is your doing! You would allow

them to stay here knowing I have ordered them home?" he roars, face turning molten as a vein bulges in his neck.

"Unlike you, I understand they are adults and respect their decisions as such. They will stay as long as they like. I am not one of your children; I am king here and I do not bow to you." Damian's voice is calm and deadly, the slight twitch in his jaw the only indication of the rage that is bubbling under his cool veneer.

"If you allow this wedding to happen, it will be a declaration of war. Are you prepared for those consequences?" Triton's breathing is ragged, his control on the verge of snapping.

Damian, as cool as ever, merely shrugs. "Are you? We have some rather powerful allies." His hands sweep around the room. "Including my grandmother," he reminds him.

"You will pay for your insolence, *boy*," he snarls at Damian before storming out of the room.

We collectively let out a breath, some of the tension in the air disappearing with Triton's departure. Aegir is leaning up against Damian's desk, arms folded across his chest, ankles crossed. "That went..."

"About as expected?" Cas finishes.

"Pretty much," Aegir agrees. "I dread telling Nerine, I want tomorrow to be perfect for her."

"It will be, we will make sure of it. She will be surrounded by people who love her. Is her family attending?" I ask.

"Her mother is, her father is not," Aegir says sadly.

"We will make it a perfect day, I promise," I wrap an arm around Aegir's waist and give him a squeeze as he hugs me back. It's the first time we've shown affection to each other, and it warms my heart.

"This isn't really how I planned this, but since I threw it out there already and you all are all here, I feel it's as good a time as any." Cas suddenly looks nervous, and I look at him curiously as he walks toward me.

"Oh shit!" Delphin exclaims, and as I look around the room, I see huge grins on everyone's faces except Damian, who looks a little worried.

Cas stops in front of me and takes my hands, Aegir backing away to stand between Nereus and Delphin.

"Layla, from the moment we met all those years ago when your smart mouth put me in my place, you've captivated me with your strength, your bravery, and the incredible compassion that guides your heart. Together, we've faced some of the hardest days of our lives and emerged stronger, our bond unbreakable. You are my confidant, my greatest ally, and the love of my life. I can't imagine a future that doesn't have you by my side, sharing in every adventure, every challenge, and every joy. You already know you are it for me. There never has been, nor ever will be, anyone else but you. You own my heart, my soul, and every fiber of my being. Be it the mortal world or our world here, there is no place where you and I don't exist. I want to spend every day of this life with you and then follow you into the next. Will you marry me and let me spend the rest of our lives showing you how much I need you, want you, and love you?"

My heart stops. Everything around me fades away as he gets on one knee and pulls a small box out of his pocket. He opens it, and inside is the most beautiful blue diamond I've ever seen. It's a simple setting, the large center stone surrounded by smaller diamonds. The band is platinum, and it circles around and rises into what looks like a wave, the crest holding the stone in place on either side.

"It was my maternal grandmother's ring. If you don't like it, we can get you something else." His eyes are shining with love. My ability to breathe has not yet returned, and I just stare at his outstretched hand.

"Damnit, Layla, say something and put the boy out of his misery," Damian teases.

"Yes." The word is a barely audible whisper.

"Yes?" Cas says, hopeful.

"Yes!" I say louder, and he scoops me in his arms and kisses me with a fierce possessiveness that makes my knees weak. Everyone surrounds us as Cas slides the ring onto my shaking finger, and tears slide down my cheeks.

Congratulations surround us and I'm smiling so hard my cheeks hurt.

"Let's not officially announce it until after the wedding, I don't want to take away from Aegir's big day, but I couldn't wait any longer. I've been holding onto the ring for weeks." He breathes a sigh of relief.

I laugh and kiss him again. Fusing my mouth to his, molding my body into him, leaving no space between us as he deepens the kiss, thoroughly devouring me.

"It's true, he has. We've been wondering what the hell was taking him so long," Damian says with a smile on his face.

Cas and I break apart, breathless. "You all knew?" I ask in wonder. I had no idea he planned to propose, and I am surprised they were all able to keep it quiet.

"Everyone knew," Delphin pipes up.

"Wow, I am impressed that you were all able to keep it a secret and shield it from me." I look back and forth between Cas and Damian. I thought it a little curious they had been shielding so much lately.

V growls, and it startles me. I had forgotten she was in the room. *If the sea prince hurts you, I will rip his head from his body.* Damian chuckles, and I look at him, I guess Chaos relayed the message.

"I love you too, V," I say through our bond. No need to let Cas in on her threat—I want to just enjoy this moment.

"Now, if you all don't mind, I am going to take my fiancée to our room to do some celebrating before we have to help with setting up for tomorrow." He picks me up, throwing me over his shoulder as I squeal, and he swats my ass. Cheers go up around the room, making me giggle. It must have been a lot of fun to grow up with so many brothers.

"Cas, put me down!" I kick my feet and he smacks my ass even harder this time. I'm wearing my midnight leathers etched with runes in case I needed to enhance my powers if Triton decided to act like a fool and do something really stupid. Something about him spanking my ass, combined with the feel of the leather, makes my clit throb painfully.

Making it to our room in record time, even with the additional weight of me over his shoulder, he kicks open the door, slamming it behind us before tossing me down on the bed. He towers above me, pupils blown, breathing ragged as his hungry gaze rakes over me.

Anticipation sends a shiver down my spine. "Cas," I whisper, "Come here."

He removes his clothing before kneeling on the bed. He grabs my ankle, unlacing my boots and tossing them across the room. He then peels off my socks, holding my foot, grazing his teeth along the sensitive arch, making me gasp, and I try to yank away from him, the sensation too much.

"Unless you want that ass spanked so hard you can't sit for the next week, I suggest you sit still," he growls. Fuck, I love it when he's all bossy, my pussy clenching at his words.

I'm trying so hard to be still, but it tickles so much when he switches to the other foot my instincts take over and I jerk away again.

He moves so fast I don't know what's happening until it's too late. He flips me over and yanks my pants down past my ass, pulling me over his lap as he brings his hand down on me hard. It stings so good, and I moan as he runs his hand gently over what is no doubt a bright red handprint on my backside.

"I told you to be still," he murmurs as he leans down and kisses each ass cheek before yanking my pants down the rest of the way.

He turns me over again, pulling my shirt over my head and unclasping my bra. He takes a nipple into his mouth, and the feel of it is like throwing a match to gasoline. My entire body is on fire, and only he can douse the flames. I arch into him, threading my hands into his hair as he slides a hand slowly down my body. The need for him makes me feel crazy with want. He's going so damn slow it feels like torture. I roll my hips, but he keeps his weight off me, determined to prolong the torture.

For the love of the gods, I would give up all my power, sell my soul even, for him to touch me where I need him the most. To fill me so I can't tell where I end, and he begins.

"Cas, I need you," I plead.

"Patience," he whispers against my skin as he trails kisses up my neck. His hand lightly brushes over my clit and the hypersensitive skin throbs with need. "More, Cas!" I run my hands over his back, digging my nails into him, marking his skin.

He moves his large frame down my body until his mouth is so close to where I want him, I can feel the warmth of his breath there. I thrust my hips upward, and his lips brush ever so slightly over me, making me ache painfully with need.

Wrapping an arm around each of my thighs, he holds me in place so he can lick slowly from my entrance to my clit, the sensation sending a shockwave through me, making me whimper.

"You taste so fucking good. I could spend the rest of our lives on my knees, worshiping you, head buried in your pussy, and be a happy man." He latches onto my clit, sucking gently as he slides a finger inside of me. I'm already so far gone it only takes me mere seconds to come undone. The feel of his mouth and the possessive way he takes me causes an explosion of pleasure that spears through me so hard and fast it borders on painful, my body heaving, heart galloping in my chest so loud it thunders in my ears. Each wave brings a new jolt of pleasure until I am completely spent, my body limp and boneless. He keeps licking and sucking, devouring me with his teeth and tongue as I come down until it's too much, and I'm begging him to stop.

"Oh, you want me to stop?" He rises over me and quirks a brow questioningly.

I can't form words, so I just shake my head.

"What do you want, Layla?" He's rubbing his cock back and forth over my clit, coating himself with the orgasm that drips down my thighs.

"I want you, Cas." I grip his ass and raise up to grind myself on him.

"You already have me, sweetheart. I want to know exactly what you *want* from me." He sucks my bottom lip into his mouth, and it sends a new rush of desire straight to my core.

"I want you to make love to me," I say to him, and I see surprise flare in his eyes at my choice of words. I usually tell him to fuck me.

"Look at me, Layla." I meet his gaze, so much love is shining there my heart feels like it may burst. "You are mine," he growls. He rolls his hips, entering me in one swift thrust, burying himself to the hilt, locking us together. My eyes flutter closed. "Eyes on me, Layla. I want you looking at me as I make love to you."

I open my eyes at his command. Sweat is beading on his forehead, and I am deliciously aware of the feeling of him sliding in and out of me so slowly it's driving me insane. The sensation of him filling me feels so damn good. It goes well beyond the physical, knowing that in this moment, our bodies are joined, and we are one being, two souls connected in a way that goes beyond description.

He buries himself fully and he stills, eyes locked on mine before he peppers kisses all over my face. The maddening pleasure just from our connection alone is so intense I may explode. I know there is nothing I would not do for this man. I would tear the world apart with my bare hands to make this feeling last forever, for there to be nothing except me and Cas. After what feels like an eternity, but in reality, has only been a few seconds, he finally begins to move inside of me again and I sigh.

"*Thank fuck*," I whisper into his mind, and he chuckles. I don't trust myself to speak words out loud at the moment.

"You feel so damn good." His breathing is getting strained, and his control is close to snapping. I place my hands on his cheeks and bring his mouth down to mine, kissing him slowly. It's a languid dance between our tongues, licking and sucking in a way to purposely draw out pleasure.

I feel that pressure start cresting toward release as my hips begin thrusting up to meet his of their own accord.

"Harder, Cas," I whimper and slide my hands down, raking my nails across his ass. He lets go of his control and starts pounding into me like a man possessed, like keeping himself leashed for that long makes something snap inside of him when he finally untethers it, pounding into me so hard he nails me to the mattress as I moan beneath him, urging him on.

"You like it when I fuck you rough, don't you?"

"Yes!" I gasp out.

"That's my good girl, you take my cock so well." His grunts between each word let me know he's close. His words shoot straight to my core, tipping me over that edge, tumbling down as wave after wave of pleasure has me crying out his name, clinging to him as my orgasm begins to fade and he continues his punishing pace.

"Fuck Layla, I'm going to come. I'm going to fill that perfect little pussy of yours until I'm dripping down those soft thighs." He thrusts one more time, even harder, and I feel him throb inside of me as he moans and bites my neck. "Fuck, I don't what it is about you that makes me feel like a damn animal." He grinds his hips into me again before rolling to his side, pulling me with him.

"Wow," I say, breathlessly.

"Yeah, wow," he agrees and kisses the top of my head as we lay there, wrapped in each other's arms, basking in this moment of pure happiness.

Chapter Twenty-Six

DAMIAN

Security is my main concern for this wedding. After what happened at my birthday celebration, the idea of having another big event has my nerves on edge. Not only do we have to worry about my uncle, but we also now have to worry about Triton. I've only been ruler here for a matter of months, and I'm making enemies left and right. Maybe I'm not cut out for this job after all.

I rest my head in my hands, elbows on my desk, trying to come up with a way to make sure my people are safe while we draw a huge target on our backs by defying Triton.

"Chaos, any suggestions on how to keep everyone safe tomorrow?" He twitches his ears and cocks his head, studying me from where he lays on the floor next to my desk.

"Your grandmother will be here; do you not think that will be deterrent enough?"

"Maybe? I have no idea what Thanatos may have planned. He wants to overthrow her, and while I don't think he can do it without Layla, I can't be certain he won't try."

"There will be enough power here to keep everyone safe. Caspian is

231

able to shield the entire palace and its grounds, he just has not realized it yet."

"That's interesting, I will have to have a chat with him today and see what he can do. I'm not as worried about the people here as I am the city."

"Can you ask Nyx to shield the city with darkness?"

"I'm not even sure she is powerful enough to cover that kind of distance."

I hear laughter in my head before Chaos says, *"I would not say that to her. The Godslayer could achieve it alone if she was more confident in her powers. Maybe the two combined would help her realize her own strength."*

"You may be on to something." I mull it over and decide I will speak to Grandmother on the subject as soon as she arrives. For now, I need to meet with the head of our security, who is currently five minutes late. I stand to go find him as he comes rushing in.

"Sorry I'm late, your mother stopped me." He gives me a sheepish grin, and I breathe a sigh of relief, thankful it was nothing serious that kept him. He's been the head of security for as long as I can remember and always kind to me and Mother. We quickly go over the plans for the palace and the town. Nyx is bringing some of her men as well, so we will have double the forces. I feel marginally better as I head out to see where Mother needs me. There's a small army of people bustling about, setting up tents, doing lawn maintenance, and draping everything that sits still in decor of varying shades of blue.

In the midst of it all is my mother, the loveliest conductor, creating the perfect masterpiece around her.

"Hello, Domain!" She kisses my cheek as she approves a list someone is holding out to her. "What can I do for you, love?"

"Just seeing where I can be of service." I look around at the chaos, utterly bewildered at how she manages to know exactly what every person is doing.

"I have it all under control! Why don't you relax? Take Anika down to the beach. I'm sure Umbra and Onyx would love an excuse to go flying for a bit. You look tired."

"Thanks for nicely telling me I look like shit." I smile at her, and she swats my arm.

"Shoo! Go enjoy yourself, I am in my happy place right now. I see Anika look at those dragons longingly often enough that I know she will happily accompany you."

With purposeful strides and excitement filling my veins at the prospect of spending some time with Anika, I make my way into the castle to either find her or Chaos. I check her room and she's not there, nor is she in the nursery.

"Chaos, where are Havoc and Anika?"

"We are all in the Dragonhold, Audra is here as well."

I smile, I should have known. Audra and Anika are both fascinated with the dragons.

I practically sprint to my room to change out of my jeans and throw on a pair of athletic shorts. I stop by the kitchen and pack some lunch, so excited about the possibility of an actual date with Anika that I quickly toss items in and head to the Dragonhold.

I hear the low rumble of approval coming from one of the dragons as feminine voices are cooing to the massive beasts as if they are nothing more than puppies. Anika and Audra both are scratching Drayvhn's neck and chin, his eyes closed as his massive head leans into their hands. His deep purple scales shimmer in the light and he sighs contentedly.

"Hello, ladies," I greet them, a note of teasing in my tone as they both jump like they have been caught doing something wrong.

"Damian!" Anika cries, walking over to me, threading her arms around my waist, and leaning up to press those sweet lips to my mouth. I savor the smell of sunshine and flowers that cling to her. She leans back enough for me to drink her in, her red curls pulled into a braid, but several defiant strands have escaped and fall around her face. The slight dusting of freckles across her nose and cheeks has gotten darker in these warm summer months, and I have an irresistible urge to count them, but I kiss the tip of her nose instead. A grin spreads across her face and pleasure lights up her eyes.

"Hi." My voice is low and husky as heat fills my veins at her closeness. "Can I interest you in an afternoon on the beach? We can take the dragons for a ride, escape for a little while?" I suddenly find myself nervous. Until this moment, I didn't realize how much I wanted her to say yes to this.

Her entire face lights up and she bounces on the balls of her feet. "Yes! Wait, shouldn't we be helping with the wedding?" Her brows furrow and her lips tug downward, causing my heart to lurch.

"Mother has declared she has it under control. It was her idea that I take you, actually." She beams at me again and all is right in my world.

She looks back at Audra. "Audra, are you okay if I leave you for a bit?"

She shrugs, "I'm fine, you go have fun!"

"How are you settling in?" I shift my attention to her, still a little wary but warming to her presence.

Stroking Drayvhn's nose, she replies without looking at me, "Okay, I guess. Everyone is nice enough, and *he* hasn't tried to bother me anymore."

I assume the *he* she is referring to is her father. "Thor will be here for the wedding; be prepared and please behave. If you want to bash his head in after the guests leave, I'll happily let you do it. But he is one of the few that can help you learn to control your powers. He's going to be working with Layla, so you won't have to be alone with him."

"I know," she grumbles, "she told me, and I said I would think about it. I have a decent amount of control as it is." She raises her arms, clouds roll in right above the Dragonhold but nowhere else. She snaps, thunder booms and lightning strikes. She waves her hands like she's batting at a fly, and the clouds dissipate like they were never there.

"Fascinating," I say in wonder. "What else can you do?"

She walks out of the building, motioning for us to follow. "Stay there," she demands, and Anika and I both stop in our tracks as she walks further away. She points at a nearby tree; lightning flashes, hitting a branch and snapping it off. She picks it up from where it landed and carries it to the middle of a pile of rocks near the base of the mountain.

I watch Audra in silent awe, her ability both thrilling and terrifying. She closes her eyes, a serene expression masking the storm brewing beneath her skin. Sparks dance and flicker across the surface of her skin like errant whispers of a gathering tempest. When her eyelids flutter open, her eyes have transformed—glowing white, intense, and otherworldly, mirroring the raw power at her command.

With a graceful, deliberate motion, she raises her arms, the air around her crackling with electric anticipation. In a heartbeat, she unleashes her power. A surge of pure energy bursts forward, a brilliant arc of white-hot lightning that strikes the target with precision and ferocity. The branch, placed precariously atop a pile of rocks, stands no chance against such force. It splinters explosively, disintegrating into countless fragments that scatter like ashes caught in a windstorm. The display sends a clear message of her formidable power, and a shiver of respect runs through me, mixed with a flicker of caution at the sheer potential of her abilities.

"Holy shit," Anika whispers.

"Yeah, you took the words out of my mouth," I tell her.

Audra walks back toward us and while I thought she would be smug, instead, she looks rather pensive.

"I think you are correct in your assessment; you have an amazing command over your power," I tell her, and a small smile plays on her lips at the praise.

She crosses her arms around herself protectively. "It's weird being able to use it freely here. I'm so used to hiding it."

I nod, "I would say that Layla feels the same way. She had a little more freedom because she had Rio and Cas, then me, but she probably gets it," I say, kinder than the tone I usually take with her. She suddenly looks as young as she is, and vulnerable. She comes off all tough, but I need to remember she is still very young, and life has not been kind to her.

"She does." She nods and then pulls herself out of her thoughts, her face brightening. "You guys go have fun! I'll go find Layla. And Damian..."

"Yes?"

"Will you teach me how to ride them at some point?" Her head jerks toward the Dragonhold, a hopeful look on her face, her blonde hair whipping around as she seems to hold her breath, waiting for an answer.

"Of course, we might see if we can find you a Thunderwing Dragon. These are all Shadow Dragons, with powers similar to Layla's and my own. I don't wield the night, but I have powers that can be enhanced by theirs. You would be better off with a dragon that is suited to your particular powers. I'll have Umbra see if there are any Thunderwings without riders." I nod to her and offer her a smile. Her entire face lights up and I sigh. Looks like we are adding another stray to the family. We have quite an eclectic collection of misfits around here. Secretly, I don't mind, and the fuller the house becomes, the more Mother seems to glow.

Anika and I mount the dragons, me on Umbra and her on

Onyx, the only other grown dragon in our midst that has not chosen a rider. Dragons will accommodate other riders, but they tend to favor the ones they have claimed. The two juveniles won't claim riders until they are grown, which given the rate of growth lately, will be soon.

Flying always brings me a sense of joy and peace that's hard to put into words. It's so quiet—the white noise of the wind makes it easy to either quiet your mind or give you time to think. Unlike in the mortal realm on a motorcycle, where you must concentrate on the road, dragons do all of the work and you can just relax, unless, of course, you are in a battle, then you must work as a team.

But today's ride is quiet. I sneak several glances Anika's way, and I can tell she is enjoying the simple pleasure as well. Before long we are landing on a pristine beach with white sand and crystal blue water shining out as far as the eye can see.

We spread our blanket out on the sand, kicking off our shoes, getting comfortable, enjoying each other's company and conversation.

"This is the edge of your kingdom, right?" she asks me.

"Yes, the sea here is ruled by Njord. His son and daughter rule the land where the safehouse is near the portal we normally use. Freyja, his daughter, was once Odin's lover and Thor hates her because of it. On Earth, you would have known them as Norse gods. They all had a thing for Vikings back in the day. There's a rumor that Thor and Freyja were also lovers, and when Odin discovered the betrayal, he cast them both out." I wink at her, popping a grape into my mouth.

"My parents never really spoke of their lives here or told me stories like that. I knew some basics, but that was about it. Not really having strong wielding abilities, they struggled and wanted more for their lives. My cousins, Lucien and Phoebe, told me our line is descendants of Apollo, but my parents never mentioned that.

I have more light-wielding ability than they did, but sometimes I wonder if it's because I practice."

"So, a lot of this is all new to you as well?" I'm curious what it must have been like to grow up as one of us on Earth.

"Yep. I never really felt like I fit anywhere. Layla was the first person outside of my parents that I met from here. Well, she's not really *from* here, but you know what I mean. Then there was Rio and Cas. Rio wasn't from here either, was he?"

"No, Rio was half-human, born on Earth, but his father was involved, and he spent quite a bit of time going back and forth. I don't know for certain, but I think his father was Hephaestus. Cas might know more."

"What do you think about Cas and Layla being engaged? I see the little lines in your forehead and the scowl that seems permanently plastered on your face when you watch them together," she asks, a genuine curiosity tinting her tone.

I let out a deep, exasperating sigh before responding. "It's not that I don't like Cas, but I was there with Layla when he was gone. She was a shell of herself. Her hurt consumed me. Being able to feel what she was feeling when she wasn't shielding well enough almost brought me to my knees. I know he loves her; I do. But he also hid so much from her, and I don't understand that. I guess I am just worried about her getting her heart broken. I would do anything to protect her. What do you think about it?" I turn to face her, propping myself on my elbow and resting my head on my hand.

She gazes out across the expanse of water, her expression thoughtful as she gathers her thoughts before speaking. "I like Cas, and I love Layla," she begins, her words measured and deliberate. "They've always been meant to be, it was clear to me from the start."

There's a quiet certainty in her voice as she continues, a conviction born from years of friendship with them both. "He loves her like nothing I've ever seen. If you knew what she put him through, and yet he stuck it out, you would probably feel differently."

She pauses, her gaze lingering on the horizon as memories flicker through her mind. "It's harder for me to be objective because I've known them both for so long," she admits. "But in my eyes, even when they weren't a couple, they were. He's always belonged to her."

A hint of sadness touches her words as she acknowledges the things they've been through. "Has he screwed up? Of course he has, we all do," she concedes. "But at the end of the day, they love each other. And for Layla, loving someone and giving them the power to break her heart is the hardest thing she has ever done."

I think about her words for a moment and wonder what it really is that bothers me so much about the match. I can't quite put my finger on it. I push it to the back of my mind and focus on the beautiful woman lying here with me.

"Want to go for a swim?" I wink at her and grab her waist, pulling her close enough for me to kiss her.

"You didn't give me time to grab anything, I don't have a swimsuit," she says with a reproachful look.

"Look around, Anika, no one else is here. You can go naked." I smile and wiggle my eyebrows at her, causing her to laugh as she smacks my chest. I grab her hand and keep it there, over my heart. She's so damn beautiful it hurts. Her fiery red hair, pale, milky skin, and green eyes are a combination that I can't get enough of. Add in her temper and sassy mouth, and I'm a goner. I lean in and kiss her again, feeling her fingers curl over the material of my shirt.

"I can feel your heart racing," she whispers against my lips.

"That happens any time you are near me, love." I kiss her again. What I wouldn't do to be able to spend every minute of every day exploring that plump, pillowy mouth. Devouring her, taking in her little moans as I delve in deeper, sliding my tongue across hers, nipping that bottom lip that makes me think of all kinds of sinful, deviant things. I wonder what I've done to deserve this kind of happiness.

"I could wear my underwear and bra, right? It's no different than a bathing suit." She pulls back, and there is no mistaking the lust in her hooded gaze. The way she is biting her bottom lip is about to make every ounce of control I have disappear.

"That works," I say huskily, hopping up to strip down to my black boxers and watching as she shimmies her shorts down those long, perfect legs. She pulls her top off next, a groan escaping me as I close my eyes, trying to not throw her down and fuck her in the sand. When I open them again, she's smiling at me.

"Race you!" She takes off like a shot, laughing and breathless, splashing through the surf before she dives into the water, me hot on her heels.

I grab her around her waist and bring her body flush with mine, water beading along her skin as we lock eyes and our mouths collide, hot and hungry for each other. She wraps her legs around me and presses into me as close as she can, arching her hips into me. I can feel her nipples pebble under the thin fabric of her bra, and I pull the material down to feast on them, licking and lavishing them with attention.

"Yes, Damian, fuck, that feels so good." She throws her head back, arching into my mouth, begging for more, threading her hands in my hair, scoring my scalp with her nails. She's rubbing herself against me in earnest now, desperate to relieve that ache that is building hot and fast. I slide a hand between us, under the fabric of her lace underwear, until I find her clit, swollen and needy. I rub her hard, not wanting to take my time. I need her to find her release quickly so I can bury myself inside of her, the need for her burning through all my common sense. She rocks against me, needing more, her breaths coming faster as her release slams into her, her thighs clamping around me like a vice.

My patience is gone. I don't wait for her to come down before I release my cock, shove her panties aside and slam myself into her. She gasps in surprise and is so tight around me I can already feel my balls drawing up, the need for release thrumming through my veins. She feels so damn perfect, like a silken glove around me.

The warm water slides back and forth across our skin, somehow making this even hotter, or maybe it's because we are out in the open, where anyone could happen upon us. They can't see anything, but it wouldn't take a genius to figure out what we are doing with the way we are moaning and moving against each other in the water.

I kiss her neck, gripping her ass with both hands, grinding her against me as I fuck her.

"Fuck Damian, I'm going to come, don't stop!" she says into my ear, and damnit if it doesn't make me feel like I am on top of the world knowing I am giving her this pleasure. I feel her pussy tightening around me as her body seizes and shakes, rocking her hips against me through her release.

Groaning, I lose all control, pounding into her with deep, powerful thrusts, harder and harder as I chase my own release. I'm looking into her eyes, mesmerized at how damn beautiful they are, all soft and warm, drawing me into their depths like a siren. Her mouth is parted, and I can't help but kiss her as I thrust into her one last time, groaning with the power of my release, spilling myself inside of her.

"Fuuuuck," I grind out as my cock keeps emptying into her, feeling so fucking good. It finally eases and I rest my forehead against hers, panting, legs trembling.

I pull my head back and look into her eyes once more, raising a hand to her face and tucking a wet piece of hair behind her ear. The last few days have my chest cracking open, my heart feeling raw and exposed in this quiet, perfect moment with her.

"I love you, Anika." Her eyes go wide and panic blooms in my chest. I didn't mean to say that. It completely came out of nowhere. I've barely come to terms with my feelings for her; while I know she feels for me, I don't know if she's there yet, and the last thing I want to do is make her feel pressured to return a sentiment she's not ready to declare. I've never said those words to a woman outside of family before, but I can't take them back now, and I find that I don't want to.

Suddenly, she threads her fingers back into my hair, gripping a handful, and pulls my mouth back to hers. The greedy way she is kissing me feels like she is fucking my mouth with her tongue. She pulls back and we are both breathless. Looking into my eyes, wetness shining in hers, she whispers, "I love you too, Damian. So, so much."

The knot that had formed in my chest has loosened and we are kissing once more. Our bodies are still joined, and I'm instantly ready for her again as we spend the rest of the afternoon making love at the beach before reluctantly heading back.

I feel lighter than I have in weeks, and I can't stop grinning. I love this woman so fucking much.

Chapter Twenty-Seven

LAYLA

"Where's Damian?" I demand as I walk into the room and see almost all the boys lounging around.

"He took off with Anika," Brennan says as he tosses a cheeseball to Delphin, who catches it in his mouth, and everyone cheers.

I roll my eyes but can't help but smile at the big goobers. Delphin's grin at his achievement and flashing dimples remind me so much of Cas. I throw my hands on my hips and look at them all reproachfully.

"Boys, why are you all in here instead of helping?"

Aegir looks down, Brennan gives me a sheepish grin, Delphin just gives me what I assume is his best panty-dropping smile, a smile that I am certain has gotten out of countless amounts of trouble in his lifetime, while Nereus rubs his hand across the back of his neck. Cas pushes up from his chair and walks over to me, putting his hands on my waist before speaking.

"Well, we may have been fired." He gives me a grin that is similar to Delphin's, but his makes my panties wet and makes me want to climb him like a tree. It's that adorable little mischievous grin that usually means trouble of the good kind. Today, however, I'm guessing that's not the case.

"Fired?"

"Um, yeah, fired," he says sheepishly, looking adorably embarrassed. I see the slight glassy look in his eyes, and a smile slowly creeps across my face. I do believe Caspian may be drunk, a sight I've never had the pleasure of seeing before.

"What did you all do?" I stare each of them down, none meeting my eyes. "Cas?"

"Well, we kinda got a jump on the bachelor party. We started drinking, and then we may or may not have started competing to see who could do their assigned chores the fastest and it may or may not have resulted in things being broken." I've never seen so many giant men blush, but here they all are, these boys of mine, covered in muscles and tattoos, every single one of them capable of breaking people in half, blushing and looking embarrassed like they are a group of twelve-year-old's that just got caught staring at a pair of boobs.

"What am I going to do with the five of you?" I cluck my tongue and shake my head, but it's so damn hard to really be mad at them.

Cas pulls me flush with his body before brushing a kiss over the shell of my ear, making me shiver. "I have a few ideas," he says, his voice rough and husky.

My entire body shakes with laughter, and I place a hand on his chest, "Back it up, big boy, we have stuff to do. Before you all run off tonight, I need to talk to Damian, so no sneaking off for guys' night until I have, understand?" He's making it really hard to concentrate as he nips along the skin of my neck.

Delphin shoves Cas away from me and takes me in his arms. "Layla, when are you going to dump that asshole and run away with me?" He spins me around the room before Cas grabs his shoulder and tosses him onto the couch.

"Mine," he growls and Delphin is cracking up.

"You are such a possessive asshole," he tells his big brother.

"Hey now, leave the baby alone, Cas. I like knowing I have options." I wink at Delphin, and he pretends to swoon.

Brennan groans, "Can you two stop pawing at my sister? So gross." We all laugh at that before I wave and quickly slip out of the room while they good-naturedly argue amongst themselves.

I need something to do. Today was supposed to be a busy day, but everything seems to be under control, and I am restless as fuck. I have shit I need to tell Damian, but I can't even be mad at him because, more than anyone, he deserves some downtime. V pads along with me as we head outside.

"Let's go play with dragons, V."

She snorts, *"I'm not sure playing with fire is a smart thing to do, Godslayer."* The humor in her voice is something I don't hear often, and I friggin love it.

"Aww, what's the matter, Vengeance? Can't take the heat?"

"Dire wolves are not afraid of dragons."

"What exactly are dire wolves afraid of?"

"Baths." She gives a full-body shudder, and I roar with laughter.

"I have literally seen you jump into a lake and go fishing! You are not afraid of water!"

"No, water is fine. Baths are different. It's degrading to smell like flowers."

"Okay, okay, no more flowery soap for you, but I draw the line at no baths, you stink."

She growls at me, and I ruffle her fur as we make it to the Dragonhold. I'm pleasantly surprised to see Audra here, quietly watching the dragons with deep longing in her eyes.

"Hey, Audra! What's up?"

She gives me a small smile, "Just checking out these crazy beasts. You spend your entire childhood dreaming about things like them. It's kinda a mind fuck to be staring at one, ya know?"

"Trust me, I get it! I saw one for the first time just a few months ago. I've known about them for a few years, but knowing and seeing them are two different things."

"Does it ever piss you off knowing this was all here and you didn't get to experience it before?"

I shrug my shoulders and stick my hands in my pockets, not really sure what to say next, thinking about my words.

"Sometimes, yes. Cas, Rio, Damian, and even Anika were coming back and forth, and I felt like they were a part of some secret club I wasn't good enough to be in. There was so much about this side of me that they knew and I didn't. I don't think it ever really pissed me off, but it did make me feel very alone."

The curve of Audra's shoulders is heavy with an unseen burden, and the lines of her face are etched with a sorrow that seems to weigh her down. Though her features are usually animated and fierce, now they are softened by a profound sadness, her eyes distant and unfocused as if lost in memories too painful to bear.

"You okay? You wanna talk about it?"

Still looking up at Drayvhn, she begins to speak, "It's just been hard. It was always just me and my mom. She was beautiful and men would flirt with her all the time, but she never looked at a man twice —she was still waiting on my father. She was still waiting on him when she died. She spent her life pining after a man who walked away from us without a backward glance. She never got to experience real love, never got to take a vacation, never really got to enjoy life, and then she was gone. And here he was, a man who had everything he could ever want, while mom worked two jobs and was still barely able to keep food on the table. It hurts."

I put an arm around her shoulder, and she leans into me. "She did know love; she obviously loved you, and you loved her. I bet if you could ask her, she would tell you that she wouldn't change a minute of her life, that you were worth all of it."

"Would your mom have said that?"

"Gods no, my mother was a mess and kicked me out when her piece of shit boyfriend came onto me, and I beat the fuck out of him. I had nowhere to go, so Rio took me in. I never spoke to her again, and when she died, a part of me was incredibly sad, not for the loss of her, but for the loss of the hope that she might love me enough one day to be better for me and Brennan."

She nods. "I see the guys all in there goofing off, and the way they are with you and it's hard not to feel a little envious. It's hard not to want to be a part of a big, loving, crazy family. I used to dream about having siblings. I remember begging my mom for a baby brother or sister when I was little." She smiles sadly, a faraway look clouding her face as she's lost in her memories.

"No need to feel envious, you'll find your place here. You can be a part of this if that's what you want, Audra. No one will force you to go back, but if you want to, I will make sure you can return to the mortal world. I don't give a fuck what Thor says."

Her lips turn up just a little, but her eyes still have that haunted look that cracks my heart open for her. Both of our heads jerk toward the open wall of the Dragonhold when a roar sounds in the distance, and we hear the thunderous cacophony of dragon wings as they beat against the air creating a symphony. With each stroke, the sound reverberates through the surrounding landscape, filling the air with the rhythmic pulse of their descent. The rush of wind and the flap of enormous wings combine to create a primal, awe-inspiring melody that announces the dragons' arrival, commanding attention that instills a sense of wonder. Audra's face is alight with rapturous envy. As soon as the wedding is over, I'm teaching this girl to ride.

The graceful way they land shouldn't be possible given their girth, but they make it look like a well-choreographed dance, movements practiced to perfection.

Smiles are plastered on both of their faces. A slight pink flush graces Anika's cheeks from the sun and Damian's hair is a delightful, rumpled mess. They look so relaxed I almost want to put this conversation off, but I can't.

"Cousin!" Damian says after a smooth dismount. He throws an arm around me and kisses the top of my head.

"Hi, guys! Did you have fun?"

The color on Anika's cheeks gets brighter and I can't wait to pull details out of her later. Eww, wait, I forgot she's sleeping with my cousin. Dammit. Who am I kidding? I'm still going to ask for details—I'll just pretend it's about someone else.

"We did," Anika says, sliding a glance at Damian as she smiles.

"Good, you two deserve it. Now I need to steal Damian for a few minutes, we need to talk."

"Good, I actually need to talk to you about tomorrow too. Where's Cas? Chaos gave me an idea earlier that I want to run by him."

"Cas later, me now." I grab his arm and start pulling him away. "Anika, can you have Audra help you with the dragons while I steal your man? It's important royal duties and stuff."

She laughs and waves us off, "Yes, you go take care of important royal duties. We've got this."

We get far enough away from them, and I whirl to face Damian. "Did you know dire wolves can kill immortals?" I hiss softly.

I can tell by his face that, no, no he didn't know this information. I can also tell by his expression that he is checking in with Chaos to see if I am a lunatic, just going around making up crazy shit in my head.

His face goes slack, "How did I not know this? No wonder they have been hunted to near extinction. We cannot let anyone else find out about this—they will kill them."

"No shit, Sherlock, why do you think we are out here discussing this away from everyone else?" I wince after the words leave my mouth, I trust all the boys and Anika, of course, but this feels like something I don't want to burden others with knowing.

"Well fuck."

"Yeah, that's kinda what I was thinking. Now, why do you need to talk to me and Cas? The boys are all a little tipsy. I'm not sure how that's even possible. I've seen Cas drink most men under the table and barely be buzzed. He has a freakishly high metabolism."

"Ahh, they probably got into the stash of Olympian Fire I brought out for the wedding. It's a type of spirit that would probably kill mortals and can knock an immortal on their ass pretty quick. You better stay away from it, understand?"

"No problems there! I'm too much of a control freak to drink much anyway. Now spill, damnit, the suspense is killing me. What is your idea, jackass?"

"Chaos thinks you and Cas have the ability to shield the palace and the city. I thought maybe we could try it out. Grandmother will be here in the morning, and if you can't do it alone, he thinks you can do it with her helping you."

Panic grips my heart. I don't have enough control over my powers to shield that kind of area. Darkness is the only thing I wield with the utmost confidence, and the wedding is happening at dusk, so I might be able to pull it off, but I've never tried anything that would use that much power at once other than killing Moros, and I had to draw strength from Damian to accomplish that.

"What about being in the wedding? Won't it be hard to shield while I'm distracted?"

"Most of us can shield like it's second nature, without even thinking about it. You are able to shield your thoughts without thinking about it now, so I don't think it would be much different. Let's grab Cas and see if he's sober enough to test the theory."

The only way to describe what we walk into is pure, unadulterated pandemonium.

Chaos.

Madness.

Mayhem.

Whatever word you want to describe it, it's insanity. There's a game of sorts underway that involves scooters. The boys appear to be in teams and when they reach a certain point, they drink and move on before tagging in the next member of the team. Damian's jaw hangs open as Brennan and Delphin nearly take out a housekeeper when they round the large kitchen island. Brennan yells a quick "sorry" while Delphin flashes a flirtatious smile.

There's so much shouting going on it's hard to tell who is saying what. The raucous laughter that fills the space as they dash and disappear in and out of rooms, following whatever course they devised, is infectious.

"Damian! Quick, tag in!" Brennan shouts. Damian raises a brow, turns toward me with a quirk of his lips, and is off, joining in the melee. Groaning, I quickly abandon ship before I end up a casualty of whatever war they waged on each other, leaving them to their boys' night fun. We can worry about shielding in the morning.

I decide I should hunt down the ladies to get our own night going. A night I anticipate will be much, much calmer than whatever the boys have going on.

Fuck, was I wrong.

Chapter Twenty-Eight

DAMIAN

"Damian! You boys need to be up!"

Whoever is screaming my name and beating on my door is going to die a slow, agonizingly painful death. I swear it.

"Do *not* make me come in there!" The pounding gets louder as the fog in my head starts to lift enough to register the groans and grumbles from around my room.

"Damianos, this is your last warning!" the voice screeches.

Shit. Realization dawns. Mother is at the door, and we are all supposed to be up preparing for a wedding this evening.

"Coming, Mother!" I yell as I use every ounce of my willpower to order my legs to slide off the bed, hoping they agree to bear my weight. My foot comes down on something that grunts, and I peer over the side of the bed to see Nereus passed out on the floor, half-naked, with tattoos I didn't know he had on full display, his large frame stretched out on his stomach, clutching a pillow as he mumbles something unintelligible.

I step over him and the other bodies I can't seem to recall how they ended up crashing in here and crack open the door to peer at the tiny, terrifying banshee standing in the hall.

"Yes, Mother?"

Her hands on her hips she gives me a withering stare. "Do you have any idea what time it is?"

"Not a clue, but I am fairly certain you are about to tell me," I deadpan.

"It's nearly two in the afternoon." She purses her lips and stares me down as my face pales. Holy hell, I had no idea it was this late.

"On it, Mother, we will be down shortly. Food?" I ask, giving her my best sad, puppy dog face.

"You better have them all up and in the kitchen in twenty."

"Yes ma'am." I salute her as she storms off down the hall.

Turning back to examine the contents of my room, I can't help but wonder what the hell happened last night. There are some snippets of memories I can grab from the recesses of my mind, but most of it is fuzzy. All four of the other men are passed out in various poses and places around my room, except Delphin. I navigate through the minefield of various large bodies splayed on the floor and make it to my bathroom to find him passed out in my tub. Why the hell is he wearing makeup and a tiara? I run a hand across my short facial hair and wonder once again what the hell happened.

"Rise and shine, princess," I say to Delphin as I try to rouse him. A deep rumbling snore rolls through him and I snort with laughter. I turn the cold water on and watch his body twitch once, twice, and then a third time as I see him start to come back online. His eyes fly open as he jumps out of the tub, his ass soaking wet.

"Jesus, what the fuck, Damian?" he bellows. I watch him as he turns toward the mirror that takes up nearly half the wall behind him, my smile spreading as he catches a glimpse of what he looks like.

His eyes flare wide, mouth hanging open as his arms fly out to his sides. "What the actual *fuck*? Who did this? They are *so* dead!" The indignant look on his face makes it a million times funnier than it already is, and I am almost double over with laughter.

A sleepy-eyed Nereus joins us, and the moment he sees his baby bro in his best drag queen get up, he falls over onto the floor, holding his stomach as he howls.

"Fuck you both!" Delphin growls as he searches the bathroom for a rag. The rest of the crew files in to see what the commotion is about, pandemonium ensuing once more. I stand back and watch the chaos for a moment, laughter shaking my whole body. For years, this place was filled with fear. With dread. Laughter didn't fill these halls, and a lonely ache in my chest was a part of who I was.

Now that ache is gone, I feel a different sort of pang, one that symbolizes love and caring for the people surrounding me. I have come to understand that those years of fear and loneliness have been replaced by these people. By friendships, by family, by bonds that go deeper than blood. We seem to have, somewhere along the way, chosen each other, and damn if that doesn't hit me hard in the chest. I love the chaos they bring, the fullness that fills this space. They are loud, messy, and unapologetically themselves. I can't imagine a world where this no longer exists, and I realize that before, I was just surviving. Now, I feel like I am actually living.

A loud, thunderous burst erupts from Delphin's ass as his face contorts, and a rancid smell fills the room, burning itself into our nose hairs.

"Aww, shit!"

"Mother*fucker* you stink!"

"Check your pants dude! That was *not* normal!"

Everyone fights to get out of the room as they hurl insults, elbowing and shoving each other to try and make it out alive. No one in their right mind would believe this room was filled with a bunch of immortal princes. It's more reminiscent of a biker club in the back of a dive bar, and now it smells like something crawled up someone's ass and died.

"Break it up, boys, Mother has given me strict orders to have you in the kitchen to be fed in about ten minutes, and you do *not* want to piss her off today."

They instantly go still, sober expressions on their faces. They know better than to upset Mother, and while she is quite scary when she's pissed, it's more about the affection they feel for her than anything.

"I suggest everyone go take quick showers and then meet downstairs. I have no idea what the hell we got into last night, but we can piece it together as we eat. Now get your asses moving!"

All jumping into action at once, the room is cleared out in seconds, leaving a huge mess behind them. I follow my own advice and hop in the shower, making it out in record time.

Food is laid out on the large wooden table that can seat twenty. I used to think this table was a huge waste of space, but if we keep collecting strays, we may need an upgrade. As the boys file in, they descend on the assortment like rabid dogs. They can pack away food like nothing you've ever seen and love to fight over things even though they know more can be brought out. I think it's more about the spirit of competition, but growing up an only child, the dynamics between brothers is still a mystery I am trying to unravel.

"Aegir, how you feeling? Are you ready for today?" I ask him.

He smiles and nods enthusiastically. "I can't wait." His eyes dance with excitement. He doesn't seem to be quite as hungover as the rest of us.

"You have any idea what the hell happened last night?" I raise an eyebrow, rubbing a hand back and forth across my freshly trimmed beard as I look around the room, everyone's eyes on Aegir.

A slow smile spreads across his face. "You all got shitfaced, and I had to babysit."

"So how the fuck did I end up in princess drag?" Delphin demands.

Aegir throws his head back and laughs. "That was Audra. You kept hitting on her and said you would do *anything* for a kiss. She took that shit seriously."

"Wait, what? Did we kiss?"

"Yes, but it was a small peck, and then you threw up all over her shoes."

"Oh fuck, you are making that shit up," he moans as he flops back into his chair and buries his head in his hands.

"You wish, it's all true, baby bro," Aegir snickers.

Mother comes into the room, a whirlwind of instructions as excitement radiates from her. "Damian, your grandmother has arrived. You told me to let you know when she was here, so she's waiting in your office with Layla. Aegir, you are not to see Nerine before the ceremony, understand?" He nods at her when she pins him with a glare. "You will need to go back to your room and get ready to be married. I'll come get you in about an hour with further instructions. Nereus, Brennan, and Delphin, you will be coming with me when you finish eating. Cas, you are going with Damian."

We all nod our heads and murmur acknowledgment of our orders before she breezes back out of the room, a dreamy smile playing on her lips. I feel another presence enter the room behind me and see Delphin stiffen and his eyes narrow. Ahh, the lovely Audra has joined us.

She sashays her hips, grabs an apple, and slides her ass onto the table almost directly in front of our current resident beauty queen. I wonder what he did with his tiara?

The smirk on her lips as she sinks her teeth into the apple has me glued to my seat, waiting for the drama to unfold. The other boys must have the same idea because all eyes are on the two of them.

"Hi, pretty boy. Fun night?" she asks as she wiggles her eyebrows at him, kicking her feet back and forth as they dangle off the side of the table.

"It was, we got our very own drag show performance," Aegir teases.

Delphin's eyes never leave Audra's, but he raises his middle finger to his older brother, causing a round of catcalls and howls of laughter from around the room to erupt.

A grin still plastered on her face, she taunts Delphin, "Aww, come on, pretty boy. You know that face is a ten out of ten, even while it's puking on my favorite pair of shitkickers. You're just pissed that smile that usually causes ladies to drop digits and possibly panties didn't work on me."

"Damn, I like her," Nereus whispers. I have to admit, she is highly amusing and the way she is tying Delphin in knots is fun to watch.

"Audra, if I were not already getting married today, I might drag you to the altar instead," Aegir chuckles, and none of us miss the way Delphin's eyes darken as they swing over to stare at his brother.

"That's my cue to skedaddle." Hopping off the table, she pats Delphin on his head like a puppy and skips out of the room, still munching on her apple.

"She really is a bigger handful than Layla. You are so fucked," Cas says to Delphin as he stands to walk around to where I am. "Come on, Damian, let's get this show on the road." He claps my shoulder before I rise, and we head to my office.

Opening the door, the first thing that catches my eye is Layla sprawled out on a couch with her arm covering her eyes. Grandmother is sitting at my desk, hands folded in her lap while she seems to be lecturing Layla.

"Well, you should have known better. You won't find any sympathy from me; medicate and hydrate," she orders her.

"Rough night, cousin?" I ask, curious as to what they got up to.

"Yes! It was so stupid. I thought Nerine was this sweet, quiet, mousey thing. The fuck she is. She's crazy, so is Audra. Those two together are insanity times infinity."

Cas and I look at each other, our faces mirroring our confusion. "What happened?" Cas asks.

"Audra talked us into going to Earth. There were strippers and alcohol. She swiped some from the boys. I think there might have been a limo and the police."

"The police?" What the hell did those crazy vixens do?

"Yes! The police! Keep up! Audra and Nerine were hanging out of the sunroof of the limo. The police pulled us over. I had to fuck with his mind, which I wasn't even sure I could do, but apparently it worked because he let us go. Then they decided they wanted to go to see strippers, but not guy strippers, girl strippers. And somehow, we all ended up dancing on poles."

Caspian growls deep in his chest, "You did what? Were you naked?"

"No, I wasn't naked! I had on a dress. You know the one, the blue one with the slits on each side."

"The one you wore on your birthday? Please tell me you were not on a pole in that thing; it looks more like lingerie than actual clothing." The poor boy looks a little green. He covers the distance between them, kneeling on the floor next to her, taking her face in his hands. "Did anyone touch you? I swear to the gods, Layla, if anyone laid a hand on you, I will fucking kill them."

"Well, no males laid a hand on me, but those damn horny women were all up on me. You should have seen it. The men watching were throwing money at us like crazy, and the club owner offered us jobs. Anika slapped my ass, and one old guy almost had a heart attack. Then Audra plumped up Nerine's boobs on the stage and ran her hands down her ass, and someone slipped her a hundred-dollar bill in her G-string."

"Who's G-string?" Cas pales.

"Audra's. She stripped down to her undies and worked that pole like her life depended on it. That girl is freakishly flexible and is built like a brick shithouse. Then they got bored, and we went to the club. Marcellus will be here in a bit, by the way."

"Marcellus?" Cas squeaks out.

"Yes, we got a private room, but before you panic, nooo, I did not do anything with anyone. I am all yours, big guy." She pats his cheek. "But Thelma and Louise, AKA Nerine and Audra, talked a few of the guys into putting on a show for us, and they put all those dollar bills we earned stripping to use, stuffing them into some really hot guy's underwear. I think they were gay, though."

"Is that all?" I am almost afraid of the answer.

"Mostly. We danced and then came home. Delphin puked on Audra and she made him into a princess. He was kinda cute." She lets out a long sigh and snuggles into the pillows on the couch.

"Sounds like quite a night." Grandmother seems highly entertained by this story and the panicked look on Cas's face.

"Well then, I guess now that we are all caught up, Grandmother, Chaos gave me an idea on how to protect the city tonight, as well as the people here. I'm sure you heard about what happened a few days ago when Triton visited?"

She frowns, "I did, and if he attacks here, he will pay dearly for it. If he ever insults Layla the way he did again, I will rip his tongue out, use it to wipe his own ass when he inevitably shits himself and then put it back in his mouth." That she says it so seriously makes me shiver.

Cas leans over to me and whispers, "Now I see where Layla gets her violent streak." I raise my eyebrows and give him a slight nod. I can't imagine the amount of graphic violence the two of them would be capable of inflicting if they teamed up.

"I don't think he will, knowing you are here. Triton isn't that stupid. As far as Thanatos, I have employed every resource I have, and it seems that Layla's father is laying low for the moment, but I'd rather not risk it. Chaos thinks you can shield the city with the night and that Cas can shield the palace. He thinks Layla could do it on her own, but she's never shielded an area that large and hasn't practiced much with her focus divided, which it will be during the wedding."

Grandmother is quiet for a moment, drumming her fingers, lost in thought before she speaks.

"Layla," she says quietly, but the command in her voice is evident. "Go do as I said, medicate and hydrate. We are going to see how well you can shield. Caspian, can you handle the grounds on your own?" She arches a brow at him.

"Yes, I believe I can. I haven't tried, but my powers have grown exponentially in the last few months, and I have an easier time controlling mine than Layla."

"Let's walk outside and see what you've got, young man."

We all get up, Layla heads to the kitchen, and Cas and I follow Grandmother outside. "Show me what you can do. Shield the grounds and we will see if it holds." Cas nods to her, and he scans the sky above him, closing his eyes and pushing power above us. I feel an odd weight pass through me, then it settles, but the distinct hum of power is still there.

"Damian, you are more sensitive to power than I. Can you feel it?"

"Yes, Grandmother, I believe so."

She nods, "You can wield fire, correct?" She says it more as a statement than a question, but Cas answers.

"I can."

"Send a fireball up into the sky above us, let's see what happens."

He holds out his hand, concentrating on growing a fireball big enough to push into the air above us. When he is satisfied, he pitches it, and within seconds, I can see it dissipate, a blue pulse radiating from around where it looks like it hit an invisible wall.

"How easy is it for you to hold?" She looks at him like he's a puzzle she's trying to solve.

"It's as easy as breathing. It only uses a small fraction of my power." He's quiet as he says this, and while I've known for months that he was almost as powerful as Layla, this surprises even me.

Satisfied, grandmother looks at him, a smile tugging at her lips. "Well done, boy. I am thoroughly impressed."

Chapter Twenty-Nine

LAYLA

Chugging water, I get back in just enough time to hear Caspian admit how easy it is for him to shield the grounds. A little shocked, a seed of doubt settles inside of me. For reasons I can't understand, he doesn't share this stuff with me. I'm always an open book when it comes to my powers. It makes me wonder what else he might be hiding, and it pisses me right the fuck off.

"Layla, I'm going to teach you how to imbue an object with power. Damian, what is at the most central point of the city?"

"It's your temple, Grandmother. The idea was for everyone to be equally as close to you." His eyes light up and one corner of his lips curve up when he tells her that.

She looks delighted as she claps her hands, "Wonderful! Come, sweetheart. Boys, go make yourselves useful and stay out of trouble!" She laces an arm through mine, and I find that I like the comfort of her presence.

"I thought I was going to learn how to shield?" I ask, confused.

She blows an extremely undignified raspberry, and I think I might love having her as a grandmother. "Why work harder when you can work smarter? I will teach you to shield larger areas, but for now, this will be easier and will last longer than the night. With the two of us, it should be strong enough to hold for at least a few weeks. It takes a great deal of effort, but it's similar to the way Damian can ward places and dampen powers, he just can't manage large areas. It will take a great deal out of you, so you might need to rest after to be prepared for the ceremony tonight."

"Why aren't we having Damian help?" I had forgotten about his ability to ward things.

"I need him to be at full strength this evening; he will be reading people, and it can be taxing. We need to know if anyone is plotting against his claim to the throne. With that many people in a confined area, it will drain him by the end of the evening to leave himself open for that long. His powers are a fairly well-kept secret, and most people don't naturally shield themselves the way he has taught you to do."

Okay, that makes sense. "Grandmother," I hesitate to ask the questions I want to ask, but there's not really anyone else I can get answers from, so I press on even though doubt settles in my chest, "will you tell me about my father? Was he always an asshole? Do you think there was ever a part of him that loved my mother? That cared about me?" The questions rush out all at once, and I mentally chide myself for the word vomit I just spewed all over her.

She stops and faces me, holding my hands in hers as she lightly runs a thumb back and forth across my skin. Taking a deep breath, her eyes meet mine and there is so much sadness and conflict in their depths that I know the answer before she can say those hurtful words I'm expecting but desperately hope aren't true. I don't know why I want to be wrong about this, why I want to think there was, at least at some point, something redeemable about him. Maybe it's because I want to know that I came from something that was good, at least for a time.

"Layla," she says with tenderness, "he never cared for you or your mother. I wish I could tell you differently. He and Moros were always power-hungry shitheads, even when they were young. I blame the influence of their father, but I also shoulder the burden of their shortcomings. My list of failures is long, and my love for them made me overlook a lot of their misdeeds. When I tried to step in, it was too late. He and Moros wouldn't listen to reason. When I gave them rules to abide by, they were furious and rebelled. Until you came into power, I doubt he even remembered you existed or your mother's name. I'm so sorry."

The hurt I feel surprises me, even though this isn't new information. My heart feels heavy. For myself, but also for my mother and what she later became.

"Did you know about me?"

"Not always, but once I discovered your existence, I didn't yet know if you had powers, and that made it difficult to interfere. We are supposed to be keepers of your world. We did a better job when the mortal realm was young and it was new to the gods. It relieved some of the boredom of immortality. We, too, have a creator, and when we decide to move on from our world, we will answer to Him. We were to be guardians, but after a while, people would get angry with us when things did not go the way they wanted, so we spent less and less time on Earth, and beliefs faded. Demigods were not meant to exist, so unless they showed powers not meant for the mortal realm, we were not to reveal our world to you. Aetheria is forbidden to mortals, but occasionally I bend the rules." She gives me a wink, and I know Brennan is on both of our minds.

"When you found Rio, I was able to keep an eye on you and planned on making an introduction when I thought you were ready. My main goal was to keep you out of your father's hands, even if that meant keeping my distance. You have no idea how thrilled I was when you and Damian found each other. That boy has the kindest heart, even if he only shows it to those he cares about. How he turned out nothing like his father is a miracle, one I am thankful for daily. The same goes for you. I am proud to be your grandmother."

I grab her arm again, tucking mine into hers as we begin to walk, lost in my own thoughts.

"Layla, what are you thinking about?" Her voice is kind and soothing and while I love the family I have found with Damian and Enthralia, I still feel starved for family connections, and I desperately want to build something solid with my grandmother.

"I'm just not sure how I am supposed to feel. Sometimes, everything seems too big to label or even process. I grew up thinking my stepfather, the man who did unspeakable things to me, was my dad. I would curl up in my bed at night and cry, begging God to let me die or, at the very least, let someone come save me. My heart would hurt so much I really felt I would die from the pain, and I shouldn't have felt that way. I knew I wasn't like other kids. I felt wrong somehow like I was dirty or tainted. Unclean. I saw how kids at school were treated by their parents and none of them dealt with the things I did. We went on a field trip once and this girl, Jaime's parents, went with us. The way they spoke to her, listened to her, and treated her had tears welling in my eyes, and I ran to the bathroom so I could sit in a stall and cry."

Nyx presses into me a little and tightens her grip on my hand. My chest aches with every breath I take as emotions clog my throat and tears escape down my cheeks.

"The day I found out he might not be my father, a little seed of hope began to grow. I thought maybe, just maybe, my real father was out there and was everything I had dreamed he might be, or that the blood that ran in my veins wasn't that of someone so damned evil they could do the things that my stepdad did to me. Imagine my disappointment when I found out that not only would mine use me for his own gain, but he has also killed innocent people just because he can. He puts no value on anyone's life, much less mine. I am nothing more than something to be used by both men who were supposed to protect me and love me. It fucking sucks.

"Then throw my mom into the mix. I used to think she was strong, and she would often protect me from my stepdad. But as I got older, I realized she should have never let it happen in the first place, but it took me a long time to see that. After I killed him, she became a shell of a person. Instead of being free of him, she acted broken, and I never understood it. Like losing him was just too much for her to handle, even though she wanted to leave him. I was so happy when she started planning to leave, I thought, finally, we can be happy. It was a relief to think she loved us enough to want to take us away from him, but she didn't. Sometimes, it makes me feel broken in a way that I can't come back from. Like all the pieces of me will never fit back together the way they are supposed to, or maybe they were screwed up from the beginning based on who I am and where I came from."

A sob escapes me and my body shudders. Something breaks inside of me, and I can't stop it. The insecurities, the doubt, and all the pain have finally hit the point of no return. The dam I had built to keep it all in has been demolished and I can't help but buckle from the force as everything I've avoided dealing with comes crashing over me, making it hard to breathe. I hit my knees, bending over, resting my hands on the bricked road as I fight to regain control. Nyx bends down next to me, gently rubbing circles on my back until finally sitting on the ground herself and pulling me into her arms.

"Shhh, it's okay, you are okay. You are not dirty or tainted. You are beautiful, loving, and strong. You are nothing like your parents and you never will be. Look at the way you have protected your brother, how you are there for the family you and Damian have been building. The same blood that runs in you also runs in me and in your cousin. Do you think Damian is somehow evil or unclean?"

"No, Damian is awesome. He cares so much about everything and everyone, even when he's playing the part of royal jackass." I sniffle and furiously wipe at the tears still freely falling.

Grandmother laughs and I feel her entire body shake as she holds me. "I've seen him as a royal jackass, and he can play that role to perfection, but you are right, that boy always cares. So much that I don't know how he doesn't crumble from the weight of it."

She pulls me back up and while I'm still a snotty mess, I feel a little lighter than I did before. There is still one thing weighing me down.

"Grandmother, Cas doesn't talk to me about his powers. It probably wouldn't bother me as much, but he and Rio used to keep me in the dark all the time. I trusted that Rio knew what was best, or he would say he couldn't tell me. It bothers me when Cas hides shit. I learned most of what I know about myself from Damian. Today is a perfect example. I had no idea he could do that. None. We are supposed to get married, but I don't know if I want a relationship where I have to wonder if my partner trusts me with the truth."

She frowns, her eyebrows knitting together as her eyes narrow. "You need to have a conversation with him. Don't let it fester. Think about what you want to say, wait until you can talk to him with a clear head, and lay out your concerns. How he reacts will help you sort your feelings out."

"But aren't we supposed to be like 'fated mates' or some shit? Doesn't that mean we are supposed to be together? What if I don't like what he has to say? Don't get me wrong, I love him more than I ever thought humanly possible, but things like this make me think that love isn't enough if he doesn't trust me or won't be open with me. That's not the kind of relationship I want."

"Fated mates aren't set in stone. We really don't know much about it. It's more of a legend. It's been so long since we have seen it, and even then, it was more of a guess than a certainty. The fact that your powers grow with your relationship does indicate some kind of tie to each other, but not even fate gets to dictate the decisions you want to make for yourself."

Her words make me feel better. Having your life decided for you by forces beyond your control is a lot of pressure. I don't like not having a say in my own fucking life.

I feel something brush against my leg, a familiar presence that fills me with a feeling of comfort. I don't even have to look to know it's V.

"Hey, girl," I say to her as we near the temple.

"I felt your distress. I understand your feelings but know I would not have chosen you if you were not someone deserving. You are strong, brave, and fiercely loyal. I have trusted you with secrets about my kind, knowing you were worthy."

"Thanks, Vengeance. I can't imagine my life without you." I lay my hand lightly on her as we stop, looking up at the beauty of the temple that was built to honor my grandmother. It's a little surreal, kinda what I would imagine being related to Taylor Swift might feel like.

A shadow looms above us. I tilt my head back and see Drayvhn flying overhead.

"Looks like your dragon also senses all is not well with you," V states.

"Well shit, now I feel guilty for worrying everyone," I mumble. *"I'm okay, Drayvhn, just having a bit of a pity party."*

I can feel his relief, even though he doesn't respond. He doesn't land but stays in the air, close enough for me to feel his presence.

"Ready, Layla?" Grandmother asks as her gaze softens when it meets mine.

"Let's do this," I say with more confidence than I feel.

I let out a shaky breath as she reaches for my hand.

"We are going to let our power flow into the temple. You will stretch your shield out to encompass the building and imagine pushing directly into the stone. The building is already etched with runes. All temples are built with ones that symbolize the powers of the gods or goddesses they represent. Those runes will absorb the powers and once we fully charge them, for lack of a better word, they should reach far enough to cover the city."

"Sounds simple enough."

She takes my left hand, placing hers on the stone, I mimic the motion with my right hand, and she gives me a little nod.

"Now close your eyes and picture yourself pushing into it like I said."

I do what she asks, trying to calm my mind and reach for my powers. They've changed. I barely noticed it at first, but now it's distinct enough that it's hard to ignore. Instead of them feeling like separate things inside me that I can reach for, they have coalesced into one large entity inside my mind. I have to intentionally pull out the type of power I need from that singular source. In this case, I feel like maybe I should try to tap into it as a whole.

I reach for it and feel the familiar rush as it surges forward along my skin. Pushing it through my fingers into the structure is easier than I thought it would be. The stone warms beneath my hand, a pleasant hum filling the air as everything else seems to grow silent. The birds quiet, the wind dies, and even the insects stop their singing chatter. All around us everything holds its breath as we work.

Power flows stronger and faster than before, pouring out in a torrent. In the back of my mind, it registers that Grandmother has dropped my hand and is shouting at me. I can't hear anything over the buzzing in my ears as I feel my body drain. A heaviness settles into my bones, making it impossible for me to break away or even move as more and more power rushes through me.

A surge of a different type of magic barrels into my brain, violently breaking the connection as I sag against the wall, falling to my knees.

"Godslayer! Your power! Are you well?" Vengeance. She broke through the connection to my power to stop the flow. Still trying to catch my breath, I assure her I'm okay.

A thundering roar sounds overhead, wind from flapping wings as they descend, stirring dust around us as Drayvhn lands, calming me further, knowing he is here. Standing on wobbly knees, I turn to Grandmother. She is studying me with a look of concern and curiosity on her face.

"Is it done?" I ask, leaning on V for support as I try to steady myself on legs that feel like they are made of jello.

"It is. You could not shut off your power."

"Yeah, I'm not sure what happened there."

A roar sounds again, and Drayvhn has lost all semblance of patience. *"She will ride home with me!"* The shout reverberates through my head, and I know V heard it as well.

"Drayvhn says I am riding home with him, he seems a little pissed," I say as I try to get my legs to work.

"I gathered that." Nyx looks at the dragon with narrowed eyes as he bares his teeth and growls deep in his chest. "Dragon, you may want to remember who is queen here and who rules the shadows from which you were made."

He snorts in what sounds like disapproval but quiets.

"Layla, are you sure you will be okay riding back on him?"

"Yeah, I'm sure. V will head back with you." She nods at that as I make my way onto Drayvhn's back.

"You wanna tell me what that was about, big guy? Why would you not let her just snap me home?" I opt to speak to him through

269

our minds rather than have this conversation where my grandmother can hear it.

"She should have cut your power off herself. She is capable. Your body cannot handle anything magical now, you need rest." He leaps into the air, beating his wings as we climb higher and higher.

"I'm sure she would have; V just beat her to it. Did it work?"

"Yes, the lands are warded. No undead will be able to enter, nor your father. It does not mean there still is no danger within, or danger that can enter the wards. There are still enemies to fear."

"So, what you are saying is basically I need to keep my eyes peeled and not let myself get comfortable?"

"Yes, though I do not sense anything amiss, nor do the other dragons or the wolves. Be careful, but I think it is safe for you to enjoy the night."

I'm too exhausted to think much more about this as we begin our descent. Damian is running full speed to the field where the dragons usually land, his long legs eating up the distance.

"Layla!" he mentally screams, pure panic in his tone.

We hit the ground, and I slide off the dragon right as Damian reaches us, scooping me into his arms and holding me close. I can feel his heart thundering in his chest beneath my cheek.

"I'm fine, you big goober! Well, other than the ribs you might crack if you don't stop squeezing the fuck out of me," I cry against his chest. "Why are your panties in such a twist?"

"Chaos told me that Vengeance had to save you from being consumed by your magic. He said you couldn't cut it off." He pulls me back and looks at me as I sway on my feet.

"Damnit, Layla! You are about to pass out. Come on, let's get you to bed. You need to rest before the ceremony." He sweeps me up into his arms, cradling me like I'm a toddler and I'm too tired to fight him.

As we make our way back to the castle, I can't help but notice how the yard has been transformed into a fairy-tale paradise, with strings of twinkling lights draped between the ancient oaks and elaborate floral arrangements bursting with colors at every turn. Two separate tents have been erected, one where the ceremony will take place, lined with chairs and artful arrangements at the end of each row. The other is set up with tables for the reception and is still currently under construction.

"Everything looks gorgeous," I say sleepily as he makes a rumble of agreement. "The warding worked."

"I know, I'm very proud of you, now rest," he demands.

"So fucking bossy. Where's Cas?"

"I'm sure he will be here shortly."

"No! I'm...I'm not sure I want to see him right now. I just want to sleep. Tell him I'll see him when I wake up and don't let him near me right now, okay? Promise me."

I feel Damian stiffen at my words; his arms tighten around me. "Everything okay, cousin?" he asks softly.

"Yeah, I'm just tired," I say as my eyes close, and sleep overtakes me.

Chapter Thirty

DAMIAN

Setting Layla on her bed, I slowly back away, watching her for a moment as she sleeps. My heart still hasn't stopped thundering in my chest. The fragility of Layla's half-human side is always a terrifying unknown. It's time for Grandmother and me to have a conversation about what needs to be done to ensure Layla is immortal, even if she doesn't agree to be her heir.

I turn to leave and almost run right into Cas. "How is she?" he asks.

"Worn out, she needs to rest, so let's leave her be—V will guard her." Damnit, now I'm using the nickname for the wolf.

He takes one last look at her sleeping form before walking over and kissing her hair, then following me out the door.

"Enthralia let me know Marcellus is here—he's waiting in your office," Cas informs me with a heavy sigh. I know the two of them are friends, but Layla's history with him must make it just a tad uncomfortable for Caspian. I know I sure as hell wouldn't want to sit across from someone who had fucked Anika. I would probably rip his throat out.

We enter the office, and Marcellus stands to hug Cas and shake my hand. "Cas! So good to see you!" His enthusiastic greeting doesn't match the worry in his eyes.

We all sit, and I grab a bottle of spirits my father kept in his bottom drawer, Nectar of the Gods. It's not quite as potent as the shit the boys got into last night but will help with the conversation we are about to have.

"Tell me about the killings," I insist.

"First, I need to tell you that there have been rumors the clinic will be attacked. You need to evacuate the people there."

"What the *actual fuck*?" I bellow. Jumping out of my seat, I pace the room while the workers and the residents there run through my mind. Ryanne. Layla will never forgive herself if her father kills that girl. We have to get her out.

Marcellus continues, "He's picking places now, not homes. He's trying to make a larger impact with each strike and he's getting bolder. It's a matter of time before he starts attacking humans."

"Cas, how long do we have until the wedding?" My mind races, heart hammering against my ribs like it's trying to break free. Every second feels like an eternity, each tick of the clock a stark reminder of the potential danger. The thought of the clinic—a place that is supposed to be a haven—being the target of an attack constricts my chest, squeezing until I can barely breathe. Images of the place, of the families we've sheltered there, flash through my mind in a relentless torrent. I can't focus, can't think straight. Panic claws at my insides, demanding action.

"We have about two hours. Can we get there and get them out fast enough?" Cas asks.

"You stay—you need to be here for your brother if I don't get back soon enough. I also need you to be here in case something happens here. *Fuck!*" I really need to be here. Layla also can't go.

"Go get Brennan and Audra. They don't need to be here for the wedding preparations. Hurry! Marcellus, you are also coming with me."

"Why is Layla not coming?" Marcellus questions.

"Because she can't," I snap as I get up to leave.

Cas takes off at a dead run, and Marcellus stands and follows me out of the room. I can't breathe. Tugging at my collar, I try to ease the constriction.

"Here, let me." Marcellus reaches a hand to my arm, gently wrapping his fingers around my bicep. A warm feeling spreads through where the contact is being made, and I feel a lightness bloom in my mind. He lets go, smiling at me as I rub over the place where his fingers had been.

"What was that?" I ask in wonder.

"I can heal small things and soothe emotions. Not anything major, but relieving stress is my specialty." He winks at me and his reputation at the club with women suddenly makes so much sense. "You are a Seraphel, I have no idea how I missed it before."

We both look up when Cas rounds the corner with Audra and Brennan in tow.

"I filled them in as much as I could. Now go so you can hurry up and get back! I'll tell Layla where you are if she wakes before you return," Cas yells as we all make it toward the portal.

We hit the door running, making our way to the safe house.

"Hurry, Marcellus, does the club still have party buses?"

"Yeah, and as far as I know, one is free tonight."

"Perfect, here's the keys to the SUV in the garage. Go start it, I'll be there in a minute." I grab the keys from a hook and throw them across the room as I run and grab a gun and cell phone I use when in the human world, out of my safe. Most of the idiots my father had working for him were from Aetheria but not immortal. I abhor guns but find them necessary from time to time.

Once the gun is secure, I meet the rest of the crew in the garage.

Marcellus is in the driver's seat, and as much as I hate it, to save time I'll let him drive us to the club.

"Drive fast, Marcellus, I'll shield the car so we won't get pulled over." Audra is unusually quiet in the backseat with Brennan. I use the ride to fill them in on what we are doing, mainly to help keep my mind busy.

"Marcellus will drive over in the party bus; it should hold everyone from the clinic. We will get everyone loaded and back to the safe house to portal over."

I dig out the phone and call the clinic. Mila picks up on the second ring. "Damian! It's so good to hear from you, it's been a while!"

"Listen to me, Mila, I don't have time to explain. I need you to get everyone in the clinic packed up and ready to leave for Aetheria. You have about twenty minutes. We are on a time limit, so twenty minutes is about all I can give you." I hope she can hear the urgency in my voice.

"On it, you can explain later, I'll have everyone ready to go." She hangs up, and I feel a massive amount of relief.

Twenty-two minutes. That's how long it takes us to get there. Twenty-two minutes where every single horrible possible scenario played on a loop through my mind. As soon as the vehicles are in park, we all fly out and into the clinic. I throw up a shield around myself and Brennan.

"Audra, can you shield yourself?" I ask her.

"Yeah, Layla taught me."

"Good, shield now. Marcellus, you too."

Mila comes running through the lobby with the girls in tow. Ryanne's eyes meet mine, and I see relief replace the panic.

I start barking orders, "Brennan, put Ryanne in the SUV with us, start loading the others on the bus. Mila, how many are left?"

"We only have three residents at the moment and four workers.

I've called everyone else and told them to stay away. One worker, Tenley, wants to go with us. She's quite attached to the two-year-old we still haven't placed, Ryker. But the other two want to go home, I'm assuming that won't be a problem?"

"I'd rather them come with us so we can keep them safe, but I won't force them. And you?" I raise a brow at her.

"I'm coming with you."

"Good, now let's go."

After dropping the workers off, we make it back to the safe house and get everyone through the portal safely, with nearly an hour to spare.

"Audra, can I trust you to get Tenley settled into one of the suites in the nursery with Ryker and the little girl? Then put Ryanne in the room next to you and Mila across the hall? I'll come check on you all after the wedding."

"I got you." She smiles as she herds them toward the stairs to lead them to their rooms.

"Let's go get ready for a wedding, boys." I run up the steps to grab a quick shower and get dressed. I'm expected to look like a king tonight, which is bullshit. As king, shouldn't I be able to wear what the fuck I want? I pull out a suit my mother had custom-made that is similar to Layla's midnight leathers with power-enhancing runes sewn in. I'm ready in record time, looking way more put together than I feel.

I make my way down the hall and stop to knock on Layla's door. It's thrown open with a force that startles me, Layla fastening on an earring as she looks at me with relief. I look past her and see Anika sliding on a pair of sinfully high heels, adding several inches to her already tall frame. My pants get a little tight thinking about what she would look like in just those shoes and a pair of panties.

"Thank the gods it's you," Layla mumbles.

"As opposed to...?"

"Cas."

"You need to elaborate. Are you avoiding Caspian?" Her words from earlier, when she made me promise to keep away, have me worried something bigger is at play here. I walk past her and shut the door as she turns away, muttering under her breath. I look at Anika, raising a brow. She shrugs her shoulders and shakes her head. Hmm. Whatever is eating at Layla hasn't been disclosed to her either.

"How are you feeling, cousin?" I move to stand in front of her, grabbing her chin and titling it up so she has to look me in the eyes. I see wariness there and I reach for her mind. She's locked down tight. Good.

"I'm better. Still don't feel like I am one hundred percent, but I'm okay," she says reassuringly, wrapping her fingers around my wrist and moving my hand from her face. "I do have a favor to ask."

"Name it." She knows I will give her anything she asks for.

"When everything from the wedding is settled, can you take me home for a few days?"

I look down and my midsection, thinking surely there is a knife sticking out of my stomach. The hot flare of pain is searing. I never knew a simple sentence could gut me the way hers does.

"Home? Layla, this is home." I can't hide the tinge of hysteria coating my words. How does she not see this as home? Does she plan on leaving?

Her cheeks flush as she quickly corrects her statement, "You know what I mean. I want to go back to Earth, just for a few days. I...I need some space. I need to be able to think."

"Do you want me to just take you or stay with you?" I'm terrified to leave her alone there, afraid she won't come back.

"No, if you don't mind, I want you to go with me. I need your help. Anika, do you mind if I steal him for a few days?"

"Not at all! Is there anything I can do?" Anika asks, she's obviously worried for her friend.

"You can stay here and help keep the boys and Audra in line."

"You got it," she says as she walks over and hugs Layla.

Both women are dressed in a shade of ocean blue. Layla, as maid of honor is a slightly different dress than Anika, but they both look lovely. Anika grabs her things and as she strides over to the door, I notice the slit in her leg that goes to almost the top of her thigh. My breath catches as my eyes roam over her body, the dress hugging every luscious curve. One shoulder is left bare, and I wonder exactly what she's wearing under it.

I grab her hand and drag her across the hall to her room, throwing the door open and grabbing her in my arms as I kick it closed again. I press her up against it as she gasps.

"Damian, don't you *dare* mess up my hair or makeup!" she warns, swatting at my shoulders.

I reach through the slit and hook my fingers around the scrap of lace that are her panties and yank hard, ripping the fabric. She yelps, then groans as I slide a finger into her.

"We don't have time for this," she moans as her hips rock into my hand.

"Then you better come fast," I whisper as I bury my head in her neck, kissing her skin, reveling in the smell of her. I slide in another finger and use my thumb to put pressure on her clit. A few moments later, I hear Layla's door open, and I double my efforts. I'm rewarded with Anika's cries in my ear as she clenches around my fingers, her body shuddering as she finds her release.

I pull my hand away, bring it to my mouth, and start to lick it clean. Anika grabs my hand, looking me in the eyes as she wraps her lips around the fingers that she just came all over and sucks them like she's sucking my cock.

"Fuck, woman. You're killing me here."

"I'll make it up to you later," she purrs as she moves away from me and opens the door, slipping out before I can grab her.

I take a deep breath and follow her into the hall, Layla leaning against the wall, a grin spread across her face, eyes alight with mischief.

"Damian, I'm going to start calling you the minute man. That was the quickest quickie in the history of quickies," she teases.

Anika's laughter fills the hall as we start to walk. "It wasn't a quickie." Anika's face turns several shades of pink as she defends me.

"Oh damn, look at you being a martyr. At least your balls will match the wedding decorations," she cackles. I shove her, and she nearly topples over on the spiky heels she's wearing. I grab her arm and pull her into me.

"You're lucky Mother would probably kill me if I messed up your hair, you little brat or I'd put you in a headlock right about now."

I check on Mila and the others, making quick introductions before we head downstairs. Everyone seems to be settling in well, but I hate that I have to rush off so quickly.

Guests are beginning to arrive, and my palms start sweating, thinking about the role I have in the wedding. As ruler of this realm, I will be officiating. Thankfully, Aegir and Nerine have opted to write their own vows, so my lines are limited.

As we approach the hall leading to the exterior, a door suddenly swings open ahead on the right, startling us. The sounds of giggling vibrate through the walls as my mother steps through the door, looking devilishly rumpled. I stop dead in my tracks, as do Anika and Layla, as Thor walks out behind her, grabbing her around the waist and pulling her in for a kiss. A primal roar leaves me as I lunge for Thor, tackling him like a linebacker.

"Damian!" Layla and Mother yell at the same time. I feel hands pulling at me, but I pummel my first into Thor's face before I'm thrown across the room, landing in a heap against the wall. I launch myself at him again, but this time, Layla pins me with shadows, leaving me unable to move.

"I will kill you for touching her, you piece of shit!" I scream as I fight against the bindings.

Mother comes over to me and looks into my eyes, "Damian, I am a grown woman capable of making choices for myself, I love you for wanting to protect me—I do, but can you please refrain from acting like a barbarian? If you are upset, we can talk this out, but this is my choice. I have given myself freely. I am a woman who has spent too long being afraid to live. I need you to trust me, can you do that?"

"But Mother, one of his powers is seduction. How can you say you give yourself freely? He literally hit on Layla days ago."

"I am aware of his powers, and he had no need to use them, I promise. We have a wedding to get to. Can you please not punch my wedding date again?"

I glare at Thor. "Damian, I would not disrespect your mother, I have known her for a very long time, and I care for her."

"Let me go, Layla," I growl. My mother walks away from me, and Layla moves into my line of sight.

"If I let you go and you act a fool, I will pin you somewhere incredibly uncomfortable for the rest of the night, and those balls will stay blue, won't they, Anika?"

"Yes, they will," she says with deadly calm, arms folded across her chest as she glares at Damian.

"Don't tell me you are on *his* side?" I say to Anika, hurt that she doesn't understand why I am so upset.

"I am on your mother's side. As a woman myself, I would be pissed if someone beat the shit out of you because they thought I wasn't capable of knowing my own mind," she tells me with a hint of defiance in her voice.

Well damn, if that thought doesn't settle me right the fuck down. "Fine, let me go. I will behave."

Mother nods at Layla and she releases me. Anika walks over, pressing a quick kiss to my mouth as she straightens my clothes. "I know this is hard for you," she whispers, "but think about how long it's probably been since she has found joy in the arms of a man. Let her have this, let her feel alive and like a woman."

I soften a little and hug Anika to me before moving toward my mother and Thor.

"I'm sorry, Mother," I say as I pull her to my chest, kissing the top of her head. "I truly just want you to be happy, I just worry about you."

"I know, love, I know."

I release her, turning to Thor. I hold out a hand and he shakes it.

"Well, at least you weren't balls deep in someone else's woman, just someone's mother," I grumble. "You hurt her, I will let Layla kill you." I put every ounce of menace behind those words as I possibly can.

An icy look passes over Layla's face, it's a look I recognize—I've seen it on her father's face more than once. It's a look of warning, one that lets me know there's a storm brewing beneath her seemingly calm exterior.

Walking up behind us, she looks him dead in the eye and says, "Look dude, I like you, I really do, but I *love* her. For you, I'd knock a fucker out if I needed to. For her? I will end you and not break a sweat. Got it?"

"Ah, yes, message received. Crystal clear."

Mother, with tears in her eyes, pulls Layla into a tight hug, "I love you too, Layla. I may not have carried you, but you are mine. You are everything I could have ever wanted in a daughter."

They pull away and wipe at their eyes, everyone laughing as we finally make our way outside. Layla grabs my arm as we walk, stopping me in my tracks.

"Thank you for finding me, Damian. For giving me a family. You have no idea how much it means to me, how much you all mean to me."

I nod, squeezing her hand, throat too tight with emotion to form words. We begin walking again, and like I have a million times before, I think about how thankful I am.

Chapter Thirty-One

LAYLA

Everything is perfect. Damian has Audra controlling a breeze that blows lightly through tents on this hot July night, keeping everyone comfortable as they are seated, waiting for the ceremony to begin. The light of day is fading, but the area is covered in thousands of twinkling fairy lights, making this already magical realm look even more fantastical. In a matter of moments, I will be fetching the bride and butterflies are having a party in my stomach as I send up prayers to whoever will listen that tonight goes beautifully.

Grandmother winks at me from across the yard, trapped in conversation with a man I don't know but who looks like a pompous ass. She looks gorgeous in a sparkling navy gown that reminds me of twilight.

Hands wrap around my waist as Cas whispers in my ear, "You look beautiful tonight, I've missed you." He nuzzles my neck and I sigh. I still feel uneasy about the conversation that we need to have, but at this moment, I just want to enjoy the feeling of happiness that permeates the air and not ruin it with the intrusive thoughts that have been occupying my mind lately.

"I've missed you too," I say. It's true—I do miss him, but I need him to trust me and talk to me. "How's Aegir?" It's kinda weird thinking that the woman marrying Cas's brother was supposed to marry him.

"He's so excited he's bouncing off the walls," he chuckles, his breath tickling the skin at my neck. "Last time I checked on him he —" I feel him freeze; his breath catches as his eyes are locked on a woman across the way.

"Cas?" I question, turning to look at him.

"My mother is here." He grabs my hand and takes off sprinting, letting me go once we are close enough to her that he can swoop her into his arms, twirling her around in a circle.

"You're here!" Laughing, he sits her down and looks at her. "Aegir will be so happy! *I'm* so happy! I've missed you!"

Her face is alight with joy as she laughs at his genuine enthusiasm. "I have missed you too, son! Where are your brothers?" Her voice is beautiful. There's a melodic lilt to her words that makes me want to close my eyes and just listen. It's like hearing a favorite song for the first time—one you know will stay with you.

"The boys are around, I'll find them shortly, but first, there is someone I have been dying to introduce you to for years now. Mother, this is Layla. Layla, this is my mother, Nerissa."

"Ahhh, I have heard so much about you! It's nice to finally put a face to the name!" She moves in to hug me, enveloping me in a strong embrace. This is a woman who is utterly confident in herself, and it shows in the way she moves. I thought the boys looked like their father, but they look so much like her. The blue of their eyes, the dimples, even her beautiful golden skin and blonde hair. This family seriously hit the genetic lottery.

"Hi, it's nice to meet you too. We had no idea you would be

here." I am thrilled she is here, but I can't help but worry that her presence will bring trouble.

"Like I wouldn't be here for my son's wedding! I don't care what that grumpy old bear says, I would have liked to see him try and stop me! Caspian can tell you, his father doesn't cross me often. He may think he wears the pants in this family, but I have many ways beyond brute force to get my point across. How else do you think I survived raising those boys of mine?"

I think about how much of a handful they all are now as adults. I bet she is tough as nails to have survived their shenanigans.

Damian walks up with a smile and greets Nerissa before telling me it's time to get started. I excuse myself to fetch Nerine. I open my mind up as I head into the castle and reach for Damian.

"*Are you surprised she's here?*" I ask.

"*Not at all. She comes off as a perfectly poised member of royalty, but under that, I hear she is as feral as you. Now shield yourself like you're supposed to,*" he replies.

"*Yes sir!*" I state and close myself off once again.

Nerine is waiting in a makeshift dressing room on the first floor. I walk in and am taken aback at how beautiful she is. Her hair is swept up elegantly for the wedding, the pale gold tresses so light they're almost white, shimmering like strands of fine silk illuminated by the sun. Each lock is pinned neatly, yet a few loose tendrils escape, tenderly framing her delicate face. They catch the light with a brilliance that borders on ethereal, giving her an otherworldly appearance as if her locks were spun from sunlight.

Her beautifully bronzed skin from living a life on sun-drenched islands sets off the white of her dress and brings out the vividness of her pale green eyes. She is so perfect she looks like she can't possibly be real, but maybe a sprite or woodland pixie, ready to create mischief.

A memory of this perfectly regal princess gyrating on a stripper pole like a seasoned stripper pops into my mind, making me smile as I catch her eye. Her lips twitch, fighting a grin like she knows the turn my thoughts have taken. Aegir is going to have his hands full with this little minx.

"Wow, just wow. I don't even have words to tell you how ridiculously beautiful you look right now. That boy isn't going to know what to do with himself when he sees you walking down that aisle. That dress is fire!"

She's chosen a simple dress, but it is a breathtaking sight to behold. The sweetheart neckline gracefully highlights her feminine curves, drawing the eye to her breasts that are all but spilling over the top. The gown cinches at her slender waist, accentuating her hourglass figure. Each seam seems to caress her form, hugging every contour in a mesmerizing embrace. Adorning her waist is a belt encrusted with glittering jewels, adding a touch of decadence to the otherwise simple gown. As she moves, the fabric sways, casting a radiant glow around her, making her appear as if she's stepped out of a dream.

My eyes are drawn to a woman standing in the corner of the room that I hadn't noticed before, too caught up in Nerine.

"Layla, this is my mother, Mariselle."

"Nice to meet you, Layla. Nerine has told me wonderful things about you. Thank you for welcoming her and treating her like family."

"Layla is engaged to Caspian," Nerine says, a smile playing on her lips.

"I see, I am happy for you, and thankful. I would rather my daughter be married for love than business." She winks at me, and I relax. She places a delicate crown upon her daughter's head before stepping back to admire her with a smile on her face.

"Perfect," she says as she claps her hands together and Nerine beams. "I think we are ready, let's get you married!"

With moments to spare, we hustle to our designated places, the anticipation buzzing in the air like electricity. The music begins and I'm given my cue to start. I link arms with Cas, feeling oddly nervous. I've never been to a wedding, much less in one. Anika and Nereus fall into step behind us, their expressions a mix of excitement and nerves, while Audra and Delphin follow suit, their movements fluid and practiced.

"I can't wait until you are walking down an aisle to me," Cas whispers as he squeezes my arm. I smile, but my stomach churns. As we reach our positions at the front of the aisle, I steal a glance around the room, taking in the sea of faces turned toward us. Joy and love fill the space, chasing away my nerves, making it impossible to feel anything but happy.

My eyes are drawn to a beaming Aegir, nervous energy pouring off him as he waits for his bride. His excitement is infectious, and it makes me wonder how in the hell Triton could even think about robbing them of this kind of love.

Then, with a hush falling over the room, Nerine makes her grand entrance, looking radiant. Beside her walks her mother, a smile gracing her lips despite the absence of Nerine's father. It's a bittersweet moment, tempered by the love and support that surrounds her.

Finally, the crowd stands as Nerine makes her way to Aegir. She is absolutely glowing, her smile stretched across her face, her eyes bright and shining with happy tears. I turn to see Aegir, and the look of awe as he watches her is a wondrously beautiful thing. It makes my heart hurt in the best way, and I feel the prick of tears form in my eyes as I desperately try to hold them back for fear of ruining the masterpiece Anika created with my makeup. I've never witnessed a moment like this, where so much love is openly on display, and I wish I could bottle it to revisit when my soul feels heavy with grief.

I'm lost in my own thoughts when suddenly Damian's commanding voice brings me back into the moment as he begins the ceremony.

"We come together to celebrate love and to unite these two souls in eternal companionship. May the bonds forged today be as enduring as the mountains and as deep as the roots of the earth. Just as light cannot exist without shadow, let your lives be intertwined in harmony and balance. In the presence of the elements that govern our lands and the ancestors who watch over us, I ask you both to pledge not just your love but your truest selves to one another."

Nerine and Aegir recite simple vows to each other that are sweet and heartfelt. After getting to know her wild side, I almost expected something a little friskier out of her, but she kept it very princess-like. Before I realize it, Damian is wrapping things up, and it's almost over.

"Let the magic that flows through Aetheria bless this union so that your hearts may always find light even in the deepest shadows. By the power vested in me by the ancient laws of Aetheria and the throne of Shadowfell, I pronounce you bound in the sacred trust of marriage. May your unity be a beacon that guides you through all realms and all times. Aegir, you may now kiss your bride!" Damian says the last line with enthusiasm and Aegir doesn't disappoint, sweeping Nerine up into a searing, swoon-worthy kiss as the crowd goes wild, cheering as the couple finally breaks apart.

The hours pass and guests finally start to leave. Delphin and Brennan have been valiantly spinning ladies around the dance floor, one after another, but even they have disappeared. Nerine wanted to honeymoon in the mortal realm, claiming she could see this world anytime she wanted, so Damian just left with them to portal to Fiji.

Anika and I grab some drinks and head over to a table to sit and keep an eye on things as they wrap up, but overall, the night has, thankfully, been perfect.

"May I join you ladies?" Grandmother asks, settling herself into a seat next to me.

"Of course. Did you enjoy yourself? I didn't see you much."

"I did, everything was beautiful." She pauses a moment, her lips pressed into a tight line. "Layla, Damian told me you asked him to take you to Earth for a few days. Do you think that's wise with your father running amok there?"

"Damian will be with me, and most of the time, we'll be in the safe house. I just really need some time to think. I need some closure with Rio's death, too. It's time to start packing his house up. Thor said I need to conquer my fear or some crap to be able to control my power. To do that, I need to sort some things out in my head. What happened earlier is a perfect example of me not being able to keep control, and Thor won't even continue our lessons until I get my shit together."

"If you need anything, even if it's just an ear, you can have Damian send for me, or he can bring you to me. I would like to show you around my kingdom. Hopefully, it will be yours someday." She stands to leave, and I rise to hug her and thank her again for everything as we say our goodbyes.

Sitting with Anika once again, we are quiet for a few minutes before she asks, "What's up with you and Cas?"

I lean my head back, looking up at the stars, and groan. "I feel like it sounds stupid."

"Layla, I have been with you and Cas since before there was a you and Cas, so just spit it out."

"Ugh, *fine*. When I saw what he could do with shielding this place, it just kinda hit me that he still doesn't tell me shit like I think he should. Between him and Rio, they kept me in the dark for years. Damian is the one who told me who my father is, who my grandmother is. He is the one who really helped me test my powers and push their limits. I get why they did it to a point, but Cas and I

291

are engaged. We are supposed to be equal partners. Best friends, lovers, I want it all, and right now, it feels like you and Damian are my best friends, and I'm just fucking Cas."

She frowns but nods her head. "I get that, he does seem to keep you out of the loop more than he should. He can't use the whole 'I want to protect you' BS because how is that protecting you? If anything, it leaves you unprepared. Have you talked to him about this?"

"No, I'm going to. I just want to get my head on straight first, which is why I want to leave with Damian ASAP, so I don't explode on him and make things a billion times worse."

"I'm going with you." V barges into my thoughts, slamming through my barriers like they don't exist.

"Um, no ma'am, you will give the humans a heart attack," I argue back.

"I will stay inside. I am going with you. It's not a request." And with that parting comment, I feel her block me out, effectively ending that discussion.

"Damian's back," Anika says, a slow smile spreading across her lips as he strides toward us, eyes glued to Anika, sliding down her crossed legs, the slit completely exposing the bare skin all the way up to damn near her ass cheek.

"Anika Williams! You trashy little whore! Are you wearing underwear?" She's one of the only people in this realm who has a last name. That's because she was raised in the human world, like me. Apparently, her parents went with the most generic one they could find in an effort to blend in. Here everyone goes by their first name, then who their daddy is. Like Cas is Caspian, Triton's son or son of Triton. I'm not sure I'll ever get used to it.

She looks at me conspiratorially and whispers, "I was until he ripped them off of me in my room earlier." Her cheeks heat and I wink at her.

"That's my cue to skedaddle. I'll let you two get your freak on while I go talk to Cas. Damian, come get me when you are ready to leave."

He doesn't bother responding. Instead, he hauls Anika up into a bone-melting kiss, and for a moment, I consider finding Cas, throwing him on my bed and riding him like a cowgirl.

I open my mind and search for him. *"Hey, where are you?"*

"Helping clean up a bit, what's up?"

"Meet me in our room?"

"Be there in five, leave the dress on."

I close myself back off and think about my options here. We really need to talk, but it wouldn't hurt to soften him up a little with a quickie. *Ugh, no. Bad girl! You are mad at him.* Yeah, I am, but I've always been able to separate sex and emotion. Sex is a great way to give myself a momentary reprieve from the constant runaway train of my thoughts.

I reach my door, and the minute I open it, Cas is there, hauling me against the hard lines of his chest as he threads his hands through my hair, claiming my mouth in a savage kiss. It's desperate, needy, and hot as fuck. I let myself be lost in the moment, sinking into the kiss as his mouth dominates me and my brain shuts down. The only thing existing is the feeling of desire currently running rampant through me.

He's ditched his jacket, and I am desperately trying to get a hand in between us to undo his buttons. I need the feel of his skin under my fingers.

"Shirt. Off. Now," I say against his mouth. Without breaking the kiss he moves back a little and rips the shirt, shoving the sleeves off of his arms as my hands caress his massive shoulders, feeling his muscles bunch under my fingers with every little move he makes.

He nudges my legs apart, planting a thigh in between them as he pulls the fabric of my gown up until he finds what he's looking for.

"Fuck, Layla, have you been bare under here all night?" He slips a finger inside of me and smiles against my lips.

"I didn't want to risk a panty line with as thin as this fabric is. Cas, I don't want to play around, I'm already soaked. I just want to fuck you. You can either get with the program, or I can pin your ass and take what I want." I bite his earlobe and he shudders.

"I think you should pin me. Take what you need. Use me to get yourself off," he whispers as he shifts to give me better access to kiss along his neck.

I pull back from him, my eyes narrow and I smirk, throwing him onto the couch and pinning him in a sitting position. He licks his lips in anticipation, straining at the bonds as he arches his hips, ready and waiting to be fucked.

I stand in front of him, bending at the waist to undo his pants, freeing his beautiful cock. I can't resist wrapping my lips around the head and sucking appreciatively for a moment, moaning at his sharp intake of breath.

I release it with a pop of my lips and smile at him as I lift my dress to straddle his hips. Using my hand to slide his cock from my entrance to my clit, I drive myself closer to the edge of my sanity. He arches up into me, and I take the hint, sliding myself down onto him, relishing at the feel, closing my eyes to savor it for just a moment before I start riding him.

I wrap my hands around his neck to give myself something to hold on to as I start fucking him in earnest, the sound of our grunts and slapping skin filling the room as Cas whispers naughty things in my ear.

"Pull your dress down, let me see your tits."

I oblige, yanking it down and pulling my boobs out of the strapless bra so he can watch them bounce as I ride his dick. I grab one in my hand and raise it up to his eager mouth as he pulls the nipple with a gentle tug, pushing me closer to coming unglued.

I drop the bonds and beg, "Touch me, Cas, rub my clit." He slides one hand between us and starts rubbing tight circles where I need him most while his other hand digs into my hip as he meets me thrust for thrust, his breaths coming faster.

"I can't hold on much longer, Layla. You feel too fucking good, I'm going to come." Sweat blooms on his skin, and I can see the strain on his face as he tries to hold back. He lets go of my hip and takes a nipple into his mouth again, giving it a little tug with his teeth. That does it. My body detonates as I dig my nails into his shoulders and scream out his name, convulsing around him as he comes with me. He groans and bites my neck, slowing his pace, leisurely rolling his hips as he helps me ride out the last waves of my orgasm.

I drop my head to his shoulder and he wraps his arms around my back as we lay there, recovering. He kisses my head and lazily runs a finger down my spine and I sigh, so utterly content in this moment.

"You've seemed a little off today, everything okay?" he asks and immediately all the uncertainty, anger, and general unease I have been feeling slams back into me, ruining the moment.

Fuck.

I pull back a little and look at him. "I'm going to Earth for a few days with Damian, I want to start closing up Rio's house and check on a few things." I feel a pang of guilt because now I'm doing the exact thing I'm pissed at him for, not being one hundred percent honest. But how am I supposed to tell him I need a few days to sort out my feelings about him hiding shit before confronting him so I can be levelheaded during it without having that conversation right now? So, half-truths for the win.

"I'll go with you," he says, confusion in his eyes as he tries to puzzle out why I didn't ask him in the first place.

"No, we need you to stay here in case something happens. You need to keep the boys in line and help get the newcomers settled. We will only be a few days, promise. I need to do this on my own, Cas."

"But you're not, Damian is going with you."

"Yeah, that's because I can't go alone with my father out there, Grandmother would have my ass." I move off him and start packing a bag before stepping into the shower. I half expected him to follow me, but he doesn't, and when I come out, he's gone.

Chapter Thirty-Two

DAMIAN

Layla sits on the couch, lost in her thoughts, as I move through the safe house, checking what supplies we might need. It feels a little weird to be here. It's even weirder to have V's massive body lying on the living room floor, but the damn wolf is as hardheaded as her person. We've been in and out a few times, but I haven't actually spent real time here in months. I strip the sheets and throw them in the wash before replacing them with fresh ones, thinking about a certain redhead that was in my bed at home not an hour ago.

I hear movement coming from the kitchen and I see Layla in there wiping things down. She's been rather quiet, which is worrisome. Normally, I don't have to wonder about what she is thinking, she says everything that pops into her head, but since we've been here, she has barely spoken, a haunted look in her eyes.

"It's crazy how much dust accumulates in a few months," she mutters.

"I know. We'll get some basics done and then get some sleep, or would you rather watch movies? There's some popcorn in one of the cabinets and some Pepsi in the fridge."

"Why don't we have television in Aetheria? It's weird. I didn't realize how much I missed movie nights until just now."

"I'm not sure? Maybe because we have dragons and magic? We have a theater where we can see plays and listen to live music. I'm sure we could arrange to have television if you'd like."

"No, when we were there, I didn't even really notice it. Plus, it gives me an excuse to come here from time to time. I'll go pick a movie. Do you want something funny, bloody, or romantic?"

"Let's do funny. Have you seen *Stepbrothers*? I heard the boys talking about it, it sounds hilarious."

"Perfect, then we are following it with *Bridesmaids*."

I busy myself with the popcorn, wondering how long I am going to give her before I drag her down the basement and spar with her until she gets out the feelings that seem to be weighing her down.

The timer for the microwave dings as I hear the opening credits coming from the living room. Dumping the popcorn into a bowl, I grab some drinks and join her on the couch. She's curled up in the corner closest to the television, and I take up residence in my favorite spot at the opposite end of the couch, stretching my legs out to rest on the table in front of me.

"If you want popcorn, get your ass over here. I know better than to hand you the bowl, you're a greedy pig," I tease her as she scoots closer, tucking herself into my side as she snatches a handful of popcorn.

"I'm not a pig, I just really like popcorn." She sounds indignant, but she pokes me in the side as she says it, a smile on her lips.

I kiss the top of her head. "Don't poke my ribs, you little brat, you know I hate that."

"Duh, why do you think I did it?" she snickers, and some of the tightness in my chest loosens. I hope she doesn't want to come back here to stay, and if she does, I have no idea what I will do about it because I can't imagine not having her around, and I won't abandon my kingdom now that I've taken the throne.

"Layla, you aren't thinking about coming back here forever, are you?" There's no point in worrying about it when I can talk to her.

Vengeance growls at my question.

Layla stiffens and moves over enough to turn and face me. I try to keep my face neutral, but she can read me better than most. The two of us are bonded in a way that goes deeper than anything I've ever known. It's different from her bond with Cas or mine with Anika. It's the bond of family who have survived living in the depths of hell, being tormented and tortured by those meant to protect us. We are such similar creatures, both desperate for family, for the love we were denied. There is a familiarity between us that feels like she is a part of the very fiber of my being. I don't always understand it, but I don't need to, it's comfortable for us both.

She pauses the movie and sits in silence for a moment.

"I won't lie, Damian. The thought has crossed my mind, but I love my life there and know I can come here when I want. Your mom has been more of a mother to me than mine ever was, and I want to be in her life. I know you can't leave Shadowfell for long, and I would miss your annoying ass too much. It's so weird, but you feel more like a brother than a cousin. I feel closer to you than I do Brennan, I just worry he might want to come back, and then I have no idea what I'll do. I feel like I'd have to choose between the two of you."

The wolf growls again.

"Plus, I wouldn't think of leaving V." She looks at the wolf affectionately, and V settles.

She pauses. I give her time to collect her thoughts, staying quiet, thankful she wants to stay.

"Nyx wants me to be her heir, and that terrifies me. I can't even control my powers. Cas wants to marry me, and I have no idea what that will mean if his father does decide to make him his heir after all. Would that mean we would have to live in his kingdom? I want to stay in Shadowfell, I don't want to rule anywhere. I just want to be in the castle with the crazy family we've made there. I even want all the boys to stay, and Audra. There are too many 'what ifs,' and so much has changed in such a short amount of time, I'm spiraling."

I sigh, pulling her back into me. "That is a lot of things to think about—I can understand why you feel like you need space. I have no idea what I would do if you decided to leave, though."

"Enough talking for tonight, I need to laugh, back to the movie."

She's asleep in twenty minutes, curled into my side. I'm not about to move her, she looks so peaceful, I carefully shift myself so I can be comfortable, grabbing a blanket off the back of the couch to throw over her as I settle in to get some much-needed rest myself.

Screams shatter the silence, echoing through the darkness like a chilling refrain. Panic grips me as I search for their source, my heart racing with dread. It doesn't take long to realize that the screams are coming from Layla. Terror courses through me, twisting my gut as I navigate the world that seems to be burning around me.

Flames leap from either side as everything distorts. I struggle to make sense of what the hell is going on, the cacophony of screams growing louder and more anguished with each passing moment. It feels like I'm drowning in the chaos, unable to find solid ground amidst the swirling confusion.

With a sudden jolt, I snap awake, my heart pounding against my chest. Layla's screams pierce the silence. My hands tremble as I gently shake her awake. My voice is a desperate plea as I try to pull her from the grips of her nightmare.

"Damian, *no!*" The terror in her voice sends chills down my spine as her keening wail fills the space. "No! Let go of me! *Let go!*"

Vengeance is next to us, whining and nudging at Layla with her nose.

"Vengeance, can you not pull her out?" The wolf looks at me and I wish like hell that Chaos was here.

"I'll take that as a no. Layla, it's me, it's Damian, you're safe," I say over and over again, hoping to get through to her. Finally, her eyes shoot open, and I can see the moment the haze of the dream clears from her mind.

"Damian," she sobs, throwing her arms around my neck, hysterically crying as I wrap my arms around her. "He took you. He took you and I couldn't stop him." Her body violently shakes against me, and I pull her into my lap, rocking her like a child as she clings to me like I might disappear.

"It was just a dream, sweetheart. You're fine. I'm here, I'm okay." We stay like this for what feels like hours before she finally quiets, little hiccups escaping from her every now and again, making me smile. She seems so small, curled against me like this, fragile and childlike. It's a strange juxtaposition compared to the fearless warrior I normally see her as.

Her breathing steadies and I realize she has fallen back to sleep. I carry her into the main bedroom, settling her in, then turning to leave the room.

"Don't leave me," she begs, her voice soft and full of uncertainty.

"If you want me to stay, I will."

She builds a wall of pillows between us and settles in, reaching her hand across, searching for mine. I let her take it, and we lay like this, holding hands as she falls asleep once more.

THE SOUND OF WATER RUNNING WAKES ME AS I SLOWLY remember where I am. I look to my left and see that Layla is already out of bed, I'm guessing she's in the shower. Heading to the kitchen, I see what I can scramble up for breakfast.

Nothing. Looks like we will be making a run to the store. I open the back door to let Vengeance out to do her business.

"V, you should be able to feel where the wards end. Do not leave the safety of that area, humans will flip the fuck out if they see you." She makes her way outside on silent feet as I head to the guest room to get dressed.

When I emerge, Layla is in the kitchen, letting V back in. She looks tired but ready to tackle the day.

"There's not really much to eat here, you want to head to the store, or should we eat out?" I ask.

"Both?" she asks hopefully.

"Done." I smirk.

We spend the morning eating and shopping, chatting about everything and nothing. Watching her carefully, I try to anticipate her needs, but she seems content. We both relax in the easy camaraderie we share when together. As we pull back into the house, it's lunchtime, I fix us some food as she puts away the things we bought, tossing a large steak to Vengeance, which she catches in midair.

"Do you talk to Anika about important things?" she inquires, the question taking me off guard.

Do I? I'd like to think so, but if I'm honest, sometimes things happen so fast I just act. "I try to, but sometimes I must make choices before I have a chance to speak to her. If you're asking because of Cas, let me just say that my relationship with Anika is still new. You and Cas have known each other for years. Anika and I are still in the 'getting to know you' phase, and while I know I love her, I'm smart enough to understand we still have a foundation to build."

"Wait? You're in love with her? Does she know this? Dude! That's awesome!"

"She is aware." I let my smirk speak volumes.

She lets out a most unladylike squeal and launches herself at me, hugging me tight.

"If there is anyone in this world that is good enough for my best friend, it's you. But I'll still kick your ass if you hurt her," she threatens, thrusting a finger into my chest, but her face is all smiles.

"What if she hurts me?" I feign mock horror, placing a hand over my heart.

"Then you probably deserved it," she says sweetly, booping me on my damn nose, flashing her teeth before walking away with a skip in her step.

"Get back here, we aren't done talking about this," I growl, I want her to work out these insecurities she's feeling before they consume her. One thing I know about her is that she needs to talk things out. She gets in her head too damn much to let anything sit and fester. It will eat her alive.

She whirls around, "Let's do this in the living room, bring the alcohol."

I follow her onto the couch, handing her a glass of bourbon. She swirls the amber liquid, staring at it like it holds the secrets to life in its depths.

"Talk," I demand.

Her hand stops moving, and she lifts her gaze to meet mine, anger swirling in those deep brown pools that look exactly like my own eyes. She's pissed, which is what I wanted. Better than the uncertainty that's been swimming there lately.

"He hides shit from me, and I need to talk to him about it, but I'm not sure how to do it without it being a major fight because when I think about it, I feel hurt and pissed. I don't know how to do this whole relationship thing. We've always just fought things out and I don't want to do that anymore with him. I want him to trust me enough to tell me shit. I shouldn't have to find out randomly when something comes up. I definitely don't like it when other people know, and I'm left in the dark like I'm not important enough for him to talk to about it."

"Is this about him being able to shield the palace?"

"Yes. I had no idea he could do that or that it came so easily to him, just like I had no idea he could wield fire. It didn't occur to me until later to be mad about that one. His brothers didn't seem surprised, not even a little. I don't want to marry him if he can't treat me like an equal. I should be the first fucking person he tells shit to, not the person that has to find out by other means. I know I have zero experience with relationships, and I wouldn't know a healthy one if it bit me in the ass, but I do know I don't like the way this makes me feel, and I am not going to just be okay with it because something somewhere decided we are 'fated' to be together. That's bullshit." Her hands are waving all over the place as she talks, her face getting red the angrier she gets.

Thunder crashes overhead and she winces, her face going from angry to embarrassed in two seconds flat. I throw back my drink and pour myself another.

"Layla, you have to do what you think is best for you, fate be damned," I take another drink. "You need to talk to him, yes. Lay out all your fears and concerns. I'm exceptionally proud of you for being self-aware enough to know you needed space and time to think before having that conversation with him. It shows you care about your relationship and want to get it right. But honestly? What do I know? I'm in the same fucked up boat as you and have no idea what relationships are supposed to look like."

She starts giggling and can't seem to stop, tears streaming down her face as she clutches her sides. "What the hell is so damn funny?" I ask her.

"We are so fucked up," she says between breaths.

"That we are, cousin, that we are," I agree as I throw back the rest of my drink and laugh at the absurdity of the two of us trying to navigate love when neither of us was ever shown what it's supposed to look like.

Chapter Thirty-Three

LAYLA

On our third day in the safe house I am ready to tackle Rio's. Damian and I have watched all kinds of movies, played board games that often ended up in arguments, and trained until I was too tired to move.

I walk into the guest room, and a pang of guilt washes over me for stealing the master bedroom from him, but he's kinda a stubborn ass and wouldn't take no for an answer.

He's still sleeping.

I take advantage of the moment and just stare at him. My heart swells with emotion as I imagine what my life would be like right now if he hadn't come storming into it.

His face looks so much younger and relaxed like this. His normally serious expression is gone, as if sleep has removed the heavy burden he carries through his waking hours. His lips are slightly parted, the full sculpted lines softening in sleep. The seemingly permanent furrow in his brow is gone, and his normally perfect hair is delightfully rumpled, even if he is in desperate need of a haircut. It's definitely long enough to rock a man bun now, as is

Cas's. I make a mental note to tease them both about this later, even though I kinda like the idea of Cas trying that look out.

Sighing, I almost feel guilty for what I'm about to do.

Almost.

Doing my best to restrain the giggle threatening to break free and give me away, I grab a pillow and whack him in the face with it.

"Get up, we have shit to do!" I squeal as he grabs the pillow from my hands and launches it back at me.

"Asshole," he mumbles.

"Do you remember that one time we were here, and you would *not* let me sleep? Paybacks a *bitch*! Now up! We're going to Rio's today." I saunter out of the room, calling over my shoulder, "You have ten minutes before I come back in here with ice water." I hear him groan as he throws another pillow at my retreating back.

I'm sitting at the large, gray wooden table with my legs tucked under me, diving into my bowl of sugary goodness when he joins me, snatching the box of cereal to pour himself some as we eat in silence.

"Are you sure you're ready for this?" he finally asks.

"No, but it's time." V growls from her spot on the floor and I roll my eyes. She's not happy any time I leave the house without her, but it's hard to take a wolf that's nearly two hundred pounds out in public here.

"Then we go. Do you have keys?"

"No, he installed a hand scanner, and my hand should be scanned in. I've never actually been inside, which I always felt was weird, but I thought Rio didn't really feel comfortable being alone with me since I was a teen girl or some shit. We always spent time at the gym and did family stuff at Nova's."

An hour later, we pull into the drive of a tiny house on the outskirts of Boston. I've only been here a handful of times, just for Rio to either bring something out or for him to run in. I've never left the driveway. It's weird being here, and it feels like his grumpy face is going to walk out of that door at any moment. A lump forms in my throat as we sit quietly in the comfort of the SUV, Damian waiting for me to take the lead.

I stare at the red bricks, the white door, and the grass that's over a foot tall. "We should cut the grass," I mumble absentmindedly. It seems wrong somehow that we've let his house fall into a state of disrepair. I know it's only been a matter of months, but it's as if we are being disloyal to him somehow, forgetting him by not taking care of something as simple as his home.

Sucking in a deep breath, I open my door and head up the walk, Damian falling in step behind me. I reach out and wrap my fingers around the handle of the screen door and feel my heartbeat thrumming in my chest as I pull it open.

The pad on the main door looks more expensive than the entire house. There's a small part of me that hopes this doesn't work, so I don't have to do this right now, I'd give anything to walk away and not face this. Invading his space like this is too final, too much of a reminder that he's not coming back. My hand trembles as I press it to the scanner, closing my eyes as I take deep breaths. It whirs to life and a small click has my eyes popping open as the panel turns green and the door swings open a few small inches.

I slowly push it the rest of the way, anxiety overwhelming my senses as I step into a small living space. On the left wall, there's a well-loved leather couch, and to the right, a giant, wall-mounted television. Under it is a table lined with pictures of me, Rio, Brennan, Nova, and Cas through the years. Tears well in my eyes as my fingers drift over the faces behind the glass.

"Go grab the supplies from the car. I want to take these pictures with us," I tell Damian, my voice thick with emotion. He says nothing, but I hear his retreating footsteps and the opening of the screen door. All my pictures were destroyed when the gym was bombed, so discovering these is like finding an unexpected treasure, a well of emotion threatening to crack open my chest.

I make my way through the next room, smiling at everything that reminds me of Rio, from the neatness of the space to his weird fascination with coffee mugs with snarky sayings. Nova would give him a new one every single birthday and Christmas. The memories flood my mind, making me smile.

Moving into his simplistic bedroom, I find more pictures. There's one of me and Rio when I was about fifteen and he's training me to box. I remember Nova taking it, tears springing to my eyes at the memory as I clutch the frame to my chest in a hug. I open his drawers, feeling like I am invading his privacy, before reminding myself that he's gone—he doesn't care about privacy anymore. I know what I'm looking for as I paw through the neatly folded items.

I find it, my hand caressing the softness of the well-loved cotton T-shirt. It's an Aerosmith shirt from Rio's first ever concert and it was his all-time favorite. I pull it out and hold it up to my nose, smelling the scent of his laundry detergent. My heart aches a little that it doesn't smell more like him. He always either smelled of sweat when at the gym or like the only cologne he wore when he dressed up for family events. What I wouldn't give to have him rub his smelly armpits in my face right about now. What used to feel like an act of terror now causes a pang of longing.

The sounds of tape being strung over cardboard can be heard from the living room, where Damian must be constructing the boxes we brought to pack things in. Gratitude fills me, thankful he is here with me for this, I couldn't have faced it alone.

I continue my perusal, finding another favorite shirt hanging in the closet. I take it down, throwing it on the bed to keep as well. The next stop is the bathroom and I hit the jackpot when I find a half-full bottle of his cologne. I carry it back to his room, adding it to my pile as I take a whiff, inhaling the spicy aroma, and close my eyes, pretending for a second that he's here with me.

Damian pulls me out of my reverie when he walks into the room and asks me what needs to be packed beside the pictures in the living room.

"So far, just the stuff on the bed." I head toward Rio's office and gasp when I open the door, my feet rooted to the spot. Damian comes up behind me and lets out a low whistle as he takes in the sight before us.

I scan the room, taking in the rows of monitors, futuristic-looking tech devices, and files. I knew he was good with technology, but this is some next-level space station kind of shit. My feet finally shuffle my body forward as I study the monitors.

"Is this security footage?" I turn to Damian and see the confusion on his face.

"I believe so, but I'm not sure why some of these places are being monitored or even where they are."

Under the monitors are wall-to-wall cabinets. The counter on top of them is littered with different files. Damian walks over and picks one up, studying it with a frown on his face. I open a drawer, Damian leaning over my shoulder to see what's inside. More files.

I thumb through them as he grabs a few and has a seat at the table that occupies the middle of the space.

"These are all files on people from Aetheria," I state, confused as to why Rio has them. I pull open a few more drawers, and bingo! My name is typed in bold black letters across the top of a file. I yank it out, tucking it under my arm as I frantically search other drawers until I have a collection going.

Slamming them down on the table, Damian looks up at me with raised brows. I stare at him, my hands shaking. I grab a file and shove it under his nose.

"These are all files on *us*." Hurt and anger burn through me. I plop down in the seat and start thumbing through it. Everything about me is in this file. Everything. It's factual and devoid of any emotion.

"Highly volatile and unable to control powers fully," I read and Damian snorts.

"Well, it's not wrong," he smirks.

"Fuck you," I let my glare speak volumes.

I flip through more of it—even my relationship with Cas is in here. What the hell? I throw it across the table and pick up the one on Cas. More of the same crap. My eyes roam over the list of powers, and my blood turns to ice.

"Damian," I whisper, my hands shaking as I pass it over to him.

"Suspected powers beyond water wielding: Shapeshifting or illusion manipulation, energy manipulation, elemental control beyond water, telepathy beyond that of a high born, magical binding and sealing." He runs his hands over his face, flipping through a few more pages.

"Fuck."

"Yeah, that's a lot," I say.

"Threat level: high, recommend continuous monitoring," Damian tilts his head—a look of confusion washes over his features like a shadow. He grabs the folder with my name on it and reads the same statement.

I flip through a file on Audra and say, "Yeah, it says it on Audra too, and each of our files is labeled with the term 'Legacy,' besides yours. What do you think that means?"

"Isn't it obvious? Each of you is the legacy of a mortal legend. So, you are all legacies of legends. I assume that's why they have you labeled as such."

"So why wouldn't yours be labeled that?"

"Either they didn't know enough about me or don't consider

my father enough of a legend to label me as one. He's not well known here in the mortal realm."

I read through more before responding, "They don't have much on you, they weren't even sure of your powers. I guess Rio didn't have time to update it."

"Or he kept it out for a reason." Panic flares in Damian's eyes as he snatches the folder with my name on it, frantically flipping through it. He stops on a page, his eyes darting back and forth as he reads. "Oh, thank the gods," he says with an exhaled breath.

"What?" I walk behind him, peering over his shoulder to see what he's looking at. It's my list of powers.

"Being able to kill gods isn't on the list," wonder fills my words. Was Rio trying to protect me by keeping that a secret? I'd like to think he was, but he died less than a day after I killed Moros, so it's a question I'll never have an answer to.

Damian shoves away from the table and studies the monitors. "I think they have been watching the people they have files on." He clicks a few buttons, and the view changes angles or to different people altogether. "The safe house doesn't appear to be on here, but check this one out."

It's the house where I first met Damian, well, where I was sent to *kill* Damian and ended up captured instead. That is, until he let me and Cas go. "Aww look, D, it's the place where we first met." I pretend to wipe a tear from my cheek, and he rolls his eyes.

"Did you just call me D?"

"Sure did. I like it, I think it's gonna stick," I tease. "Hey, big D!" I shout, deepening my voice. "I can't wait to tell Anika to go get the D."

"No, just no," he says while shaking his head.

"It's gonna stick," I say in a sing-song voice.

He sticks his tongue out at me.

We really are overgrown children. Wonder if it says that in our files?

"What is up with you calling everyone by their first initial?" he grumbles.

"I can't do it with everyone, like C wouldn't sound right for Cas. Or A. Some letters just aren't cool like that. Cas has almost always called Brennan, B."

"Call Delphin, D, he would probably love it."

I nod my head in agreement, "That is probably true. I could call you Big D and him Little D!" I clap my hands with excitement.

"Wouldn't that defeat the purpose of shortening the names?"

"Would you hate me calling you Big D?"

"Yes."

"Then it's totally worth it."

He stops clicking and looks over at me, an angry glint in his eyes. I give him my widest smile. His eyes soften.

"Do you know one of the things I love about you?" he asks.

"Nope, but I am sure it's my sparkling personality."

"It's your ability to be able to take shitty situations and still joke around. I know you're pissed about that list in Cas's file. I know reading Rio's notes on you hurts, and I know you're worried. I can see it in your eyes, and yet here you are, poking fun at me."

"I can't always do it, sometimes things are too much."

"I know, but I still love that you can sometimes. It means that you haven't let all this break you down. You have already been teetering on the edge. I've been over here in a panic, thinking this was going to tip you over that ledge, but like always, you show me how capable you are."

I hug him and he rests his chin on my head.

"You ready to call it a day, Big D?" I whisper against his chest, fighting the urge to giggle. He yanks my hair, and I jump out of his reach.

"Yeah, I think we've seen enough for now." He grabs a few of the files to take with us, and I do the same. When I confront Cas, I want his file with me.

Back at the house, Damian asks, "You ready to go home?"

"Yeah, I think so, one last movie night? We can go back tomorrow?'

"That works."

"Can we skip training? I don't think I have the mental energy for it tonight."

"Me either. Hungry?"

"Starving, you cooking?"

He looks at me like I've lost my mind. "You think I trust you to cook? Of course, I'm cooking."

I pretend to be insulted, but I know I'm shit in the kitchen, and of course, he's ridiculously good at every damn thing. I bet he could knit if he wanted to, even with those giant man hands.

We spend the rest of the afternoon eating dinner and irritating the crap out of each other, which is one of our favorite pastimes when we are together.

We decide on *Aqua Man* for our movie, even though I'm usually more of a Marvel girl. I don't argue because, hello, Jason Momoa is just gorgeous.

"Holy shit! I just realized something." I turn to look at Damian, my mouth open, eyes wide. He looks at me quizzically as I grab my phone, another thing I don't miss when we are in Aetheria, and search frantically for what I am looking for. Ha! Found it.

"Look! I knew you reminded me of someone." I hold my phone in his face, a picture of young Jason Momoa on the screen. "Other than your eye color and the eyebrow scar, you could totally be brothers."

"I have more muscles," he deadpans, looking back at the screen.

That's fair, he does. Plus, he's better looking, if that's possible.

Jason just busted into a ship with no shirt on when Damian's phone rings, startling us both. No one knows we are here except people at home, and they don't have a phone, so who the hell is calling?

He looks at his screen, "It's Marcellus." He presses the accept button and puts it on speaker.

"What's up, Marcellus?"

"Damian, thank the gods you're still here. You need to get here ASAP. Bring Layla. Her father is here. Fuck, hurry." We can hear screaming and pandemonium in the background. I look at Damian, our eyes meeting for the briefest of seconds before we jump into action.

"Go home, get help. I'm going and taking V with me."

"No Layla! Wait for me to get back!"

"Damian, you know I can't. People could be dying. Go! You're wasting time and we need backup. You portal directly into the damn castle. It won't take you ten minutes, you will be right behind me. Now *fucking go*!" I yell as I run into my bedroom to throw on some jeans. Dammit, I wish I had my leathers. My stomach feels like lead. Moving as fast as I can, I grab the keys. V is already waiting by the garage door. Running to the SUV, I open the hatch, and she jumps in.

Slamming it back shut, I fly into the driver's seat and take off, thankful we left my vehicle here as well so the boys can take Damian's. The drive is a blur.

V gives a little whine when I take a corner fast. "How you holding up back there?" I forgot she's never been in a car before.

"Are you auditioning for a part as a stunt driver? Don't be angry if I vomit."

Apparently, my girl suffers from motion sickness.

Chapter Thirty-Four

LAYLA

I pull into the parking lot on two wheels, making it to the club in record time. My phone dings, and I risk precious seconds I feel like I don't have to check it.

Damian and the crew are on the way.

I let V out and surround us in shadows, shielding our minds and presence as I call to my powers, sending darkness racing into the night to tell me what's waiting inside.

My father is there, waiting, while others do his dirty work. I have two ways I can play this. I can sneak in somehow with a giant wolf or just kick the door in and be all like "surprise motherfuckers" and start knocking people out.

Option two feels like the right choice.

"V, we're going in hot. You ready to bite some asses?"

A low, menacing rumble so deep I swear the air around us vibrates is emanating from my wolf. "I'll take that as a yes. Here goes nothing."

I throw my arms wide, power rippling through the air as the

door bursts into splinters. I can hear people inside screaming as we enter, V staying glued to my left side. I feel my power surging along my skin, ready to be unleashed, shadows swirling around me, the ebb and flow of them following my movements.

Glass from broken bottles crunches under my shoes, tables are flipped over, pictures sitting on the floor with broken frames.

"V, watch your feet, there's glass everywhere." I stick to communicating through our link to not give away her presence. I don't care if they know I am here, but I'd rather not risk her any more than necessary.

The hairs on the back of my nape stand up, and I feel someone flying through a door on my right. I whip out a tendril of darkness and grab the intruder as V lunges.

"Layla! It's me!" I recognize Marcellus's voice.

"V! Stop!" She stills but keeps growling.

"Layla, where's Damian?" Marcellus breaths come out in short pants, a gash on his head bleeding down onto his handsome face.

"He'll be here any second. Where is Thanatos?"

"I'm not sure. There's so many people hurt, we have to get them out."

I nod. "Get out of here, Marcellus, now."

"No, Cas would never forgive me if I left you. I'll be okay. Come on, we can't waste any more time."

My instincts are screaming at me to leave, but I hear people crying, and my conscience won't let me walk away. We move deeper into the building, Vengeance disappearing into a corner of the room, stalking her own prey.

"Be cautious, Godslayer, something doesn't feel right." I feel V's thought in my mind right as an open door comes into view, and beyond it sits my father.

"Daughter, so good to see you." His face shows no hint of

emotion as he looks at me. I step into the room, Marcellus tight on my heels. As soon as we are both in the room, the door slams behind us. I turn, trying frantically to open it, but it won't budge. I throw my power into it, but I can barely feel it. I only know one person capable of dampening my power this way.

Damian.

The sting of betrayal tastes bitter in my mouth, hurt and anger warring inside me for dominance.

"Where is that fucking asshole?" I say through gritted teeth. I hear Vengeance snarling and tearing into flesh as screams erupt from beyond the door.

"Call your wolf off before I have her killed," my father snaps.

"You touch her, and I will gouge your eyes out with my fingers, then shove them down your fucking throat."

The sound of something large being thrown against the door startles all of us as the cold grip of terror squeezes my heart.

"V, stand down," I yell as rage boils in my blood, chasing away the fear.

"I will not! I will rip their heads from their bodies and bathe in their blood!"

"Vengeance, I need you to stand down. I mean it," I say out loud for my father's benefit, but then silently say to her, *"I need you to wait for the boys. Keep them safe, please, V. I don't know how or why, but I think Damian may have betrayed us."*

"Don't be ridiculous. You know better than that. I am insulted you think Chaos would have chosen him if he were capable of such a thing. I'm disappointed in you, Godslayer."

Guilt spreads in my gut. The snarling quiets, and I study the man before me. "Where is he?" I say again, less sure about it being Damian who betrayed us but wanting to keep up the ruse.

He cocks his head, studying me. "Who, exactly, are you referring to?" His fingers drum on the side of the chair he occupies, and it pisses me off to see that nervous tick.

I do the same thing.

My stomach churns, knowing I have something other than looks in common with this asshole.

"My powers are dimmed. I only know one person whose powers can negate my own," I snarl, crossing my arms and setting my feet. It's what Rio used to call my fuck-around-and-find-out pose. Remembering Damian's words from our first meeting, I level a glare at my father while I dig deep inside of myself, reaching for my power, trying to break free from this magical bond that has me wondering if this is what men feel like when their dicks won't work. Impotent is the only word that seems to come to mind.

It's there, but it's being shielded behind a thick fog, one that seems to be clearing the closer my mental self gets to it. Thanatos is saying something that I don't catch, snapping me back into focus.

He's speaking to Marcellus, who has moved out from behind me. "Marcellus, no!" My mind thinks he's somehow sacrificing himself for me, putting himself in harm's way. Reaching out to grab his arm, he looks back at me and grins as he moves out of my reach and takes up the space next to my father.

My mouth gapes, opening and closing like a fish floundering on land. Finally regaining some damn sense, I snap my mouth shut and stare at him as his face lights up, delighting in his duplicity.

"You have got to be shitting me, you stupid fuck." I'm dumbfounded. "Why Marcellus, why? I thought we were friends."

"Your father promised me you if I helped him." He shrugs his shoulders like it should be obvious.

"The fuck? I thought you and *Cas* were friends."

He sneers and rolls his eyes. "That spoiled asshole doesn't deserve you, Layla. He brought you to me because he knew I could give you what he couldn't. He just handed you over and watched me fuck you. Is that really the kind of man you want to spend the rest of your life with? He's lied to you and manipulated you, and he will eventually cave to his father's demands and leave you behind to claim his crown."

For a moment, I have no fucking idea how to respond to him. I *liked* him. We were friends, he was someone I trusted. I'm a godsdamned idiot.

Finally, my brain starts working again. "You have lost your damn mind. Like seriously lost it. So what? You think I'm just going to skip off into the sunset holding your hand and live happily ever after?"

"Cas has done nothing but lie to you. He knew who your father was for years and didn't trust or respect you enough to tell you the truth. He lied to you about his engagement, about his powers, he even lied to you about *your* powers, Layla. Between him and Rio, I'm not sure which one of them lied to you more. They purposely kept your other powers dampened."

The shock on my face must be obvious because he tilts his head back and laughs. The sound carries a slightly manic edge that sends chills down my spine.

"Yes, Layla, they knew about your other powers, at least your potential, likely before you did. They didn't want you to know because they were afraid of you. Do you see anyone trying to keep Cas from his powers? Why do you think that is? You're a smart girl, think about it."

"They were afraid if I became too powerful, they wouldn't be able to control me," I whisper. A coldness seeps into my bones, etching itself into every fiber of my being. "That's why they wanted to keep me away from Damian. They knew he would tell me the truth."

"Correct. We had planned on taking you at the clinic, but when you didn't show for the rescue, we had to come up with a new plan.

I just need time to show you how much they have been manipulating you, then you will see," he says, a crazy, unhinged look in his wild eyes.

Marcellus starts to speak again, but my father interrupts. "Speaking of your brother, I believe he just entered the building. Marcellus, make sure to keep the sea prince busy. I want to speak to my children."

Marcellus's green eyes meet mine, and I see worry there. I'm so thoroughly confused. He holds my gaze for a moment more before walking out the door. I think about bolting out behind him, but the door glows with runes I'm guessing are meant to keep people either in or out. I reach a handout, and sure enough, a jolt goes through me.

Directing my attention back to Thanatos—he is watching me like one would a caged lion. There's a wary curiosity in his stare, his preternatural stillness makes my skin crawl.

I tilt my head, studying him in return. "Why did you call Damian my brother? Hit your head one too many times? You kidnapped my brother last time we met, and you saw how well that turned out for you."

Loud banging from behind me has me wincing, but Thanatos doesn't even look surprised. Opening the door, Damian burst into the room, snarling and baring his teeth, wrapping me in his arms, then shoving me behind him as he faces off with my father.

"Hello son, it's time the three of us have a nice little family chat." He waves to the sofa for us to sit as the door slams again, locking us in.

"Don't call me son, *uncle*." His face is contorted with rage as he growls the last word, his cold fury palpable.

The side of his mouth lifts as he stretches his arms out and looks utterly at ease. "It's time to clean a few skeletons out of the family closet. You may not like it, but you are *my son*. My brother, being the useless weasel that he was, couldn't seem to sire children. He tried for years to get your mother pregnant and failed. Desperate for an heir, he convinced me to breed her instead. We sought out Loki, and he used his magic to turn me into your father when your mother's fertility cycle hit. I spent three glorious days fucking her over and over again. Her little cunt was so damn tight I was almost sad when she fell pregnant, I was hoping it would take a few tries. Oh, don't look so shocked, I made it good for her. Your father was a twat that needed violence to get his limp dick to work. I made her scream in pleasure, her nails raking down my back as she milked my cock like a good little whore."

Primal screams filled the air as we both lunged for him. Damian got to him first, slamming his fist into his face as he howled with rage.

"Don't." Punch. "You." Punch. "Ever." Punch. "Speak." Punch, punch, punch. "Of." Punch. "Her." Punch.

Someone steps into the light, seemingly appearing from thin air. I recognize him. "Anteros." He doesn't seem to hear me as he touches Damian on the forehead, and he collapses.

"Damian!" I rush to his side, checking him over to make sure he's okay.

"Don't worry, Layla, he is merely asleep," the giant says as he squats down next to me, scooping him up and placing him on the bed.

"I'm so confused. What the fuck are you doing here?" The last time I saw him was last year on my birthday and while I wasn't really worried about getting to know him, I remember how sweet he had been to me.

"Wait, are you working with my father too? Both of you? Were you working with him when we fucked?"

"By the gods, daughter, do you have to be so vulgar? Did your mother not teach you to behave like a lady?" Thanatos has the nerve to look annoyed with my upbringing.

"Are you serious right now? Cause I kinda can't tell. Did you hear the words that came out of your mouth before Damian beat the shit out of you? Pot," I say, pointing to him, "Meet kettle," I say, then point to myself. He looks at me expectantly, still waiting for a response to his moronic question.

"Umm, she was too busy worrying about whatever douchebag boyfriend she had at the time, and I was too busy trying to avoid them getting handsy to pay attention in etiquette class." I look at him like he's lost his mind, then turn my attention back to Anteros.

"Were you working for my father when I was sucking your cock, and you were coming in my mouth?" I look over my shoulder at my father with a feral grin, throwing a wink his way just because I feel like being a petty bitch.

"Yes."

Well, I wasn't really expecting him to give me an answer quite that easy. I need to change tactics. I can feel my power rising, but it's taking time to break through the layers of whatever is binding me.

"Why?"

"I'm a half-breed like you. No one cared about me until I came into power, and like your brother there, I can bind powers and read minds. My mother never wanted me and resented having to raise me. My father never bothered to claim me, leaving me a part of two different worlds and belonging to neither. Your father wants to change things for people like you and me, give us a place where we are accepted, where we matter."

My brain can't process everything going on. Damian is my brother keeps flashing in my head like a neon sign, eclipsing all else.

Looking at Thanatos, I say, "I don't believe you."

"It doesn't matter if you believe me or not—the truth is the truth. My mother knows, you are more than welcome to ask her. He *is* your brother."

"Why are you telling us now? It's been kept hidden for over a hundred years and now suddenly you feel the need to come clean? What changed?"

"My brother is dead, there is no need to keep it any longer. I will not challenge his claim to Moros's kingdom; will not publicly claim him."

"You want him to join your cause." The revelation hits me like an avalanche, burying me so deep under its weight I'm encompassed in darkness, my chest refusing to expand.

"Yes," he draws out the word, nodding at me, a smile playing on his lips. Damian's lips, my lips. The contents of my stomach threaten to make an appearance.

"And if he doesn't?" My voice is so quiet it barely carries, but he hears my words nonetheless.

"Then I will claim him, he will lose his kingdom, and his mother will learn the truth of his parentage." He says it matter of factly, a bored expression on his beautifully cruel face.

Taking a deep breath, I close my eyes, feeling my power finally heed my call, sizzling along my skin. I'm not going to make the same mistake as last time; this this fucker is going to die.

I lower my shields for a moment to relay a message to Cas and Vengeance. *"Be prepared, I'm about to blow shit up. Don't trust Marcellus."* I don't wait for a reply before closing myself off once again. I just pray they are all safe.

Before I can act, a deafening boom rattles the building. Thunder reverberates through the walls, shaking the foundation as the protections placed on the door falter and it bursts open, Audra standing in the now gaping hole, eyes glowing white, lightning dancing along her fingertips. Cas and Delphin both flank her, bloodied and clad in black leather, looking like the very definition of angry gods.

My head swivels to the left, eyes drawn to V in the background, ripping flesh from a body as she growls, blood splattering in an arc, raining down on her, covering her gray fur.

I meet Cas's eyes, and relief replaces the cold anger there for the briefest of seconds before they shift, and panic flares as he looks over my shoulder.

Cas turns to see Anteros, his eyes going wide as they land on an amulet around his neck.

"Layla," Cas says as he looks back at me. "Where is the gift I gave you for your birthday?" I look at him like he's lost his fucking mind. Is now really the time to be asking me this?

"I lost it when the gym was bombed, I never opened it."

His eyes close for the briefest of seconds before they meet mine again and his voice fills my head. *It was a dragonstone pendant. It gives the wearer certain abilities, depending on the person. Anteros is wearing it.*

I turn and see Anteros pick up a still unconscious Damian, and in a movement so quick none of us have time to react, he grabs my father, and they just disappear. They wink out of existence and are just gone...like they were never even there.

"*Fuck!*" screams Cas. "Apparently it gives him the ability to fucking teleport!"

"Damian!" I scream, running over to where they were just a second ago. I whirl around the room, eyes frantically searching. "No, no, no, no! Please no! Damian!" I bellow before hitting my knees, burying my face in my hands. I failed him. I failed everyone again. My power is burning through me, my blood boiling me from the inside. Arching my back, I fling my power upward, ripping a hole through the building as debris rains down on me, power streaming through my body, storm clouds rumbling outside while lightning flashes and thunderclaps so loud my ears ring from the sound.

Cas runs to me and puts a hand on my shoulder but is thrown back the minute his skin touches mine. My teeth rattle with the force of the power pouring from me, the pressure ripping me apart molecule by molecule.

"Stand back!" I hear Audra shout through the noise and then I feel a jolt shock my system. My body convulses and everything goes dark.

Chapter Thirty-Five

AUDRA

Rolling my shoulders, trying to ease the tension there, I take a deep breath. Staring at Caspian through narrowed eyes, daydreaming about taking that letter opener on Damian's desk and stabbing it through his peepers just to shut him the fuck up.

Finally, I can't take it anymore. I snap, "Shut your fucking mouth, Cas. If I have to hear another damn word out of you right now, I can't be responsible for my actions. I knew she would survive the lightning, you dumb fucker. She can wield it like I can. It wouldn't kill her any more than water can kill you, so you can quit your stupid fucking ranting. It stopped the power flowing through her. It was going to burn her alive if I didn't do something, so instead of yelling at me, how about a damn thank you?"

He stares at me, body vibrating with emotion, hands clenching and unclenching at his sides, his jaw flexing.

"Check yourself, Cas, I'm not going to tell you again. In case you forgot, it was your stupid friend that got her into this mess in the first place." Lightning sparks along my fingers. I have no problem knocking him on his ass, he's about to find that out the hard way. "What you should be concentrating on is how we are going to get Damian back, how the hell we are going to tell his mom he's been taken, and what we are going to do to support Layla when she wakes up because you and I both know she's going to blame herself and be a complete wreck about it. Instead, you're standing here with a stick up your ass."

"Shut the fuck up, Audra," Delphin snaps at me from where his pretty ass is lurking in the corner.

I don't bother with words; I just storm over and deck him in the jaw. I'm so sick of his attitude. His head snaps back, jaw tightens before turning back to look at me, rubbing his hand over where my fist connected. Fucking prick. We stare each other down, both seething.

"Both of you stop," Cas gripes. "She's right. We need a plan."

"What we need is my grandmother. I have questions she needs to answer, questions that may help us get Damian back."

We all turn to see Layla in the doorway, her eyes clear and full of fury as her aptly named wolf stands by her side, teeth bared, still covered in Marcellus's blood.

Check out this preview of book three, *Magic & Mayhem*.

Layla

Lost. I feel utterly and completely lost. He's been gone for seven days. Seven days of not knowing if he's safe. Seven days of not knowing if he's alive. Seven days I haven't been able to sleep for more than a handful of minutes at a time. Seven days of torture. Seven days of feeling like a failure.

During the first few days, anger fueled me. I've spent countless hours hunting, capturing dozens that had any ties to my father and killed them all. Slowly. Mercilessly. I spent those days covered in blood, the rage inside me morphed into a bloodthirsty beast that couldn't be controlled or contained.

And still, I have no answers. I'm no closer to finding him today than I was seven days ago. My power burns inside of me, a fire raging under my skin, demanding to be satiated as the hunger for vengeance consumes me.

This is my fault.

Guilt wars with the anger, and today, both of those emotions have been beaten into submission by the depths of my despair. I feel as though I've been torn apart, my very essence shattered into countless fragments that litter the landscape of my soul. Each piece carries the weight of my sorrow, cutting deep into the fragile edges of my spirit with every heartbeat.

I'm enveloped in a suffocating darkness, consumed by a profound sense of loss and anguish that threatens to swallow me whole. It's as if a storm has ravaged the very core of my being, leaving behind a desolate wasteland of broken dreams and shattered hopes.

I try to gather the pieces of myself, but they slip through my fingers like grains of sand. I long to feel whole again, to find solace in the embrace of a forgotten happiness that now feels like a distant memory. But no matter how hard I try, the pieces refuse to fit together, leaving me trapped in a never-ending cycle of misery. How can I ever feel whole with such a large piece of myself missing?

I'm adrift in a sea of sorrow, lost in the labyrinth of my brokenness. I cling to the fragile hope that I'll be able to find him and put myself back together again. But for now, I'm left to navigate the jagged edges of my shattered soul, praying for a glimmer of light to guide me out of the darkness.

The scalding heat from the shower burns my skin as I sit naked, my knees pulled to my chest, head buried in my arms as sobs wrack my body. I'm so tired, but how can I rest when he needs me? How can I face his mother, his people, our family, knowing I failed them all?

So lost in my grief, I don't hear anyone enter the room until the door to the shower opens. "Fucking hell, Layla! You're burning yourself!" Cas reaches in and shuts the water off, my skin already beginning to heal. His hand grabs my arm, trying to haul me off the floor.

Panic overtakes me. I will not let him take me from here. I know he wants me to go back to Aetheria and regroup but there is no fucking way in hell I am leaving here without Damian. Not happening. I yank my arm away from him and rise to my feet. Exhaustion and lack of food over the past week have taken their toll and I stumble, Cas catches me and hauls me into his arms.

"Let me *go*!" I thrash wildly, punching, pulling and kicking him as he drags me out of the bathroom. "I am *not* leaving here without him!" I see Audra and fury surges in my veins. "If you so much as *think* about throwing a lightning bolt at me I will not hesitate to *rip your fucking head off*, understand me?" She puts her hands up in surrender and backs away from me as I manage to land a punch right to Caspian's face.

"Layla just fucking stop and listen to me!" he bellows.

Calling to my power, I try to shove it at him, but I'm too exhausted. I have nothing left so I fight dirty, grabbing his hair and yanking, scratching his face, a primal scream erupting from me as I try to escape his grip.

"This is your fault!" I scream as he hauls me over his shoulder and I kick and punch, flailing around with zero grace, just hysterical panic. "If you and Rio hadn't kept my powers from me, then maybe I would have been able to break through when they dampened my abilities faster and I could have stopped them! I didn't have enough time! I wasn't strong enough! You took that away from me because you *didn't fucking trust me*! If you had trusted me then we wouldn't have been here for them to take him in the first damn place! I will *never* forgive you if we don't find him! *Never*!" I rip my engagement ring off and fling it across the room.

Cas stills and I stop my assault, my energy spent as I start sobbing again. He slowly sets me down, grabbing a blanket from the bed to cover my nakedness. Putting his hands on my shoulders he looks me in the eyes.

"Layla, what are you talking about? What do you mean, you wouldn't have been here if I had trusted you?" His voice is calm, measured, but there is a hint of panic behind his words.

"We were here because I was pissed at you, and I needed time to think." I cover my face with my hands, hating myself.

"Why?" he asks, confused.

"Because you never told me about your new powers. Every time I found out it was through someone else, not you. Then Damian and I found files at Rio's, and it listed a shit ton of stuff you never told me. Marcellus also had quite a bit to say about how you and Rio lied to me and hid things from me. I didn't like the way it made me feel, and it made me question us. I wanted to clear my head before I talked to you about it."

His hands fall away from me, and I look up at him. His face is pale, shock registering across his perfect features.

"Layla-"

"No, Cas. Just stop. I don't want to hear your excuses; I don't want to hear some bullshit apology. I want to get my brother back." I'm shivering from head to toe, the crash from the adrenaline rush hitting me harder with how drained I am.

"You're brother?" Cas questions as his eyes widen and his brows shoot up.

"Well, I guess your father is responsible for dropping that bomb," Nyx says from the doorway. "It's time for us to have a chat, we've been trying to get to you for the last week, but in your tantrum, you had it shielded so well, not even I could break through."

My eyes narrow. "You lied to us."

"I know." Her eyes soften a little, which pisses me off even more.

"Where were you last week when I was ready to leave and Enthralia sent for you?" I ask through gritted teeth.

"I was there within an hour, Layla, you refused to wait."

"That was an hour too long. Damian had already been gone for two at that point."

"You can't very well be angry, I was there as soon as I could get there, then we tried to portal to this house, and you had it sealed. I'm not even sure how you managed that, so we had to portal elsewhere and upon arriving here, we couldn't get near the house. Your wolf was beside herself when we couldn't bring her with us. Your dragon as well as Damian's have been searching our world high and low with their wing along with the wolf pack. We will get him back, Layla. Now get dressed and meet me in the kitchen." She walks out and leaves me burning with rage, mad at everyone and everything.

Audra

Fucking hell. I've never seen anyone as pissed off as Layla. Not that I can blame her, this is some fucked up family drama. Cas and I take a seat in the cozy kitchen at the large gray table, Nyx following suit. The fact that I'm sitting across the table from a fucking Prince, and not just any prince, but the fucking eldest born son of Triton, as well as the most powerful goddess and ruler of Aetheria, Nyx, is a total mind fuck of epic proportions.

I miss the days when the most complicated thing in my life was getting people's orders right or kicking some asshole out of the bar when they had too many drinks. It's like I'm in some fucked up dream I can't seem to wake up from. A dream with dire wolves, dragons and legendary figures with crazy powers and abilities.

The last time I was in this house I was being kidnapped. Now look at me, less than two weeks later hanging out with these crazy assholes like it's normal. My life is so fucked up.

"So, when are the love birds being picked up from their honeymoon?" I ask, trying to ease the tension.

"Well, Damian was supposed to pick them up at the end of this week, but since he's not here, and I need to help Layla find Damian, I asked Thor to take Nereus to get them."

I tense at the mention of my father. He doesn't seem like a total douchebag, but I still can't just ignore how he left me and my mom to struggle all our lives while he lived in the lap of luxury. Fucking Thor. I doubt he would have even bothered with me at all if I had taken after my human mother and never developed powers.

I look at the intricate tattoo on my right forearm, a set of roses, with my mother's name woven into the design over and over. Rose. My grandmother named her after her favorite flower, the rose, because she said roses were the most beautiful thing she had ever laid eyes on until the day my mother was born.

My mother really was beautiful, inside and out. Lovely cinnamon colored hair, freckles that made her always look younger than she was and eyes the color of whiskey. I miss her so much, her absence a constant ache that has become as familiar to me as breathing.

Growing up, I always wished I looked like her, but unfortunately, other than my nose and my slight build, I am almost a carbon copy of my father. Same honey blonde hair, same sky-blue eyes and golden skin. It must have been hard for my mother to look at me and always see him.

Footsteps echo through the hall and a moment later, Layla enters the room. She looks like shit. Paler than normal, deep, dark circles under her eyes that give her a haunted look. I worry she may pass out from exhaustion as she takes a seat next to me. Poor Cas looks like he's about to snap he's wound so tight, and Nyx's lips are drawn into a thin, straight line. I haven't felt this much tension in a room since the time a guy walked into the bar & grill and saw his wife in a booth making out with his sister. Talk about awkward.

"I assume you have questions." Nyx begins, clasping her hands together and sitting them in her lap, eyes on Layla.

"Why didn't you tell us he was my brother?" She spits out, even through her exhaustion, I can feel anger rolling from her in waves. Thank you, baby Jesus, she's too tired to wield her powers, because she can barely control them as it is, being this worked up, she would probably burn the house down, or kill one of us.

"I saw no reason to jeopardize his claim to Moros's throne. I can't think of anyone better suited to rule than he is, and the people there love him and his mother. Then there is Enthralia, I did not want to hurt her, she's been through enough."

"Do you honestly believe she doesn't deserve to know the truth? If I were in her position, I'd be furious, and so would you! You had no authority to withhold that from her! At the very least you should have told Damian and me that we were siblings! He could have still ascended to the throne; after all, he's your grandchild! Even if you were worried about my father's heir making a claim, you could have confided in us." She bangs her hand on the table, causing Cas and Nyx to flinch. This kind of drama is reminiscent of the days when Jerry Springer was still hosting his television show. Good ole Jerry, I used to think that shit was staged, now I'm not so sure.

"Layla, I'm sorry. I can't change what has been done in the past, we just have to move forward and find him." Nyx says as calmly as she can. "We've heard that you have been attacking your father's men, leaving a bloody trail of death in your wake. How are you even finding those men?"

She's silent for a moment before she finally speaks, almost as if she's considering how much she wants to share. "Rio has files at his house. Damian and I discovered them. He has one on each of us," she waves her hand across the room, indicating me and Cas, "and the groups he had been watching. So far, it's gotten me nowhere."

"Hold up, someone fill me in here, how is he your brother?" Cas queries, clearly confused as fuck. I feel ya, dude, I can't keep up either.

"Moros couldn't get Enthralia pregnant. He begged Thanatos to help give him an heir, they went to Loki, she went into her fertility cycle, Loki transformed Thanatos to Moros, he fucked the shit out of her for a few days and knocked her up. All caught up now?" Layla looks at him expectantly.

Poor guy's eyes are wide as saucers, he obviously wasn't expecting to be in a real-life episode of *Paternity Court* today. Thanatos, you *are* the father!

He shakes his head before continuing. "Ok, well moving on, how many men of his have you killed?" Cas raises an eyebrow. He told me a little about how sadistic Layla can be when she's pissed and hunting. It makes me wish I had been with her.

"I lost count. Over fifty in four different states surrounding us."

"Did you question them at least?"

"Do you think I'm stupid?" she snaps at him, "Of course I did! It got me *nowhere*! I tortured the fuck out of every single one and made the others watch so they would know what was coming for them! I'm no closer to finding him, they knew nothing!" she screams, the surge in emotion causing her power to flare enough that the lights flicker as lightning sizzles along her skin and shadows race from the corners of the room.

I watch them volley back and forth, a verbal tennis match where Layla seems to be ahead in this particular game. My eyes are drawn to her hands, the tremor there. "Layla, you are about to push yourself past the point of no return. You need food, and rest. I'm going to take Damian's bike and do a little digging of my own. Do you have any of those files with you? Let me help and let Cas take care of you, or you will be no good to anyone."

"How do you expect me to eat? To sleep? To pretend like everything is normal when I have no idea if he's dead or alive? If he is alive, he's waiting for me to come save him. He's fucking *waiting* and it's been a godsdamn week! We're sitting here twiddling our thumbs and he's...he's..." she bursts into sobs again; Cas tries to reach out to her, but she swats his hand away. After a moment she finally calms.

"Let me help you, Layla. Damian has given me a home, taken me in like I belong. You have been kinder to me than anyone has in a long time. Let me help." I quietly plead with her.

She looks at me with bloodshot eyes for a moment and I hope I am conveying the sincerity of my words well enough that she will let me in, let me help. Finally, pushing back from the table she marches out of the room while Cas starts rummaging through the fridge to find her something to eat.

"I'm going to put shields back up around the property. Layla's have faltered because she's exhausted. Thankfully, it got us in here, but it also leaves you all vulnerable. Cas, a few days ago you said Marcellus knew about this place, do you think he told Thanatos?"

"Possibly, but if he had, I think he would have been watching it and tried to take her as soon as the shields failed. Marcellus only knew for a day or two before everything went down. We also have no idea what kind of powers besides teleportation Anteros has from the dragonstone."

"Anteros has *what*?" Nxy hisses.

"I had given Layla a dragonstone pendant for her birthday. Apparently, she never opened it, and it was at the gym when it was bombed and thought it was lost. Anteros was wearing it."

"Fucking hell," Nyx whispers.

"I hoped he knew and would come for me, and how was I supposed to know Cas gave me some magic pendant? I was pissed at him for being engaged." Layla says as she walks back into the room, handing me a stack of files and a laptop.

Nyx sighs at Layla's stubbornness. "The good news is, unless he has someone with powers like Layla's, he can't kill Damian, he's immortal, and chances are, he doesn't want to."

"We didn't think he had someone with Damian's powers either, yet he did. And while he might not be able to kill him, he sure as shit can make him wish for death," Layla states as she begrudgingly takes food from Cas.

Flipping through the files, I open the computer and start running some searches. I may or may not have some mad skills when it comes to computers. Hacking is one of my top three favorite ways to break the law.

"Layla, are these men you haven't been able to locate, or ones you have taken out? I can hack almost anything, including security cameras all over the city. I don't want to waste my time with ones you have already taken care of," I explain.

"Those are the ones I'm still looking for. The others had addresses already listed. Rio has some software on that laptop that you should be able to use to help you with the search. I tried to use it, but while I can work a computer, Rio was a genius when it came to that stuff, so it's a little over my head."

"No worries, I'll take a look at what he has on here, if it's not what I need, I have programs I can install. I'll get locations and if they are close enough, I'll do some scouting. But only if you promise me you will get a few hours of sleep and eat."

"Fine," she grumbles, "when did you get so damn bossy?"

I just smirk and get to work. This is the calmest I've felt since Damian was taken. I haven't known this bunch of assholes for very long, but I like them and feel a connection I haven't felt since my mom died. I want to do what I can to help.

A crick in my neck brings me back to reality, standing to try and stretch it out, turning my head from side to side. True to her word, Layla is asleep. Everyone has scattered to take care of different things, and the house is quiet. A glance at the clock on the microwave startles me, I've been working for two hours and hadn't realized it.

Making my way through the house, I hear whispers coming from the garage.

"We can't take her back to Aetheria, she will lose her shit and hurt someone. You saw how she had this place shielded. Had she not worn herself into exhaustion, we would have never been able to get in here and you and I are the only two beings with even a fraction of her power. If we couldn't get in, no one could." Wait, that's Cas, is he planning on trying to get Layla back home without Damian? There's no fucking way she will allow that.

"Keep your voice down," Nyx hisses. "If she wakes and hears you, then there's no way we will get her away from here. You cannot let Thanatos get his hands on her. It will be the end of our world. Her fate isn't sealed, the legends foretold she will either be our salvation or our destruction. We have to make sure it's not the latter."

"It may mean leaving here without Damian. Can you live with that? Will she be able to? I don't want to hurt her, but if I have to choose between the two, I am going to choose her every time, no question, even if she hates me for it later."

"I would prefer to leave with both of my grandchildren, but if we have to choose, we choose Layla."

What do they mean the legend foretold? And why do I feel like they are betraying Layla with this information? The sound of footsteps has me moving my ass, something telling me to play dumb and not get caught eavesdropping.

Back in the safety of the kitchen, I wait until I hear the interior garage door open and shut before I walk out of the kitchen, nearly running directly into Cas in the hall.

He startles and eyes meet mine, guilt shining in those deep blue depths as he gives a nervous laugh. "Sorry, Audra, I wasn't paying attention."

"You're fine, I found some of the info I was looking for, so I am going to borrow Damian's bike and check out a few of the addresses while Layla sleeps."

He nods, obviously distracted, "Yea ok, that sounds like a good idea. Be careful on that thing."

I cock an eyebrow at him, and he laughs. "Ok, ok, fair enough, I know you can handle a motorcycle and can zap anyone to ash that crosses you."

Acknowledgments

As always, to my bestie, Michelle: Thank you for being my rock and getting me through the hard days. You know every dark secret I have and love me anyway.

To my oldest: You have given me my all-time favorite human, for that, you can be my second favorite. Thank you for him, staring at him is my new favorite pastime. (He's never allowed to read my books, EVER.)

To my tattoo artist: Thank you for turning my books into beautiful works of art on my body. You defiantly make the top ten of my all-time favorite people. Plus, you are all kinds of fun and indulge my fantasies, so that's an added bonus.

To my editor and cover designer: You two rock! I love working with you, you make everything perfect!

To Nancy: I love having you in my life! Thank you for being such an amazingly supportive friend!

To my mom: I'm not sure what I would have done without you this past year. Thank you for everything, and for not disowning me when you read book one, lol.

To the readers: You all are amazing, thank you for reading my books! As a book lover myself, I hope you enjoy these characters and this world that lives in my head!

To the higher power I pray to and hope hears me: I'm really sorry for being such a degenerate, but I'm glad you love me anyway.

Made in the USA
Monee, IL
01 November 2024

69105572R00195